INDIA ON FIRE...

a land of whispered challenges growing to a shout across the blazing plains.

India under the British Raj, a glittering, clumsy military machine ruled by senile generals and corrupt colonels overcome by claret in the bloody evening of an Empire.

But there were men like Lang, a daring young British officer, who were willing to shatter tradition with a new kind of honor—to mount impossible charges, destroy impregnable forts, wrest victory from screaming odds of ten thousand to one . . .

"A really stupendous novel which brings the Indian Mutiny vividly to life—the shame, the glory, the appalling apathy and desperate courage of the British Raj."

—*Kenneth More*

FOLLOW
THE
DRUM

James Leasor

A DELL BOOK

**For The Drummer
and all who follow him**

From the Writer to the Reader

According to the *Concise Oxford Dictionary*, a novel is a 'fictitious prose narrative of sufficient length to fill one or more volumes, portraying characters and actions representative of real life in continuous plot.'

Follow the Drum is a novel. But, because fiction can only ever hold a mirror to real life, I would like to say here and now that the important incidents described in my story all took place.

Most of my characters were real people. And to those who were not, I have given real experiences from the lives of others, both Indian and British, who were involved in the tragic and heroic events that form the background to this story.

Looking back at these events from an age obsessed with leisure, amusement and 'rights,' it is difficult to believe that Indians could be blown from guns without arousing an outcry from either side; or that an Indian officer could be ordered to shoot his own son and not demur; or that two young British officers could ride out with fifty men and, through sheer audacity, capture the most wanted man in all India—although at that time he was surrounded by thousands of his own subjects.

Words like duty and honour and bravery and service held a depth of meaning for British and Indians alike in that long-lost world which many today will find hard to believe.

I hope that this preface may make their understanding easier.

J.L.

1

After that night, long after it, whenever Lang saw the moon paint still water silver, or smelled the scent of roses on summer evening air, the years would melt away, and he would be nineteen again, on the evening of his engagement party at Five Mile Place.

Looking back, it seemed odd that he had only seen the great house for the first time that evening, arriving by hired carriage with his mother; although then this had not seemed in any way unusual.

He had been immensely impressed by its sheer size; but so was everyone who first saw the terraces and balustrades, the stone statues, the temple-like follies built in cypress groves—and the five square miles of land from which the house took its name.

And he was to marry Arabella, the girl who one day would inherit it all. Their children would boat upon this lake, and ride across this park, and one day maybe he would hold an engagement party like this for them.

Across the shimmering lake, Lang saw the house, lit by flares. Hundreds of candles caged in coloured glass jars flickered in trees, like glow-worms. Above the poplars that lined the drive, owls and bats, driven frantic by the lights, fled silently, dark, sinister parentheses in the sky.

He turned to his mother and squeezed her hand; he could imagine what this moment meant to her. That her only son, for whom she had scrimped and saved through so many lonely years, should be marrying into the wealth that this party represented, was as astonishing as if she were marrying into it herself, after years of little money and other people's cast-offs.

Lang still felt secretly bewildered by the prospect. Only days before, he had been commissioned into the Bengal Army of the Honourable East India Company—that extraordinary commercial complex which had started in the reign of Queen Elizabeth with a few trading posts around the Indian coast to store Eastern spices, much valued for their ability to keep meat edible during English winters, and which now virtually ran the country.

He looked at his mother, and, mirrored in her proud eyes, he saw the house with its Palladian front and carved pillars of gentle Dorset stone, mellow in the lamplight. She had willed this for him; she must have done; there was no other explanation. He could never have accomplished it alone.

'You will marry well one day, Richard,' she used to tell him when he was still at school. 'You'll get a commission first, of course. Your dear father was a major. With the right wife, you'll rise to be a general.'

'Yes, mama,' he had replied, not really listening. The right wife. To Mrs Lang this described Arabella MacDonald perfectly; rich, an only daughter, her father a colonel who had married a rich wife himself.

Every time Lang had looked at the faded brown daguerreotype of his own father that his mother kept in a silver frame on her dressing-table, he had re-affirmed his decision to be a soldier. This was the life he had been born to: a soldier's life, following the drum. But—marriage? This was another thing altogether, although, as his mother explained, intricately bound up in the first.

The coachman flicked his whip over the arched backs of the horses. Iron tyres growled on gravel. As they went forward, the music grew louder, and he saw the red and white marquees, lit within by trembling flames. alive with music.

Many of the guests were officers, who wore mess dress, blues and scarlets, brave with burnished shoulder chains and gold epaulettes. The women were in crinolines of white and blue and pink, with flowers in their hair.

Among them moved butlers and liveried footmen, expertly, and without fuss. But then they were not just servants hired for the evening, but regular staff. No one and nothing was hired here; everyone and everything was theirs—and one day would be his. That is what marriage meant—the *right* marriage, of course, as his mother insisted.

Arabella. It seemed incredible that he, with so little money, brought up in a small terraced house his mother rented cheaply in Torquay, should ever have met her, let alone be her future husband.

She had been walking out with Mrs MacDonald along the sea front, looking out across the fishing boats beached on the shingle when a gust of wind had blown her hat away. He had picked it up, bowed, and returned it.

Her mother had thanked him, and somehow he was invited back for tea. Mrs MacDonald and Arabella explained that they had but lately returned from India. They had rented a house in Torquay for a month; the colonel was in the country seeing to some matters connected with his estate.

Lang explained that he had been born in India; his father had been a major in the Bengal Army.

'What regiment?' Colonel MacDonald had interrupted his wife when she told him about the meeting.

'Fifteenth Native Cavalry Regiment. Barrackpore.'

'Hm. Nothing special. Sort of regiment you'd join if you hadn't much money. They don't keep up much style.'

'That's what I thought. But he's a good-looking boy. Tall. Nice eyes. And a lot better than, than—the others.'

'Oh, my goodness, yes.'

The others. An Indian princeling she'd fancied herself in love with. Fancy, an *Indian!* Of course, he was rich, no doubt, and well born, and you might dine with that sort of person once or twice in a year if you were stationed near their palace. You might even permit them to lend you and your friends a dozen elephants with howdahs and half a hundred beaters for a tiger shoot, but that was the extent of your relationship; distant, correct, formal. Like two people playing a game, each knew his place and the iron rules and etiquette involved.

And there had been someone else equally unsuitable; a sergeant in his own regiment. Incredible, of course; he was quite a good-looking fellow in a common sort of way: father, a Sussex farmer. Good soldier, but nothing else about him. Well, there was one thing: his physique.

Colonel MacDonald had seen him bathing in a river, naked. The man had certainly been impressive; chest like a barrel, whang as big as a policeman's truncheon, sack well filled.

That's what had attracted his daughter, he realised; the physical side of the man. Perhaps it was the same with the Indian? He'd heard all the bazaar talk of their astonishing sexual appetites; how their women derived pleasure from sex—an extraordinary proposition by European and Christian standards and values, of course, but nevertheless believable as regards heathen natives. MacDonald had the authority of his own regimental surgeon for believing that Arabella was no longer a virgin.

'Of course, colonel,' the surgeon had added, rather embarrassed, but trying to be reassuring; after all, he needed a good report from the colonel for his own promotion. 'Of course, these young girls play tennis now, and some ride astride instead of side-saddle. And this sort of unaccustomed exercise can produce the same physical results as—ah—sexual congress.'

'But in this case, surgeon-major, what do *you* think?'

'I hesitate to say, sir, but in view of the young lady's warm personality, and a certain full-bloodedness about her private parts, I would consider that she has had intimate experience of some kind.'

Obviously, the sooner Arabella was safely married, the better; and this subaltern Lang seemed an ideal choice; safe, uninfluential—and Colonel MacDonald could still exercise some control over his career.

So, although Lang still could not understand how—for he never guessed that Mrs MacDonald would approve of such meetings, let alone encourage them—he had met Arabella again and again, and then quite frequently. A chaperone always accompanied them, of course, and gradually it became accepted that he was courting Arabella, and that they would marry. And then, because the MacDonalds were returning to India, their engagement was announced; Richard had been carried on the tides of wills stronger than his own, and had not objected. After all, it was probably, as his mother insisted, a wonderful thing.

Her own life had not been easy: his would be infinitely better—if he married Arabella.

'Yes, mama,' he had agreed, and of course he wanted it to be better. But what did they both mean by better?

To Mrs Lang it meant being waited on, living like the MacDonalds, who rang a bell and a manservant instantly appeared, a genie in a swallow-tail coat. A life without washing-up; no scrag-ends, no more mending and letting-out or down. No more scrimping. Ever.

To Richard, a better life meant a chance of adventure, the opportunity to extend himself, to stretch his mind, to achieve something—he was not quite sure what. It never occurred to him that these two definitions did not have the same meaning.

The coach jerked round the last bend in the long drive and so Richard missed—if indeed he would ever have detected in the darkness—a slight movement among the dark-green laurels and purple rhododendrons.

The couple in the bushes lay watching the coach jog on towards the house, like a cut-out silhouette. Then Arabella turned to her companion, and stroked his chin slowly.

'Didn't hear that at all,' she laughed. 'Must have had my mind elsewhere.'

'Not only your mind,' whispered Garroway and kissed her neck, biting her ears gently, running his hands down over her shoulders, cupping her bare breasts in his hands, feeling the nipples harden under his palms. Arabella strained up against him. He leaned over her, pulling up her skirt and their mouths met, tongues fencing, as he covered her body with his. She arched up under him.

'I love you,' he said untruthfully, looking down at her intently, as though he wanted to imprint in his mind how she looked with the clouds scudding across the moon, 'You bitch.'

'That's *why* you love me.'

'Then what about this boy Lang?'

'Oh, that's Mama's and Papa's doing. They want me to get engaged to him. So I am. It's being announced any minute.'

'My God, and yet you're doing this now, with me?'

'With no one else. At least, not at this moment. Know something, Ian?'

'What?'

'You talk too much.'

Then there was nothing but their own movements and

heavy breathing, and her long sobbing sigh of exultation, and they lay panting in each other's arms.

Suddenly, she struck Garroway in the middle of his back with her clenched fist, a small imperative blow.

'Get up,' she hissed, wriggling away from him.

Garroway rolled to one side and knelt on the outspread blue and red cloak and watched her, listening.

'Do me up. Quickly.'

'Why the hurry?'

'The band's stopped.'

She was sitting up now, fumbling with the hooks and eyes of her bodice. He picked up his cloak, shook it, and brushed it as best he could with his hands.

'What about me?' Arabella asked petulantly. 'Are there any leaves or grass on my dress?'

He brushed down her skirt at the back, and then pulled her to him fiercely. She shook herself free.

'Not now.'

'You *are* a one.'

'I know. But that won't help either of us unless we hurry. I'll go first.'

She stepped out of the bushes on to the gravel path and walked swiftly towards the house. A plump man with a swinging lantern was coming down it. The butler.

'Miss Arabella?' he called tentatively. His eyes were weak and he had mislaid his spectacles.

'Yes, Charteris.'

'The colonel is calling for you, miss. He wishes to make an announcement.'

'I took a walk,' she said. 'It's lovely by the lake.'

Charteris said nothing. He wondered who had been walking with her by the lake; and how long they had kept walking.

Garroway watched them go up the drive, and then came out of the bushes. He lit a cigar, pulled out the comb he kept in his left breast pocket, combed his hair and walked towards the house. The nearest table was packed with glasses of iced champagne, bubbles rising. He picked up a glass, drank it greedily. Then he drank a second, and carried a third glass towards the edge of the crowd that had now gathered around the steps of the house.

At the head of the steps stood Colonel MacDonald and

his wife. The colonel wore mess dress, a tall, white-haired figure with small eyes, his face flushed with drink and self-importance.

Arabella would be a rich bride. And money, like food, was all the more desirable when you hadn't enough of it. Garroway picked up another glass of champagne thoughtfully from the tray of a passing waiter.

Trumpeters played a fanfare and Arabella's uncle, a short fat character showing a lot of starched cuff and stiff shirt front, held up podgy hands for silence.

'My lords, ladies and gentlemen,' he intoned ponderously. 'It is with great pleasure that I introduce my brother-in-law, Colonel MacDonald, our host here tonight, who has an announcement to make of the highest importance.'

He waved one hand to MacDonald, like a barker in a fairground. The colonel bowed.

'I would like to welcome you all,' MacDonald began. 'Not only to this party which Bertha, my wife, and I are giving on the eve of our departure to India for our last tour of duty, before we return to stay here—I hope for ever—but also for another, and happier, reason.

'Our daughter, Arabella, is sailing to India with us. When she comes back here again, it will not be as Arabella MacDonald, but as the wife of an officer of the East India Company's Bengal Army, as Mrs Richard Lang. It gives us the deepest pleasure to announce her betrothal to Richard tonight.'

The colonel turned, and Lang stepped forward. He stood as tall as the colonel, his face pale in the hissing naphtha flares. Some guests began to clap, but not many; they didn't know this young man. Mothers, with sons they would have liked to see married to a girl with such rich expectations, looked at each other with raised eyebrows and shrugged their shoulders, pretending to clap their hands, careful not to let their palms touch.

'Richard also sails next week. But unfortunately not in the same ship. However, we will meet him again in India, and we have already made a provisional date for the wedding in June next year, at the church of St James's in Delhi.

'Richard Lang is a young man who, I am sure, will go far. His father, the late Major Ralph Lang, tragically had

his career cut short by an untimely death in the service of
John Company and his country. I know that Richard will
carry on in his father's tradition. And I know, also, that
all of you here will join me in wishing the young couple
great happiness in the years ahead.'

'Hear, hear,' shouted Garroway from the edge of the
crowd, the effects of four glasses of champagne moving in
his veins. He raised his empty glass ironically. People
frowned at him. Some of the women stayed looking, for
he was handsome: dark thick hair without a parting; a
Spanish-style moustache drooping on either side of his
mouth; a slightly sardonic gleam in his brown eyes as he
turned and toasted the women who stared at him. They
looked away, embarrassed that he seemed able to read
their thoughts.

Richard and Arabella now stepped forward. They
bowed and smiled and were holding hands.

'My lords, ladies and gentlemen,' called the colonel,
glass in hand. 'I ask you now to charge your glasses and
join me in a toast of long life, health and happiness for
my daughter and her future husband.'

The glasses went up with murmurs of: 'Hear, hear,' 'I
second that.'

Several guests later remarked that Arabella's left hand
was behind her dress, apparently brushing away a few
blades of grass and crushed clover petals. But only one
person in the crowd knew how they came to be there.

The maid bustled into Lang's room carrying a polished
copper can of hot water, pulled the curtains, wished him
good morning, sir, respectfully, curtsied, poured some
water into the white china bowl let into the marble slab
beneath the window, and withdrew.

Then a footman, with a dirty, pock-marked face under
his white wig, walked into the room gravely, carrying a
silver tray of tea, wafer biscuits, and an apple already
sliced. He laid the tray down reverently in his white-
gloved hands on the table by the bed, like an offering on
an altar.

Lang slid out of bed and crossed to the window and
looked down at the twenty-acre lawn that stretched to the
drive. A dozen gardeners, all wearing green baize aprons
and trousers tied with string below their knees, were care-

fully picking up the scattered debris of the previous night;
pieces of bread, lobster shells, broken glasses, white linen
napkins, a discarded fan. Other bearded men, in dark
coats and black bowler hats, were expertly lowering the
marquees. A few ragged little boys scuttered like two-
legged animals among the men, picking up crusts and
dropped rolls, cramming them into their mouths hungrily.
What they could not devour, they carried away in their
shirts.

Lang poured himself a cup of tea without milk or
sugar, drank it thankfully, then washed, shaved, and went
downstairs for breakfast.

The dining-room was empty. On the sideboard stood a
row of polished German silver domes covering plates of
bacon rashers, rind already removed, sizzling on silver
grills above blue-flamed spirit lamps.

He picked up a plate, already warm, put on two rashers
from the grill, a couple of eggs from under the next
domed dish, kidneys, fried bread, then poured himself a
breakfast cup of coffee, and sat down at the table.

The Times and the *St James's Gazette* were waiting on
polished brass stands, with their folds ironed, and the
pages sewn in with white thread, so they would not fall
out when the paper was opened. An under footman had
been downstairs at half past five to do this, and then had
prepared breakfast for the first and second footmen, the
butler and the housekeeper.

Lang ate quickly, glancing through the overseas pages
for any headlines about India. A dispatch from Calcutta
mentioned vague unrest among the sepoys. Of course,
these newspaper writers had always to keep looking out
for 'trouble somewhere to provide something to write
about.

The writer, like most of his kind, was obviously a clerk
or doff-hat, who knew very little of military matters. Otherwise how could he claim that, in a number of regiments,
sepoys had complained formally to their commanding officers about being ordered overseas to Burma, since this order was contrary to the terms of their enlistment, which
explicitly stated that recruits would only serve within Indian boundaries?

Some high-caste Hindu sepoys viewed this prospect of
overseas service with great alarm, not on the grounds of

personal danger, but because of spiritual contamination.
As Brahmins, they had been taught by their priests that to
share a plate, a bed space or a drinking vessel with a man
of lower caste, contaminated them eternally, so that they
would have no part in the glories of the after-life.

To cross the sea in a ship with others of low caste or,
worse still, no caste at all, or with *bhistis*, who drew and
carried water for washing and drinking, or sweepers, who
emptied latrine buckets, was comparable, in European and
Christian terms, to asking a man to share his bed with a
leper, with one fearful difference; they knew no cure for
the disease, either in this world or the next.

The writer listed further reasons for the disaffection
which he claimed should be causing more concern than it
was in Calcutta, the capital of India, and in London. The
East India Company, which frequently acted as though it
was the government instead of being simply a commercial
concern, had recently annexed the Kingdom of Oudh, a
province about the size of Scotland, midway between Ne-
pal and the North-West Frontier. From this kingdom the
Company's two armies, in Bombay and Bengal, had drawn
most of their recruits, for soldiers had privileges in Oudh
which civilians could never achieve.

In any legal dispute, for instance—and India had
many, because leases and wills and agreements were frequently only verbal—soldiers could be assured of help either in the courts or out of them by the British Resident
himself. Very few Indian lawyers, however honey-
tongued, would risk accepting a dubious case when they
knew that the judge and the defending lawyer were both
British and that neither could be bribed. Now, native
judges were to be appointed in their place.

The East India Company had assumed control of Oudh
because the old king was insane and his kingdom was, in
fact, controlled by robbers, who grew wealthy through le-
vies paid under threat of assassination. The Company had
feared revolution, which would very seriously affect their
revenues and profits, already the lowest they had been for
years. But instead of giving this genuine reason, they produced an unconvincing excuse that an old treaty with Britain had never been ratified. No one in Oudh believed
this, and few thought that the move was simply commer-

cial: they believed that more sinister motives lay behind it.

So, at a stroke of whose pen no one really knew, the East India Company had not only alienated their own armies and their own families, but had spread unrest and apprehension for the future among people who had previously been proud to serve.

Richard threw down the paper irritably. It was rubbish, of course. These newspaper writers whipped up trouble where none existed. India was a hot country, and in hot countries you always had disputes and disagreements of some kind. He'd learned this from his history lessons at Addiscombe, the East India Company's college. A hundred years earlier, Indians had been similarly shocked when, through entirely humane motives, the British had forbidden the old Hindu custom of *suttee*, in which, to show their love and fidelity, widows would fling themselves on the flames of their husband's funeral pyres and burn themselves to death.

Then the Company had stopped parents murdering unwanted baby girls, also a Hindu custom, which kept roughly constant the ratio of boys to girls—a most serious necessity in a country of primitive standards of agriculture.

The arrival of missionaries preaching the Christian faith had caused more alarm, among Hindus and Moslems and Sikhs alike. Until then, they had all believed that the British were only interested in trade, and kept the peace in India simply so that they could do more trade at greater profit and disadvantage to their European rivals, France and Portugal. Now they thought that the British were intent on Christianising the country—and by force, if need be.

But then, Lang's tutor had asked his class rhetorically, what could you expect from heathens, niggers, people who could not read or write? What, indeed?

As Richard went out of the dining-room into the inner hall, a side door to the garden opened, and Colonel MacDonald came in. His face was puffy, his eyes red, as though they had been sandpapered.

'Ah, Richard,' he said. 'Up early, eh?'

'Not as early as you, sir,' Richard replied dutifully.

'Hope you slept well?'

'Yes, sir.'

'I'd like a private word with you,' MacDonald continued.

Lang followed him into the library.

'Sit down,' said MacDonald; more an order than an invitation. 'Expect you're pretty tired after last night, eh?'

'Not really, sir. I danced most of the dances with Arabella. One with your lady wife. Two with my mother.'

'Very fitting ratio,' said MacDonald approvingly. 'Drink?'

'Not so early in the morning, sir.'

'Never too early for me. Medicinal purposes, of course. Settles the stomach. Keeps the vital juices working. Persuades the blood to pulse more agreeably around the body.'

MacDonald poured himself half a tumbler of neat whisky, drank it in two gulps, gave a soft, wet sigh and sat down behind the desk.

'We'll speak man-to-man,' he announced. 'No rank, eh? First, about Arabella. She's a very high-spirited gel. Rather like a yearling filly. Headstrong. Always had her own way. Only child. Follows her mother. You were very young when you were last in India, but you're a man now and I can tell you that the heat in India sometimes does odd things to the ladies, bless 'em.

'They may be cold in temperament in England. Indifferent to our, ah, *advances*. Lacking as you might say, in ardour, even. But out there, the heat and the curries and a strong moon and the lonely feeling of being one of a handful of Europeans, amongst literally millions of natives—it all seems to charge their emotions. They become wayward, difficult, passionate. Not as one imagines *ladies*. As opposed to doxies. You get my meaning?'

'Perfectly, sir.'

'Good. I'll be frank with you. When we were out there last, Arabella formed some idiotic attachment to some Indian princeling. You'll meet these fellers. Rich as Croesus. Charming. Educated over here. Just like one of us. Except, of course, for the colour of their skins and the fact they're heathens, worshipping gods of stone and wood. Which, of course, we can't do with.

'Mind you, we *mix* with these fellers, you know. Oh,
yes. Our ladies even dance with them. And they're very
hospitable in their own homes—palaces really. Ask us
back to dine. Have wonderful horses, and literally thousands of retainers.

'Fellers like the maharajahs of Patiala and Ahmed-
nagar. Then there's Baroda and Nana Sahib, the Maharajah of Bithur. Actually, the Government says he's not a
real rajah of the blood—only adopted. So they won't allow him a salute of guns like the others. Bit short-sighted,
I say, for he's just like the rest. Hospitable. Pleasant.
Well-disposed. God knows how rich they all are, and
they're all, well, *gentlemen*. Wogs, if you like, of course.
Worthy *oriental* gentlemen. A compliment in a way. But
you'll form your own judgement.

'Anyhow, I was saying that Arabella became rather too
involved with one of these chaps, and so we brought her
home. Commander-in-Chief's lady wife thought it might
be a bad example otherwise, you know. I admit you get
rankers who marry Indian women out there—damned
good looking they are, too, some of them—but not the
colonel's daughter. Got to draw the line somewhere. Do I
make myself plain?'

'Perfectly, sir,' Lang said for the second time.

MacDonald opened a drawer in his desk and pulled out
an envelope.

'Well,' he said thankfully, 'that settles that. Glad to get
it off my chest. Best to be frank. Nothing hidden. Now, to
the other matters. I know your father was a very honourable officer. But, of course, he's been dead for ten years.
And you'll not know many people who can give you a
push in your career when you need one. And if you
haven't got money in India, then you need good friends,
who'll help you—and perhaps you'll be in a position later
on to help them. Turn and turn about. The law of life.

'So I've racked my brains to see who I knew out there
who might be able to help you. And I've come up with
two.'

He opened the envelope.

'Both young men. Well, youngish. In their late thirties.
One's a bachelor, one's married.

'The bachelor's Nicholson, John Nicholson. Irish. Fa-

ther was a Quaker doctor, who caught fever from a patient and died. Left a widow and seven children, and
nothing else.

'Nicholson was sixteen. So what did *he* do? He left
school, got on to his uncle in the East India Company—
see what I said about friends?—and became a cadet, then
an officer, in the Bengal Infantry.

'He's an odd feller, rather a lone wolf. But I believe
he's highly thought of. In fact, I *know* he is. Feller in my
club last week said he's bound eventually to be a general.
Maybe even governor-general. He knows him well. So I
got him to write this letter, introducing you.'

'Thank you, sir,' said Lang. 'As a matter of fact, my
mother knows his mother slightly. They both live in
Torquay. She's also writing to him to say I'm coming out.'

'Oh, well, perhaps I'll tear up this letter, then?'

'No. Please don't. It was most kind of you to get it for
me.'

MacDonald pushed the letter across the desk petulantly.

'Now, the married man. Again, I don't know the man
personally—one can't know *everyone* personally—but I
think he'll be useful to you. His brother's a parson. Bishop
here knows him. So I got him to write this note to him.
Name of Hodson, William Raikes Hodson. Was at Rugby.
Cambridge. Evidently fooled about, wanted to be a lawyer, but did nothing—didn't get a degree, I mean—so
came down and also joined the Bengal Army.

'Now he's married some woman older than himself.
Think she's a son by her first husband. Boy must be in his
late teens now. Funny feller, Hodson, apparently. Good at
things you wouldn't expect an officer to be good at.'

'Like what, sir?'

'Like being a mimic. Man can memorize pages of *Pick-
wick Papers*. Takes all the parts himself. Odd, don't you
think?'

'Unusual, sir.'

'*Bloody* unusual. Some of the best officers I've served
with couldn't even *read*, unless it's a cheque—or a race
card. I believe he's been in some sort of trouble out there,
money or something.

'It's damned easy to run into debt in India, Richard, believe me. You never pay cash. You sign chits for everything. They don't come in till the end of the month,

maybe not for three months. Sometimes they're sold by
one trader to another at a discount. Then they'll all come
in at once.

'So you borrow money to pay them, and the interest is
high—or maybe you are asked to show a favour to someone instead. If there's a contract some native contractor's
very anxious to get, for instance.

'So you've got to watch yourself with money. Don't
think Hodson's a *rogue,* mind. I wouldn't give you his
name if I thought he was. Just expect he was careless.
Most of us are, about money.

'Anyhow, he's been seconded to the Intelligence Department. Bit of a backwater, I'd say. Not work for a gentleman. I take Napoleon's view. His spy-master, Schulmeister, ferreted out the secrets that helped him win both Ulm
and Austerlitz. Napoleon gave the man money, of course,
but Schulmeister wanted an honour as well. Napoleon
naturally wouldn't consider the idea. "I cannot honour a
spy," he said. And he didn't. Quite right, too.'

'But, what about this Hodson, sir? Isn't he an officer?'

'Of course he's an officer. A lieutenant. But mind you
he's thirty-five or -six. Or maybe even older. He should be
a captain by now. He would be. Even a major—if he had
money.'

'So all promotion goes by money? You've got to buy
it?'

'Well, not *all,* but it helps, doesn't it? Dammit, you've
got to run your polo ponies somehow and pay your bills,
haven't you? Say you're the colonel of a regiment, and
you've got two young fellers, equal in everything else—
but one can put five hundred pounds into mess funds, or
five thousand. Then he's got a better chance than the feller who can't put in anything. *Must* have. That's obvious,
surely?'

'I don't think I have much of a chance, then. I've nothing except my pay.'

'That's why I'm giving you these contacts, Richard,' said
MacDonald coldly. 'You make yourself pleasant and useful to them. They speak well of you—and you could find
yourself in a position where their good influence is as
good as money. Or almost. Which means promotion. And
promotion means success. And that's happiness for Arabella and you. It's a vicious circle.'

'Certainly sounds a bit vicious, sir.'

'What do you mean by that?'

'Nothing, really. Just a bad pun.'

'Too early in the morning for jokes. Well, I'm going to London for a luncheon today. So I'll say good-bye to you now, Richard. Or rather, as the French say, "au revoir." See you again in Delhi. You know your posting yet?'

'Fifteenth Native Cavalry. Stationed in Barrackpore.'

'Oh, yes. My wife told me. Near Calcutta. Bit dead-and-alive up there. Humidity's terrific. Curious thing. Civilians wear a white dinner jacket in Calcutta and black trousers. Go across to Bombay and they wear a black dinner jacket and white trousers. Deuced odd, don't you think?'

'Yes, sir.'

'Well, nothing much more. Are you taking out any guns? Do much shooting?'

'I haven't got my own gun, sir.' Lang did not add that he could not afford one. His father's twelve-bore had been sold long ago.

'Pity. Get some damned fine shooting with these maharajah fellers. Don't use any dogs. You have native boys to pick up your birds for you. They are just *like* dogs, you know. I remember once, duck shooting, we all went to lunch, and I looked out of the window and, damn me, there were half a dozen natives swimming away for dear life in the lake to retrieve the ducks.'

'Do they like it, sir?'

'*Like* it? Never asked 'em. Don't see why they shouldn't though. Keeps 'em cool. Anyway, you don't ask natives if they *like* something. You just tell 'em to *do* it.

'You have my address? Headquarters, Special Detachment, Delhi. In the Red Fort. My job's to look after the old King of Delhi, who's really only a king in name. An old fool on the Company's payroll, surrounded by concubines and eunuchs, and women he can do nothing to except look at. But he's very useful to the Company. A kind of totem for the Indians.

'The Company's got an agreement that they won't keep any British troops in Delhi, except the small detachment I'm in charge of. Sort of guard of honour.

'The nearest British regiments are about forty miles away, across the desert at Meerut. They can reach Delhi

in a couple of days' fast marching, so everyone's happy.
The Indians have their honour and pride and prestige—no
foreign troops in what was their capital for hundreds of
years—and we have the country and the trade. A very satisfactory distribution. I look forward to our meeting
again, Richard.'

'Yes, sir. And thank you for the letters.'

They shook hands. The colonel stumped off up the corridor, and left Richard looking out of the window at the
lawn. Both marquees were down now, and workmen were
carrying the poles, like huge battering rams, towards the
carts.

Did all successful people think so much about money,
he wondered; or perhaps the colonel thought about it so
much because it wasn't his money, but his wife's.

He knew she had come from some family in the north
of England. Cotton-spinners or mill-owners. It was wise to
marry a rich wife, if you hadn't money yourself. As his
tutor at Addiscombe had advised his class once: 'As officers and gentlemen, you don't *talk* about money. You either have it or you haven't. But if you haven't got it, then
you make it. And if you can't make it, then, dammit, you
marry it.'

Looking out over the lawn, towards the sweep of trees,
Lang suddenly realized that people could also say he was
marrying for money.

Was he?

2

Queen Victoria was expecting her seventh baby.

The courtyard of Buckingham Palace had been laid with freshly washed sea-sand to quieten the grind of iron tyres beneath the windows, although her private apartments were on the other side of the building overlooking the garden and the lake.

The special saluting guns of the Royal Artillery stood with horses bridled and limbers fitted, ready to move instantly to the Park, the Tower of London and to Fort Belvedere, out near the village of Sunningdale on the Southampton Road, to fire the Royal Salute of forty-one rounds as soon as the birth was announced.

One room in the Palace had been set aside for the event, and all the furniture inside it was draped with white sheets in an attempt at asepsis. The Queen's two nurses, Mrs Lilly and Mrs Innocenti, were already installed in their own quarters, and had discreetly fixed up a small Chinese screen in a corner of the room. Behind this stood a complex cluster of strange glass globes and bulbs and raw metal barrels hung with red rubber bladders and pipes. This was the anaesthetic machine.

The new baby would be the second royal baby to be born in something less than agony. Queen Victoria had inhaled chloroform four years earlier, in 1853, for the birth of her sixth child, and this unexpected Royal innovation had set a seal of acceptance on six years of unrewarded research and experiment by Dr James Young Simpson who, still only in his forties, had struggled all this time

unavailingly to influence the course of painless midwifery
by the use of chloroform and ether.

A sitting-room was also ready for those Ministers of the
Crown who had to be present by custom. There, within
earshot, but tactfully not within sight of the Queen, they
would satisfy themselves that the child was actually born
to the Queen, and was not some other baby introduced il-
licitly.

This tradition stemmed from an ancestor of Queen Victoria, the sickly wife of King James II. All her children
had died in infancy, and when, in July, 1688, she gave
birth prematurely to a son, some politicians put about the
rumour that he was not a real Royal prince, but a humble
child smuggled into the Palace in a warming pan.

Lord Dalhousie, the recently-retired Governor-General
of India, knew all about these preparations for the imminent birth. The servants' papers had been full of these details for days. One didn't read that trash for pleasure, of
course, but sometimes a headline caught the eye.

Some men, no doubt, would have felt flattered that the
Queen should still ask to see them at such a time, but not
Dalhousie. A political opponent had told him once that he
was vain as an ugly woman, and this was quite true. He
was as conscious of his dignity as of his lack of inches.
He was pleased he had retired as Governor-General of India. People in England were not at all concerned with India, thousands of miles away, when they had so many
worries at home: mass unemployment, the rising cost of
bread, demands to raise the school leaving age to eleven,
and other irrelevancies of this sort.

Only the government was mildly concerned—and then
simply from motives of fear. If the Company grew too
rich and powerful, it could become a threat to their own
existence. So could any general revolution in India, if
British subjects were massacred, and the public at home
asked why this had not been foreseen and prevented.

His successor in Calcutta, Lord Canning, was more to
their taste: always ready to listen to the Indian side of any
dispute. Personally, Dalhousie was well out of it all. He'd
served for ten years; he'd earned the good things that
would now be his.

His coachman turned into the gold-topped gates of the
Palace, and the polished iron tyres struck sparks from the

gravel. A footman in Royal livery stepped forward smartly, and bowed low as he opened the silver-handled door
with Dalhousie's crest in gold as the carriage halted outside the main doors.

His own footman jumped down from his place on the
box with the driver and saluted the open carriage door.
Dalhousie waited for a moment—there was no need to
hurry, you had to show these fellows who you were; they
respected you more for it—and then he climbed down
slowly, studiously ignored them, and walked up the red
carpet into the Palace.

A butler stepped forward and bowed. Dalhousie stood
on the points of his shoes in the subconscious hope of add-
ing an inch to his stature, handed over his white gloves,
his rolled umbrella and his polished silk hat. The butler
took them, and passed them on to a second servant, who
materialized behind them. Then a third footman appeared,
in breeches and tail coat, wearing a powdered wig. He led
Dalhousie along a tiled green-walled corridor lined with
marble busts of long-forgotten kings and queens and
statesmen, opened the door of a waiting room and bowed
again.

Dalhousie went into the room. The Prime Minister,
Lord Palmerston, was waiting for him, wearing his favourite dress of green trousers and blue coat, his whiskers
carefully dyed to conceal his age. He was a vain man, but
cheerful: only days before he had won a general election
by seventy-nine votes, the biggest majority since the Re-
form Bill twenty-five years previously.

'Good morning, Prime Minister,' said Dalhousie.

'Morning,' replied Palmerston. 'Thought you were going
to be late.'

He lived in a huge house just across the Park, in Picca-
dilly, and allowed himself six minutes for the short walk
to the Palace.

Dalhousie took out his gold watch ostentatiously.

'Eleven fifteen is the audience. It's eleven eleven, Prime
Minister. Precisely.'

Palmerston grunted. He had all the big man's con-
descension for someone much smaller: everything about
Dalhousie irritated him.

'With the birth expected any day, it's a wonder Her
Majesty will see you at all,' he said.

Dalhousie said nothing. Instead, he prowled round the room on his toes, looking at ornaments and paintings that did not interest him; anything rather than have to face Palmerston. Or rather, not face him, but because of his height, be forced physically to look up to him.

A flunky wearing velvet knee-breeches and a white wig and jacket with gold buttons embossed with the Royal crest, a splendid outfit contrasting strangely with the sour smell from his pustuled and unwashed body beneath these fine clothes, opened the door.

'My lord, Prime Minister,' he said adenoidally, looking from one to the other. 'Her Majesty will see you now.'

Some ancient knight from the shires, white-haired, pink-cheeked and trembling, a Gentleman of the Household, now appeared, and bowed deeply to both visitors. Palmerston bowed to him in return. Dalhousie bowed, but carefully to no one in particular.' Then they all set off down the corridor, unconsciously falling into step.

Queen Victoria waited in an audience room small by the gargantuan standards of palace architecture, no more than forty-foot square. It had a ceiling painted by Cellini, embossed with gilt and blue cherubs against white Italian clouds scudding before a sunnier sky than London had ever seen. The curtains were drawn, so that the room appeared dim, almost at half-light. The small, puffy-faced woman of thirty-seven who awaited them, her clothes skilfully arranged around her by personal maids to minimize the fact that she was nearly nine months pregnant, sat on a throne decorated with lions' heads, gilded and built into the arm rests.

She nodded as the three men stood in the doorway, the courtier in front of the visitors. They all went down on their right knee before her.

'You may enter,' she said, stroking the ears of the lions. They felt very smooth to the touch, almost like real gold. Would a real lion's head feel so silky? She must ask Albert: he would know; he knew everything.

Her voice was thinner and less regal than Dalhousie had imagined it would be. When he raised his head he looked into her hard small eyes, set in curiously white and waxy flesh, the face of someone who rarely saw the sun. It was as though one of the marble heads in the corridor outside had suddenly become animated.

'Well, my Lord Dalhousie, pray come forward,' Queen Victoria told him. He took two paces into the room. The carpet was so thick that it muffled all sound of his movement.

'And how, pray, did you leave our Indian enterprises?'

Dalhousie took a deep breath, realizing that the question was entirely rhetorical. Queen Victoria wanted a quick answer, not the long, involved, carefully balanced statement he had rehearsed to himself in his study until he knew it by heart. Well, he would give her what she wanted.

'Your Majesty,' he replied sonorously, measuring to each syllable the weight it deserved, 'if I were asked to prophesy, I would say that this year will be one of unparalleled peace, prosperity and goodwill throughout the length and breadth of all India.'

3

The early morning sun, gathering strength for another burnished day, when the mercury in the barrack-square thermometer would boil in its bulb, blazed across the parade ground, throwing long shadows from the three cannons across the dry dust.

They were old siege guns with muzzles eight inches across, big and black as bear-holes, barrels intricately carved with serpents and fiery heads. Brought out from their artillery store, polished and sanded, black-spoked wooden wheels re-lacquered, leather release straps oiled, bronze on their barrels buffed, they stood in line, ready for their terrible purpose, barrels pointed to the sky at their highest angle of elevation.

Behind them stood the artillerymen in their full dress uniform, brass helmets, tiger-skins, and black leather breeches. Alongside each cannon lay newly sawn stakes of wood formed into crosses, about twelve feet long and four feet across, with mule-loading ropes coiled near them. Behind the gunners, on two sides of a square, stood two rows of British troops in red coats and white shakos. They were armed and carried their loaded carbines at the slope. On the third side of this hollow square an entire Indian regiment had been paraded, unarmed. Behind them again, stood three ranks of British troops, and then the muzzles of other artillery.

Subedar Ram Gupta, with thirty years' service in the Bengal Army of the Honourable East India Company behind him, and now within sight of his pension, stood to attention in front of his men on his last parade, his mind numbed by the prospect of what was about to happen.

Late the previous evening, he had returned to Barrackpore from leave, from spending three months in his village with his wife and daughters near Cawnpore, nine days' march away, to hear the astonishing news that the regiment, *his* regiment, which had been both mother and father to him since he had joined so many years before, was to be disbanded. This might seem incredible, but it was true. And, worst of all, three old comrades were to be blown from guns. Alive.

Ram Gupta could find no English officer to tell him anything about his future, or why this astonishing and terrible decision had been reached. The colonel and adjutant, to whom he usually had instant access, were—so the regimental clerk told him—with General John Murphy, the divisional commander. All junior officers were in their quarters—sheltering in case of violence.

'Violence from whom?' asked Ram Gupta in bewilderment. Was he going mad, or was this some elaborate hoax?

'From us, subedar sahib,' replied the clerk, grinning. His teeth, dyed red with betel juice, made his mouth seem full of blood, and gave him a sinister cannibalistic appearance.

'*Us?*'

'*Jihan.* We will be the masters soon. It is written.'

'Where is it written?'

'In our stars, in our hearts. You have been on leave too long, subedar sahib. One regiment has already refused the new cartridges and has been disbanded. Now it is our turn.'

'But, why? *What* cartridges have been refused?'

'The new issue. For the new Enfield rifles the English are giving us to replace the Brown Bess muskets. The cartridges have to be greased with cow fat and pig lard, and a twist of paper bitten off before we fire them.'

'I don't believe it. The cow is sacred to us Hindus. As the pig is unclean to Moslems. The English would never be so foolish. They know our beliefs.'

'The old ones did, subedar sahib, I agree. But not the new officers we have now. Not a fish's tit do they care for us. They cannot even speak our tongue, but need an inter-preter.'

'That is true,' Ram Gupta agreed reluctantly. But did this also mean that the new English officers were so igno-rant that they would deliberately insult and offend all the sepoys of both major Indian religions by insisting they used this grease? Surely not?

Man cannot determine at what hour or place he enters this world, but sometimes others decide when and how he will leave it. And the greatest defilement of all, the ulti-mate horror that paralysed Ram Gupta's mind as he clenched and unclenched his hands at the sides of his trousers, was the unspeakable way these men would pass from this world to the next—from the three siege guns.

How could refusing to go against their religious teaching bring such an ultimate punishment? Was there indeed truth in the bazaar rumour that the English planned to convert Indians to Christianity by force?

Ram Gupta's eyes, narrowed against the bright sun, tried to draw some comfort from the familiar back-ground: the parade ground itself, rough as a rasp; the thatched barracks, with mango trees behind them, their branches trembling and feathery in the growing heat. How many hundred of times had he stood thus before his men under the roasting sun, proud of his position and rank!

Ram Gupta stood still as an iron man, not a muscle moving, eyelids barely blinking, although sandflies stung his neck, relishing the salt sweat that streamed down beneath his heavy shako.

The heavy serge hand-me-down red coat he wore (too tight under the armpits, because the local Indian tailoring contractor, who had copied a British design intended for cold climates, had defaulted on the amount of cloth) con-stricted the circulation so that he had no feeling whatever in his arms. Behind him, and on either side, in open or-der, boots polished like ebony on bare feet, their flesh beneath their uniforms soft with sweat, the rest of the reg-iment also waited as rigidly, their shadows shortening as the sun climbed up the sky.

The nine hundred men with whom Ram Gupta had served for so long might also have been statues, carved from dark stone, except for their grey hair. Many were in

their fifties, and some even in their sixties, for promotion
came slowly in the local armies of the Company. British
officers could buy it—if they had the money—and set
prices were laid down and adhered to with no bargaining,
for gentlemen did not bargain. Four thousand pounds for
the command of a regiment; two thousand pounds for a
captaincy; a thousand for a quick commission to provide
a gentleman's career for a feeble-minded younger son.

Indian sepoys tried to advance their humble rank by
judiciously bribing regimental clerks, who might then
plead their case for promotion with their superiors, or by
giving presents to the Indian mistresses of British officers,
who could speak kindly of them to their lovers.

But, even so, for naiks and havildars and subedars, as
for lieutenants and captains, promotion often came so
slowly in this hard, hot land that death overtook their
chances. Now, disgrace had overcome them all.

A small group of British officers rode slowly out
towards them from the shade of the barracks. The polished steel of the subalterns' drawn swords signalled wild
messages from the rising sun.

The leading officer was a major of fifty-five, sweat already spreading its dark stain on his back and beneath his
armpits. He turned to an Indian interpreter who ran barefoot alongside the horse, his feet hard as iron, never feeling the sharp flints of the barrack square.

Although the major had served for nearly forty years in
India he could still only speak *charwallah* hindusthani. He
knew enough for his meagre purposes and his personal
pleasures: to summon his Indian mistress to his bed, to re-
buke a *bhisti* for running his bath too hot. But for the dis-
agreeable and shocking task ahead, he needed professional
assistance.

He reined in his horse and turned to the interpreter.

'Put it in their lingo as I speak it,' he said briefly. 'Understand?'

The interpreter nodded. He was a grey-haired man in
his sixties, wearing a white dhoti that looked like a shroud
when the wind flapped its length about his thin, brown,
scaly legs.

'Right,' began the major. 'There is no need for me to
tell you once more why you're here, but I will.

'You're here to be disbanded as a regiment. To be

struck from the Roll of Honour of the East India Company. You are being disbanded because you have refused a lawful order to accept the new ammunition which all the armies in India, the Bengal and the Bombay Armies of the East India Company, *and* the British Army, are being issued with.

'Three of your number have also deliberately refused a further order, to embark for service in Burma. This is mutiny. The punishment for mutiny is death. Since the army is in the field, the sentence is to be fired from guns.'

His horse broke wind and scraped its shoes on the ground; the flies were annoying it. The major tugged irritably at the bridle.

'Where are the prisoners?' he shouted.

'Here, sir.'

Three sepoys came marching out from the barracks between double guards of British corporals. Their ankles were shackled with iron chains. They held them up as they walked, still keeping in step with the other troops; years of training were not easily forgotten.

A British sergeant-major, marching to one side, pace-stick under his right arm, wheeled them round in front of the nearest cannon, and kept them marking time. Their knees came up like pistons; six boots hammered the hard earth as one.

As they came in front of the muzzles of the three guns, he halted them. They turned to face the inner empty square, the huge mouths of the guns gaping blackly behind them.

'Prisoners in position, sir!' the sergeant-major reported.

The major raised his sword to return his salute.

'Have they anything to say?' he asked.

The prisoners shook their heads. The prospect of what awaited them within minutes had drained their minds of all thought and the power of speech. They stood numbly, eyes wide with horror. A wave of unease. like a wind in dry leaves before a storm, trembled across the ground.

A British lieutenant dismounted from his horse behind the major and crossed to the prisoners, spurs clanking. He carried a small knife in his hand. With this he ripped the brass buttons from the men's jackets. Smiths and armourers went down on their knees with hammers and huge pincers to nip the shackles. Other men pulled off the prisoners' uniforms, picked up the three wooden crosses.

The prisoners were naked now, except for loincloths. Their heads were shaven, because of their caste, save for long tufts of hair which distinguished the Hindu from the Moslem. Hindus believe that, at the moment when the spirit departs from the body, it is by this cord of hair that it ascends to the other world.

The punishment was the long-established way of dealing with mutiny, under the old Mogul Emperors, and was equally dreaded by Hindus and Moslems, for both their religions declared that it destroyed the human soul as utterly as the body.

The Hindus believed that unless their corpses were burned to ashes, or consigned to the sacred waters of the Ganges, they would have no after-life. The Koran taught that all true believers must be buried unmutilated. Only those who had lost limbs fighting the infidel would be excused this strict condition.

No one was quite sure of the next orders: there was no recent precedent for them, but somehow the men had to be tied to the poles, so the sergeant-major had evolved orders of his own.

He did not relish his part in this business, but orders were orders; they were his life. If you started questioning orders or not obeying them, you could end up like the poor devils in front of him.

British privates carried up the crosses and began to rope the prisoners to them as tightly as they could, panting with their exertion, constricting all circulation. Then they picked up the stakes, four men to each one, and bound them to the mouths of the three cannon.

The sepoys were totally incapable of movement, except for their heads. Their foreheads were rigid with wrinkles, eyes white and staring in their heads, as they awaited crucifixion by cannonfire.

The sun was coming up now over the thatched barracks, and to one side, and unseen, a drum began to beat. For the prisoners, these beats marked their last seconds of life as they ticked away.

One shouted hoarsely, desperate for reassurance as he stood on the brink of eternity:

'For the faith! For the faith! Remember us!'

Another sepoy called back his reply from the ranks of the sepoys on parade.

'We will remember! We will remember!'

For a second there was silence, then a faint bubbling sound as the middle sepoy lost control of himself; his sphincter muscle relaxed and faeces oozed down his legs and on to the ground.

'Light tapers!' came the order.

The gunners struck the flints on tinders; little flames trembled on the ends of the wax tapers they held.

'Siege gun demolition party, prepare to fire! . . . *Fire!*'

As in one movement the three tapers went at the same time to the flash-point of each gun. For a second that stretched, it seemed to the watchers, for hours, nothing happened.

Those nearest the guns could see the tiny flames tremble like candles. Then, with one monster voice, the three guns spoke.

Their muzzles belched out huge sheets of orange flame, ringed with black oily smoke, and from the vortex of each explosion streaked the splintered stakes with the prisoners tied to them.

They were still alive, and they screamed as they hurtled through the air. The cannons had been primed with half charges, lest full charge should disintegrate the bodies completely, and so the prisoners were only flung for about three hundred yards.

As they began to fall, everyone on the parade ground could see how the blast of the explosions had blown away the flesh from their backs and their legs and blackened the bones.

The three bodies dropped within yards of each other. The stakes stood on end for one moment and then fell to one side. The sharp, familiar smell of burnt cordite was replaced by the stronger smell of burnt flesh; crisp, oily, sweet and terrible. Three men had passed into eternity under the eyes of thousands.

The firing party presented a fearful sight. They had neglected to put up back-boards to the guns, so the recoil had flung back pieces of raw, burning flesh, spattering their faces and covering them with blood and calcined remains.

The burial party came round at the double, carrying bamboo stretchers and folded grey army blankets, to pick up the remains of the men; strips and gouts of red, raw flesh, burst bowels encased in shreds of bloodied loincloth. They put them on the stretchers, stakes and all, covered them with blankets, and double-marched away.

Ram Gupta could barely believe what his eyes had seen, a nightmare come to life, and yet it was true. It had happened, and he had been a part of that happening.

How different had been his dreams when he had first joined as a recruit! His uncle, a havildar in the army, had told him stories of strange places and customs, of forced marches and charges, of spoils to be shared out after each victory. He had never been in any defeat, not his uncle.

So the bugles spoke in Ram Gupta's blood. He heard their voices and they would not be denied; despite the warnings of his priest about losing caste and the agony of his mother about losing a son for ever.

After weeks of argument and entreaty, his parents had given him their reluctant tearful blessing, and carrying a cloth bag in which his mother had sewn six gold mohurs, the currency of the ancient Mogul empire, still in use in remote places, and his own special brass bowl and string, for none but a Brahmin could cook or draw water for a Brahmin, Ram Gupta had set out to offer himself for enlistment. He had followed the drum and this was where his road had led him.

From the edge of the parade ground, through the horizontal slatted blinds of an ante-room in the officers' mess, General John Murphy, the Divisional Commander, stood watching the scene through field glasses.

He was a short, fat, bald man, with the pink bubbles of sweat rash streaking his chin. He had cut himself shaving that morning, and a piece of blood-soaked cotton wool still stuck to his wrinkled, sodden flesh.

Behind him, hovering like an uneasy satellite, stood his chief of staff, Colonel Jack Whitehead, with a handful of captains from rich families. Beyond them again, like lesser stars, stood mess orderlies in white uniforms, wearing thick red and gold belts burnished with the crest of the regiment. Tables were packed with soda-water bottles, marble stoppers in their necks, and buckets of ice, with whisky and claret in glass decanters.

These mess servants would be without jobs, too, at the end of the day, but their future seemed hazy and unreal, even to them; the present was what mattered. The regiment was still their mother and father.

Above their heads, tapestried punkahs flapped to and fro, guide ropes slopping through greased holes in the far wall to a little hut outside, where the *punkahwallah* slept, one end of the rope tied to his right ankle. Even in sleep his leg moved mechanically, a limb with a mind of its own.

'A bloody shame,' the general said to no one in particular. 'But we'd no other choice.'

He thought of the start of this whole disgraceful business, on a Sunday afternoon some weeks earlier when a sepoy in barracks, Manghal Pandy, fuddled through smoking *bhang*, a type of Indian hemp, had seized a rifle and challenged anyone to fight him.

The quarter guard thought he was mad, and took no notice. A British sergeant-major heard the shouting and came out of his bungalow in a great state of anger, asking what the hell he thought he was doing. Pandy shot at him, missed and then clubbed two young British officers who had tried, without much enthusiasm or effect, to reason with him.

Somehow, General John Hearsey, the Area Commander, heard of this shameful shambles, and taking his two sons as companions, galloped to the scene.

He had served all his life in India. He knew that appeals to reason were useless in such cases, so, shouting to his sons to keep him covered with their rifles, he walked over to Manghal Pandy—who promptly turned his rifle on himself. But instead of committing suicide dramatically, Manghal Pandy only shot himself in the calf.

As soon as the guard saw how the general's action had swung the pendulum of initiative, they arrested the wounded Pandy. He had been court-martialled and hanged, but somehow his name lived on: the mutinous men, who had just been executed, were all to be referred to by Indians and British alike as Pandies.

'It *is* a very serious step, sir,' agreed Colonel Whitehead, his careful monotone voice cutting through Murphy's thoughts like a blunt sawblade.

Whitehead never disagreed with anyone too firmly in

case the other person's opinion proved right; that way, he
kept his options open, and had acquired a reputation for
sagacity. He had survived malaria attacks only to fall vic-
tim to chronic indigestion, chewing soda mints after every
meal.

Oddly enough, the regimental medical officer's treatment for malaria—shaving Whitehead's head to his skull,
and letting blood regularly—had only weakened the man
further.

'Of course, it's serious,' the general agreed irritably.
'But what else could we do with mutiny? We can't hang
'em all like Manghal Pandy. Or shoot 'em from guns. Not
a whole *regiment*, damn' nearly a thousand men. I mean,
it's not, well, *feasible*.'

'That mutiny, sir. It was only a technical point,' insisted
Whitehead. He had read the law of sedition in the Army
Act the previous evening. He felt ready to stand up, how-
ever briefly, for a small exchange of fire over definitions.

The general lowered his glasses. His eyes were heavy
and dull over pouches of flesh; grey hairs grew like goose-
berry bristles in his nostrils.

'Everything in military law is only a technical point, if
you want it that way, Whitehead. But if we let those niggers get away with refusing orders, next thing the whole
army all over India will be doing the same thing. *And* engaging Indian lawyers to plead their case.

'One, they've been ordered to serve overseas in Burma
and they've refused. Two, they've been ordered to load
with the new cartridges, and they've refused that, too.
You can't have a clearer cut case of disobeying an order—two orders. The shortest definition of that is one
word. Mutiny. The Judge Advocate agrees.'

'No doubt, sir. But, with respect, the terms of the
sepoys' recruitment specifically state that they would never
be ordered to serve outside India. The fact that we have
tried to force them to do so because we need men in
Burma does not alter the case, sir. Brahmins believe they
lose caste if they go to sea.'

'Don't tell me what they believe. I know that as well as
you do. Better, for I've been soldiering longer. When we
get more missionaries here, who can teach them the Christian gospels, they'll forget all this heathen nonsense.'

'Possibly, sir, but meanwhile . . .'

'Meanwhile,' said the general firmly, 'I'll have a drink.'

He held out his right hand. A *khitmagar* instantly placed in it a glass of claret. Murphy drank deeply, put down the half-empty glass on a tray, and turned back to Whitehead. Soon the wine would make him foolish, then lecherous, in an ironic, feeble way, for he had been impotent for years. But now it made him feel at ease, in command of a situation he could neither understand nor control.

'You can say what you like, Whitehead,' he announced with finality. 'But there was nothing else we could do. *Nothing.*'

Wasn't there? thought Whitehead bitterly, irritation lighting a new flame to burn his tortured stomach. There probably isn't now, but there was years ago; maybe even months ago. Also, blowing sepoys out of a cannon as a warning to others seemed as bad to him as using a convicted thief as a human plough, drawn along between two bullocks, a punishment favoured by indigo-planters farther north.

You couldn't break up a regiment of men who had served together loyally, literally from boyhood, and send them walking back to their villages, as far as a thousand miles away, without pensions or even references, and expect life to go on for them, or for you, as though nothing had happened.

He had reported so many earlier signs of disaffection to the general, but no one had wanted to admit them. They were like unwelcome clouds on a summer day. Everyone pretended they weren't really there, or if they were that they would blow over.

The Indians were convinced that the British intended to break down their whole system of life and belief, for they saw evidence on every side. In the proposal that girls as well as boys should go to school; by encouraging people to travel by the new railway trains, so that men of high caste had to sit with those of lower caste, or even the untouchables who had no caste at all, and so were beyond every point of human contact; in plans to irrigate India from the sacred waters of the holy river Ganges.

How could anyone believe that these final insults of mixing cow fat and pig's lard to produce a lubricant for a new sort of cartridge were not also deliberately and calcu-

latingly introduced as part of this whole system of tearing
down the ancient tapestry of belief and social order?

Whitehead had told the general of other uneasy tales,
but Hearsey and Murphy had both dismissed them all as
rumours; foolish gossip. Only old men believed them. Yet
they were old men themselves.

One rumour declared that, within a hundred years from
the first great battle on Indian soil between Englishmen
and Indians—the Battle of Plassey, when Clive, a sickly
clerk with the Company, commanding nine thousand
men, had defeated a force thirty times as large—British
power in India would wither and die.

Now a hundred years had run. Was the evening of an
empire also close at hand?

Other Indians spoke of chapattis, thin round pancakes,
tinted with red dye, that strangers had asked them to pass
from hand to hand, from village to village, as a sign and
token of unrest; red for blood, red for danger—and also a
simple way to discover how long a message would take to
travel across the country.

And there were further, more violent, signs of discord:
fire arrows that set aflame the thatched roofs of English-
occupied houses. Poison inexplicably appeared in wells;
villagers grew reluctant to be out after dark, lest some
nameless horror overcame them.

Whitehead had served in India for twenty-five years.
Never had he encountered so many symptoms of unrest.
Some, yes; all, no. He felt an unease in his guts that had
nothing to do with indigestion. Within hours, these disbanded sepoys would be setting off for their homes, each
one an ambassador of discontent, exaggerating what had
happened, to minimize his own embarrassment, to give
himself more importance. Village elders would listen
gravely, nodding their heads at yet another instance of
English duplicity, another reason to distrust them.

Whitehead picked up the general's glasses, and focused
them on Subedar Ram Gupta. Surprise showed in his face.
The man was crying.

Tears for his shame, for the bewildering, unbelievable
sadness of what was happening, rolled down his cheeks
and darkened his sweat-stained collar. He could see nothing but his own misery.

What could he do now for a living? He had no trade

apart from soldiering. He was the product of years of service, of discipline and military knowledge. Nothing, except death in the end, could ever rob him of these. But could they be put to any purpose?

He could become a professional robber, a *thuggee*, to travel with others of that kind, waiting their chance to fall in with a caravan of merchants. Then, while their companions slept, they would garrotte them, gouge out their eyes, cut off their testicles, and seize their goods, their camels, their horses, and sell them for what they would fetch. And then go farther along the road to wait for the next rich travellers.

Or he might find service with a native prince, but these already employed hundreds, sometimes thousands, of retainers. The King of Oudh, although deposed and in Calcutta, still maintained several thousand armed men around him.

As Ram Gupta stood, imprisoned in gloom and dejection, he remembered another name that a relation, Dhost Sitapur, had mentioned to him on leave. The Nana Sahib, the Maharajah of Bithur, a small town about eight miles out of Cawnpore.

This maharajah, so Dhost Sitapur had said, was a just, generous man, and he should know, for he was in his service. Although the maharajah was not born of noble blood, as a matter of family pride he had maintained all fifteen thousand of his adoptive father's old retainers.

Surely then, he could make room for one more? He would go and ask his advice. The thought that he had someone to see, some plan for the future, warmed Ram Gupta's cold, bleak thoughts. Now that his regiment was no more, he might find, in Cawnpore, a new friend, a new father.

The silver had been cleared away and the two men sat, at their ease, facing each other across the white tablecloth. Candles in porcelain holders threw trembling shadows on the walls. The only sound was the faint barking of a wild dog, miles away, and the tireless whirring of the cicadas.

Both men were tall, broad-shouldered, with muscular hands, heavily bearded, black moustached. But one had a pale skin and pale blue eyes, cold as chips of broken ice. This was John Nicholson, the British Deputy Commissioner in Peshawar, a small town up on the jagged, often disputed frontier, between India and Afghanistan.

Across the table, his guest, now adjusting his huge turban, was Gulab Singh, the Maharajah of Jammu, a part of Kashmir; a man whose power among his own people, the Sikhs, was only equalled by Nicholson's astonishing influence over them.

Both men were thinking: John Nicholson of an incident as a little boy when his mother came into the nursery and found him lashing the air with a knotted handkerchief.

'I am trying to get a blow at the Devil,' he had explained. 'He wants me to be bad. If I could get him down I would kill him.'

This sense of evil as a living entity, the obverse of goodness, still possessed him, eating into his thoughts, making him fight desires, whether sexual or ambitious, as though they were evil forces to be overcome, never to be pandered to. His life had been one long struggle: he believed it would continue so to be. He hated inefficiency and bureaucracy to such a pathological degree that sometimes, even now, he would seize one of the buff folders, thick with political and Intelligence memoranda, and carefully bound with thick pink tape, and boot it across his office like a football.

At seventeen, he had sailed for India to join a regiment in Meerut. On arrival, a servant stole his forks and his spoons, which he could ill afford to replace. Posted to Karnaul, up-country, another thief cut a hole in his tent and stole his pistols, his trunk and dressing-case, and some money. Most officers were so rich that they condoned such petty theft. Nicholson was poor, and could not. He complained that such standards of behaviour should not be allowed.

His colonel considered that such complaints were unbecoming to an officer and a gentleman, and only to be expected from those unaccustomed to servants. Therefore, as much to be rid of him as anything else, he sent Nicholson off with a corporal and a few men on a political mission to the frontier.

Nicholson was given no provisions, but carried a note from the British political agent, a weak, vacillating colonel, addressed to the headmen of all the villages through which he would pass, asking them to supply him with food at the current rates.

Nicholson was astonished when two headmen laughed in his face; this was before he realized the contempt they held for the colonel.

'You will provide this food and I will pay you the fair price,' Nicholson told the third headman he met. 'And you will bring it *now*.'

'And if I do not, sahib?' asked the headman, smiling insolently at this boy.

'If you do not, I will flog you myself, and everyone in your household. You have up to three to consider your decision.

'*One!*'

The headman looked to left and right. Nicholson's corporal had dismounted; so had half a dozen sowars. This boy might just mean what he said. Certainly, he was tall and his eyes were like knife-blades.

'*Two!*'

Nicholson picked up a horse-whip and cracked it in the air like a gun.

'I will get you the food, sahib,' said the headman quickly.

News of this incident travelled on the evening drums along the frontier. Old men, puffing the blue smoke of opium pipes, remarked that an English*man* was here, not someone to be fooled or trifled with.

Nicholson's mission was completely successful, and he obviously had such a gift for leadership that he was seconded from the regiment for other political duties.

He learned native dialects. Where a weak magistrate would side with an influential landowner against a tenant in the hope of future favours—or lest he or his servants were attacked—Nicholson sided with no one. He stood on the side of right.

Sometimes he was posted back to military duties, and once he wrote to his mother, so disgusted by the poodle-faking of his brother officers, the nickname by which adultry was dignified in the hill stations, that he admitted: 'I dislike India and its inhabitants more every day, and would rather go home on £200 a year than live like a prince here.'

His brother officers found him morose and self-centred. He lived by Old Testament laws; and Old Testament laws were harsh. But while he spared no evil-doer, he never spared himself.

Out on patrol, to drive back groups of marauding tribesmen who had been stealing corn from villages, he would chase them into the hills and disperse them and then kill them, one by one. Other officers would simply have ridden round the village in a show of force, and returned to base as soon as possible.

The Sikhs came to admire Nicholson because his qualities mirrored their own. Originally, they had been only a religious sect led by a Hindu who preached a new faith, partly taken from Hindus, partly from Moslems, and partly opposed to both. Under their leaders, or Gurus, every man was trained to arms, and every man came under oath not to shave or cut his hair, and to carry a knife, a comb in his hair, and to keep his body clean as his spirit.

Understandably, each Sikh felt that they were a race apart, a ruling race. Yet twice they had fought the British and twice the British had beaten them.

In both battles Nicholson won the commendation of his superiors and of the Sikhs, because he was brave and fair. They nicknamed him 'Nikal Seyn.'

Some even believed he was Brahma brought back to earth by reincarnation, and formed a sect to worship him. When Nicholson heard of this he had the men flogged. They admired him all the more, for he combined the precious god-like qualities of courage, chivalry, a complete disinterest in personal wealth or promotion, and an inner spiritual belief that he was born to rule and lead.

Once, a superior found Nicholson ill with fever in his tent, his face puffed and flushed with a high temperature.

'What do you wish done?' Nicholson asked him.

'Had you been fit, I should have wished to send you to secure Attock, but that is out of the question. Someone else must go.'

Attock was a fortress fifty miles away. Nicholson rose from his bed and started to buckle on his uniform, swaying dizzily.

'I will start tonight,' he said.

Within hours, he was leading sixty Pathan horsemen and twice as many sepoys on foot. He rode so fast that only thirty riders could keep pace with him, and the infantry was sixteen hours' march behind. Without waiting for either group to catch up, Nicholson crossed the Indus River in the early morning and rode right into the Fort—through the front gate!

The Sikhs were so astonished that they capitulated; they believed he must be the advance guard of an immense force. Nicholson had so few men with him that he had to order the Sikhs to arrest their own leaders. Such was the hypnotism of his character, his tremendous physical presence, and his complete lack of fear, that the Fort fell without a shot being fired.

Thereafter, Nicholson received one assignment after another: to subdue this local insurrection; to preside at some Court of Justice where no judge dared to make a fair decision; to protect a village from enemies who would destroy their crops.

Nicholson's thoughts flitted across his years in India, like one of the night moths fluttering round the candles . . .

Gulab Singh was also thinking. Of his youth in the hills; of half-forgotten skirmishes and other pictures from the past; of prophesies about imminent insurrection which he had heard from holy men sitting in the mouths of caves.

Nicholson and his guest had discussed the present tension in the country, and the signs of unrest on every side that only men blind in mind and eye could fail to see.

'Do not think that this animosity is only shown to you English,' said Gulab Singh reassuringly. 'Alas, one of my best cooks tried to poison me—*me*—his maharajah!'

Nicholson smiled.

'And what did you do?'

'I had him brought before me,' said Gulab Singh. 'He admitted his offence, so I had to make an example of him. I ordered my guards to separate the skin of his head from behind the neck to the throat. Then they flayed his head and pulled up his skin over his skull.'

Nicholson's face twisted in distaste.

'Then did he die?' he asked politely.

'Oh, my dear Nicholson, *no*. He lived for weeks!'

And the Sikh sat back in the hard wooden chair, shaking with laughter at the memory.

'You are a cruel man,' said Nicholson.

'It is a cruel country, a cruel world.'

'Tell me,' said Nicholson, not disagreeing. 'On whose side will your Sikhs be if there is trouble between the English and the Indians?'

'I cannot speak for all, only for my own. We will be with your people, Nikal Seyn. Unless you look like losing!'

He roared with laughter at his own wit and stood up.

'I shall be leaving you, Nikal Seyn,' he said. 'I have a journey to make tomorrow.'

They shook hands. Nicholson followed him to the front door. A drum was beating somewhere, and in the village a mother crooned to a child who had awakened because of a bad dream.

Gulab Singh's orderly waited by his horse. The maharajah jumped into the saddle, dug in his spurs and was away without a backward glance.

For some time Nicholson stood in the doorway, wondering about the future: his own and India's. Then he went into his house and closed the door behind him.

4

Hodson pushed aside the bead curtains on the bedroom door, and came out on to the scrubbed wooden planks of the veranda.

He was a tall, slim man with blond hair and pale blue eyes, who walked on his toes, as though suddenly expecting to have to break into a run. His forehead was wrinkled, so he appeared to be perpetually scanning the hot bright horizon. Actually, he had suffered from his schooldays with severe headaches, but only recently had an army doctor diagnosed eye strain, and suggested he should wear tinted glasses.

Hodson put on a pair now and, resting his hands on the flaking paintwork of the rail, looked across the little compound, beyond the bungalows of other subalterns in the First Bengal Fusiliers, towards the parade ground and the Himalayan foothills beyond. He wanted to know whether the group of men who had been squatting under the banyan tree near his porch the previous evening were still there.

They were.

Hodson swallowed, and ran his tongue over dry lips. For a few moments he had tried to delude himself that he had only dreamed about them. That they had no existence outside a nightmare. Now he knew he carried the nightmare with him. He was in debt and worried, and, for the first time in his life, unsure of himself.

He watched, expressionless, as the men rose to their feet, dusted down their pantaloons and *dhotis* deliberately, and came towards him. They were all plump and middle-aged. Their leader wore a white pugri, not a fold out of place even after ten hours' vigil, and had little gold pieces let into the sides of his nostrils. His gold earrings jangled as he walked. He was Bisharat Ali, a money-lender.

He gave Hodson a large salaam, bowing deeply with exaggerated respect that made the salutation an insult.

'What do you want?' asked Hodson, knowing quite well what they wanted: the payment of their bills. And he wanted nothing more than to pay them, to get them off his back, for ever. But on two hundred and fifty pounds a year, after his demotion from a staff rank which had earned him nearly five times this amount, after the fearful medical bills for his wife, Susan, when they had lost their baby daughter, he had no money left. Nothing.

They knew that, all of them. They could have bought and sold him a hundred times over. They knew that, too. But Hodson was still an officer, an English officer, and therefore, by definition, a gentleman. He would have to pay them eventually; their money was quite safe. They knew that as well, but they needed to show their power.

'Sahib,' Bisharat Ali began sonorously, 'I do not like to raise the subject of money again with you. I know you have been through great trouble and sadness. But it is money that we need to pay our debts, to buy rice to fill the bellies of our children. Otherwise we would not have come to you. Is that not so?'

He turned to his companions for confirmation.

'*Ji, Ji,*' they said, nodding their heads in agreement. Hodson hated them all. They came here two and three times a week, squatting in his courtyard for hours on end, talking to his bearers, who passed on their gossip to the bearers of other officers, so that everyone knew that Lieutenant Hodson, formerly Major Hodson, was in debt to Indian money-lenders, and smiled at the knowledge. Hodson had no private means: the other officers had. He had to live on his pay; they used theirs as small change. The situation was as simple as that.

'You'll get your money,' he said shortly.

'But when, sahib? That is the question.'

'How much is it?' asked Hodson, as though he did not know.

'Two thousand rupees basic loan, sahib. With interest,

two thousand four hundred and fifty rupees, sahib.'

Bisharat Ali was now standing under the veranda, so close that Hodson could smell the spices on his breath.

'I would not have troubled you, sahib,' he said insolently, 'were I not leaving for my own village of Khurkund within the next few days. I need the money for my journey.'

'You lie, Bisharat Ali,' said Hodson. 'You are rich enough to own a palanquin and as many horses as you wish, to have as many women as you want. You do not need my money for your journey. But I will pay you, I promise you.'

'But *when*, sahib?' they called after him as he turned away. '*When?*'

He swung around at them.

'I don't like owing you money any more than you want me to keep owing you money. Or rather, you *do* want me to owe it, because of the interest. Twenty per cent—how often? Every month? All right, you'll get it. I've told you. Now—*go*.'

He stormed back into the bedroom so fiercely that the beads rattled on their thin strings like loose teeth behind them.

His wife stirred in bed and rolled over, her face puffy with sleep. For a moment, he looked down at her tenderly, watching her, wondering about their insolvency, remembering, as another nightmare, the slow death of their daughter.

Since then, Susan had miscarried twice. The surgeon had told him that she would probably never have another child. And yet what was there to interest her when he was away on service if she had no child to watch grow up? The whole dreary boredom of their life together depressed him: two people diffidently putting out feelers, tender antennae towards each other, seeking, from an aching empty loneliness, some common meeting place of love; and without success.

'Who were those men, Willie?' Susan asked drowsily.

'No one.'

'I heard voices. You were shouting. Why must you raise your voice so?'

'They were from the bazaar. After the money we owe them.'

'We?'

'Oh, all right. *I* owe them.'

She closed her eyes and sank down on the pillow as
though she could physically blot out the prospect of another day of depression and unfulfilment, another day
nearer the grave.

She had been dreaming about her dead daughter, Olivia, named after her husband's favourite sister. The child
had been teething, when suddenly she started a temperature. Nothing serious, the only European doctor within
eighty miles had assured her.

But it was very serious to the Hodsons. Olivia refused
all food and began to pine, so that they decided, on the
impulse, money or no money, to take her up to the hills,
to Murree, to see whether the cool, clear air would help
her.

For a fortnight, she lay, pale and lifeless as a china
doll, head turned away from the light. No doctor could
advise anything; their stock cure of bleeding her was so
manifestly absurd that they only suggested it hesitantly,
for they had no other treatment to propose.

On the fifteenth day after their arrival in Murree, Olivia's life left her so quietly that, for several hours, neither
Hodson nor Susan, who had taken turns in sitting by her
bed, noticed any change in her appearance.

But what was the death of a subaltern's child? she
thought bitterly now, burying her face in her damp pillow.
English children died every day in every army station.
That was one of the many penalties of the climate and the
country. Cholera. Typhoid. Malaria. Jungle fever. You
came to accept death, and you started another child as
soon as you felt able.

But what if, like her, you couldn't? If all your desperate
dreams of another child ended in a tin latrine bucket of
blood and slime, carried away, buzzing with bluebottles,
by an indifferent sweeper? What if you came to dread the
act of love, fearing it only as a prelude to more pain,
more draining weakness, another disappointment?

She had been married before, to a lawyer, much older
than herself; they had one son between them, now in his
teens. But their life together had been drab, cold, precise—always with her husband keeping one cautious eye
on what other people might think of this behaviour or

that. They had lived in Guernsey—the gentle climate suited them both—and then Willie Hodson had arrived on the island, newly commissioned from Cambridge into the Militia, amusing, witty, able to mimic anyone, quite the antithesis of her husband.

When Hodson received the posting to India for which he had been waiting, they wrote to each other every week. Then John died unexpectedly, and it had seemed to her only natural that she should travel to India, too, on what little money he had left her, and marry William. Looking back now, from this shabby bungalow, it seemed incredible that she could have naïvely imagined that their feelings would be the same for each other after eight years. For what exactly *had* their feelings been in Guernsey? Simply, that they had some things in common; that they were complementary in others; that, possibly, perhaps, if she were not already married, they might have made a life together.

Susan Hodson realized now that this ban to a fuller relationship then had only heightened their attraction for each other. Without this artificial stimulus, they could have exhausted their interest in each other within days, for what had seemed a romantic liaison in Guernsey, was not the same in India. Susan was five years older than Hodson, and five years when he was twenty-eight did not seem such a big gap as it did eight years on.

Each thought that the other had changed, and of course they were right. What neither wished to admit was that they had also changed themselves.

Hodson watched his wife and could guess her thoughts. He wanted to say something to comfort her, to reassure her, but he did not know what or how, so he said nothing, and walked out again on to the veranda.

Somewhere, somehow, I've gone wrong, he thought. In my career. In my marriage. I push too much. I try too hard. Yet that's the way I'm made. There is no other way I can go about things.

He gripped the wooden rail tightly. It felt warmer now. The day was charging itself with heat. In an hour it would be too hot to be out in the sun without some covering for the head.

One of the money-lenders had reminded him of his father, a clergyman, who had saved to send Willie to Rugby, and could never understand why his son would not follow his own cautious theories, why he wanted things to happen now, not tomorrow.

He used to excuse his son's impatience by explaining: 'The boy has bad headaches. They make him hasty, but he's got a first-class mind. He'll settle down and make a very good lawyer.'

But I never made a lawyer, thought Hodson on the veranda. I've never made a success of anything. I'm thirty-six and I'm still a subaltern. I *should* have been a bloody lawyer. I couldn't be worse than I am now.

At school he would fight anyone, regardless of age or size, if he felt he was in the right. It never occurred to him that he might be beaten, so he rarely was. Now, he wondered whether he was not beaten at last.

He had gone to Cambridge, meaning to read law, but the play on words, their different shades of meaning, close yet infinitely separate as onion skins, was not for him.

If I'm going to be successful, and I've *got* to be successful, he had told himself time and again, then I'll have to do it myself, my own way. With the sword, never with the pen.

But by then he was twenty-three and had no qualifications or training. The last resort was always the army. But not the British Army, for he had no private means to help support a regiment's pack of hounds or string of polo ponies. All that was left was the Indian Army, to become what was contemptuously called, in England, 'a black officer.'

He was obviously too old for the Company's-school at Addiscombe but his brief training in law had not been entirely wasted, for he discovered a clause in the Company's regulations that explained how men who had held commission in any other force would be automatically entitled to one in either of the East India Company armies.

His father wrote to every influential man connected with his church; one helped to secure Hodson a commission in the Channel Islands Militia, something the Company would accept. In Guernsey, he had met Susan and now, forcing himself to be honest—he always found it easier to be honest with himself when he was alone—he wished they had never met.

What had happened to turn that young girl into the

drawn and jagged woman in the room behind him? How could something that had seemed magical under the pale watery sky south of England, become tawdry and irksome when transposed to the dry heat of central India? Was he to blame for this transformation?

It wasn't his fault, he told himself fiercely. But if it wasn't, then whose was it?

When he was with her, he was quiet and reserved, anxious to anticipate her complaints and her wants. But when he was away from her, on his own, on detachment, he became cheerful, gregarious, a different person altogether, building in his mind a completely illusory character to come home to; a gay, witty, passionate, amusing woman.

But when he returned, and rode up to their bungalow, and she came out to meet him on the veranda, they would see their mutual disappointment mirrored in each other's eyes.

For while he had been away, Susan had also been assuring herself that her husband was successful; not just a man who tried so hard to make her happy; and who did not succeed.

Hodson could feel a headache growing. He had so many worries, he *must* keep a clear head. That was what Henry Lawrence always used to say, 'A clear head, a clear eye, a clear mind.'

Sir Henry Lawrence. A family friend introduced Hodson to Lawrence, then British Resident in Lahore, and they had taken to each other at once; they spoke the same language of adventure and initiative. Lawrence had arranged a posting for Hodson to a new regiment, just formed, the Guides. This was one of Lawrence's own ideas; five hundred infantry, three hundred horsemen, travelling light, ready to strike anywhere quickly.

Because of the enormous amount of baggage that accompanied every British soldier in India, everyone in orthodox units was allowed one coolie, sometimes more, to carry most of his kit. Otherwise, in serge uniforms, breeches and heavy shakos, with carbine and bayonet, they would have been unable to march at all in the burning heat.

Each officer had, in addition, two camels to convey his personal belongings; some had ten, and a colonel might need twenty. All the mess plate was also carried on each campaign, plus mess furniture, which was liberally interpreted as including armchairs, carpets, candelabra, even a piano for mess nights. And the mess bar travelled complete, with machinery for making soda water to mix with whisky, and ice to keep drinks cool.

Then there were *bhistis* to draw water, *dhobis* to wash linen, cooks to prepare meals and sweepers to dig latrines. Most of these camp followers were married with children and in-laws and other relations, plus pet monkeys and parrots in cages, and dogs and cats and mongeese.

On the march, a battalion of nine hundred combatant troops could have twenty times as many non-combatants strung out for twenty miles.

With the camels, elephants, mules, spare chargers, with gharries to carry pregnant women and the sick and wounded, plus ration and ammunition wagons, and elephants to draw cannon, it was no uncommon thing for the head of the column to be bivouacking for the night after a day's march, while the tail had barely left the previous night's halting place.

Such a slow, cumbersome, inefficient method of travel signalled an army's intentions to any potentially hostile force hours before they made contact. And the troops in red coats and blue trousers, with white blancoed belts, straps and pouches, blazed like multi-coloured macaws against the burning sun of the desert, targets to be seen miles away.

Lawrence's intention was to have a force which could strike so quickly and be away before the troublemakers realized who or what had hit them.

Hodson entered into the spirit of this. He wrote home to his brother, a parson like their father, and asked him to send out nine hundred sets of uniform in drab cloth, known in India by the Persian word, *khaki,* to give them camouflage against the rocks of the desert. He also asked his brother to send out, at Hodson's expense, three hundred carbines so that the Guides would be able to outshoot any known opposition.

In the past, when a village was being terrorized by marauding Afghan tribesmen, weeks could pass before the regular troops could arrive to restore order and courage among frightened peasant people. And by then the looters could be miles away, over the border. Now, Hodson's

Guides were there within hours, and retribution was swift and drastic. Because of this, terrorism declined rapidly.

This success in keeping the peace brought Hodson a new and totally unexpected problem.

Henry Lawrence had a younger brother, John, Chief Commissioner for the Punjab. He was not close to Henry, and of quite a different outlook. He was also envious of his brother's success and, because Hodson was one instrument of this success, he disliked him intensely, although they had met only briefly.

Once, at a dinner party in Lahore, Mrs Lawrence remarked to the table at large, to show her own dislike of Hodson: 'Mr Hodson, we know, will *never* marry, save for money and ambition.'

Hodson smiled and raised his glass to her.

'At any rate, madam,' he replied, 'I will not sell myself cheaply at Indian rates.'

Many senior officers followed John Lawrence's lead in disliking any break with convention. The more efficient a regiment became, the more inefficient they would be made to appear. And after all, *soldiering* was their profession, not fighting. Who the devil was this fellow Hodson with his new ideas and his men all scruffily dressed in drab instead of in traditional scarlet?

They wanted to bring him down quickly, because they felt that if they did not, he might soar out of their range. They knew the contempt in which he held them, and feared that if ever he reached a position of power, he would remove them from their sinecures; as indeed he would.

Some officers were too fat to mount their horses unaided, others employed deputies to go on parade while they lay abed, fuddled with drink. A brigadier, who hoped shortly to become a general, firmly believed that one minute's exposure in the noon-day sun meant instant death to his men. He, therefore, made them parade at night. Other senior officers would not entrust any message to the new electric telegraph, but insisted on using native runners or even carrier pigeons, which were easy prey for kite-hawks.

It never occurred to Hodson that anyone could envy him his small success in the Guides. Other officers, with money or influence, or both, had secured staff appointments within months of joining the army. The only influence he had was that Henry Lawrence liked him. But then Lawrence fell ill and went home to England to recuperate, and the Guides were asked to investigate the attempted murder of a young British officer.

All evidence pointed to an attempted political assassination by a border chief, Khadar Khan, who had a considerable and deserved reputation for such deeds.

Hodson arrested Khadar Khan on a charge of attempted murder, confiscated his property, and put him on trial. Khadar Khan engaged eloquent Indian lawyers, and for week after week, then month after month, he managed to postpone his trial on the excuse of illness or the absence of an essential witness. When he finally faced trial, the principal prosecution witnesses had been intimidated, and testified to the impossibility of Khadar Khan being involved; he was making a pilgrimage to a holy place at the time. The judge was old and weak, and anxious to be rid of the case; he dismissed Khadar Khan.

Hodson immediately returned Khadar Khan's property, but Khadar Khan, recognizing an adversary worthy of some attention, who would no doubt cause him more trouble in the future, at once declared that bags of money and family jewels were missing. Clearly, Hodson had stolen them.

Up and down the country, in army messes, middle-aged majors with pot bellies and red noses, eyes watery as under-poached eggs, seized this unexpected weapon to strike Hodson, who was a hundred miles away at the time, and so knew nothing of these accusations which followed him to Murree, where he watched his little daughter die.

On the day after her death, Hodson's detractors struck their first direct blow against him. His adjutant, MacFarley Turner, whom he had left in charge of the Guides while he was on leave, refused to sign a financial statement.

Instead of informing Hodson, he forwarded the statement to John Lawrence's Military Secretary, declaring that some amounts did not tally, and that Lieutenant Hodson's conduct in keeping them in this way was not compatible with his rank as an officer.

The whole argument hinged on the way in which the Guides, and many other cavalry regiments, accepted new recruits, a custom known as the *sillidar* system. Recruits used their own horses and paid a deposit against the issue of uniform and weapons, to minimize the risk of wild tribesmen arriving from the hills, ostensibly as recruits, receiving carbines and then taking off with them on some private mission of revenge. When the soldiers retired, and handed back their carbines, their deposits were returned.

Turner claimed that a recruit had arrived with a horse worth one hundred and fifty rupees. When the man was shortly afterwards discharged as unsuitable, Hodson had kept the horse himself and made him buy another for two hundred rupees.

The accusation was that Hodson had pocketed the difference—fifty rupees, about three pounds ten shillings. Hodson denied it. Lawrence's Military Secretary complained that the accounts were not written intelligibly.

'Of course they're not,' replied Hodson heatedly. 'They're written in Persian.'

'Why?'

'Because they are personal documents. These are confidential details.'

'If there is nothing irregular in the accounts, then what is there to hide, Mr Hodson?'

'There's nothing whatever to *hide*,' retorted Hodson. 'These are simply personal details, not for everyone's eyes.'

'Mr Turner thinks differently.'

'Possibly. He thinks differently from me about many things.'

'Are you criticizing Mr Turner?'

'I'm criticizing no one,' replied Hodson, his mind still numbed by his own personal tragedy. 'Mr Turner has applied for a posting, anyhow.'

He'd be glad to lose him. A fat, lazy man with green pig-eyes flecked with matter at the corners, and a wife taller than himself, always complaining that her husband had been passed over repeatedly for promotion.

The Military Secretary knew that John Lawrence would welcome this chance of humiliating Hodson. If he did not give it to him, he would be furious; and then the Military Secretary's own hopes for promotion would suffer.

If, on the other hand, he recommended that a Court of

Inquiry should investigate the whole affair, then he would absolve himself from all responsibility. Accordingly, the Military Secretary ordered that such a Court should be set up.

This produced several predictable happenings; Lawrence was delighted; the Military Secretary received almost instant promotion; Turner was given indefinite leave, and immediately moved to Peshawar, where the Court was to meet, where he spread stories of Hodson's extravagances, his inability to keep records, and the fact that the rolls were in what he called 'a frightful mess.'

Hodson was astonished at the importance being given to such a trivial matter.

'Of course the rolls are in a mess—if you judge them by London book-keeping standards,' he agreed. 'The Guides are there for fighting, not for keeping books. And what about Turner himself?'

'Well, what about him?' asked other officers, rather coldly.

'He's not much of an officer, in my opinion,' said Hodson.

'Then why didn't you report him?'

To explain that if he had reported him he might have been sent someone even worse, was no satisfactory answer. No one had seen Turner drunk as he had seen him drunk. No one appeared to know that he owed money in the mess. The president of the Court turned out to be a friend of Turner's and posted an unprecedented order at the Guide's regimental depot urging any man of any rank with a grievance or complaint against Lieutenant Hodson to come forward with it.

Such a situation was intolerable; but Hodson still felt it was beneath his contempt. He was convinced that truth would answer all these ridiculous charges. And so it did, in the end, at a price he had never imagined: his own reputation.

The Court of Inquiry took four months to reach their decision; and even then it was vague and inconclusive. While the keeping of the rolls was, in their view, 'far from satisfactory,' they admitted that every anna had been accounted for.

By then, Hodson, suspended from the Guides during

the Inquiry, was without a job. Everyone had heard the charges against him; no one seemed to have heard he had been acquitted.

He applied for this job and that, but somehow they were always filled. Finally, in despair, his savings gone and in debt to Indian money-lenders, the only people who would advance him money, he secured a posting to a mediocre British regiment, the 1st Fusiliers. Here, instead of £1,200 a year with the Guides, he was on the lowest basic rate for his age and rank—£250 a year, and even this was paid three months in arrears.

During all these months of worry, Susan was concerned with her own unhappiness, not her husband's. She took to her bed, crying herself to sleep, too ill or too miserable to take an interest in anything.

The gaiety that had attracted Hodson to her in Guernsey had gone. Susan now appeared locked inside a fortress of her own making. He could only enter by paying tribute of some kind, either flattery about her looks, by giving her a present, Kashmir shawls or something else he could not afford. The fault was as much his as hers; they should never have married. He had been swayed by a woman's tears; there were neither rewards nor punishments for this basic mistake, only consequences.

The C.O. of the Regiment knew Hodson's reputation as a man of action, and decided to sidetrack him into a harmless backwater where he could not bombard him with ridiculous suggestions for more rigorous training (as if British troops were natives, and expected to carry their own kit and travel light!)

He put him in charge of the Intelligence Department, where Hodson had a small office of his own and could sift reports from government agents and informers. It was not gentleman's work, of course, but then was Hodson *really* a gentleman?

Hodson knew he could receive no promotion until some announcement was publicly made of his acquittal. In desperation, he travelled up to Kurnaul near Amballa, where the Bengal Army's commander-in-chief, General the Honourable George Anson, had his house and his staff. As Hodson wrote home to his sister, he felt he had three choices: 'I can do nothing and endure a wrong for ever; I can appeal to the commander-in-chief, or I can shoot my-self.'

He chose the middle way, and wrote out an official ap-plication to see the Honourable George, as the com-mander-in-chief was nicknamed.

'Has he any money—or friends?' asked Anson again, when his A.D.C. had explained the reason Hodson sought the interview.

'No, sir. In fact, I believe he owes money.'

'Poor devil. Well, I'll see him, but he can't expect me to do much. I mean, can he?'

'No, sir.'

Anson was plump and elderly, bored by forty-three years' service, which had started as an ensign at the Battle of Waterloo, but had included no other action since then. He did not want to become involved in some subaltern's complaint. In any case, he was fully engaged in other more agreeable matters.

His wife was in England, and the wife of another youn-ger officer—anxious for promotion, even at the cost of being cuckolded—was acting as his official hostess. Anson was savouring that Indian summer of the ductless glands that affects the prematurely senile in warm climates. She made him feel young and virile and clever; and he knew all too well he was none of these things.

So Hodson waited, in limbo. On a veranda in a shabby, unpainted rented bungalow, camel dung spread odorously on the floor and watered every day to keep down the mosquitoes; with a wife haemorrhaging almost constantly, lying in a shaded room, weeping for the child she had lost, for the baby she would never bear.

Here he was, with his creditors waiting for him, his en-emies watching him. He had borrowed heavily to pay Susan's medical bills; there was nothing left. Within weeks, possibly even within days, his financial ruin would be universal news. He'd be finished then, for ever. Not to have money was bad enough; to owe it was worse, unless in mess bills or to tailors; but to borrow it from Indians was unthinkable.

'Hodson,' they'd say, over their ports and brandies. 'He had a bit of bad luck over that business in the Guides. But he was rotten all through. A cad. A bounder. Pushed his luck too far.'

They'd give him a pistol, one of the new American Colts, and one round. A shooting accident. 'But in the end he did the only decent thing. Died like a gentleman. Even if he wasn't one.' That way there would be no scandal, and a military funeral afterwards.

The hypocrisy of the whole system was what Hodson hated most—yet, ironically, as an officer, he was pledged to defend it. The system virtually murdered a man, then gave him a funeral with military honours, reversed arms, and the Last Post sounding for the glorious dead.

Hodson turned back again towards the bedroom, hammers of frustration beating in his head. A voice called from the edge of the thick bushes that ringed round the bungalow.

'Sahib!'

He turned.

Rajib Ali, a former Moslem priest, one-eyed and of infinite loyalty, whom he had recruited into his Intelligence Department, salaamed him.

'What is it?' Hodson asked shortly.

'I have news for you, sahib,' said Rajib Ali. 'Of trouble.'

His one eye rolled like a white billiard ball in his skull. He did not wear a patch over the other, and the hole was hollow, like a cave in his head.

'There's trouble everywhere,' Hodson replied. 'I do not wish to hear of more. I would like some good news.'

'It is written,' said Rajib Ali. 'Out of tears comes forth joy, and out of weeping comes forth laughter.'

'Only sometimes,' said Hodson, thinking of Susan and their dead daughter, their dead dreams. 'What specific trouble do you speak of now?'

'I hear that some regiments in the east have refused to take ship over the sea. They will not use the cartridges that are greased with unholy fat.'

'I know all that.'

He had seen the Intelligence reports about this. There was nothing new here.

'I also hear that some princes are like captains of ships who, facing the dreaded monsoon storms, trim their sails both ways. They wish to stay out of trouble should the Indian sepoys lay down their arms and refuse to obey orders.'

'Possibly, yes.'

'This could be a time for you, sahib. It will be a time for new leaders. Not old weak men any more.'

'That will be the day.'

'Indeed, yes, sahib. And it is near at hand.'

'Possibly,' said Hodson, unconvinced.

He turned to go into the bungalow, and an officer riding past them on a charger waved to him.

'Hodson!' he called accusingly. 'It's the ninth. Remember?'

The ninth? Hodson looked at him blankly. The other officer was a Captain Birdwash, with a reddish face and small blue eyes. And although the hour was early and it was not yet hot, he was already sweating unpleasantly.

'Those two hundred chips you owe me,' Birdwash added sharply, jabbing the air towards him with his crop. 'Hadn't forgotten, had you? You promised to repay by the ninth.'

'I'll give you a cheque.'

'That's settled then. See you in the mess before lunch?'

'Yes, of course. I do apologize.'

He stood, hands limp at his sides, watching Birdwash ride off towards the parade ground. He was orderly officer that morning.

Two hundred rupees meant nothing to him. Birdwash played that on the fall of a card. But, if Hodson gave him a cheque and it was not honoured, he was finished. Two hundred chips. He had to find it somehow. And soon.

He went into the bungalow, but not into his bedroom. Instead, he sat down on a cane chair, his elbows on his knees, his head in his hands.

There must be *some* way out. He had already applied to go on service to Persia, where a British expeditionary force could not find enough officers, but his application had been delayed. He had no cards left to play. Nothing.

Hodson had not prayed since he was a boy, for in spite of his father's calling, he neither believed nor disbelieved in any over-ruling omnipotent providence. But if there was a God, surely He would understand?

'Give me another chance. I have had chances already, I know, and I have lost them through my own fault. But next time I will do better. Please give me a next time.'

He opened his eyes. His headache had receded.

'Willie! Willie!'

Susan was calling from the breakfast-room. Her voice sounded high and querulous. Breakfast must be ready.

He stood up, clenching his hands to force himself to keep calm so that she would not suspect how worried he was. Then he went into the breakfast-room. He did not like to keep her waiting.

5

Amid the many temples outside Cawnpore, with green-slimed stone steps that ran down to the sluggish Ganges, which Hindus believed would bear all their souls to Paradise, the palace was the largest building.

The air near the river hung heavy with afternoon heat, and the wind slept. Temple bells tinkled faintly like tired tin cans. The river, the most sacred in all India, lay flat and oily, a serpent a mile wide, reflecting the shimmering amber sun.

On its banks at this exact place, unknown years before, Brahma had finished creating the world and then had offered the sacrifice of a horse to mark the end of his design. Somehow the pin of Brahma's slipper had become dislodged, but a watchful disciple had found it, and built it into one of the steps of the principal temple.

As a result, every November, an annual festival brought thousands of pilgrims from all parts of India to worship at this most sacred shrine. During this festival they would cram the banks of the sacred river, thick as flies on carrion, sleeping in skin tents and reed shelters or out under the stars. Their camp fires would darken the evening skies with smoke, and their chantings drown the ringing of countless bells. But now all this activity lay six months away; both banks of the river and the village of Bithur were empty. The fields stretched, yellow with mustard flowers, into the misty, lazy foothills. Only one man stood upon the steps of the palace, hands clasped behind him.

He was of medium height, plumpish, sallow-faced, his

head and chin shaven in the style of the Mahrattas, one of the most famous fighting races in India.

He appeared to be the only man in the village, the only living figure on a sun-dried landscape, but, because he was Nana Sahib, the maharajah, eyes watched him through slits in doors and holes picked by sticks and fingers in mud walls. For apart from the pilgrims once a year, he was the only other provider. Fifteen thousand pensioners depended entirely on him, plus half as many other retainers.

Nana gave a sigh of boredom. He was to hold a dinner party that evening for the commander-in-chief of the British forces in Cawnpore, General Sir Hugh Wheeler, and for other officers and their ladies, and the prospect depressed him.

The conversation on such occasions was invariably the same: small items of local and unreliable gossip; complaints about servants and the high cost of living, the long delays of letters from England, even though most mail and packages to India now travelled from London to Marseilles by train, by boat to Alexandria, then camel caravan to Suez and on by steamer to Bombay—several weeks less than the old voyage round the Cape.

When he was asked out in return, the maharajah would meet the same people he had entertained in his own palace, because there were no others.

The emptiness of this social life irritated him. Yet he needed to cultivate these English officers, with their watery protruding eyes and receding double chins and paunches strapped in with bandages. If only he were rich, as they imagined he was, he would not have to bother with them at all.

His sambur-skin *chaplis* flip-flopped over the snowy marble floors as he walked, hands still behind him, head down, through a vast hall walled with mirrors, beneath French glass chandeliers that dangled dangerously above his head on silver chains.

He paused at the doorway of a huge room, hung with tapestries, with crossed tulwars on the walls, and giant green-shaded oil lamps suspended from the ceiling above two billiard-tables in the centre. For a moment, pursing his lips, he thought he would play a few games against himself—he was by far the best player in Cawnpore, if not within a hundred miles radius. But playing on his own was not much fun; living on his own was equally dull.

He moved listlessly across the tessellated floor of the hall and into the dining-room, another vast chamber, its floor almost completely covered with a Persian carpet. The twenty-foot table in the center of the room was laid for dinner, the magnificent damask cloth, which had been sent out specially from England, stiff and white as frozen snow. The forks and spoons on it were silver, but the knives were yellow, bone-handled ones he had bought cheaply in a job lot in Calcutta; salvage from a sunken ship.

The wine glasses were a strange inelegant mixture of crystal goblets originally intended for champagne, and round, thick-bottomed tumblers, bought from an American commercial traveller. And, at each place, instead of a starched and folded table napkin, his servants had laid a small bedroom towel. The side plates were stamped with the arms of the Ninth Lancers; the salt cellars were cheap silver plate, and did not match.

None of his guests would ever remark on this, of course. They regarded what would be unforgivable rudeness in a poor man, as simply an endearing eccentricity in a rich one. For where else within a hundred miles or more did a native prince, so well disposed towards the British, allow them the use of his special carriages, or his saddles for camels and horses laced with silver, or his elephants with howdahs, which he would generously offer them for hunting? He even had his own zoo, with rare specimens of deer and antelope and tigers, which he was delighted to show to their children.

But the maharajah was not rich. He was not even a maharajah. His palace was hung with shields and swords, many of them inlaid with gold and rubies, but he had little real money. The whole place was in pawn to money-lenders, who had advanced him sums at huge rates of interest because he assured them that one day he would have money.

He frequently gave what he called 'entertainments,' like the one being prepared for that evening, but since he spoke no English, he could only move among the guests smiling and bowing, and raising his eyebrows inquiringly at what they said. It would be another wasted evening so far as he was concerned.

Yet Nana Sahib felt that if he stayed on friendly terms with them all, maybe one might one day influence the East India Company, and see that he received a pension, so he could afford to maintain the old retainers that honour and dignity demanded he kept.

How could these old men live if he did not feed them? It had never crossed his mind, or theirs, that they should seek other employment in the fields, working for other masters.

His whole unhappy situation arose because he was adopted; because the Company's lawyers had used every loophole, every ambiguous clause in contracts and agreements, to exclude him from what he was convinced should have been his.

The British had defeated his adoptive father, Biji Rao, at the battle of Seoni nearly forty years before. Under the terms of surrender Biji Rao had to resign his title in return for a pension of eight hundred thousand rupees a year and a home, as the Company's lawyers put it, in 'Benares or any other sacred place in Hindustan.'

Finally, after making various proposals which the English refused to accept, the old man settled, at their suggestion, in Bithur, not a situation he would have chosen, despite its holy associations. It was unhealthy, too near the river, with swamps: cold in winter and very hot in the summer. But he was in his sixties and the British thought he would not live long. Also, they wished to keep him in a remote area where he would have little chance of fomenting trouble or raising an army to fight them a second time.

Biji Rao had sired two sons. One had died within days of his birth; the other lived for only a few months. He had many wives, concubines and mistresses, but he could not produce a male heir. So, thirty years earlier, he had adopted two little brothers. The eldest was Dhondo Pant, known as Nana Sahib, and the younger took the nickname of Dada Sahib; the grandmother and the grandfather.

When Biji Rao died, his huge pension died with him and although his will left everything to Nana Sahib, there was, in fact, very little to leave.

Nana assumed that the East India Company would continue paying him a pension, but they did not do so. Their profits were down and their expenses had increased. They were therefore most anxious to cut down on any expenditure that was not absolutely essential. Their lawyers argued that he was not a son of the blood; their contract had been with Biji Rao. Nana had therefore no claim on the Company either legally, morally or materially.

Nana sent petitions to the Governor-General in Calcutta, then to the directors of the East India Company in London, but without result.

He had inherited gold mohurs and other coins and ornaments worth a considerable amount if he sold them, but he felt that this inheritance was only his to hand on, like the baton in a relay race, to whoever might succeed him.

As it was, he had to sell nearly two-thirds of the gold coins to pay his father's debts. He incurred great loans at five, ten, fifteen per cent compound interest, unreducing, and irreducible under the fierce harsh terms of the Indian money-lenders.

Finally, in desperation, as his capital melted away, he sent a personal emissary to London to argue his case. This emissary, Azi Mullah, was strangely qualified for this task. He spoke English only because he had been educated at the government school in Cawnpore. He had then become a table servant with an influential English family, where he had learned English customs and manners.

Then he took a job as tutor to the children of a brigadier, but was speedily dismissed because he was found accepting bribes from bazaar shopkeepers to steer custom towards them.

From then on, Azi Mullah was out of work—until he presented himself at Nana Sahib's palace, and was given the job of interpreter.

This unlikely ambassador arrived in London with fifty thousand pounds in gold sovereigns, and Nana's orders to do the best deal he could with the East India Company's directors.

Azi Mullah soon realized that his cause was futile, and decided to put Nana's money to his own use. He bought a house in Belgravia, and another in Brighton, and promoted himself to prince.

As a charming young man, dressed in oriental costume,

with gold rings on his fingers, a silk neckerchief at his
throat, his dark face alive with amusement and witty
sayings, he became much sought after as a guest at parties
and balls in the big houses recently built on the Bayswater
Road overlooking the Park. Many hostesses then discovered with delight that his talents were not limited to the
drawing-room; he became as welcome in their beds as at
their dinner-tables.

All too soon, Nana's money ran out. Azi Mullah, lacking other employment or capital, had to return to Cawnpore. In his report to his employer, he naturally did not
mention his own extravagances. All the expenditure, he
claimed, had been necessary in the form of bribes in cash
or kind. But the despicable English had taken the money
and then not done what they solemnly swore they would
do.

Nana Sahib then sent his nephew, Kalyan Singh, to
London. This young man was due to return any day, but
from his letters it seemed he had achieved nothing either.

So Nana was back into his old unsatisfactory routines
of entertaining officers and their ladies, hoping, but by
now not quite so optimistically, that one would say a kind
word for him to an influential director of the Company.

An Eurasian came through the hall towards him. This
was Mr Todd, a pathetic half-caste, who had arrived in
Cawnpore from Calcutta as a clerk when the Grand
Trunk Railway was being built up to the Frontier.

When the railway was finished, and Todd was out of
work, he had joined Nana to read English newspapers to
him, to put into English any letters and petitions he might
send, and to translate the replies. He was a small, harmless, sallow-skinned man, with sunken cheeks and a
shabby white duck European suit. He wore no socks under his sandals. No one knew his first name, or even if he
had one. He was simply Mr Todd.

'I have just heard from General Wheeler, sahib,' Todd
announced. 'He will not be present tonight. Regrettably,
his wife has a migraine.'

Nana shrugged. Wheeler was an old bore. He was no
loss.

'Anything else?'

'There is a man to see you, sahib.'

A man. A petitioner, no doubt. Someone who wanted

money, a chit to be written, a grievance to be resolved.

'Who is he?'

'He says he is a subedar. Ram Gupta. He has walked from Barrackpore, near Calcutta to see you. It is a long way, Nana Sahib. Six hundred miles.'

'Why has he come?'

'His regiment has been disbanded.'

'What is that to me?'

'He seeks your advice.'

'Does he seek money, too?'

'No, sahib. He does not ask for money. He is a proud man. He also looks an honest man.'

'The biggest rogues often look honest men, Todd. I'll see him, but come in after he has been with me for five minutes, so I can be rid of him.'

Nana hated to break off any conversation. He lacked the incisiveness to tell a guest, or even a supplicant, that the interview must end, that he had other things to do.

He walked into his study. Ram Gupta came in after him and bowed.

Two weeks had passed since he left Barrackpore. He had slept this last night in his relation's house near Bithur, risen early and washed in the sacred river to bring blessing on his trip. Then he put on his best starched white dhoti, darkened his caste mark on his forehead, oiled his hair, shaved, and now he was ready.

He was unused to the splendour of the palace, and awed by it, for all his life had been spent in encampments or tents or army barracks with undecorated stone walls.

Truly, if Nana Sahib was as rich as this place made him appear, he would also have power and could speak for him. The thought gave him confidence. For the first time since that terrible last parade, he felt at peace.

Nana acknowledged his bow.

'What did you want to see me about, subedar sahib?' he asked.

'I have more than thirty years' service in the Bengal Army, Nana Sahib,' Ram Gupta began, emotion making his voice tremble. 'I came back from leave in my village to find the regiment was disbanded. Men were blown from cannons. It was the worst day of my life.'

'Why did these things happen?'

'Because of follies that were not my doing. The English

have a new rifle, the Enfield. It takes a new sort of cartridge instead of the old powder and ball. The cartridge case is made of paper, and has to be bitten and rubbed with grease. The grease is the fat of pigs and cows.'

'It is impossible,' Nana Sahib said sharply. 'The English are not fools.'

'So I thought, Nana Sahib, but it is true. My men refused to accept these cartridges. They also refused to serve overseas without special pay, as is their right. So the English disbanded the regiment and executed those who had refused first. There have been other cases in other regiments. Other men have been shot from guns, or crucified in the heat of the day on the wheels of gun-carriages.'

'Why do you come all this way to see me?'

'I do not seek money, Nana Sahib, but men speak well of you. I have a relation in your service, Dhost Sitapur.'

'Ah, yes. Did he ask you to come here?'

'No, sahib. You are a man of wisdom. I came myself to ask what you think I should do.'

'That is a difficult question. You are, how old?'

'Fifty-three, sahib.'

'It is difficult at fifty-three to put down new roots, to learn new skills. Tell me about the regiment. There were a thousand men in it?'

'About that number, sahib. They will all now be in their homes. All without employment.'

'Did they expect to be disbanded?'

'No, sahib. It was the worst possible thing. We have all given years of our lives—for nothing. We gave them for the hope of a pension, for security in our old age, and now we have nothing. Others are rich and we are poor.'

Yes, thought Nana, and other maharajahs are rich and I am poor. The old ruler of Mysore fought the East India Company for years, and when he was finally killed, they showered his descendants with money, *and* a palace to call their own. Even the king of Delhi, the ruined descendant of the great Mogul, had been removed from the dungeon where he had expected to end his days, awarded a huge pension, the insignia of sovereignty, and the Red Fort in Delhi as his home—while he had nothing. Why? *Why?*

'Are there any other regiments in the same position?'

'Many, sahib.'

'Why?'

'Principally because the sepoys have no fear, sahib. Let me give you an example. I tell you, a low-caste man breaks into a house. He steals some jewels, and maybe he threatens the householder.

'He is caught—and what does he get? A year in prison. That is no punishment for him, sahib. It is making a holiday for him. For twelve months he is better fed, and housed and clothed than he ever has been.

'A sepoy does not require many rules to live by, because some can read one thing into rules and some another. He should look up to his commanding officer as he looks up to his god. The army has been my mother and father to me, but this is not so now.

'The English have divided their power. The adjutant has some, the commanding officer has some, the commander-in-chief a little more, the Governor-General in Calcutta a lot more. But they all have to ask someone higher before they can make decisions. Maybe they finally have to seek permission to do something from a director in London, thousands of miles away, who has never served in this country. That is not only not right, Nana Sahib, it is madness.

'Let me tell you a thing. There was in my regiment a havildar, who was insolent to an officer. In the old days, ten, fifteen years ago, he would have been flogged and the matter forgotten.

'But now, sahib, while they still flog English troops in the English regiments, no one must flog an Indian in an Indian regiment. He has a clever officer to defend him— and he goes free, to laugh in the beard of his commander.

'Now the English seek to convert us to their own religion. It is not good any longer, to serve in the army . . .'

'So what will happen, subedar sahib?' Nana interrupted Ram Gupta. The fact that others had problems took his mind off his own, but brevity also had its merits.

'There have been many theories, Nana Sahib.'

'Tell us some of them,' ordered a voice behind him.

Ram Gupta turned. Azi Mullah had come into the room through a side door, and stood, soft and dark, smiling rather superciliously, his teeth red with betel nut.

'He is my friend,' said Nana Sahib. 'You are free to speak.'

The subedar bowed.

'Then I will say what I have to say,' he said. 'For a long time we thought that the British were invincible. But they are not, sahib. In the Crimea, three years ago, they were very foolish. A whole ship arrived there loaded with left boots. No right ones. They had summer clothes for a winter climate, and the wrong ammunition for their guns. Officers brought out their packs of fox hounds. Only the bravery of the ordinary British soldiers saved them from disgrace.

'And then there was Kabul. Nearly five thousand troops, and three times as many camp followers, lost in the snow. And at the end, the King, whom the English had put off the throne of Afghanistan, was back on it again. This would not have happened in the old days. And, look at last year, Nana Sahib—seizing the Kingdom of Oudh.

'Telegraph wires carry messages from one town to another, so that what we speak here today is known within the hour in Calcutta and Bombay. That is magical, but it is not good.

'I tell you, there is government flour on sale in the bazaars that contains ground bone. Any man of any caste who eats it is defiled. I know that forbidden lard has been mixed with butter. Even the ghee we have now is not pure like it used to be. I have heard that drinking wells have cow flesh in them.

'All these changes mean that sepoys are worried and uneasy. It was prophesied that the English would only last in power in India for one hundred years after the Battle of Plassey. It is *now* one hundred years, Nana Sahib. That is why I come to ask what I should do?'

'What shall we tell him?' asked Nana Sahib jocularly. The man had begun to bore him. He had heard too many soothsayers and their prophecies and auguries, and he did not believe any of them. They spoke rubbish; fodder for empty minds and simple people.

'I think we might give him some good advice,' said Azi Mullah slowly. 'Let him wait outside while we discuss it.'

Ram Gupta bowed and backed out of their presence.

'What do you mean?' Nana asked, when they were alone.

'We can use this man,' said Azi Mullah. 'He is loyal, but he is simple. You will never get a pension from the

Company unless you are in a position to *force* them to pay. I have seen the letters from your nephew, Kalyan Singh. Like me, he has no progress to report. No one in authority has done anything, or will do anything, *unless they are made to.*'

'How can we make them?'

'We will send this subedar from village to village to contact sepoys who have come back from his regiment, and other regiments. We can pay him a little money. A few gold coins to buy his loyalty, to make him think he is doing something worthwhile. The important payment to such a man is payment in the mind. And then you, Nana Sahib, you go down to Delhi and see the old King there. Sound him out on the great things that are going to happen.'

'He is old. He is not concerned now about what will happen in the future. He has no future.'

'Even so, every man has his pride. No man thinks of himself as dying. The King is a figure around whom others will rally and follow. He is like a flag, the colours of the regiment. It does not matter that he is old.'

'There are no British troops in Delhi.'

'I know that. They are in Meerut. You can travel there, too. We will appoint a spy in each regiment, who reports back to us. If we can advance this movement of unrest a little bit, then the English will grow worried.

'Nearly three hundred thousand Indian troops are under arms in our country, and only twenty-seven thousand British troops. And they all take so long to move from one place to another with their baggage trains and mules and elephants to pull the guns. And what of their magic telegraph line? They can have a thousand miles of wire. But cut out only one half inch and it is all as nothing.

'We will know from our spies when various regiments plan to revolt, if they do so. If not, we can say they plan to do so. Then we go direct to the Governor-General, Lord Canning, Nana Sahib, in Calcutta and we make our proposition.

' "We do not wish to cause any trouble to anybody. We just wish to rule our people in peace and prosperity. But we need the pension to which we are entitled, Governor-General. Then we can use our influence to stop this unrest instantly!" '

'But can we?' asked Nana. 'Can we?'

'Of course. Because it is as nothing. Who are these so-called mutineers? A few wretched sepoys, hungry and miserable, fearful because they believe their religion is being tampered with. We can give them assurances that this is not so. The English will help us—they will be anxious to do so. And if we do not use this chance, others may.'

'What others, Azi Mullah?'

'I think the Russians. I came through Crimea on my way back from England. I had many talks with Russians. They would like a foothold in India. They could come through the passes in Afghanistan very willingly. This is a move the English fear. That is why they keep so many of their troops up on the frontier, and great stocks of arms. In case the Russian bear should wish to come south from the snows to the sun.'

'It is as you say,' said Nana. 'Bring back the subedar sahib. I will speak to him again.'

6

On the morning after her return to Delhi, Arabella MacDonald lay late in bed, looking at the ceiling.

The room was one she had slept in since childhood; everything in it marked some memory in her life. The crimped starched cotton cover on the bedhead she had embroidered when she was ten. A washstand stood in one corner, a square of muslin edged with glass beads over the water jug to keep out flies and insects, necessary in the weeks before the monsoon, when they blundered blindly about in the heat. Her governess had given her that for her twelfth birthday.

At the side of the bed was a small table, and, on this, her *chota hazri*, the small meal, the pre-breakfast sustenance; a pot of tea, a biscuit, half an apple, brought in by the Indian woman who used to be her ayah, her nurse, and who was now her personal maid.

Arabella had not touched the tea. She lay, her hands folded between her legs. She had been dreaming of Garroway and the other man, the Indian; their bodies had been covering hers. The timid knock of the ayah had splintered the embracing warmth of her dream. She rolled over in the wide soft bed and looked at herself in the dressing-table mirrors. There were three mirrors, and three Arabellas looked back at her.

She was beautiful. She moved up her hands and smoothed her firm breasts, caressing the brown nipples. Then she moved her hands back down to the warm secret apex of her body between her legs. She lay watching herself, stroking herself, feeling the muscles tighten and her heart began to drum more quickly.

Garroway. He *was* a cad, as her father said; and yet there was something about him that made other men say nasty things. He had a rakishness that other men either envied or despised; he was all male. Those men who criticized him were half-neutered by dull, older wives, emasculated by the drag of families, by duty, the lack of money or courage; or they simply lacked virility, and hated him because he had what they lacked. Arabella did not hate him. She wanted him.

She would be married in a few weeks; Mrs Lang. A nice enough boy, but was that enough? He had never made love to her. He was not the sort who would, and yet he might be persuaded. But if you had to persuade someone, was he worth persuading? And this inexperienced youth was the man she had agreed to marry; to bear his name and his children.

There were other considerations, too. She derived enormous pleasure from sex, and this was something no English woman in her class would admit. A harlot might, or a doxy, a rich man's Continental mistress, or a country whore who otherwise might ruin her eyes as a seamstress; but not a colonel's daughter, not a lady. How could she explain her need to a young man like Richard, probably innocent of such matters, maybe even shocked by them, when she could not discuss it with her own mother?

Mrs MacDonald was only anxious to get her daughter off her hands, in case there was a scandal, for there had been other men in her life, to use the quaint saying. There would be others yet; many others, and in her body, too.

Why was it that women were supposed to find no joy in sex? Why should it just be their wifely duty to submit, to endure the sudden rush of life in their direction when there was so infinitely much more to it? Were they never to know the rapturous explosion in the mind and body and the blood, for which *any* risk, *any* scandal, was worthwhile?

She heard voices outside and listened, not caring who they were, or what they said. She recognized her father's voice, but the man to whom he was talking, who was more querulous and pedantic, measuring out each word as though it cost him money personally to speak it, who could he be?

Then she remembered; she had met him on the previous evening; the new parson at St James's, the Reverend Geraint Ponsonby, a thin, pale, precise, careful man who had so obviously never done a foolish thing in all his life, or a brave and generous one, either.

She listened to him now.

'But, colonel, you say you have no troops here in Delhi?'

'No *British* troops, that is. Plenty of Indians, of course.'

'But, why not, pray? You have here in Delhi, so I understand from General Hewitt, at Meerut, when I passed through last week, the largest arsenal in the British Empire. You have hundreds of mines and engines of war of every description—explosives, gunpowder, shells, cannonballs. The largest arsenal in the Empire means that it is also the largest in the world—yet you've no one to defend it?'

'Well, that's not *quite* true,' said MacDonald, in the condescending way officers use to civilians, who do not know the arts of war. 'This arsenal—the Magazine, we call it—is in a very strong fortified position, you know. Huge wall round it. Special detachment of eight British engineers inside. And we've got the whole garrison at Meerut, which is only forty miles away—only two days' march.'

'Why *only* two days? A lot can happen in two days. God made the world in six days, and rested on the seventh. And why do you keep the men *there* when the Magazine is *here*? As the Old Testament says, Where your treasure is, there should your heart be also.'

'It's not as simple as that, you know, padre. The East India Company has a Treaty with the King of Delhi. He's only a titular king. Last of the Mogul strain, the descendant of the great Mogul Emperors who ruled from here to Europe in their time. It's a matter of pride for him that he doesn't have alien troops in his city.'

'But, surely it's a matter of expediency for us, the British, that we *do* have them here? After all, we're not aliens in India. We run the place.'

'Well, in a *sense* we run it, padre, I agree. But we

didn't want to take it over. We've rather been forced to become more involved in politics than we ever wished, simply in order to stay in business. I mean, if we hadn't advanced and annexed whole provinces, then the Portuguese or the French would have been here instead. Or even the Russians. There's always that threat, you know, from the north. They keep looking over the border at this fertile country, and they would rather like to come in.'

'Understandably. I quite see that, colonel. But all that you say only underlines my own belief that we should have English troops here in the city.'

'As I said, padre, it's basically a matter of tact and pride. And we can get them here very quickly. We're not all fools in the army.'

'I'm not suggesting you are, colonel, although I must say some of the senior officers I've seen do seem a little lacking in imagination. But then they're largely men of great physique, and you know what Bacon wrote about tall men?'

'No, I'm afraid I don't.'

' "It is with tall men, as with tall houses. The top storey is ever the worst furnished." '

Arabella heard her father's short laugh of politeness, and then the clop-clop of hooves as they rode away.

She smiled and went on stroking herself, softly at first and then more strongly, shutting her eyes, imagining Garroway thrusting into her, or that young Indian prince; smelling the scent of their hair and their sweat.

For a long time there was no sound in the room and then, when her sob of exultation came, she lay back, brow damp, still looking at her reflection, three times reflected. Who is the real me? she thought, relaxed at last, stretching her long limbs like a cat. *Is* there one?

7

The day smouldered bright as a burning glass by the time they reached the edge of the parade ground.

Lang reined in his horse, and the animal tossed his head and stamped his feet and twitched his tail against a cloud of blue flies.

The orderly who had ridden with him from Barrackpore looked across at him anxiously.

'You recognize the place, sahib?' he asked hopefully.

He could neither read nor write, and they had been on the journey for nine days and nine nights.

'Yes,' Lang told him, with a conviction he did not feel. 'We've arrived. This is Meerut.'

It was the end of a journey from England that had taken him nearly three months.

First, he had travelled by train across France to Marseilles, then by steamer to Alexandria and across the Egyptian desert by camel caravan to Suez. Here, another steamer carried him down the Red Sea, and across the Indian Ocean to Bombay. A stay in port of three days to disembark a British regiment beginning its overseas tour of duty and to take on coal, then south under brilliant sunshine, through seas alive with dolphins and silver flying fish to Ceylon, and north by east to Calcutta.

At Bombay, a young Indian had come aboard; tall for a native, lean, and with a grace about his movements that was almost animal. He was obviously wealthy—his clothes were European, well cut and the rings on his fingers had clearly cost hundreds of pounds. They had sat at the same table in the saloon, and Richard learned how Kalyan Singh had met Arabella MacDonald, a charming English lady and, of course, her father, at the home of an East Indian Company director in London.

Kalyan Singh appeared so Europeanized that Richard found it hard to think of him as Indian; only his skin and his eyes and his slightly Welsh accent gave him away.

His relations in India were rajahs or maharajahs, Richard wasn't quite sure which, and did not like to inquire too closely because this would show his ignorance.

On the voyage, he told Richard so many facts about India that he found difficult to accept, but did not like to be thought rude by contradicting—such as the sun not really being injurious to people. You had to protect your head from it, of course, but there was no need to wear the heavy greatcoats and spineheads on which the army insisted. Also, water was drinkable, despite what English doctors said. And far more Europeans died through drinking too much claret in the middle of the day than from drinking bad water. He also advised Richard to learn Hindusthani thoroughly, so that he could speak to sepoys directly, and not through an interpreter, whose own views, or even an inflexion in his voice, could change the meaning of what he said.

As they anchored off Calcutta in the yellow Hoogly River, Richard suggested that Kalyan Singh should stay for a few days with him as his guest in the mess.

'The officers' mess is not an hotel,' replied Kalyan Singh, smiling. 'You may also discover that an Indian civilian is not welcome.'

'But that's absurd. You're a prince, aren't you?'

'Rank makes a difference, I admit,' agreed Kalyan Singh gravely, neither confirming nor denying, 'and I appreciate your offer. But I have a long journey to make. To Cawnpore, to see a relation. Nana Sahib.'

'Is he a maharajah?'

'Yes and no. He's the adopted son of the Maharajah of Bithur. On extremely good terms with all the English there, of course. He was their guest of honour at the regimental ball in Cawnpore just before I came away. His stepfather received a pension from your East India Company, but it died with him. I've been in London trying to negotiate a pension for my uncle.'

Richard did not understand money. He had been
brought up never to talk about it; only Jews or people in
trade did that. Money was like sex; always in the background, but never a subject of conversation between
gentlemen. The fact that Kalyan Singh was willing to discuss the matter of his uncle's pension embarrassed him.

'Did you have any success?' Richard asked him reluctantly.

'No luck at all, old man. I placed my bribes. They just
took the money—and did nothing in return.'

'You placed *bribes?*' repeated Lang, shocked.

'Of course. Everyone has their price.'

'Come, come. I don't believe that. I haven't a price.
And neither did my father. Nor my future father-in-law.'

'In India, such probity is rare. Indeed, when it was put
to Warren Hastings how much money he had accepted in
bribes, he replied that he was amazed at his own moder-
ation in accepting only a quarter of a million pounds
when he could easily have taken twice as much.'

'I find that hard to believe.'

'I don't,' said Kalyan Singh, smiling. 'And remember,
I've lived here all my life.'

All around the ship, as they lay at anchor in Calcutta,
yellow water sucked and chuckled. The current carried
past a splintered wooden box, a spar, bloated bodies of a
pig and a dog, and then something covered with sodden
rags, eyes bitten out by the sharp-toothed fish; a native's
body.

Across the heaving Hoogly River, the coastline trembled
in the morning sun, bright as a fanned flame. The Strand
was thick with the carriages of rich Europeans; coachmen
up front, and a little Indian boy, the *chokra*, ready to hop
down and open the door, riding the rear axle underneath.

As Lang watched, so many other memories returned.
The sight of a camel, padding in its aloof way through the
crowds, head raised disdainfully above the press of hu-
mans. Individual riders on smooth-flanked horses: European ladies wearing white muslin veils and wide-brimmed
hats against the sun, sitting demurely in their open carriages but keeping an interested eye open for any new and
handsome young officers. As Colonel MacDonald had
said, ladies changed in the sun. Perhaps men did, too—
only in a different way?

'Who did you bribe in England?' Lang asked at last.

'Englishmen, of course. They had carriages, servants. Houses in Bayswater and Kensington. Country estates in Surrey. But I could get nothing. Not one penny. So, I came back, like the prodigal son in your Bible, empty-handed.'

'What will your uncle say?'

'What can he say? I did my best.'

'He'll accept that?'

'In India, you learn to accept things. Like famine and plague and cholera, extremes of heat and cold and early death. And injustice. Mostly injustice. It is an old country, my friend. We had a civilization here when people in England were running about naked with their bodies painted blue.'

At that moment, a steward had interrupted them. An officer was waiting on the quayside to see Mr Lang.

'My name's Ogilvy,' he said.

He wore civilian clothes, and was probably a year or two older than Lang, but his face had a peculiar yellow tinge, as though it had been dyed; the skin was drawn tightly over his cheek-bones, like parchment. They shook hands.

'I expect you've heard about the regiment?'

'No. What about it?'

How could he possibly have heard? He had been travelling for months.

'It's been disbanded,' said Ogilvy brightly.

'But I've got a commission in it,' said Lang stupidly. 'Why has it been disbanded?'

'Mutiny, that's why.'

'Mutiny?'

The ground seemed to heave like the deck of the ship he had just left. Lang's mouth felt suddenly very dry. Heat trembled in the distance as though the earth itself was panting for breath.

He had sailed half-way round the world to take up a commission in a private army only to find the regiment had broken up before he reached it.

'So what happens to us? To me, especially?'

'We'll get you a posting somewhere. Know anyone here?'

'No,' said Lang. 'I have a couple of letters of introduction to people.'

'What sort of people? Not the Governor-General or the C-in-C, I suppose, eh?'

'A Mr Hodson and a Mr Nicholson.'

'Never heard of them. Sound like pawnbrokers to me. Anyhow, I'm here to take you back to the mess. I've got a couple of *doolies* here.'

He led the way to two conveyances, like horizontal sentry boxes, or sedan chairs on their sides, with wooden handles at both ends, a man standing at each handle. Lang climbed inside one and lay down clumsily on the rough horse-hair cushion, supporting himself on his right elbow.

Ogilvy was already in the other *dooli*, lighting a cigar. Coolies swung up Lang's trunks on to a kneeling camel. Ogilvy threw some coins to them; they scrabbled for them in the dust and the dung. He beat on the side of the *dooli* imperiously.

'*Chalo*,' he called. 'Go!'

They jog-trotted along for nearly an hour and then skirted an empty parade ground, where *bhistis* were carrying hogskins filled with water, spraying it out over the ground to lay the dust. A useless performance, Lang thought, if there were to be no more parades.

A handful of bungalows stood close together, as though for company. Their thatched roofs had been soaked with water to keep them cool. Outside a larger building with shutters and square doors and, surprisingly, a sepoy standing guard outside with a musket, the bearers lowered the *doolies*. Behind them the camel came up on its padding balloon feet. The keeper prodded its testicles with a sharp stick. The beast's knees trembled with rage and humiliation, as it came down reluctantly, still chewing, lips stained with green froth.

'My orderly will settle up,' said Ogilvy.

'Who do I report to?'

'The mess. Adjutant's usually in there. The colonel's gone, of course.'

Ogilvy led the way into the mess: a long room, faintly damp and musty, where water, slopped on the roof to keep it cool, had leaked through the thatch. The bar was a grey slab of slate supported on bamboo uprights. An orderly in a white jacket that reached beneath his knees, with a red and black belt six inches wide, buckled with the regimental crest, was polishing a glass behind it, and watching the only drinker, a tallish, fat man with a thick moustache and side-whiskers. Small bloodshot eyes glittered like polished red beads beneath his brows. He held a glass in his hand and turned slowly like a shaggy hunting dog as he heard their footsteps.

'The adjutant,' whispered Ogilvy.

The adjutant turned back again towards the bar, and allowed his arm to complete the movement of raising the glass to his lips, then banged down the empty glass on the counter. The orderly filled it without being asked or even looking up.

'Who the hell are you?' asked the adjutant.

'My name's Lang—Richard Lang. I've just been posted here.'

'Well, you've arriv.d too bloody late.'

'I've told him,' Ogilvy looked from one to the other, anxious to be friends with both.

The adjutant was swaying slightly on his feet, very slowly, like a tree in a wind. His movements were made in exaggerated slow motion, like a clockwork man with the spring running down. He had been drinking long before he came into the mess. He picked up the glass of whisky, drank half of it and put it down again. Some slopped on the bar counter. He put a finger in the wetness and licked it.

'Lang. I've heard of you. You've got a posting.'

'Where to, sir?' asked Lang.

'No bloody "sirs" in the mess. We're all equal here. At least, most of us are.'

He finished the second whisky. The barman poured him a third.

'Meerut,' said the adjutant. 'The most important garrison in the Empire. Know why? It guards the Magazine at Delhi. Enough explosives there to blow up half India.'

He paused, swirling his drink in his glass.

'And sometimes I don't think that would be such a bad idea, either.'

'I'm supposed to see the colonel tomorrow,' said Lang, glancing at Ogilvy.

'Too late. The colonel's gone. Off to the hills. On leave. Got no regiment, so why should he stay? It's Meerut for you, boy.'

'But I'm cavalry,' said Lang.

'I can't help what the hell you are. There's an emergency. Didn't anyone tell you? Mutiny. I've got you down for the Nineteenth Native Infantry. And that's where you're going. All your papers are made out.'

Lang frowned. What was the point of being commissioned into the cavalry if he was to serve with the infantry? Was there to be no discussion about it at all?

Ogilvy pulled him to one side.

'Don't argue,' he whispered. 'He's merry.'

'I'm not.'

'Go to Meerut and see the C.O. They've no scare about mutinous sepoys there.'

'But how do I get to Meerut? How far is it?'

The adjutant swung round on them, his fourth whisky in his hand.

'I'll tell you how to get to Meerut. You *ride* there. How far is it? God knows. Maybe eight hundred miles, maybe nine. This is a big country, India. A big, old, hot country. Indent for a horse here. We've still a few chargers left. I'll debit you five hundred rupees.'

'But I haven't got five hundred rupees.'

'You will have. When you get your pay slip from the paymaster, you'll find it's debited by one charger. "A warlike animal," is how they put it on the stores list.'

'But how do I ride to Meerut? I mean, on my own?'

'Of course not. What bloody stupid questions you do ask! You hire a servant. You've got to have one, anyhow. At *least* one. Better if you have two or three. I've got fifteen myself, and they're barely enough. Have you any money? I mean, your own money?'

'A little,' said Lang cautiously. He had twenty golden sovereigns sewn into a handkerchief in the bottom of his ribbed cabin trunk, but he did not want to admit how poor he was. Twenty sovereigns were not 'money.'

'What the adjutant means,' said Ogilvy, signalling for two beers, one for himself, another for Lang, 'is that you sort yourself out with a bearer. He arranges a couple of camels for your luggage, a camel boy, maybe a baggage guard, and you set off. We'll give you a letter to the C.O.'

'Sorry to appear so ignorant, but I was only a boy when I was in India last.'

'You're acting like a boy now,' said the adjutant. 'You mount your bloody horse, and set your bloody compass, and you bloody *ride.*'

Lang opened his mouth for another question, but Ogilvy signalled him to silence. So they stood, the three of them, drinking at the bar, while the barman went on polishing glasses, and the purple dusk poured in over the parade ground, through the windows, and no one thought of lighting the lamps.

Now he had reached Meerut. His first thought was that the parade ground might have been the one they had left at Barrackpore. It was ringed with identical thatched bungalows. The same *bhistis* seemed to be laying the same dust. The same earth was so hot that it dried almost as soon as the water was poured.

To the right Lang saw the thin spire of St John's Church, and the Venetian extravagance of the bandstand. The two camels which had carried their luggage padded up behind them and paused, blowing through their blubber lips, stamping their fleshy feet and looking about them arrogantly and impatiently.

A few Europeans, riding past on horses, pointedly ignored the new arrivals. It wasn't done to acknowledge anyone until they had been introduced formally, or until the newcomers had called on all the bungalows, not to meet the owners, but to leave their visiting cards. The occupants examined the size of the cards, and the quality of the printing, and in particular the depth of the engraving, and could then decide whether they wished to meet them.

Lang picked up his binoculars and scanned the horizon. One building was picked out with stones, whitewashed and arranged in the form of a bugle, the regimental crest of the Nineteenth Native Infantry. They headed towards it. An orderly came down the steps to see what they wanted.

'The adjutant's office,' called Lang.

'He's on duty, sir,' said the orderly. 'All officers are on special parade.'

Lang swung himself down from the horse. Dust blew out from his uniform. He was dirty, and he felt dirty. They had slept each night in dak bungalows, arranged a day's ride apart, thirty to forty miles, on the Grand Trunk Road. These bungalows were small buildings, constructed so that government messengers and mail carriers and officers in transit like himself, would have somewhere safe to spend the night. In each one he enjoyed the brief luxury of a bed with a rope mattress, a servant to fry up two minute eggs for breakfast, with chapattis and a cup of thick sweet tea, smelling of goat's milk. Then maybe a wash in a canvas bath, and off, hours before dawn, on the next leg of the journey.

He had never ridden so far in his life before. Every muscle ached. His eyes burned in his head like coals from constantly staring into the sun.

A young officer ran down the steps of the mess, buckling his sword.

'My name's Gough—Hugh Gough. Bungalow's third on the right. There's a spare bed.'

They shook hands.

'What's this parade?' asked Lang. 'Should I attend it?'

'Wouldn't if I were you. Only a court martial sentence being carried out. Be back in an hour. Use my bearer meanwhile if you haven't one of your own. Servants' quarters over there—to the right.'

And he was off to meet his groom who was bringing out his charger.

Lang walked into the bungalow. After the blaze of noon outside, it felt almost chill under the dampened straw roof. The building was little more than one large room, with whitewashed walls, rafters unpainted and pocked by wormholes as though peppered with shot.

A bamboo-framed mirror hung from a nail. There were two narrow beds, with carved wooden heads, and tables by them, covered by white clothes, each with an identical oil lamp. He picked up one lamp. It was stamped 'Property of the Honourable East India Trading Company.' The floor was earth, hammered flat, with strips of carpet near the beds.

In the ante-room was a tin bath with a lid, white inside, simulated wood grain outside. On an unpainted wooden table were two watering cans with a drinking carafe, a glass inverted on top and an enamel dish holding a bar of red soap. A washing bowl stood on four wooden legs. He filled the bowl with cold water, washed gratefully, and called to his bearer for a towel. It was hardly luxurious, but at least he had a base—unless this regiment was also about to be disbanded? The mention of a special parade made him somehow uneasy.

He was also worried about his finances. He needed to pay his bearer and the camel wallahs, and the debt that had been forced on him for his horse. He was paying the bearer fifteen rupees a month, the camel boys ten each. Then there would be fodder for his horse and more back-sheesh for the *bhisti* who drew the bath water, and for the bearer, who cleaned his shoes, and the *dhobi* who pressed his uniform and washed his shirts. He could have a hundred rupees going against him every month before he had bought a bottle of beer for himself.

Standing in the damp bathroom, rubbing his face with the towel, he suddenly realized he had come half-way round the world for less than he could have hoped to earn from any profession back home. On the other hand, here in India, with luck—and you *had* to have luck if you had neither money nor influence—he could create a career for himself. He hadn't had much luck so far, but all that would change when he married Arabella.

He went back into the bedroom. The bearer had laid out a fresh uniform for him and was squatting on his hunkers at the door, polishing his spare pair of brown boots.

Lang changed and walked towards the parade ground. He might as well see what was happening.

Out on the baking, dusty square stood two British regiments, the 6th Dragoon Guards and the Queen's 60th Rifles, and several Indian battalions. Behind the men stood the officers of the Bengal Artillery sweating under brass helmets shaped like coal-scuttles, wearing tiger-skin rolls and waxed leather breeches.

Two batteries of British Artillery, the brass on the guns glittering like glass, were drawn up behind the men. The two British regiments faced each other. The Indian troops made up the third side between them.

Gough saw Lang approaching, swung down off his horse, handed the reins to a groom, and crossed to him.

'Bad time to arrive,' he said.

'I seem to pick bad times,' replied Lang. 'My regiment was disbanded in Barrackpore before I reached it. Same thing's not happening here, I hope?'

'No, but it's serious enough, for all that. Eighty-five men refused these new cartridges that the stupid beggars in Calcutta insist on issuing. They're going to be sentenced. The general wants to make a show of them. Look out! Here he is now.'

He leapt to attention and saluted smartly. Lang followed him. Through eyes narrowed against the sun, he watched two small ponies pull an extraordinary conveyance of basketwork with iron wheels, like a swollen bathchair from some English spa.

In this, under the intermittent shade of an umbrella held by a native running at a jog-trot, lay a bloated husk of an Englishman, so fat that his sword buckle was on its last hole, and his uniform open at the throat. A little saliva trickled down from his old, weak, bluish lips on to his jacket. His fingers, fat and pink as raw sausages, gripped the sides of the buggy.

He acknowledged the subalterns' salutes with a nod that set the white feathers trembling in his shako. He was well into his seventies. That this husk was the general in command of the garrison shocked Lang.

As soon as the buggy passed, with two young A.D.C.s riding identical black stallions behind it, he looked questioningly at Gough.

'That's General William Hewitt. Seventy-five. Only time he's ever heard a shot fired was when he used to bang after duck. Now he can't even lift a rifle, of course. And he's so fat he can't mount his horse. Used to have a special squad of men to lift him up. Then one day they gave him such a heave—he weighs twenty stone—that he rolled right over and fell off on the other side! Surgeon said if he did this again he might kill himself. So the garrison carpenters made this buggy for him.'

'How did he get posted here? I thought Meerut was the key garrison of India?'

'It is. But if you marry the right person, or you own a couple of thousand acres in the Shires—the *right* Shires, mind you, nothing unfashionable—that goes a powerful long way to help you.

'Old Hewitt's been thrown out of every job he's had.

But he's well-connected. So the commander-in-chief, General Anson, just had to give him something. Our hope is that nothing blows up for the next six months. With the amount he eats and drinks, I shouldn't think he'd last much longer.'

The buggy had now reached the open side of the square. The A.D.C.s dismounted, and were levering the creature who commanded them out of his seat and up the two steps of the wooden dais. They stood on either side supporting him.

Another officer, white-haired and thin, saluted the general and then began to shout in English at the troops, pausing between each sentence, while an interpreter standing with the Indian regiments repeated the words in Hindusthani.

All Lang could hear were isolated words. 'Therefore . . . above mentioned . . . penal colony . . . in the Andaman Islands . . . transportation . . . life imprisonment . . . others having regard to . . . relative youth . . . easily led . . . twenty years . . . ten years . . . hard labour . . .'

He finished shouting, saluted the general, and marched to one side of the buggy.

A few of the Indian soldiers being sentenced scraped their boots nervously on the rough ground. From the left, Lang heard the tramp of feet, and a detachment of British soldiers, armourers and blacksmiths of the Horse Artillery, marched out carrying coils of chains over their shoulders and newly-made leg irons in raw red metal, fresh from the forge.

'Why the devil the general's doing this in front of everyone, I don't know,' said Gough in a worried voice. 'It can't do any good. If others want to refuse the cartridges, they will.'

The smiths ripped off the prisoners' boots and, as they stood barefoot on the hot, burning ground, they hammered the fetters round their ankles. Other men in the shackling party tore off the uniforms, and flung them in a heap, so that the prisoners were distinguished from their comrades by their black bodies, oily with sweat, white loincloths, and the iron shackles round their legs. Some of the ringleaders had extra chains going up behind their necks so that they could only shuffle like hobbled donkeys. Then came the command: 'March the prisoners away!'

Some prisoners bent down to pick up their boots through force of habit. They were government-issue property; they would be responsible for them.

'Detention party . . . *By* the left . . . quick *march!*'

The British troops marched easily enough, and the prisoners tried to, but the shackles tripped them and they fell on all fours and men behind bumped into them, and the rough ground rasped their bare skin and drew blood.

They began to shout angrily at the pace they had to keep up. Some flung their boots in the direction of General Hewitt, and as they marched at their own pace, they began to chant, 'For the *faith!* For the *faith!*'

Behind the British troops came a confused roar of orders and a metallic clang as shot was rammed down the mouths of the cannons. Over the bellowed commands and the rattle of muskets when the British regiments loaded, the prisoners shouted frantically: 'Remember us! Remember us!'

For a moment it seemed as though some Indian sepoys might break ranks and run to them, but they had heard the iron noises, and knew that to move meant death, so they stood firm.

The prisoners were marched off to the army hospital, the only building big enough to house so many. When they had gone the A.D.C.s helped General Hewitt back into his buggy. Gough turned to Lang, his face creased with distaste.

'Come back to the mess,' he said. 'There's nothing for us here.'

The mess, like the bungalows and the parade ground, was almost identical with the one at Barrackpore; Lang did not know then that military architects had produced only one basic design for officers' mess buildings throughout India. Every new station, every garrison throughout the land was, therefore, virtually the same.

The ante-room had a number of brown leather chairs, stained on the backs and arms by sweat, others of cane or bamboo, and half a dozen little cane tables with year-old magazines on them. A few hunting prints, showing horses with unnaturally elongated legs jumping five-bar gates, decorated the whitewashed walls. Two old officers, bald and gloomy as grave-diggers, sat side by side. Tumblers of gin fitted neatly into holes cut into the arms of their chairs. Their heads swivelled round like gun turrets as Lang and Gough came in.

'Here's Richard Lang. Just joined us from Barrackpore,' said Gough brightly.

They said nothing, but looked at Lang carefully, through pink, unblinking eyes, glazed with gin, and then glanced at each other. On the instant, as though making a drill movement, each put out his right hand, picked up his glass and raised it to his lips.

'What is your pleasure?' asked Gough.

'A Pale Ale.'

The barman opened the bottle, poured out a glass for each of them, then pushed a little pad towards Gough.

'To your time with the regiment and in India,' said Gough gravely, raising his glass in a toast. 'May you never be more unhappy than you are today!'

'I'll drink to that,' said Lang.

And often, years later, he would remember the taste of that beer, warm and strong, and see Gough's cheerful welcoming face grinning at him; and he would weep for the days that had gone, and the innocence he had then, and the friends he would never see again.

8

Nine o'clock that evening, in Meerut. A warm Saturday.

General Hewitt stretched out on a cane chair in his bungalow, his uniform unbuttoned. His huge paunch, swollen like a gross soft balloon beneath his shirt, overflowed into his lap. He lay so still, eyes closed, that a fly walked across his forehead undisturbed.

Hewitt suffered severely from gout, and his bare feet, with their knobbly, rusty-jointed toes, rested on a small cane stool. A servant stood behind him waving a fan of peacock feathers.

By Hewitt's right side was a table with two decanters of whisky, and a bottle of soda water. He had been drinking since sundown, and his forehead was varnished with sweat. He had the beginnings of a headache, and the breath rattled in his throat as though reluctant to pass in or out of his bloated body.

He felt indescribably lonely and old and vulnerable. He took another swallow of whisky and the alcohol surging in his sluggish blood, combined with the melancholy of evening, almost overcame him.

Had he been alone, he would have wept. He was a failure, and he knew it. General Anson, the commander-in-chief, had demoted him only months previously from command in Rawalpindi. He would have removed him from India altogether, but Hewitt had important family connections with several of the Company's directors, and they did not desert him in his hour of need. He was there-

fore not removed from command altogether, but was posted to Meerut; an important appointment, he had been assured.

So it was, but nothing eventful had ever happened in
Meerut. There was no reason to suppose that anything
would, unless, of course, this disgraceful and totally in-
comprehensible business of sepoys refusing orders was allowed to continue.

He had treated them harshly, he knew, but how could
they possibly imagine, in their blank minds, what agonies
of his own he was undergoing? Did they not realize that if
he failed in this last command, then he would be retired,
finally forced, despite all family influence, to eke out his
old age in some English south coast watering place?

His wife had died long ago and his family was back in
England. Like many other lonely old officers he had fallen
back on the false comfort of whisky.

He would lie in his bed, and all he wanted was sleep,
merciful and dreamless, to help him escape from his gout,
the thought of what he had been, what he could have become, and what he was; a general in titular command of
several thousand troops defending the greatest magazine
in the world. But, in fact and reality, enfeebled, physically
and mentally, unable even to mount his horse unaided; a
hulk of flesh stranded on the shore of the river of time.

He took another long swallow of whisky, and waved
away the bearer with the fan. He clapped his hands and
another servant stood soundlessly in the doorway, his face
expressionless as a stone carving.

'Bring me a pen, a table, ink and paper,' the general
commanded him. He would write his own account of the
sentences, before anyone else became critical. He would
show Anson that he had made a grave error in putting
him out to grass. Why, his firm action could well have
saved the whole Indian Army from insurrection. You *had*
to be firm with these niggers.

The servant carried in a portable writing-table, set it
down to one side of Hewitt's chair, removed the glass
stopper of the ink well, bowed and withdrew.

Hewitt picked up his pen, stabbed it in the ink like a
dagger, and drew a few scratchy lines on the paper to

make sure the nib was unclogged. Then, on a clean sheet
of paper, he began to write.

> 'To the Commander-in-Chief.
> 'Sir, I have the honour to submit my report regarding
> the sentences to be carried out on the following
> sepoys who have been found guilty of the crime of
> mutiny . . .'

Gough and Lang sat on their cane chairs on the
veranda of their bungalow, feet up on cane stools, glasses
at hand, discussing the events of the day.

The heat had long since burned out of the sky, and the
evening crackled with small insect noises; the rough croak
of lizards, the rattle of a bullfrog, the hum of wings from
some heavy night moth coming too close to the oil lamp
that glowed on the table between them.

Suddenly, Gough started up in his chair, eyes narrowed.
A voice whispered urgently from the darkness.

'Sahib!'

'Who is it?' he asked, expecting a beggar, or some other
deformed mendicant, rotten with leprosy, who would drag
in his swollen trunk on a trolley, propelling himself by his
hands, to beg for a crust of bread.

But the man who now came carefully out of the
darkness was no beggar, but the regiment's subedar, the
senior native officer, Pandit Rao, a well-built man of
nearly sixty, still in uniform. His honest, homely face
shone with sweat like oiled ebony.

'What do you want?' asked Gough, surprised. No work
was done after lunch; even tribal wars were fought, as far
as possible, in the morning. And Saturday night, of all
nights of the week, was the last on which Gough expected
to be interrupted by a subedar.

'The accounts, sahib. I've come to see you about them.'

'The accounts?' repeated Gough in amazement. 'But we
dealt with those on Wednesday. What is so important that
cannot wait until Monday?'

'There *is* something that cannot wait, sahib.'

'What is it?' Lang asked him bluntly.

Subedar Rao's eyes were pale in the sudden Indian
dusk. The rest of his body was in shadow. He clearly did

not want to be seen speaking to the British officers.

'The unhappy events today have disturbed the Native Infantry and the Cavalry. They have been to the bazaar. They feel the general's sentences are unfair. It is my duty to tell you, they plan to release the prisoners.'

'When?'

'Tomorrow, sahib. When the British troops are at church.'

'Nonsense,' said Gough, trying to sound unconvinced. 'You're joking, subedar sahib.'

'Not so, sahib. I speak the truth. I speak as I do because I have forty years' service to the Company. And my son is also in the Company's army. Now I have done my duty, sahib.'

'So you have,' said Gough. '*Salaamaji.*'

The man melted away; his bare feet made no noise on the hard ground.

'What do you make of that?' asked Lang.

Gough shrugged and lit a cheroot.

'We should report it,' he said. 'It's probably nothing. But the subedar is a good soldier. He would not knowingly pass on foolish rumours. He thinks this is important.'

'What do *you* think?'

'Old General Hewitt acted like an ass with those heavy sentences. Those men are ruined. They have lost their pensions and their prestige. But whether any others will risk anything on their behalf I just don't know.'

'And if they do?'

'As things are, we haven't got a chance. We are outnumbered here, of course—and ten times as badly at other stations. I suggest we see the colonel.'

They walked across the empty parade ground towards the colonel's bungalow, unconsciously falling in step and keeping fairly close together. It felt very empty out there in the darkness. In the distance, from the bazaar, the crack of fireworks, occasional shouts from some drunken soldier, blew in on the wind, and, as a background, the high, insistent rhythm of Indian music with the urgent pattering of drums.

Colonel Carmichael Smythe's bungalow stood fifty yards away from the nearest house. A servant answered their knock on the heavy front door. The colonel arrived, a glass of whisky in his hand. Lang had a wedge-shaped view of the whitewashed hall, walls covered with pictures of English hunting scenes; two easy chairs, with antimacassars; a table with a brass oil lamp; some Persian carpets on the earth floor. They saluted smartly.

'What do you want?' the colonel asked them sharply, looking from one to the other. What the devil was the army coming to with subalterns still in their teens calling uninvited on colonels on a Saturday night?

'My apologies for disturbing you, sir,' said Gough. 'But, as the orderly officer, I felt it my duty to report that the subedar sahib tells me he believes there is a plan for malcontents in the Native Infantry and Cavalry to release the prisoners from the hospital tomorrow, when the British troops are on church parade.'

'How do they propose to do that?' asked Colonel Smythe, sipping his whisky.

They were all three standing on the porch. The colonel was not noted for his hospitality.

'He didn't say,' admitted Gough.

'Did you ask him?'

'No, sir.'

'Did you make any other inquiries?'

'From whom, sir?'

'How do *I* know from whom? You're bringing this story to me. It's your duty, surely, to seek out the truth, find corroboration, then set the facts down. As it is, this is just an absurd bazaar rumour. Idle words, Gough. Idle words.'

'Possibly, sir.'

'Not just *possibly*. Almost *certainly*. I can act on facts, but not on rumours. Well, good night, both of you.'

As he turned to shut the door he frowned. He had seen the crest on the buttons of Lang's tunic.

'What regiment are you in, Lang?'

'Nineteenth Infantry, sir.'

'Then why aren't you wearing Nineteenth Infantry buttons, eh? You're improperly dressed.'

'These are the buttons of the uniform of my cavalry regiment in Barrackpore.'

'But you aren't *in* Barrackpore. You're in *Meerut*. Most serious offence, to be improperly dressed, Lang. Could

cast a cloud over your whole career. How can men possibly look up to an officer if he's going about in cast-offs
from another regiment, eh? Tell me that.'

Lang said nothing.

'There you are,' said Colonel Smythe triumphantly.
'You have no excuse. Do not let me see you in those buttons again. That is an order. And don't spread any of
these absurd rumours about. You'll frighten the ladies.
That is also an order.

'Spend your spare time in living up to the traditions of
the regiment. Not going about in odd buttons, calling
without prior appointment on senior officers to spread entirely unsubstantiated gossip. That includes you, too,
Gough. As orderly oficer, you surely have more important
duties to do.'

He closed the door.

They walked down the path together.

'So what do we do now?' asked Lang.

'I think we should see Brigadier Wilson.'

'Do you think it really is serious? We did not ask anyone else's views, after all. It *may* just be a rumour.'

'Possibly,' agreed Gough. 'But there is just the chance it
isn't. You know from Barrackpore the trouble the army's
facing now. Remember, Richard, there are about a hundred million Indians in India—and less than fifty thousand
Europeans. And half of them are mothers and young children.

'Most of the British troops have been out here for
twenty years. They're ridden with pox, cholera and fever.
They never go out in the heat of the day in case they drop
dead. What sort of chance do you think we whites would
have if the blacks *did* take us on?'

'I don't want to think about it,' said Lang.

'Nor does the colonel. Which is why we'll see the
brigadier.'

Brigadier Wilson's bungalow stood a quarter of a mile
away from the colonel's surrounded by a whitewashed
wall, with a sentry box at the gate. A *chowkidar*, an old
Indian watchman, wearing cast-off pieces of uniform,
stood inside leaning against the box, fast asleep, like an
old horse in his stall. He shambled into wakefulness as
they approached, and seized a great club, until he saw

who they were. Then he salaamed and beat on the front
door with his club. It was not right for sahibs to exert
themselves when an Indian was at hand.

Chains and bolts slipped and rattled; and an English orderly invited them to wait in the hall. This was a virtual
replica of Colonel Smythe's, except that the paintings were
of pheasants and partridges and trout.

Again, Brigadier Wilson did not invite them farther
than the hall but came out to meet them, a thin, worried
man, with a goatee beard.

'What is it?' he asked resignedly, as though only ill
news could bring two junior officers to see him on a Saturday night.

They explained the subedar's warning.

The brigadier listened and pulled on his beard, twisting
it to a sharper point.

'What do you want me to do?' he asked Gough weakly.

'I thought you should know, sir.'

'Well, I do know now. I don't think there's much truth
in this rumour. The general's quite convinced he awarded
the only sentences he could. I know they were strict, but
what else do sepoys expect if they disobey orders?

'I've heard rumours of revolts and mutinies and so on
for forty years, gentlemen, long before you were born.
And generally they come to nothing much. Talk is a kind
of safety valve. Thank you for telling me, anyhow. Now,
I'll bid you both good night. By the way, Gough, how are
your lions getting on?'

'Very well, sir.'

'Good. I must show them to my lady wife one day. Such
noble beasts. So symbolic of England, don't you think?'

Wilson shuffled away into the recesses of the hall. The
orderly showed the two young officers out of the door.
The *chowkidar* sprang to attention with a great clattering
of his club as they went past him.

'What's he mean by that remark about your lions?'
asked Lang.

'There's so little doing here in a military way that I've
got my own private zoo.'

'Your own *zoo*?' Lang's voice showed his surprise.

'Yes. Leopards, lions, monkeys, parakeets. You can
learn a lot from watching animals. Perhaps the brigadier

and the colonel should watch them more often. Personally, I would not consider the lion symbolic of either of
them.'

'No,' agreed Lang. 'The ass would be a better choice.'

Ram Gupta stood flattened against the hospital wall,
hearing his own heart beat and the endless grumbling
croak of the bullfrogs. Inches away, on the other side of
the whitewashed mud wall, were the eighty-five sepoys
who, that morning, had been sentenced to transportation.

He had watched the parade from the shade of a clump
of mango trees, and afterwards he had followed them, unshaven and wearing a shabby dhoti, as they were marched
off in irons. He could be any tout from the bazaar. No
one paid any attention to him.

Ram Gupta was not sure whether British or Indian
troops were on guard, so when he reached the corner he
paused, listening for any give-away sound; some curse or
comment in English or Hindusthani.

Incredibly, no guards appeared to be outside the building. What slackness was this? Truly, all discipline was in
decline.

He moved more openly now; the risk of discovery
seemed minimal. The moon was rising and the parade
ground beyond the hospital lay cold and grey and empty.
Ram Gupta put his weight against the door, turned the
handle, and walked in.

Half a dozen sepoys with muskets lounged against the
wall inside, near a table with an oil *butti* on it. Its flame
flickered weakly in the draught from the open door. These
sepoys must be the guard. What folly not to guard the
hospital with British troops who would have no feelings of
sympathy towards the Indians!

Rope-mattressed charpoys stretched side by side along
the walls with an aisle down the middle. Wooden posts
supported the main roof beams; oil lamps hung from nails
driven into them.

Some prisoners lay on their beds in loincloths, mana-
cled hands under their necks, looking at the ceiling. Others crouched in small groups at the foot of their beds,
whispering together. The guards were chewing betel nut.
They looked at Ram Gupta without interest.

'What do you want here, old one?' asked a Naik, an Indian corporal.

Ram Gupta drew himself up to his full height; the Naik was surprised to see how tall he was.

'I want what these men in their manacles seek,' Ram Gupta began, in the parade ground voice he used when he would lecture new recruits on the traditions of the regiment. 'I want justice and an end to oppression. I want the right, as in olden times, to have the ear of the officer sahibs. I want to serve with officers—as I have served for many years—who speak my language, who understand my religion, who love my country.'

The guards moved around him.

'Who are you?' asked the Naik curiously.

'I *was* a subedar in the Nineteenth Indian Infantry,' replied Ram Gupta, looking down from his superior height into the Naik's yellowish eyes. 'I served for more than thirty years. I saw my friends die in a dozen campaigns, and, only weeks ago, I saw other friends of mine die in Barrackpore. Blown from guns. May they rest in Paradise.'

Chains rattled and clanked as men swung themselves off their beds and peered towards the door. The only sound was their breathing as they listened expectantly.

'Can you speak for us?' asked someone.

'You can speak for yourselves,' replied Ram Gupta. 'Your years of service also speak for you.'

'But there is no one to listen! No one!'

'Perhaps there is no one *here*,' corrected Ram Gupta. 'But I have come from a maharajah in the north who sympathizes with your plight, for it is also the plight of all our country.

'We have no quarrel with the British. We have served them loyally. We have taken their money. We are their men. We do quarrel, however, with their policies. They are now interfering with our religion—these cartridges are only one example. They are interfering with our ways. And not understanding our customs.

'This is a time of change. I have seen roofs blaze with fire arrows. I have heard passwords from the north, from the east, from the west and the south. So have you. I have travelled the country, my friends, and everywhere I find discord. You know the prophecy?'

'There are many prophecies and many prophets, but there is only one God, Allah, and Mohammed is his true prophet,' said the Naik quickly. He was a Moslem and eager to establish this fact.

'There is only one God to you, as you are a Moslem,' replied Ram Gupta gently. The last thing he wanted at this moment was any religious argument which would weaken his rhetoric.

'I am a Hindu. Even so, we worship our own gods in our own ways, and we respect each other. We do not trespass or fight among ourselves, because our gods have different faces and different names. Nor do we seek to convert each other to our own faith, as the English seek to do.

'I speak of the prophecy made at the Battle of Plassey, one hundred years ago this month. That the British would rule for only one hundred more years. A century. So now their day is ending. Night is falling on their power. Tomorrow, the sun will rise on ours.'

'You speak in riddles,' said the Naik, anxious to show he also had a rank and a mind of his own.

'All speech is in riddles,' replied Ram Gupta splendidly. 'Our thoughts are like onion skins. We peel off one and another is there to view. I speak the truth, my friends.

'Tomorrow, you will be taken from this place. You will then travel to Madras and thence, by the new ships that need no sails, across the dark water, *kala pani*, to servitude in the Andaman Islands. There will be no return for many of you, my friends. You know that, just as I do.'

'But what use is this knowledge to us?' shouted someone. 'It's easy for you to talk like this, old one. We want *deeds* now, not talk.'

'If you mean what you say, warrior,' said Ram Gupta, 'watch for the signs. Be ready to act. I leave you now, but when I return I will not be alone.'

He had no idea who else he would bring back. The excitement of the moment had carried him away. And now the words were spoken, he could not bring them back. Like birds, they had flown from his mouth.

He turned to the guards.

'Are you with us, or against us?' he asked them bluntly.

They moved nervously. Their sympathies lay with the prisoners, which was why they had come inside the building instead of standing guard outside.

Equally, by disobeying direct orders, the prisoners had invited punishment. But was the punishment not so much for their crime, as to deter others who might follow their lead?

The guards had friends in the regimental office who had told them of reports from other stations concerning similar outbreaks of discontent; about grievances unheard and other men in irons.

They wanted to stay loyal, but to whom, or what? The English in India were outnumbered, by at least a hundred to one. Everyone knew that; the astonishing thing was that the English were seemingly unafraid. Or was it because they really *were* a superior race, as they seemed to believe, and so they had nothing to fear? Nothing appeared clear-cut; issues were neither black nor white, but grey and undefined.

Yet all agreed that it only required a concerted attack in every garrison in India and the sepoys could be in power, and who would then dislodge them?

'We will see,' replied the Naik cautiously, not wishing to commit himself too strongly. The English might have planted this person among them as an informer. Ah, yes, they were cunning. How else could they have taken over a vast country a hundred times larger than the tiny islands they called home?

Equally, he had said nothing that the prisoners could use to their advantage against him, should events turn out as this former subedar had declared they would. The Naik played for safety, and the other guards grunted their approval.

Ram Gupta bowed to them, opened the door behind him, and was gone. The night air felt cool on his face, and he was pleased deep inside him because he had spoken, not with the honey tongues of lawyers who said words they did not mean, but from his heart.

The moon had risen and now threw long shadows of trees and buildings across the parade ground. There was

something curiously ethereal about the scene. With the
only sound from the bullfrogs, Ram Gupta felt he might
be the last man alive—or else the first man in a new
world altogether.

9

Sunday morning in Meerut.

The parson, the Reverend John Rotton, stood in his church doorway, shaking hands with his more influential parishioners. Usually, he preached for exactly forty-five minutes by his German silver hunter. Today, he felt he had given his congregation short measure; his sermon had lasted for barely half an hour.

The fact was, that morning, he had had rather an odd experience, and now he was telling it at some length to three spinsters who stood with him in the doorway.

'We have this old bearer, Swami,' he was saying. 'A very sound fellow. Not a Christian yet, but none the less he possesses many Christian virtues, such as honesty and loyalty. I was almost late for service this morning because he kept coming in to see me. When I asked him what he wanted, he really didn't *know*. I got quite angry with the fellow in the end. I hadn't time to waste.'

'Perhaps he wished to be converted?' suggested the youngest spinster hopefully.

'Perhaps, Miss Montrose. But I doubt it. Really, I doubt it.'

Their carriage arrived and away they went.

I wonder what Swami *did* want to tell me? thought Rotton. Perhaps I should not have been so impatient with him? Perhaps I should have listened?

Lieutenant Garroway was drinking claret in his bungalow. It was rather better furnished than Lang's with a cord rug that fitted the main room up to the walls, and a lot of empty wine bottles piled in the bathroom.

He had been examining his bank statement, which had arrived the previous evening from the Bombay branch of Grindlays. He owed the bank four hundred and seventy-two rupees and fifteen annas. When that month's mess bill was added, the total would be nearly eight hundred rupees. And fifteen annas, of course. It would never do to forget them. The bank cashier wouldn't.

Garroway poured himself more wine, drank it quickly and refilled the glass. Wine kept the fever at bay, he had heard somewhere. He drank a great deal of it, and had never once suffered from the fever.

Now, this present problem. He must get some money somehow, but how? It would be easy if he was in the commissariat or, at least, in a position where he could influence the quartermaster, who had to buy so many tons of rice and flour in any case, and so might as well buy it from someone you recommended, as from anyone else. The difference, of course, so far as you were concerned, was that you had a ten per cent commission from your contractor.

But Garroway had never managed to fit himself into this agreeable position. People didn't trust him. He was sure they envied him his good looks, his physique, his charm. He had no valuables he could pawn for security against a loan; only himself. Only his body. He caught sight of himself in the misty mirror of Indian glass hung on the wall. His body was perfect. If only he were rich, he would have no worries, no complaints.

He sipped the wine more slowly. That woman, Rosemary Bolivar, out at Ahmnagar, ten miles away, married to a major whose family owned whole square miles of slums and mills and canal frontages around Manchester. He'd got money, her husband, but everyone knew he had nothing else. He couldn't do it at all; he was impotent. His bearer had heard arguments and tears, and when Major Bolivar had dismissed him for stealing two bottles of brandy, the man had told others what he had overheard.

Garroway had first met the Bolivars at a regimental ball, shortly before he went on leave. Rosemary invited him to call in at their bungalow on any Sunday after tiffin. He'd said, laughingly, he was too poor to ride that far.

'Perhaps I'll pay you,' she'd said, swinging her fan pro-
vocatively, as they sat out three dances together on the
mess veranda.

'My price is high,' said Garroway, not entirely joking.

'I think we could meet all demands. Provided *you* could
do the same.'

They looked each other in the eyes, and knew what
they both meant. She was bored with her husband, and his
fumbling sexual inadequacies. Life was passing her by;
Garroway's good looks, his physique, his boldness attracted her.

But like many handsome men, Garroway was cautious.
This was not the first affair he had conducted with discontented wives of brother officers, and he had experienced
one or two narrow misses in the past. You couldn't push
your luck too far: you could not afford to be discovered.

He took another sip of wine and suddenly the solution
was revealed. He would borrow a dhoti and a pair of
chaplis from his bearer, darken his face and hands with
boot blacking and ride out to Ahmnagar as an Indian.

If Major Bolivar were at home, then he would ride
back at once, and no one would ever suspect he had been
there at all.

If, however, as Garroway believed, the gallant major
was away from home on detachment, then he would call
on his wife. And if any servant saw him, he would believe
he was only a travelling carpet-seller or some such harmless person.

The whole scheme was foolproof. Delighted at his own
ingenuity, Garroway finished the glass and poured himself
another.

Lang had eaten his breakfast late. Guavas, two tiny Indian eggs, rough brown bread, a mug of tea; and now the
day stretched ahead with nothing to do, for no one
worked on Sunday. Indeed, no one worked much on any
week-day either, but here he had at least twelve hours to
fill before he went to bed again. After luncheon he would
doze on his bed and, of course, attend church parade in
the evening. And this morning he should write to his
mother and to Arabella—could a letter from her have
been lost in Barrackpore? He felt saddened that he had

not received even one from her; but, of course, to be fair, he told himself, the mail was probably still on its way. He stood looking across the parade ground at the rim of distant purple hills behind the white tents with pennants on their points; the thatched bungalows, the mess halls, the barracks. They were set in rows—lines was the word they used—as much on parade as the men who lived in them.

By noon, the sun would burn its way up the sky, and begin to roast the plain. Its heat drove most men into their bungalows, clogged ink in their army-issue pens, and made sweat trickle itchily down their backs. It lit ill-feeling, and tempers would smoulder dangerously, so that remarks that would pass unnoticed in a kinder climate, would here be seized on as deadly and intended insults.

Gough, as the week-end orderly officer, had gone to inspect the guard; he was on his own.

Lang sat down at his little table, pulled a writing pad towards him and began, without enthusiasm, to compose a letter to his mother. It would be difficult to find much to write about. Obviously nothing ever happened here.

Meerut, Sunday afternoon.

The bazaar beat back the heat like a burnished gun-barrel.

The shops were wooden huts, with open fronts and bright yellow and red signs in Indian script, with crude paintings of the goods they sold to help people who could not read. Earth alleys ran between them, trodden hard by hundreds of hurrying bare feet and the hooves of camels and horses. Flies buzzed in blue clouds over heaps of rotting mangoes and corn husks at the street corners. Here and there, stray dogs and cats had died and their bloated bodies crawled with worms. Beggars with legs as thick as their trunks, others eyeless or armless, deliberately deformed by their parents at birth to assure them of a livelihood, lay on wooden trolleys which little boys would push out when anyone passed by.

Each alley was given over almost exclusively to a single trade: cutters of hair; sweetmeat sellers; money-lenders, and so on. Everywhere, sacred cows, white and humped-backed, rooted among rubbish thrown from upper windows. They moved slowly, where they wished, and no one

restrained them, for who could say who they had been in
a former life?

Indian women, young, firm breasted, wearing brightly
coloured saris, with gold ornaments in the sides of their
noses, hurried along balancing on their heads metal bowls
of grain or earthen water pots from the wells. Little children played naked in the dust, bowling hoops or turning
over the steaming piles of horse and camel dung with
sticks.

The Street of the Harlots was different from other
streets; no sweetmeats or bangles or cut melons or guavas
were on sale. The merchandise here was more subtly dis-
played behind wooden doors divided horizontally, like
stables. The bottom halves were bolted and the tops open,
so that potential customers could see whether a face or
figure attracted them before they entered into business negotiations. Equally, the girls were unable to leave their
stalls, which ensured that all business was conducted on
the premises, and the madams ran no risk of losing their
percentage.

They sat on wooden stools, sewing or beating pulse and
lentils in bowls with pestles. Not all could practise their
profession all the time, but there was no need for them to
be idle and unproductive meanwhile. Theirs was a business, like any other.

Their faces were heavily painted, eyes darkened with
kohl or lamp black, lips reddened, cheeks rouged. All
pock marks and the pitting which scarred many of their
faces were concealed as carefully as possible with face
cream. Most wore jasmin-coloured bodices, this colour
being peculiar to their profession.

This Sunday afternoon fifteen sepoys from the Nineteenth Indian Native Regiment, some in uniform, others in
white dhotis, had drifted here. They had been drinking,
and the sun was so hot that some were already fuddled
with its heat, and desire crawled within them like worms.
They headed for the last brothel in the street, for it had a
shady courtyard shielded by a high wall from the road.
The front door was open, with a bead curtain across the
doorway to keep out flies and provide an air of intimacy.

The Naik had led the way. He had come off duty inside
the hospital early in the morning, slept for a few hours,

and then had told some friends about the strange visit of
the former subedar. The situation obsessed them; after all,
these prisoners were their comrades. They needed somewhere to talk in private. What better place than the courtyard in the last house, where only silly women might
overhear them, and could make no use of what they
heard?

The madam counted them approvingly as they passed
her; fifteen men, and only eleven girls. She scribbled a
note for four girls from another house, and gave it to a
boy to deliver. Her own girls came down from their upper
rooms and sat on the benches, talking loudly among themselves, moving their arms deliberately so that the gold
bangles jangled on their wrists, and each could show herself off to her best advantage.

The sepoys walked through to the yard, where wooden
rafters supported vines and other creeping plants. The air
was filtered by thick clusters of leaves; it felt cool and
shaded after the hot, white blaze outside. Servants brought
out hubble-bubble pipes with fresh cool water in their
bowls, and little silver caskets of poppy seed, and charcoal
braziers. Soon the men would smoke. The drug would first
soothe them, and then arouse them so that their hot las-
civious thoughts would carry them upstairs. And afterwards they would smoke again, and drink sweet tea, and
they would be happy and so would she.

The Naik nodded a dismissal to the servants, took a
long lungful of the cooled smoke from the pipe, and
passed on the mouthpiece to the men on his right.

'This subedar spoke the truth,' he said solemnly.
'Manifestly, it is unjust that our comrades should be ex-
iled for ten or twenty years, or for ever, simply because
they refused to defile themselves with unclean fat.'

'Many things are unjust but have to be borne,' replied
another, older sepoy. He had been a Naik, too, years before, but had been demoted because the adjutant had
found him drunk on two occasions. He argued now for
the sake of argument, to show he had once held authority,
to prove he had a mind of his own.

'You talk like a lawyer, round and round the problem.
But while you talk, our friends are still in irons. What *action* do you propose?'

The Naik drew on the pipe again. Air bubbled through the water in the bowl, and the charcoal glowed red hot. The smoke, cooled by the water, soothed his throat. He exhaled it through his nostrils, nodding to show he took the other man's point.

'If we went back to the hospital now with the smiths, we could cut off their manacles,' he said. 'They could all go free. In civilian clothes, they would never be discovered.'

'*We* would be.'

'If we stayed in uniform, yes. But not if we went with them.'

'So you are suggesting that we forget our oaths of loyalty and our years of service, and the prospect of our pensions, and become beggars or thuggees?'

'I am suggesting nothing,' said the Naik quickly. 'I am just saying what we *could* do.'

The hookahs bubbled like the strange, exhilarating thoughts that began to ferment in their minds.

'But what if other garrisons *also* took action to free their jailed comrades? There would not be enough British in all India to overpower us. Then we *would* be in command.'

'That is so,' agreed the sepoy. 'But what you say is madness. How could we seize power and arms, when the English control cannon and other artillery? You speak with the tongue of a fool. Numbers we have, but nothing else.'

The Naik banged the table angrily with his fist. He felt he was losing their interest; he had liked being listened to; it was a new and pleasing experience.

'You speak as servants speak. Ready to complain, but unwilling to act. Numbers we have, you say. So what else have we need of?'

He reached out and pulled a tendril from a vine and snapped it as easily as a thread.

'That is how we will be treated if we do not act as one.'

He doubled the two pieces of vine stalk, then doubled them again, and pulled. They held firm.

'You see? If all the units stand against injustice, we will prevail. *Now* do you understand what I mean?'

The others nodded; the whole issue seemed simple to their drowsy minds.

The Naik stood up.

'Then we are agreed?' he demanded dramatically. 'We will free our comrades peacefully. Then we shall petition the general personally, and send messages out to the other regiments in the stations and explain what we intend. They will be sympathetic.'

'You think so?' asked the older man doubtfully.

'I *know* so,' said the Naik, convincing himself as much as the others.

Suddenly they were all standing up, facing each other across the table, all thought of girls or tea or smoking forced out of their thoughts by the heady vision of power, just across the narrow frontier of decision.

They began to file out of the courtyard, into the hall. Behind them, the disappointed girls chattered shrilly like caged birds. Men!

The madam also stood up in her little room, but for different reasons and with different thoughts.

What had happened to make her customers leave so soon? They had paid nothing; she would be the laughing stock of her rivals, and what could she tell the other madam up the road who had sent girls in to help her? That she had let fifteen customers leave without taking one anna from any of them? As the Naik passed her, she seized his sleeve.

'Why are you going?'

'We have man's work to do.'

'Man's work? That is why I thought you came *here!*' she screamed in rage and disappointment. 'Do you not like my girls? Are they not pleasing to you? Or do you not wish girls at all?'

'Out of my way, woman,' shouted the Naik, and pulled his arm free of her grasp.

'Man's work,' she repeated. 'You are not *men*. I'd rather have the English troops here than you. Ho, they are men all right!'

The owner of a rival brothel heard the shouting, and, not knowing the reason behind it, but hopeful that perhaps she might persuade the sepoys to visit her establishment, now began to shout from across the road.

'They're here! They're here! The English troops are here! Come and prove how good *you* are!'

The sepoys were out in the street now, blinking in the

harsh sunshine after the coolness of the shaded yard. Drums of fear and anger hammered in their heads; the effect of the toddy they had drunk earlier was wearing away, leaving them fractious and dry-mouthed.

Up and down the street, lattice-windows opened, and women's faces popped out at them. Jeering girls with painted harlot lips were laughing at them. They had nothing against them personally. But men had sneered at them so often that it was pleasant to do this to them for a change.

The sepoys stood, muscles taut, eyes narrowed, expecting to hear the crunch of British soldiers' boots on the dusty road, or the crash of an opening door as they burst out at them.

Someone must have warned them they were plotting to release the prisoners!

Yet the street was almost empty; a blind beggar basked in the sun near the city wall, holding an empty alms bowl. The sepoys began to grin sheepishly at each other, relieved it was all a false alarm. The Naik looked at them angrily.

'Are you dogs that you cringe at any shout? Do you fear the English so much—when we outnumber them ten to one, a *hundred* men to one?'

'Of course not,' replied the older sepoy. 'But you will admit the shout gave us a shock.'

'A *shock?* You speak of shocks, friend. We will show who can give shocks now. To the barracks! *Huzzah!*'

The Naik gave a great roar of rage and started to run up the street. The others followed, slowly at first, then faster, so as not to be left behind. And as they ran, falling automatically into step, their feet thudded ominously on the hard earth, like the pounding of hammers.

'For the faith!' they shouted. 'For the faith!'

The cry was taken up by other sepoys who burst out of brothels and tea-shops. Some seized chairs as weapons, others ripped bamboo poles that supported awnings over displays of sweetmeats and fruit, and carried them like spears. Householders fled to upper windows, alarmed by the running feet and the shouts and the crashes as the awnings fell.

Soon, instead of fifteen sepoys, there were fifty; then a hundred, with another hundred hangers-on, all running together at an easy trot, and shouting as they ran.

From foul pits beneath shops, from rotting shacks and sheds, other men swarmed out, the sweepings of the bazaar; thieves, thuggees, cut-throats, men without homes, some even without names, who lived like beasts and now, like beasts, were out for what they could steal. They carried staves and clubs and knives and iron bars to help them in their search.

Soon a crowd of hundreds of shouting, yelling men, armed and violent, surged like a terrible tide out of the bazaar and poured along the narrow road towards the cantonment that trembled with sleepy heat in the shimmering distance.

Private Ronald Dougan of the Sixtieth Rifles saw them first. He stood outside the whitewashed guard-room on the edge of the parade ground, yawning and scratching himself. He was off duty in half an hour and was wondering how he could miss church parade. He was not a man with a religious turn of mind. But which was worse, a sermon from Mr Rotton or a purge by an apothecary if he reported sick?

Two other British private soldiers, in the cells awaiting charges to be heard on Monday morning, came out after him, hair matted, eyes flecked with matter, mouths foul with drink and sleep, chins bristly as a lavatory brush. They were to carry the latrine buckets from the guard room and empty them.

'Who are these boogers?' asked Dougan rhetorically, as he suddenly saw the men race up the road under a billowing cloud of dust. 'Sergeant!' he yelled urgently.

The sergeant of the guard came out at a run.

'What the bluddy hell's happening?' he asked of no one in particular.

'Bluddy niggers have gone mad!' shouted one of the prisoners. '*Pagal* wallahs, the lot of 'em!'

The four men stood and stared at the scene in astonishment. It was so alien to a time traditionally dedicated to drowsiness, that for a moment it seemed like a mirage or a fantasy. Heat, like toddy, did funny things to your eyes. Then the angry shouts of the running men shattered this comfortable illusion.

'Bugler!' bellowed the sergeant. 'Sound the Alarm!'

The bugler boy rushed from the guard-room.

By now, the crowd was within fifty yards of the guard-room, but they ran on past as though neither it nor the British soldiers were there. They would set the prisoners free, and then return to deal with them.

The guard, eight men with loaded muskets, their belts and pouches and cross-straps pipe-clayed, stood in line outside the whitewashed guard-room near the polished brass alarm bell which the sergeant now began to beat. Clouds of sleepy crows, alarmed by the commotion, fluttered out from under the eaves of the nearer buildings.

'Runner,' the sergeant told the last man in line. 'Report to the Orderly Officer. Tell him what's happening.'

Then to the guard: 'Prepare to fire one round of warning shots in the air! Load!'

They rammed powder and ball into their muskets, raised them in the drill movement to their right shoulders and waited.

'Fire!' Their muskets cracked like whips; more birds flew out, but the sepoys went on running. He dared not fire directly at them. This might be some religious ceremony or feast, something he could not understand. And where the hell was everyone else?

'Look, sarge,' said Dougan in amazement, nodding over the sergeant's shoulder. 'The boogers have set the buildings on fire!'

He pointed towards some of the farthest bungalows across the ground. Orange flames, edged with thick black smoke, were spreading with a crunch and crackle of the dry thatch.

'They've gone too far. That's what,' said the sergeant with finality. 'But how are we going to stop them?'

Gough opened the shutters of his bedroom and leaned on the sill. The woodwork felt warm to his touch, and the afternoon wind blew dry and hot, like an open oven when the fire is dying. In the distance, he heard faint sounds of music, for every Sunday evening, a touring German band gave a concert in the ornate bandstand. This concert marked the end of one week, the start of another; everyone on the station looked forward to it. Gough was sorry he would not hear the band, but as orderly officer, he would be making his rounds.

Near the bandstand an enterprising Italian had set up a small booth selling ice-cream, an act of commerce that older English residents frowned on as not in keeping with the strict rules regarding sales on the Sabbath. But then the man was a foreigner, so what could you expect?

The band and the ice-cream seller provided two convenient focal points for younger, unattached officers, who cantered about on their suberbly groomed horses, bowing formally to each other and casually reining-in to salute when they saw the daughters of more senior officers walking demurely in pairs.

The bachelor officers ordered their grooms to dye their horses' tails purple, blue or green. This gave the girls—the 'spins' as they were called—a chance to comment on them with amusement or surprise (and, incidentally, to recognize an officer's particular horse when it was too far away for them to recognize the rider).

Always, as dusk rolled in over the parade ground, the band ended its performance with one tune calculated to fill the hearts of all listeners with nostalgia for an England most had left for ever.

This was the moment Gough would miss most of all: the sad braying of the brass, when shadows dimmed and shrouded familiar outlines, and intensified the feeling of solidarity, of being a handful of Europeans in a huge and alien land, surrounded by millions of natives who it was their destiny, somehow decreed divinely, to teach and lead into better, gentler, more Christian ways.

Gough's mind was miles away when he heard distant shouts and the rattle of musket fire. That was odd; firing practice was never held on Sundays.

'Sahib! Sahib!'

He turned. The bearer was standing in the doorway, eyes wide with fright, saliva streaming out of his mouth in the extremity of his fear.

'The lines and bungalows are on fire, sahib.'

'On fire?' Gough repeated in amazement. He pushed past the man and ran to the front door. The runner from the Guard came bounding up the steps.

'Mr Gough, sir,' the private panted. 'Sergeant of the guard's compliments, sir, but a crowd of men have come up from the bazaar with sticks and clubs and swords, sir, and they're heading towards the hospital, sir, and what is he to do?'

His voice faded as he saw Gough looking over his shoulder. Bungalows on the far side of the parade ground were already blazing. Some men had seized an officer's carriage, and the terrified horses were being driven wildly, rearing up, plunging down again, while sepoys swarmed over the roof and hung on to the axles, like demented children with an unexpected toy.

'Richard!' Gough yelled to Lang. 'Get dressed. There's trouble!'

Subedar Pandit Rao raced towards them on a foaming horse, and reined in savagely.

'Sahib!' he shouted. 'The Indian Infantry have mutinied! They are murdering the officers! Our own regiment is arming!'

'I'll be with you,' said Gough.

'Run to the adjutant,' he told the sergeant's messenger. 'Give him my compliments, and ask him to stand-to the Sixtieth Rifles immediately.'

'Very good, sir.'

The man turned and was off.

Gough rushed back to his room, pulled on his jacket, his trousers, his riding boots, buckled his sword belt round him, and his pistol on his right thigh.

'Tell the syce to saddle both our chargers,' he ordered his bearer, who stood wringing his hands in dismay in the doorway.

Lang was dressed now, Colt revolver in his black leather holster, trouser pockets heavy with rounds. They ran out on to the veranda, to wait for the chargers, while the wooden floor of their bungalow trembled from a thousand thudding feet outside.

One man saw them, detached himself from the crowd and ran towards them. He was tall, naked save for a cloth wound round his middle, under his crotch, like a huge nappy. Above his head he waved a torch made from bamboo rods lashed together. Its flame flared for a yard behind him. As he neared the bungalow, he swung this round his head and suddenly let go.

It landed a yard short, burning and hissing on the hot, trodden earth. With a screech of rage, he picked it up again to plunge it like a blazing javelin into the thatch.

Lang's Colt cracked in his hand. The man's head jerked
back and he paused for a second, one foot off the ground,
and then slowly he sank down, rolling over in the dust.
His torch dropped beside him. Within seconds he was
ablaze, crawling, arching his back to escape the agony of
fire that devoured him.

Lang lowered his revolver shakily. He had not meant to
fire; it had been an instinctive reflex action. He felt suddenly sick inside as he smelled the sweet sickliness of
burning human flesh.

'Thanks,' said Gough shortly.

'I killed him,' said Lang.

'I hope so,' said Gough. 'Otherwise, he would most certainly have killed us.'

Gough's syce came running with their two chargers.
The animals were frightened by the shouting, their eyes
rolling nervously. Gough and Lang leapt into the saddles.

'Lock the bungalow!' Gough shouted to his bearer.
'Close the shutters and don't let anyone in.'

'What if they set light to it, sahib?'

'They won't,' Gough answered him with a confidence he
did not feel. 'We'll be back in ten minutes. It is only some
riff-raff who've gone mad. We'll turn out the British
troops. They'll deal with them in no time.'

Then they were off, horses fresh and trembling under
them, the sharp smoke from the burning bungalows making them snort and sneeze.

'Where are we heading?' asked Lang.

'Adjutant's bungalow first. God knows what's happening. But a few rounds into this lot from the Sixtieth will
steady 'em up.'

The adjutant's bungalow was ablaze. No one could live
in that inferno. Giant flames stretched hot tongues out at
them through broken windows. As they watched, the rafters caved in with a great roar of burning wood and a
shower of sparks.

If the adjutant and his family had not escaped, then
they were already dead. Had the messenger reached them
in time? Or had he been killed on the way? And even if
he had reached the adjutant in time, how could he alert
the Sixtieth Rifles?

They looked at each other in silent horror, the same
thoughts in their minds.

'The British lines,' said Gough, and wheeled round his horse.

The German band conductor saw the crowd of natives running towards the bandstand and heard their shouts, and frowned at the unexpected interruption. What could be happening?

'Fortissimo! Bravissimo!' he shouted to his band. So they played louder and louder until the Indians were on them, hacking, cutting, slicing with swords, and the music died with the musicians. And then the mob were past them, streaming towards the bungalows, and the only sound was the tap on the drum of a dead man's hand.

Suddenly, from bushes at the roadside, a band of rebels leaped at Lang and Gough waving staves, roaring threats. Their terrified horses tried to bolt. As they struggled to control them, an Indian havildar on a black gelding charged to their aid, sword in hand. The three horsemen cut down their nearest opponents, and then were through the ambush. They reined in their horses, grateful for the Indian's sudden appearance. Their uniforms hung in shreds; blood from sword nicks ran with sweat down their faces. Their bridles were nearly severed. Without his help they would have been massacred. He raised his sword in salute.

'Thanks,' said Gough, waving his blade in reply.

The Indian wheeled his horse around.

'Where are you off to?' shouted Lang.

'I could not see you murdered,' the Indian replied quietly. 'But my duty is with my comrades.'

'*We* are your comrades. You've just saved our lives.'

'My comrades are out there—fighting for theirs,' he replied—and spurred his horse towards the parade ground to join the mutineers.

Suddenly, the day began to die. Within minutes, it would be dusk. Flames from burning buildings lit up the darkening sky with a ring of fire, bright against the short Indian evening. Soon it was impossible to see any landmark; the familiar church steeple was already obscured by dusk and thick black smoke.

Gough turned off from the track, along the side of a river. On either side shadowy, furtive figures were scurrying past them in the semi-darkness, pushing handcarts, piled with belongings—either saving or looting their masters' property.

They crashed through a copse of trees, and faced the artillery lines: a row of barrack buildings shuttered and apparently deserted. As they rode towards them the thatched roofs erupted in great gouts of flame. In their glare, they saw sepoys up ladders throwing more blazing torches on to the thatch, while others smashed shutters, and tossed inside bales of burning hay from the stables.

They reined-in their horses. There was no point in going ahead. Why weren't the English troops *doing* something? Was it that no one was left alive, either to give orders or to take them?

'The general's house!' shouted Lang. 'Let's try there.'

The guard had deserted Hewitt's front gate. Unchallenged, they rode up the short drive, dismounted and beat on the front door with their swords. Mosquitoes whined around their sweaty faces as they waited.

'Who is it?' asked an English voice.

'Orderly Officer!' called Gough. 'Emergency! Open up!'

A rattle of chain and bolts and the door was open. An English orderly holding a drawn sword in his hand stood in the hall.

'Where's the general?'

'He has retired for the night, sir.'

'Even so, we must see him. Outside, there's anarchy.'

They pushed past him and went up the steps two at a time, the orderly padding after them breathlessly.

'You can't do this, sir. You can't. It's—it's—*improper, sir.*'

They paid no attention, but beat on the door of the general's bedroom. He opened it himself, wearing a grey linen nightshirt with a night-cap. An oil lamp burned on a table.

'What do you want?' he asked irritably. 'What's happening that you must come barging in here at this hour?'

They clicked their heels respectfully.

'Orderly Officer reporting, sir,' said Gough, saluting. 'The sepoys are running wild, setting fire to buildings.'

'I have been watching this disgusting business from the roof-top.'

'With respect, sir, we did report that we heard something like this could happen.'

'That was simply bazaar gossip, young man.'

Hewitt opened the door a little wider, and they could see Brigadier Wilson standing in the back of the room. He looked embarrassed at being found there, like a schoolboy in a jam pantry.

'The place is swarming with sepoys with muskets,' said Lang. 'They must have broken open the armoury.'

'Disgraceful,' said Hewitt. He turned to Wilson.

'The British Regiments can put it down easily, I am quite sure, sir,' said Wilson reassuringly.

'They haven't done so yet, sir,' said Lang. 'We can't find any of them. What are your orders?'

They all stood looking at each other for seconds that seemed beyond all measurement of time. Then the general spoke.

'Brigadier Wilson will give you your orders,' he announced. 'I have to finish my report.' Then he turned back into his bedroom and gently closed the door.

The whole darkened parade ground was now alive with running sepoys.

One group ringed the hospital building and began systematically to smash the shutters. Another crowd seized a fallen tree trunk and, using this as a battering ram, charged the main doors. They collapsed inwards with a great splintering of wood and to a roar of triumph like the breaking of a wave.

Ram Gupta led thirty men into the armoury, where all the muskets were kept chained to racks, for a musket was more valuable—and more deadly—than a man.

'Forward, the smiths!' he bellowed.

Half a dozen sepoy blacksmiths, brawny-armed, carrying hammers and pincers with handles a yard long, doubled up to him.

'Cut through the chains!' he ordered them.

The sharp jaws of the huge pincers snapped the links as though they were paper. Over their heads, muskets and ammunition were passed back to sepoys outside.

Soon the building was empty, with broken, banging doors and frightened birds fluttering their wings blindly against the rafters, terrified by the noise.

Ram Gupta had no plan, except to free the prisoners and arm his men, and then report to Nana Sahib what was happening, but for the first time in his fighting life, he had miscalculated the temper of the men he commanded.

By breaking into the armoury, by setting fire to the bungalows of some of the more unpopular officers, they had already earned themselves an automatic sentence of death—if they were caught. They had nothing left to lose but their lives. So the more they could steal and plunder now, the better.

'Back to your lines!' he bellowed, but they did not hear him.

'Form fours!' he shouted again, more desperately; but he might as well have shouted against an avalanche of burning lava from an erupting volcano.

They held muskets in their hands and were determined to seize what they could, while they could. Months and years of frustration and fears for their future; resentment at being commanded by officers half their age who did not understand them or their language or their customs, but who seemed to grow immeasurably rich while they stayed poor, had for long lit flames of anger in their minds. Their sullen indignation now burned as fiercely as the blazing roofs all round them.

Groups split up, each with their own secret targets. Someone had said that this bungalow or that contained treasure; silver or gold ornaments, or a casket of jewels. They would take these instead of their pay or their pensions. Then they would return to their villages and no one would ever find them, for who would dare to search?

So Ram Gupta stood shouting orders that nobody heeded. All his life as a soldier he had been obeyed without question, without argument, and now, having listened to him briefly, the sepoys had swept past him, out of control, on their own terrible ways. He was alone, hoarse in his throat, his mouth drying with fear at the thought of what he had helped to start. Bottles of toddy, necks smashed off, were being handed round, and sepoys were drinking so greedily that brown liquor was spilling down their chins and down their sweating naked chests.

Hundreds swarmed on to the dusty road, cut free horses from carriages and rode off bare-backed, while their comrades speared or lanced or hacked to pieces terrified families on their way to church, holding Bibles and prayer books, and all utterly unable to defend themselves.

They pushed the carriages over on their sides and set light to them, or urinated in the faces of the dead. They streamed drunkenly past Ram Gupta, throats hoarse from shouting, mouths foaming. He shouted back at them, waving his arms to try to make them listen. But he belonged to a world of order and discipline that they had left for ever.

Two horses galloped up, riderless and frightened, eyes white, trappings from their bridles trailing loose. He clapped his hands to make them swerve, and caught the second and swung himself up into the saddle. The animal bucked, but he reined it in, pulling down its jaw against the proud arched neck, until he felt its muscles admit he was master.

Then he turned the horse north, and rode through the darkened, deserted lines, through the mango swamps, out past the bazaar, on towards the hills.

Once, he stopped and looked back at the garrison. Beards of flame waved this way and that as the wind changed, and showers of sparks soared up into the velvet night as a rafter or a beam fell.

Ram Gupta turned and rode on. He would go to Nana Sahib and tell him exactly what had happened: how he had tried to rally the sepoys, and how some evil and malignant spirit appeared to have seized control of their minds, so that what he had begun he could not end.

He would ask Nana's advice. Surely he would help him? For now he could no longer help himself.

10

Sergeant-Major Herbert Black, warrant officer in charge
of the church parade of the Sixtieth Rifles, was a plump
man in his middle fifties, a hard drinker, whose wife had
died twenty years previously.

He lived in a small bungalow with an Indian mistress,
Meeta, and their two young sons. Church parade was, as
usual, at eighteen hundred hours. The battalion, wearing
their number one uniforms of light drill, were due to fall
in outside the barracks half an hour before, to be inspect-
ed, and then they would march down to church behind
their band.

Black had joined the army as a drummer boy and had
served in most ranks. He had no further ambition, save to
retire eventually to Windsor, where he had been born.
Like many men of limited imagination, Black placed great
weight on routine; in always addressing the third man
from the right marker on any parade, and asking why his
buttons weren't clean behind, and so forth.

This Sunday, several events had contrived to disturb his
accepted routine. First, Meeta was just beginning her
period, and as a result her usually placid temper had
changed for the worse. At least, this was the convenient
male explanation Black had for her conduct.

Usually, on Sunday afternoon, after a heavy curry
lunch, and much bottled beer, they would make love, and
doze and wake and make love again, and then have tea.
And he would think of England and the inn he hoped to
run when he retired.

This caused a constant undercurrent of discord between them, for Meeta knew that she would never accompany him to England. She belonged here, in Meerut, and here she would be left, like all the other Indian women who had lived with English soldiers.

She'd known this from the beginning, of course, and she would not fit into a cold climate. She felt hurt, but she knew how Herbert hankered after what he called Home. But wasn't home where your woman and your children were, where you lived and loved together? How could home be a town in a cold, grey, foggy land you had not seen for thirty years?

Black knew of her feelings, but tried to ignore them. Her present querulousness, plus the fact that their bearer had inexplicably not appeared with a tray of tea, as he always did at exactly half past four o'clock every Sunday afternoon, puzzled him. The man was nowhere to be found, which Black could not understand, for only that morning he had given him a birthday present of ten rupees—nearly a month's wages.

'Let's have you, then!' he bellowed at the British troops, falling in now, in line on the edge of the square. The familiar sound of his own voice was strangely comforting. So long as he shouted the meaningless abuse of his rank he left no chink in his mind through which worries and doubts and uncertainties could creep.

'Markers, shun!' he roared. 'To your duties, by the left . . . quick *ma-arch!*'

The men were so proud of the high polish on the toe-caps of their boots, the result of hours of smoothing the leather with a hot iron then blacking and honing them with a dry piece of bone, that the markers, who marched out on to the parade ground and stood firm, while their comrades fell in on their left in four ranks, were actually carried from the barracks to the edge of the parade ground lest dust should dull the splendid shine.

Suddenly, an officer ran up through the men to the sergeant-major. No officer ever *ran;* they rode or they walked. If they walked in a party, they deliberately kept out of step to show they were gentlemen and above such routine; only soldiers marched in step. So why hurry now?

'Get the men off parade, sar-major,' ordered the officer. 'There's trouble with the sepoys. Some have broken into the hospital and are setting the prisoners free. Fall them in again with arms and ammunition, ready to move off.'

'*Sir!*' acknowledged Black smartly.

The officer ran on towards the lines.

'Right!' roared Black. 'Back to your barrack-rooms! Unchain your muskets, and out here on parade. At the double! Last man gets two weeks' pack drill!'

Within seconds, the men were back on the edge of the parade ground. But here Black paused. Something was wrong, terribly wrong. British troops never wore their number one uniforms when carrying arms. The cleanest musket would leave an oily patch on a jacket shoulder, which no amount of beating on rocks by the dhobi man could ever entirely eradicate. He would have to send them off parade again to change uniforms, and return in their number two tunics; which he did.

And while they changed, more ruffians, eager for loot before the English drove them back to the slums where they belonged, came pouring into the cantonment.

Daphne Carter, the wife of a captain, sat in her maroon carriage in her new maroon dress, drumming her fingers impatiently on the window sill. Her husband was late. What *could* have happened to him?

They should be on their way now, or they would miss their place in the line outside the church. Unless their coach started within minutes they would be in the wrong precedence of arrival. The congregation must appear in strict order of rank and seniority to worship the Almighty. It would never do for the wife of a lieutenant to appear before the wife of a major—or, even worse, in a more splendid conveyance.

A servant came running from the house and bowed.

'Memsahib,' he explained breathlessly, 'the captain sahib has sent a message. There has been trouble with the sepoys. He said the church parade is cancelled. The troops are wanted elsewhere.'

'Nonsense,' replied Mrs Carter. 'A slight disturbance will *never* stop Mr Rotton's service. Send out my groom and syce. I will ride to church on my own.'

She sat back in the carriage. Her husband was sulking somewhere, more like, or only half awake. She thought he had drunk too much claret at luncheon; it always made him amorous, wanting to spoon, or to squeeze a breast beneath her blouse in the most disgusting way; and when she stopped him, for such conduct distressed her, he would suddenly become grumpy. What wives had to put up with, *and* deal with servants who were as much use as monkeys off the tree . . .

Those servants. Where were they? She looked out of the window again, towards the house.

To her surprise, a man was standing in the porch. An Indian, and a stranger, and, *goodness,* he held a wooden club in his hand. He wore a loincloth and a turban around his head, and nothing else. Was he a fakir, a holy man who would offer to tell her fortune, or bring her good fortune for the price of a few annas?

The flesh of his body was stained, too, in a revolting, disgusting way. What with? *Blood!* He came down the steps now, lithe as a panther, his muscles rippling under his oiled flesh.

'Who *are* you?' she called in her most penetrating voice.

For answer, he swung the club, and Daphne Carter saw his face contort with hatred like a gargoyle, wrinkled and evil, as he smashed it down on the box of the coach. The club broke on the metal rail and the man roared in rage, and thrust the jagged stump through the open window at her. She threw herself across the seat and the blow missed her. The Indian now leaped forward, and the carriage bucked and the horses whinnied as he straddled the back of the nearest. She flung open the far door of the carriage and jumped down the steps on to the gravel of the porch. Then something made her turn.

Dozens of men were creeping silently across the flower beds—*her* flower beds—towards the house. Some wore uniform, but most were like the man with the club, in loincloths. Their eyes burned in their heads like live coals, frighteningly red and luminous in the dusk.

Fear clutched Daphne Carter's throat; they were coming to kill her.

For a second, horror and disbelief numbed her brain, then the coach gave a jerk forward as the man slapped the horse's flank. The movement broke the spell.

She jumped up on the box behind him, seized the coachman's whip, and brought it down across his bare shoulders. He cowered away, screaming at the unexpected lash, and slipped sideways. Again the whip cracked like a gun, splitting open the side of his face and laying bare the bone. He slid down and fell on his back under the wheels, hands pressed to the strips of bloodied flesh.

Mrs Carter seized the reins and wheeled round the horses. She stood up—somehow to sit seemed supine— and flicked the whip above their flanks. The four thoroughbreds surged forward.

Like Boadicea in her chariot, she charged the crowd that had now swarmed across the drive to stop her leaving. Down and up, and down again went the whip, its lead tip stinging bare chests and splitting black faces.

They screamed and staggered back and fell. The bright hooves of the horses hammered over them, pounding flesh, breaking limbs. The iron tyres ground the writhing bodies into the gravel, and then she was through the gate, and still alive, and the evening air felt cold as a compress on her forehead. She sat down now, shakily sobbing with reaction, still holding the whip in one hand, the reins in the other.

Dear me! she thought. This will *never* do. And I'll still be late for church. What *will* I tell Mr Rotton when I arrive?

A hundred yards up the lane, nearer the cantonment, another wife, Maureen Dickinson, lay in bed, reading the Bible. She was not going to church, and it seemed only right and proper that she should read two or three chapters from St Luke and ponder on them.

Her house was empty. Her husband, a major on General Hewitt's staff, had already left for church, and the servants, she believed, were in the small whitewashed shack behind the house, where they were preparing the evening meal.

Mrs Dickinson was not going to evensong because she was expecting her first child in a matter of weeks. For some time she had been suffering spells of dizziness and nausea which should have disappeared months earlier. The army surgeon, a young lieutenant, lately qualified after his training, which had consisted of following another doctor on his rounds in a Soho practice for a year, had advised that she spend each afternoon in bed.

The room was plainly furnished because the Dickinsons

had no private means, and, indeed, her husband sent home some money every month to help his widowed mother in England.

Maureen Dickinson was a pleasant, kindly girl of twenty-three, only a year out from home, and still missing her parents. They had given her the Bible before she left; their names were inscribed on the inside cover, 'with love.' She had never been away from them for so long before, and each time she read their familiar signatures, she felt her throat tighten with longing to see them, no matter how briefly.

She wondered what they would be doing now at home. She put the Bible down by her side, finger on the page she had been reading, and lay back on the linen pillow, eyes closed, imagining she was home.

A small sound at the door brought her back to reality; the scuff of a foot on a raffia mat. She opened her eyes.

Two Indians, total strangers, were standing in the door, looking at her silently.

Who on earth could they be? Not men with a snake in a bag and a pipe to make it dance? She was tired of such exhibitions; she always felt sorry for the snake.

'Who are you?' she asked, sitting up, for they weren't her servants, and they were certainly not from the regiment.

They came into the room, and two others behind them. They all had wild eyes, and were dressed in what appeared to be rags, stained with soot and grey ash. They must have been near a fire, for one of the men's hair was singed. She could smell the sharp scent of sweat overlaid on jasmin oil. And something else: the smell of hatred.

'Who *are* you?' she asked again.

The first man spat on the floor, but he did not answer. His right hand came up and in it she saw a long curved knife. The blade ran red with something thick and smeary. *Blood.*

She screamed then, for these men must be coming to injure her, to do her harm and the child inside her. There could be no other explanation. The knife sang through the air and through the quilt, and bit to the bone of her right leg. Her scream changed to a gasp of pain. The blade had severed a muscle. She could not move her toes.

'Stop!' she cried. 'Stop! Help!'

But there was no one to hear, or to help.

She did not know that her servants had already parcelled up what few trinkets of value she and her husband possessed from the sitting-room—and made off with them before anyone else should seize them.

The men were smiling. It was as though the knife blow had also cut through some curtain of reserve and restraint. Now they would do as they wished. A fifth man came in behind them, holding a torch. Flames grew like a hot angry beard from its tarry end, spitting and sizzling.

One of them ripped open the cupboard and pulled out a few dresses and threw them across the bed. She put out her hands, fingers spread, to protect her stomach and the child she felt moving within her.

'No!' she begged. 'Please, *please*.'

For a second, no one moved in the room. Then one of the men picked up the Bible, fanned through the pages, and ripped the book in two, breaking the binding. The leaves fluttered down on the bed like huge confetti flakes.

The knife came down again across her stomach, severing her hands at the wrists, piercing the curled-up body of the child she would never bear.

The man lowered his torch slowly until the flame licked the bedclothes. First, it charred them, and blackened the linen with its smoke. Then the muslin began to burn; and then the bed, and the room. Soon the whole house was a roaring funeral pyre.

Sergeant-Major Black turned to his sergeant.

'I must see what's happened at home,' he said. 'You know what I mean.'

There was no need to elaborate about Meeta; the sergeant knew well enough what was in his mind. Black marched smartly off the parade ground, like a policeman who must never be seen to run. But once he was out of sight of the men he sprinted for his bungalow.

It was deserted; no light anywhere. He called: 'Meeta! Meeta!'

No answer. He fumbled in his pockets for a lucifer and lit a hurricane *butti*. She had left him, and taken the children—or had they all been carried off forcibly?

In their bedroom, nothing seemed to have been dis-

turbed. He crossed over to the crude dressing-table made
of unpainted bazaar wood. Under her Bible was a piece
of paper. He pulled it out and read in Meeta's familiar
huge childish handwriting. 'Sorry, Blackie. You would
have left me for England eventually. I have had to leave
you now. Not that I wanted to. I will take good care of
the children. Think of us. We loved you.'

So she *had* gone. But he would find her as soon as it
was light, for she could not go far; she had no money. He
screwed the paper up into a ball and pushed it in his
pocket. Then he went out and down the front steps.

A crowd of natives had seen him come in, and were
waiting for him.

'Maro! Maro! Kill! Kill!' they shouted.

He held the lamp up in one hand, his pace-stick in the
other. So the black bastards would kill him now, would
they? He saw the glint of sword and dagger blades; eyeballs rolled white like marbles and then he saw the man
leading them—his own bearer! The man to whom, only
hours before, he had given, God knew why, a tip of ten
rupees! A fortune! And this was the bastard's gratitude!

Rage and resentment boiled in Black's blood.

'Get out, the lot of you!' he roared and flung the light
at the bearer's hand. The glass broke on his skull, and the
paraffin flared like a bomb. In that second, Black leapt
down from the veranda right into the midst of the sepoys.
He laid about them, left and right, with his pace-stick,
shouting with every blow, 'You—black—bas—*tards!*'

With cries of terror and pain and alarm, the crowd
broke and ran, leaving him standing there panting, the
smell of burnt-out paraffin sharp in his nose.

He smoothed down his uniform, put his stick back under his left armpit, gripped it smartly at the end in his
hand. Then he set off at a quick march, back to his men.
Must never be late on parade.

Private Dougan came out of the guard-house, his spell
of duty over, and paused, sniffing the smell of burning.
Pity about those bungalows the bloody niggers had set
alight.

On the other hand, the church parade might be cancelled. As good an excuse as any for not appearing, and

better than reporting sick, could be that he stayed near the guard-house in case he was needed. He would use the privy round the back of the guard-post, and then hang about until after six o'clock, when it would be safe to return to barracks.

The privy was a whitewashed stone building, with a wooden door with a gap of a foot at the top and bottom; partly hygienic, and partly moral—to make sure that only one man at a time was occupying it, and then for the strict purposes of nature.

Dougan hung his jacket on the nail behind the door, and sat down on the wooden seat. A tin bucket was underneath, with a flap in the rear wall through which the sweeper could reach in to empty the bucket.

Gradually, he became aware of feet padding in the dust outside. There was something frightening about their number and their stealth, for usually only a private soldier, caught short on guard, would use this privy. Indians just squatted down unabashed in the open.

Dougan stood up, pulled up his trousers, buckled his belt and peered cautiously over the top of the door. To his astonishment, twenty sepoys waited outside in a semicircle, swords and sticks in their hands, staring at the privy. As they saw his face, one of them shouted in English: 'Come out, and we'll kill you!'

What an invitation! With horror, Dougan realized that they would simply wait until he opened the door—and then do as they said, for he was entirely unarmed.

He looked around desperately for some weapon.

The lavatory seat was nailed to the walls, the tin bucket was useless, and the hole in the back was too small for him to squeeze through.

He stared helplessly, at the door. A line of ants were walking, one behind the other, towards the hinges. *The hinges*. They were long strips of bent metal pivoting on nails, so that the door could easily be removed to whitewash the interior.

He pushed the nails up and out, and undid the latch. Then, holding the door upright, he rolled up a ball of paper from the strips of old newspapers that hung on a nail at the side of the pan. He tossed this out over the top of the door to one side.

The mutineers watched it. In that second, when their attention was diverted, Dougan gripped the door by its cross-bracing, and giving a great roar, he rushed out, keeping it in front of him like a shield—straight towards them. They scattered in amazement, and Dougan was through and away, running like a stag.

Lieutenant Garroway was riding home, relaxed, fifty ten-rupee notes buttoned inside his inner jacket pocket.

He had enjoyed a most successful and satisfactory day with Mrs Bolivar, physically and financially.

Having dressed up in Indian clothes, he had ridden out to her house. He arrived at about two o'clock and cautiously circled the white walls of her compound. Mrs Bolivar was sitting in a rocking chair on the veranda, quite alone, a cup of coffee on a cane table by her side.

'Chalo!' she called instantly and imperiously, as he dismounted. 'Go!'

She thought he was an itinerant native, eager to sell her a carpet or some beaten brassware that had probably come from Birmingham. When he ignored her command, and walked up the garden path, she rose angrily to call her bearer, but he raised his hand.

'It's me,' he said. 'I promised I would ride out and see you some time. Is your husband here?'

'No. You have just missed him.'

'Who else is here then?'

Mrs Bolivar smiled; she was not inexperienced in this situation.

'No one,' she said. 'The bearer's son is getting married. He's still in the house, but he'll be leaving any minute.'

'Fancy,' said Garroway, and his throat was suddenly dry.

'Would you like a coffee?' Rosemary Bolivar asked him. 'I can get another cup.'

'Don't bother,' he said.

He climbed the wooden steps. They were very close together. She smiled up at him, and in her eyes he saw the sultry discontent that had first attracted him. It was smouldering now, like a dying fire, when you put the bellows to it.

'Then what would you like?'

'You,' he said hoarsely. 'You.'

Greatly daring, he put one arm round her waist, and drew her towards him.

'Not here,' she said sharply, as he bent to kiss her. They drew apart slightly and walked into the big bedroom, side by side.

A daguerreotype of Major Bolivar in full dress uniform regarded them coldly from the dressing-table. As Garroway began to unbutton the thirty-two linen-covered buttons that ran down Mrs Bolivar's blouse, she reached out and turned her husband's picture to the wall. It seemed somehow more fitting that way.

Now Garroway rode back, at ease. For not only had he seduced Mrs Bolivar, she had lent him five hundred rupees. A loan, of course. Both had been adamant about that. He would never accept a gift from a lady; naturally, no officer or gentleman would ever entertain such a proposal. But his shrewd eyes had assessed the value of the silk covers on cushions, the gold filigree ornaments on her mantelpiece, the jewels he had seen in a drawer on her dressing-table, when she had risen from the bed after their first bout of love-making.

Time spent on reconnaissance, so the Army Training Manual had taught him, was seldom wasted, and he had not wasted this afternoon. He guessed now that she was rich, far richer than he had imagined, and she was also passionate, in the hungry, desperate way of the unhappy woman. This five hundred rupees could only really be regarded as a first instalment of other more important sums. He would be back to see her the following week, because her husband was on detachment up-country for ten days and the bearer, by happy chance, had another wedding (or was it a funeral?) in his family.

Suddenly, to his right, and far away, Garroway heard a distant drumming of hooves. He sat up smartly and dug in his spurs. The plain was lonely; he did not wish to be overtaken by some bunch of wild and possibly hostile tribesmen.

His horse began to canter. Then he heard a shout and a rattle of musket fire. Shots whistled over his head and split a grey rock about ten yards away.

What the devil was this? Some drunken poachers out wild-fowling?

He reined-in his horse and shouted angrily over his shoulder: 'Stop that, I say!'

To his astonishment, an English voice roared back: '*Charge!*'

The ground trembled under the hooves of a dozen horses, all racing towards him. The setting sun gleamed red on the polished blades of a dozen lances laid across the horses' necks—and all pointing at him.

My God, they were charging *him!*

'You bloody fools!' he roared. 'What are you up to?'

'You nigger bastard!' came back the reply. 'We'll cut out your black heart!'

They were mad, of course, out of their reason, but this was no time to stand and parley.

He dug his spurs in deeply and slackened the reins. His horse snorted and broke into a gallop.

In his daydreaming, Garroway had completely forgotten he had blackened his face and was still dressed as an Indian.

And, of course, he had no idea that, in the few hours since he had left Meerut, every Indian had become an enemy.

11

Lang reined-in his horse to try and find where he was. The animal was flecked with foam, lathered grey with ash carried by the wind. A horseman loomed out straight ahead of him, his mount rearing up on its hind legs; Colonel Carmichael Smythe, the Duty Field Officer.

'Where are the English troops, sir?' he asked him.

'Falling in,' Smythe replied. 'This madness will be over in minutes. Follow me.'

At that moment, Gough appeared, and the three of them rode once more across the parade ground, just missing a herd of bullocks, white and ghostly in the flickering light, as they blundered ahead of them, heads tossing and panic-stricken.

Colonel Smythe reined-in his horse, head on one side, listening. Lang and Gough stopped with him, their mounts choking with the dust thrown up by their pounding hooves, and the burning wisps of paper and straw carried on the wind.

Torches, dim glow-worms of flame, were now streaming past them out of Meerut in a long procession. The mutineers were heading south. With them went gharries and carts loaded with loot, and coolies trotting barefoot, bundles on their heads. Some horses had as many as three men on their backs, and camels groaned under giant loads of stolen furniture, paintings in gilded frames, anything they could tie on them.

Huge artillery elephants, chains above their ankles clanking as they padded by, pulled the guns out into the deeper darkness beyond the blazing town, on the road to Delhi. Within its walls was enshrined all the imperial glory of the lost Mogul Empire, that had once stretched from the Great Wall of China to the gates of Vienna. Delhi, the home of Bahadur Shah, the rightful Indian King, the living magnet of men in search of a leader; a royal totem, a son of the blood.

Delhi, the site of the greatest military arsenal in the world—whoever commanded this magazine could command the whole country. One square mile, walled in by double gates, of stone buildings crammed with barrels of powder, sacks of explosive, pyramids of cannonballs; muskes; mines and all the most modern engines of war. And only guarded by a troop of Indians with eight British technicians. It would be theirs by the morning.

A British captain galloped past, and then turned when he saw the British officers.

In the light of the distant flames they recognized the regimental buttons of the Sixtieth Rifles.

'Where are your men, captain?' asked the colonel.

'Over here somewhere,' replied the officer vaguely.

'Well, get them on the road. The sepoys are off to Delhi. Double march your men ahead of them. Stop the sepoys at the first river.'

The captain peered at Smythe and recognized his rank.

'But the head of their column must already be several miles on their way, sir,' he replied. 'They're taking up all the road.'

'Well, march parallel with the road,' ordered the colonel.

'They won't be able to see their way, sir. It's pitch dark.'

'It's also dark for the sepoys, captain. Head them off. One volley will send them running.'

'Very good, sir,' said the captain without enthusiasm, and disappeared.

'Who was that?' asked Lang.

'God knows,' said Gough.

The captain reined-in his horse in front of Sergeant-Major Black. The Sixtieth had been waiting for orders for so long that he had told them to pile arms and squat on the ground to save their strength for whenever they had to march. Now they struggled stiffly to their feet.

'Colonel's orders,' the captain shouted. 'Fall the men into four ranks, then follow the rabble.'

'What to do then, sir?' asked Black anxiously. He wanted his orders to be explicit. And also he had no stomach for a march; he was thinking about Meeta, about his sons, wondering where they were. Maybe she had known this was about to happen, and the knowledge had made her restless and uneasy.

'Send out scouts. Then double march the column until we are ahead of them. We'll fire a volley and scatter them. These fellows will run like foxes.'

'Permission to speak, sir,' called a sergeant from the darkness.

'What is it?'

'We have no ammunition, sir.'

'No ammunition?' repeated the captain in amazement.

'No, sir. We can't find the key of the armoury, sir.'

Why had this not been discovered before? A whole battalion, nearly a thousand men, had been squatting for hours on the parade ground, and no one had thought to see that they were armed.

'Sergeant-major,' he said brusquely. 'Take a detail of men, and smash the door in. We've *got* to be after these mutineers, or it will be too late to catch them.'

'It is already too late, sir,' replied Black quietly. History was on the march out there in the terrible darkness, and he sensed it, and his flesh crawled with foreboding at the widening rift of hatred between white and coloured peoples. He knew now why Meeta had refused him, why she and his servants had disappeared; their skins put them on one side, and he was on the other.

At last, the Sixtieth Rifles, five rounds issued to each man—there was no time for more to be counted out—set off at a quick march along the edge of the road to Delhi. But they were unused to marching; they had been in quarters for too long, and the night was hot, and their muskets heavy, and their hearts were not in the journey.

Also, the odds against them were prodigious. And what of their wives and families? They should be back in Meerut, ready to defend them, not chasing a disorganized rabble of thousands.

Darkness built its wall around them all. The sepoys appeared to have melted away, and no one knew for certain

where they had gone. Who could be sure they *were* going
to Delhi?

Finally, the captain halted the regiment, and ordered
them to form a hollow square, two ranks deep. Then they
solemnly fired one volley to the left, and one to the right,
the outer file kneeling, the file behind them standing.

The musket balls blazed away into the night, but although everyone strained their ears, they could hear no
shouts from any wounded army sepoys. In fact, they
could hear nothing at all but the pounding of their own
blood in their ears, and the scream of frightened jackals.

After this martial display, the captain ordered the sergeant-major to re-form the men in four ranks, and the
Sixtieth Rifles marched back to Meerut.

In the cantonment, wounded men and women were
dragging themselves painfully into clumps of trees and
bushes to hide in case their attackers returned. Horses
with broken legs whinnied and neighed in their pain,
threshing about blindly in the darkness.

Looters, from the bazaar, ran silently among the dead
and dying, picking up what trinkets they could find. They
chopped off the hand of a married woman for her wedding ring, or a girl's ear for a gold ear-ring.

The artillerymen were in their own lines, comforting
wives and searching desperately with torches among
burned-out bungalows, calling hoarsely for children who
would never answer.

Everyone with a black skin was an enemy to be shot or
clubbed or run through on sight by sword or bayonet,
even though some were faithful Indian servants who had
shielded British wives and children from the attacks of
their countrymen.

Gough, Lang and the colonel rode back wearily
through the charnel-house sights and the smell of burning
flesh, to the officers' mess. The moon had risen, and in its
pale light they saw that the roof had been burned away; a
few charred rafters were still smoking against the stars.
All the glasses had been smashed, the whisky drunk, boxes
of cigars stolen, chairs slashed or carried away. They
dismounted, and stood among ashes so hot they burned
their feet through the soles of their riding boots.

'We've *got* to warn Delhi,' said Smythe, almost thinking
aloud.

'What about the telegraph, sir? There are two operators there.'

'You know there are no British troops in Delhi, of course?' said the colonel.

'I understand that, sir.'

'So what good will sending a message do?' asked the colonel blankly. Events seemed to have overwhelmed him, to have drained him of his meagre reserves of initiative and vitality.

'If they are warned in Delhi, they can telegraph to Lahore or Amballa. There are several thousand British troops in the North.'

'I suppose you are right,' Smythe agreed, almost reluctantly. 'I can't get used to these newfangled things.'

The whole system of electric telegraphy was so new as to be quite untried. Samuel Morse, its American inventor, had sent his first message between Washington and Baltimore only thirteen years earlier. In any case, science was not a matter with which gentlemen, either military or civil, greatly concerned themselves; it was a subject for mechanics or artisans. Could a gentleman trust either it— or them—to be accurate?

'Then we'll telegraph, sir?'

'No,' said the colonel with unexpected firmness. 'Not *yet,* I will report to the general first.'

'But, sir, every minute's precious now,' said Lang.

'When you've lived as long as I have, Mr Lang,' retorted the colonel, 'you'll realize that every minute is *always* precious. Are you seriously prepared, as a second-lieutenant, newly commissioned, to take on your sole shoulders the personal responsibility of sending an alarm to Delhi, urging that British troops, hundreds of miles away, are alerted and told to march on the city? Do you realize the enormous political implications?'

'I hadn't thought of those, sir. I was thinking of the people who were murdered in Meerut today. And what will happen if we don't send the message!'

'I take your point,' said Smythe stiffly. 'But there is a right and a wrong way to do these things. We will report the situation to General Hewitt. He is the officer commanding the garrison, after all.'

'After all,' echoed Gough bitterly.

Hewitt was awake when they reached his house. His

was one of the few that had neither been burned nor raided. He sat in his cane chair, gouty foot in a huge slipper resting on a stool in front of him, a glass of whisky at his elbow. Brigadier Wilson sat in another cane chair, facing him.

'A disgraceful afternoon, colonel. And a terrible evening,' he grumbled. 'Never in all my career have I witnessed such appalling goings-on. What have you ordered, brigadier?'

'Under Section Seventeen of the Bengal Army Act, I am not empowered to give orders in a garrison when the Divisional Commander is also present,' said Wilson quickly.

'Quite right, too. What kind of orders can *anyone* give in such a situation? Our troops will show these fellers a lesson, though, I'll wager that. We'll have more sepoys in irons within a few days, mark my words. We'll teach 'em a lesson India will never forget.'

'In the meantime, sir, we would like your permission to telegraph a warning to Delhi,' said Lang.

'No alarmist messages, of course, sir,' added Colonel Smythe soothingly.

'Certainly not,' said the general. 'This is simply a local uprising. The sort of thing one gets used to hearing about, happening in *other* stations, when *budmashes* get the upper hand. But it still comes as a shock when it affects your own. By all means, send a message. No, *I* will write the message.'

He pressed the bell for a bearer. Ink, pen and cane table were brought in. He wrote out one line in his rounded script: 'I am defending my position.'

'Send this,' he said, handing it to the colonel.

The colonel handed the message to Gough.

'Mr Gough, instruct the telegraph operators to make this signal immediately.'

'Very good, sir.'

For the second time within a few hours, the two junior officers walked through the doors into the compound.

'There's no warning in this,' complained Lang. 'And it's a lie, too. He's defended nothing.'

'I disagree. He's doing a very fine job now of defending his position as general. We'll add a warning of our own.'

The telegraph office was a small building on the outskirts of the cantonment, so inconspicuous that no one imagined it could contain anything worth looting, so no sepoys had attempted to break down its door.

When they arrived, the civilian operator sat in a cane chair at a scruffy wooden table. From a Morse key in front of him coils of red, rubber-covered wire went up in spirals to china insulators in the ceiling.

'What a night,' he said nervously. 'What's happening out there?'

'I don't know,' said Lang, uneager for chit-chat.

'Any messages in from Delhi?'

'Nothing. We don't get many on Sundays. The line's closed from half past nine to four, anyway.'

'Anyone on duty in Delhi now?'

'There should be.'

'Well, then, send this message from the general. And when you have finished, I'll dictate a few words to add.'

'I have to have them in writing, sir,' said the operator. 'Those are my instructions.'

'My instructions to you are to send the message as I dictate it. The rabble seem to be heading for Delhi. We've got to warn them there what to expect.'

'Very good, sir. Top speed?'

'How fast is that?'

'Eighteen words a minute,' said the operator proudly; he had a certificate to prove it.

'Eighteen words, then.'

The operator smoothed out the piece of paper, put a glass paperweight on it, and began to tap the key to open the line, lifting his hand off it briefly until it jigged back in reply.

Five miles out in the desert stood the first of half a dozen substations on the way to Delhi; a small stone hut at the side of the road. The two other operators inside were surprised when their key began to chatter.

They had been brewing up tea over a small charcoal brazier, and while one poured the boiling water into the teapot, the other took down the message in capital letters on a Government Issue form:

'CLEAR THE LINE STOP FOR COLONEL MACDONALD SPECIAL DETACHMENT DELHI

STOP FROM GENERAL HEWITT COMMAND-
ING MEERUT STOP PRIORITY STOP EYE AM
DEFENDING MY POSITION.'

The key stopped.

'What is it?' The man poured out two cups,. added milk
from a pannikin and a china spoonful of sugar.

'From General Hewitt. Says he is defending his position.'

'Who's attacking him?'

'Maybe we'll hear. I'll pass it on up the line.'

He turned to another key, and began to tap the message
on the next stage of its journey. The needle on the volt-
meter trembled and fell back to zero. He frowned,
checked the connections to the glass electric cells that
lined one wall, and began to tap again.

'We're not getting a circuit,' he said. 'There's a break in
the line.'

'Confound it,' said his companion. 'Those tribesmen
must have cut the wire again. I saw one the other day
with a couple of yards of it in his possession. Said he used
it to make bracelets for his wives. How far away is the
break this time?'

The operator moved two insulated controls. Needles on
hair springs trembled against engraved white dials.

'According to the resistance we're getting, probably
only a few hundred yards away. Will you have a look, or
shall I?'

'I will. You drink your tea while it's hot. I'll have mine
when I come back.'

He lit the hurricane lamp and went out of the door.
Hot dust from the desert rasped his face. He closed his
eyes for a minute to become accustomed to the gloom and
glanced up at the reassuring sight of the copper telegraph
wires twenty feet above his head, on the posts that
marched away purposefully into the distance. Then he
began to walk on beneath them.

Inside the hut, his companion put a saucer on top of
the cup to keep his tea warm, and took out his leather to-
bacco pouch, filled his pipe, and sipped his own tea. What
an odd message to get from Meerut! *And* on a Sunday!
Perhaps it was a joke. Early that morning, when he was
testing the line, he had received a message saying that

eighty odd sepoys were to be blown from guns. Ridiculous, of course. One of the Meerut operators liked his drama, and the other was well known as a card, a practical joker who sometimes sent silly rhymes and limericks over the wire to test the line.

The key began to chatter again, with a life of its own. The operator wrote down the words, letter by letter, in capitals:

'SEPOYS NINETEENTH NATIVE INFANTRY HAVE MUTINIED SETTING FREE MILITARY AND CIVILIAN PRISONERS STOP THEY ARE HEADING TOWARDS DELHI STOP ADVISE APPROPRIATE AUTHORITIES URGENTLY STOP.'

The key stopped for the second time. The operator drank his tea reflectively. Outside, the wind howled over the burned-out empty plain, bending the trees by the roadside wells. The wires above the hut sang like copper violin strings.

He heard a shuffle of footsteps outside the door as he poured himself another cup. His friend was coming back. He crossed the room to the door.

It was kicked open before he reached the handle.

Three Indians with swords stood framed in the doorway. The wind blew sand in over their shoulders; the hut suddenly felt very cold.

'Who the devil?' the operator began, but he never finished the question.

A sword whistled through the air and sliced off his head.

Blood spurted from his trunk in a huge red jet, spraying the walls, dripping on to the table and the floor. As his body slid down over the table, his hand knocked over the teacups. The key began to chatter again, another message coming in from Meerut. But his dead hand could not reach his pen.

The Indians waited until the key was still, and then pulled the wires from the terminals, kicked over the charcoal brazier and threw a pile of message forms on the hot embers.

Then they went out into the darkness again to wait for

the advance party of mutineers to reach them.

They left the door open behind them. It banged to and fro on its hinges, fanning the whitening embers in the brazier into flames. Within seconds, the hut was an inferno.

12

On the banks of the sluggish River Jumna, the early Monday morning wind stirred thick clumps of reeds, rattling them like dead men's dice. The current moved strongly against the bridge of flat-bottomed boats that linked one bank with the other, making them creak and groan in an agony of strained chains anchored to the riverbed.

A handful of Hindus shivering in the cold water, performing their complicated ablutions, came up out of the grey tide. The master of their ritual, the Pujari, squatted on the near bank, under a pipal tree, with his three small saucers containing the sacred dyes of sandalwood and gypsum and vermilion. As they passed him, they bowed and he repainted their red caste marks on the middle of their foreheads. Then they went on their way to begin their work as clerks and pleaders and writers of letters for those who could not read.

High above them soared the sheer, unscalable wall of the Red Fort, the prime symbol of India's ancient grandeur, a city within a city, one of the wonders of the Eastern world.

Two hundred years before, unnumbered slaves had toiled for ten years at a cost of ten million rupees to build this palace for the greatest Mogul of them all, the Emperor Shah Jehan, the Shah-In-Shah. He had decided on this site because he found his personal capital in Agra had too dry a climate for his taste. So he had commanded that a fort with stone walls, red as blood, should be built in Delhi as his personal home. And having regard to his importance, he insisted that it should also be impregnable.

So the Fort's high ramparts brooded, bristling with cannon, a hundred and ten feet up, over the river. Around the walls slaves had dug a moat thirty feet deep and seventy-five feet wide, so that no known engine of war could ever cross it, even though it was drained as was now the case.

Further to discourage the onslaught of enemies, thousands of loop-holes were hewn in the walls, to be occupied by musketeers who, almost totally protected themselves, could bring down a withering fire on the heads of any who succeeded in reaching the moat. Siege engines and giant catapults remaining from those years, with ceremonial cannon with barrels ten inches across, emblazoned with the tongues of serpents and the heads of lions, pointed warning, deterring fingers through the turrets.

Inside, the Fort contained council chambers, audience halls, whole individual palaces, each designed and built on a gigantic scale in a splendour that benefited the home of a king of kings. They opened on to courtyards with marble and gold fountains, spouting endless jets of water scented with lavender and roses into baths and basins carved from single marble blocks. Huge rooms that had once contained treasures beyond all accounting, now contained nothing more valuable than moth-eaten tapestries and tattered curtains.

In one vast chamber, the size of a jousting yard, had glittered the Peacock Throne, made of two gold peacocks, ornamented with sapphires and rubies and pearls and emeralds, scattered with the careless prodigality of coloured sugar grains on the icing of a cake. It was shaded by a canopy of beaten gold studded with pearls, supported on twelve emerald-encrusted pillars.

Birds and beasts around it had been carved from solid gold, with jewels for their eyes and beaks and claws. The terrace of this throne-room was paved with marble, white as a snowfall. Its roof was crowned by four white marble doves that shimmered in the sun like roc eggs, a landmark for miles, to inform travellers that they were approaching the home of the Shah-In-Shah.

In the centre stone over the arched gateway that led to the harem, craftsmen had carved a sentence that was no

boast, but fact: 'If there is heaven on earth, it is this, it is
this.'

And outside the Shah's private apartments, as he lay
relaxed on his silken, scented couch, in that hour of ease
after love, a Rhapsodist would whisper tales of love and
heroism, until his droning monotone, soft as the murmur
of hives of honey-bees, soothed his master and he slept.

Through the years since this palace had been built, envious plunderers had sacked Delhi many times. The Persians stormed the city in 1738 and carried off the Peacock
Throne to Teheran, where they melted down the gold.

Then, fighting Mahrattas ransacked the palace of what
the Persians had overlooked. And then the British, seeking
not other men's riches so much as the power and position
to make their own through trade, had arrived in Delhi.

They did not particularly wish to be there, but ever
watchful of their trading rights, they had seen that the
Mahrattas were engaging French officers to lead them,
promising trade concessions to France if they could defeat
the East India Company's army. But the British troops,
better drilled and disciplined, had carried the day in a
pitched battle, fifty-four years before this particular Monday in Delhi.

The British Governor-General of that time, Lord
Wellesley, arrived to find the Shah, the descendent of the
great Mogul, an old man, withered and shrunk with de-
bauchery, crouching under a tattered canopy in shabby
clothes, his eyesight almost gone, the reluctant figurehead
of a mighty but defeated people. Wellesley shrewdly proposed to the East India Company that they maintain the
old man as a titular king because of the immense esteem
in which both Moslems and Hindus held him.

He felt that this gesture of mercy and generosity could
ease the path of future trade negotiations between the
Company and other Indians in authority, and so it proved.

The East India Company allowed the King to keep his
title, but they vested the power of administering the revenue and Customs in their own nominees, with the style
of British Commissioner.

When the old man died, his son succeeded him. It was
the wish of the Company to keep on friendly terms with
the new Shah, so they minted coins bearing the image of

the new ruler, Shah Mohammed Abu Zuphur Saraz-o-Lain
Mahommed Bahadur, and increased his pension to the
princely equivalent in rupees of £145,000 a year.

While, to the Indians, Shah Bahadur was the King of
Delhi, to the British he was an indigenous puppet, under
their control.

In fact, by this particular Monday morning, both views
were illusory. The old King commanded respect only by
reason of his illustrious ancestors. And Simon Fraser, the
British Commissioner, administering a huge area of more
than 800 square miles, was allowed no British troops
within call, apart from a small ceremonial detachment,
lest their presence should offend the King, and, through
him, his countrymen, with consequent pressure on the
Company's dividends.

In recent years, the Company's profits had dwindled
drastically, and the directors felt that, when Shah Bahadur
died, it would only be business prudence to end the pension and, indeed, the whole policy of maintaining a puppet in a palace who, so far as they could discover, was
simply an expensive anachronism. They had received all
the concessions they wanted; the arrangement had out-
lived its usefulness.

But, in reaching this decision, they ignored the human
side of what, to them, was strictly a business equation.

Old men shook grey heads over the glories that were
going. The Shah was old, and not rich as some rajahs
counted riches, but he had been born to rule; he was still
their king. Steamships and trains and electric telegraphs
might all combine to shrink the size of the world, but men
born to be kings stayed aloof and remote from such in-
ventions. In any case, the Shahs ruled in a country where
time had no meaning, where the word for 'yesterday'—
kal—was also the word for 'tomorrow.'

John Company's directors, thousands of miles away in
their offices in London, out of touch with events in India,
and ever sceptical of reports of unrest or change, because
they had seen no change when they were last in India, did
not realize the depth of feeling for the King of Delhi—or
the extent of debt into which he had sunk.

He spent his income on follies, from ornate decoration
schemes, to new and expensive entertainments involving
hundreds of actors and musicians.

Early on, he had developed a taste for expensive litigation when there was no need for law. He backed lawyers against each other, as men backed horses; but in his case, there were no winnings, only further bills to meet. These lawyers and pleaders urged him to seek more money from the British. They wanted bigger pickings themselves, and this seemed the most likely way of providing them.

So Shah Bahadur asked for an increased pension, and although this was reluctantly granted, his request hardened the Company's resolve to make sure that his pension died when he did.

To give himself some extra income, meanwhile, he rented out suites and palaces within the Fort to anyone who would pay him in ready rupees. His tenants included criminals seeking refuge from justice, receivers of stolen property, distillers of spirits, compounders of opium and aphrodisiacs, the makers of sweetmeats. He maintained whole troops of jugglers, wrestlers, dancing girls, eunuchs and slaves, most of whom he never saw, but who ate his food and drew salaries and shelter from him.

At the heart of this honeycomb of voluptuaries and beggars, of avaricious lawyers and discontented relations, the King of Delhi led his impossible life. Old and enfeebled, alone and unloved in the centre of a sycophantic crowd, he lived frugally and with few comforts.

The Red Fort had been built by a man whose power, ambition and appetites made him appear larger than life. Its present tenant seemed less than life-size, shrunken and withered like an ancient mannikin, royal only in name, dwarfed by the gargantuan magnificence around him, ekeing out his life in a room less than twelve feet square.

As the Monday morning sun moved higher up the sky, and the mists melted on the marshes, the city lay bare beneath it. Above and below the King's Palace were the Civil Lines—as opposed to the Military Lines—with the European offices and bungalows and schools and a courthouse, and then the Darya Ganj, another European suburb. The Bank lay to the west of the Palace and north of this stood St James's Church with its spire, a church from an English market-town incongruously transplanted to an alien land.

High up in his room, its floor thick with carpets, the old King stirred his thin shanks uneasily under his silk

quilt. The early morning sun threw a beam on his wrinkled face. He screwed up his eyes against its unwelcome
brillance, reluctant to face another day; his joints felt stiff
and rusty, his bladder full. He half-heard the wail of the
Moslem priest, the muezzin, from the mosque, calling the
faithful to prayer: 'There is no God but Allah, and Mohammed is his Prophet.'

The old man was awake now. He stood up, lifted a
china chamber pot from a cabinet inlaid with ivory and
mother of pearl, and made water. Then he pulled a tasselled bell rope, and the servant, who had been waiting in
the stone corridor outside, carried into the room a silver
tray with a glass containing an emetic in warm water, an
opium pill on a gold plate to soothe his nerves, and a plat-
ter of rice pilaff.

Forty years earlier, a physician had assured the King
that such a diet each morning would lengthen his days
and bring peace and contentment to his soul. Now, at the
age of eighty-two, as he sipped the bitter Glauber salts,
and then slipped the pill between his dry cracked lips, he
wondered whether a long life was to be desired when all
other desire had left him.

It was true what the Lord Buddha had said: 'From lust
comes grief, from lust comes fear; he who is free from
lust knows neither grief nor fear.' It was true, yes. But to
a man who had been ruled by his desires, a life without
lust was like a meal without salt, a day without the sun.

The King stood up now, stretching his scraggy limbs,
wrapping a robe about his hunched shoulders. He crossed
to the window and stood, hands on the warm sill. The
bridge of boats bobbed in the yellow river. Across the far
bank, in the distance, almost at the limit of his vision, he
could see a dust cloud like a hurricane, a tornado, moving
over the desert towards Delhi. Horsemen. A regiment riding at speed towards him.

The King pulled the rope again.

'Who are these horsemen?' he asked the servant who
answered him immediately.

'They are sepoys from Meerut, your Majesty. They
bring a petition. An outrider came in last night to tell us.
You were sleeping. He saw the Begum.'

'Ask Colonel MacDonald to come here immediately,'
ordered the King.

The Begum. His face wrinkled with sudden distaste at the thought of his youngest wife; her plump, scented body, her discontented face, ear-lobes elongated with gold ear-rings he had bought to sweeten her, wrists and fingers encircled with gold bangles and rings, until the gold rattled like a money-changer's purse as she walked.

They had had an argument the previous evening: she was furious that he had not persuaded the East India Company to guarantee his throne and pension for her eldest son, whom he loved least of his children.

He had done all he could, but to attempt was not to succeed, and women worshipped success.

A discreet knock outside the door; three long taps and one short one, and Colonel MacDonald came in, his sword clanking at his side. He saluted. The King nodded to him.

'Who are these petitioners?' asked the King.

'Some sepoys rode in from Meerut last night, your Majesty. These men seem to be following them. There has been some kind of disturbance in Meerut.'

'Judging by the numbers here, it would seem to be serious,' replied the King, and led him to a balcony, the traditional place where he would appear to petitioners who gathered beneath to beg for justice or advice. The bridge of boats trembled as hundreds of hooves thundered an urgent tattoo on the planks. Horsemen were riding across the pontoons four abreast. One carried a lance with a pennant attached. As he saw the King, he raised the lance in salute and shouted, 'Zindabad! Victory!'

The cry was taken up by the horsemen behind him, so that the red walls boomed back the thunder of their salute. Half a dozen of the leaders wheeled off to the left and rode directly beneath the King and Colonel MacDonald, then reined-in their panting chargers.

'We have come to fight for the faith, oh King!' cried the leader. 'Open the gates and let us in.'

The King glanced at the colonel. The man had not said, 'please'; it was an ominous sign when marks of respect were lacking.

MacDonald called down to the men: 'If you have a petition to lay before the King, do so in the approved manner, with one of your number waiting on his chamberlain. He cannot see you all.'

For a second, silence hung its shroud over the hundreds of horsemen. Then, from half-way across the bridge, one of them swung up his musket from its leather case and fired. Chips of red granite splintered above the heads of MacDonald and the old King. Another horseman fired, and then a third. Were they aiming at the colonel and the King, or were they simply firing wildly in salute and exuberance? It was impossible to know, and too dangerous to find out. They retreated into the room.

'I will inform the British Commissioner immediately,' Colonel MacDonald announced gravely.

The King nodded his approval and his dismissal.

As MacDonald turned towards the door, a royal attendant, who carried a silver-topped cane to keep away beggars whenever the King made a progress, entered the room and bowed.

'Two representatives from Meerut await for Colonel MacDonald, your Majesty.'

'Show them in,' said MacDonald, glancing in surprise at the King. Two sowars, senior cavalrymen, wearing French-grey uniforms, their faces caked with dust and sweat, saluted in the doorway.

'What do you want?' asked MacDonald in Hindusthani.

'We seek your advice, sir,' said the first earnestly. 'First, we plead guilty to grievous offences. We have killed our officers in Meerut because they insisted on our using cartridges smeared with the fat of cows and pigs. We have come here to seek justice from the King.'

He paused; he had rehearsed these words many times on the road from Meerut. Now he asked tremulously:

'Please advise us, sir, what should we do?'

'You have committed a great crime, as you well know, in killing your officers,' said MacDonald gravely. 'I do not know the circumstances, if there were any, that could extenuate such murder. But unless you cease immediately from further bloodshed, you will put yourselves beyond the King's help, or mine.'

'We only killed to defend our faith.'

MacDonald glanced at the King. His face, with a sudden nervous tic in his left eye, was drawn with worry. His old hands, thin as birds' claws, picked away at his padded robe. Colonel MacDonald guessed he was wondering how he could keep from becoming involved. Or maybe the old rascal knew more about all this than he wished to admit? You could never entirely trust these Indians.

'I will go down and speak to the men myself,' said MacDonald.

'You will not,' replied the King quickly. 'Their tempers can change in an instant. I know their moods. And remember, it is Ramadan.'

This was the Moslem festival that had already lasted for sixteen days and would continue for another fortnight. It marked the ninth month of the Moslem year, in which the Koran had been communicated to Mohammed. To commemorate this, no Moslem would eat after sun-up, nor allow a drop of water to pass his lips, no matter how hot the day or hard his journey, until the sun set.

As a result, heat and thirst and hunger drove men mad. Remarks meant as jests became mortal insults, and a friendly discussion could explode into a fight to the death.

'You wait downstairs,' MacDonald told the sowars. 'The King will see you presently.'

They saluted smartly and left the room.

'If these men seek to make trouble, colonel,' said the King, 'can you offer protection to the Begum and myself?'

'It would be my privilege, sir.'

'Possibly. But can you implement that privilege?'

'We have about twelve hundred Indian troops in Delhi, sir. They should be sufficient.'

'If they don't go with these fellows, yes,' the King agreed. 'But reasons for unrest are catching, like an epidemic. Pray see if your magic electric telegraph can send a message for British reinforcements. Meanwhile, I will speak to the representatives of these men.'

Suddenly, from an open window in a room above them, they heard a woman shout: both recognized the voice of the Begum.

'Zindabad! Zindabad! For the faith! I welcome you here as the wife of the Shah-In-Shah. It is good to know there are *men* in India, as there were men in the olden times!'

'Zindabad! Zindabad!'

The crowd's shouts echoed out across the bridge of boats into the shimmering heat haze on the far bank. They surged around the palace gates. The King winced. What a fool the woman was, to inflame these sepoys in this way.

MacDonald unsheathed his sword, saluted the King with the blade, and then ran down the stone steps to the side gate that led out by the back. As he ran, the shouts of the mutineers echoed and re-echoed, distorted by the long stone corridors of the Fort.

They were in the building already. How long would it be before they occupied it completely, and the King became their prisoner?

The King's treasurer, Munshi Jeewan Lal, who also acted as an occasional intermediary between the King and the British Commissioner when confidential financial matters were involved, stood under the pillared porch of his house. He was waiting for his palki, a carriage drawn by two horses, both perfectly matched in colour and size, with his groom and a footman, in his personal livery, to take him to the court. As he waited, plump and scented and self-important, his thick hair oiled and black as a raven's wing, a servant plucked discreetly at his right sleeve.

'Well?' asked Jeewan Lal irritably. He hated being touched by inferiors; you never knew where their unwashed hands had been.

'It is unsafe for you to travel, Munshi Sahib. My brother-in-law has just come in from the bazaar. He says the city gates are closed. There is looting. Thousands of sepoys have ridden in armed from Meerut. They have surrounded the palace.'

Jeewan Lal was too experienced a courtier and too successful a banker to let emotion or surprise show in his face, but now he could hear faint shouts and the crack of muskets, and screams; and, once, a rumble as though a stone wall or building had been brought down. Perhaps the man was speaking the truth?

'Go to the Fort yourself,' he ordered the servant. 'Report to Colonel MacDonald. Ask him what is happening. And then let me know.'

He nodded dismissal to his coachman, and turned back to the coolness of his high-ceilinged hall. He had not made his fortune by being rash or in any way impetuous. If there were potentially dangerous missions to undertake, then it was better that underlings should make them. Otherwise, what was the point of employing them at all?

* * *

MacDonald had tethered his horse to a hitching post in the courtyard outside the rear wicket gate of the palace. Already, the sun was up and as he spurred away, the horse's hooves stirred the dust into a long feathery trail. Astonishingly, the street was empty. Usually, at this time of day, it was packed with dhobi-men, bundles of washing piled on their heads, running at the curious jog-trot of the Indian peasant towards the river-bank; and women would pad by, carrying brass bowls of rice on their heads. Now even the kitehawks had deserted it, and only a few chickens picked querulously among piles of rubbish and fruit peelings under the trees.

Then Colonel MacDonald's heart lifted, for he was not quite alone; another horseman was galloping towards him, a soldier in French-grey uniform, sword in his hand. As he approached, the colonel recognized him with relief as a havildar with whom he had once served. He would know what was happening. MacDonald reined-in his horse so sharply in his anxiety to stop that the animal reared on its hind legs.

'Havildar!' MacDonald shouted.

The other horseman also stopped and wheeled his charger round in a circle. His eyes were wild, his face streaked with sweat.

'What is all this disturbance?'

The havildar said nothing, but slid his sword back inside its long cavalry scabbard, and faced the colonel. Suddenly, MacDonald saw that he had drawn a pistol from a saddle holster. Without a word, the havildar raised it and fired.

The ball caught the colonel in the chest. He gave a great gasp of surprise and pain, and then rolled forwards and sideways off his horse. His left foot entangled in the stirrup and he hung upside down, blood from his fearful wound pumping down his neck, his face, his arm, into the dust.

The havildar sat for a moment watching him, to make sure he was dead. Then he put away his pistol, and cut the stirrup leather with his sword, and whacked the colonel's horse on the flank with the flat of the blade.

As it galloped away, he dismounted and turned over the colonel's body with his foot. Then he bent down, ignoring

the raw red mass of flesh and pink splintered bone, and
went through the dead man's pockets for his purse, his
wallet, his coins and his keys. Then he mounted and rode
on up the road towards the Fort.

Behind him, above the feathery tops of the palm trees,
vultures began to glide in on stretched and stinking wings.

Mrs MacDonald poured herself another cup of tea. Really, it had been the most extraordinary morning she
could ever remember.

First, out of all their inside and outside servants, not
one had appeared for work. Although Mrs MacDonald
had rung the bell and clapped her hands and called, 'Kói
hai,' which usually brought her maid or the housekeeper
or the under-housekeeper or any of the half-dozen other
personal servants who attended her, running to see what
she wanted, now there was no one. The house was empty.

'Arabella! Arabella!' she called.

'Mama?'

'Where's everyone?'

'I don't know, mama.'

'It's not a religious festival today. Perhaps there's a big
funeral and they've all gone to it?'

They walked through the tiled hall into the sitting-room
that overlooked the garden. Every other morning at this
hour gardeners would be out watering the plants in the
parched earth from hogskins filled at the well. But now
the garden was empty, the earth dry and cracking. No
smoke came from the chimneys on the low roofs of the
servants' quarters across the compound. The two women
looked at each other in perplexity, fear beginning to
flicker in their eyes. There was something uncanny in the
emptiness, in the silence, something different from every
other morning they could recall.

'Where's Papa?' asked Arabella.

'The King sent for him. He should be back in a minute.
Here he comes now! He'll know what's happening.'

They both heard the familiar clip-clop of the colonel's
horse and turned in relief. The horse stopped, as it always
did, in the porch. They ran into the hall and opened the
front door.

The colonel's horse was riderless. One stirrup was cut
off, and on the horse's near foreleg, blood had dried and

caked and cracked. The animal stood, head down, mouth frothed with foam.

'There's been an accident,' said Mrs MacDonald, suddenly calm. She had not lived nearly all her married life in India, with its procession of famines and crises, of cholera or plague, without becoming stoic. Something terrible must have happened in Delhi and all the servants had run away to escape it. They were like children. But if only one of them had *told* her. And what about her husband? She patted the horse's flank comfortingly. If the animal could only talk.

'What's happened to Papa?' asked Arabella.

'He may have been thrown. Or perhaps the horse ran away with him. I just don't know. We had better get a bed ready for him.'

'No,' said Arabella. 'Let's get away from here.'

'Get away? Why?' asked her mother.

'Listen!'

They both stood still. From the bazaar they could hear shouts and cries, and bangs that sounded like fireworks at an Indian wedding, growing louder, coming nearer. The colonel's horse began to tremble in alarm, muscles rippling under its sweating skin.

'We'll lock the house,' said Mrs MacDonald. 'Then we'll go next door.'

George Todd, an engineer involved with the telegraph system, and his wife, Jasmine, lived there.

They bolted the front door, went out of the back door and locked this from the outside. Mrs MacDonald put the key in her purse. They shut the front gate, hurried along the path to the side gate, out into the street and through the next wicket gate that opened into the Todds' garden.

Mrs Todd opened the front door herself. Her house was much smaller than the MacDonalds'. After all, Mr Todd was only an engineer and Mrs Todd quite an ordinary person from the Midlands, without private means. Usually, they had no social contact with officers and their ladies, apart from a polite word of recognition if their carriages passed on the way to church, for each layer of English society in India knew their place and kept to it; making sure, of course, that others they considered to be of a lower order also kept to theirs. Mrs Todd was a plump, cheerful woman, and obviously surprised to see

her two visitors. The colonel's lady and her daughter had
never called on her socially before.

'There is something wrong,' explained Mrs MacDonald,
as though explanation was necessary for such a call, unan-
nounced and uninvited. 'All my servants have disappeared. And my husband's horse has just come in covered
with blood with a stirrup missing.'

'And your husband?' asked Mrs Todd, her homely face
creased with concern.

'I don't know. He went to the Fort. He has not come
back. There must have been an accident. And all this
shouting and yelling in the street. I—I just wanted to be
with someone.'

Mrs MacDonald's voice trailed away. She felt lonely
and frightened, and she didn't even care if Mrs Todd was
socially beneath her.

'Come in, do.' Mrs Todd opened the door. 'I'll make
some tea.'

'Thank you. Is Mr Todd here?'

'Not yet.'

Mrs Todd instinctively glanced sideways at the clock in
the hall to check the time. This clock was her most valued
possession. She had brought it out from her parents' home
in Lichfield when she was married. All that polished wood
and intricate carving, and the solid feel of it, the reassuring, unhurried tick, tock, tick, reminded her of home.

'He'll be back in ten minutes or so, I expect. He's at the
telegraph office.'

'I don't understand these things,' confessed Mrs
MacDonald.

'Nor do I,' admitted Mrs Todd. 'It's a wonderful inven-
tion, though. It's almost like being able to speak to
Meerut.'

Meerut. General Hewitt. The MacDonalds had been at
a dinner party in Delhi when he had been chief guest, before they went on leave. He commanded thousands of
British troops. One volley from the muskets of British infantry; one charge from their horsemen, sabres bright and
sharp as razors, and all the trouble would be over. The
niggers would soon kowtow.

'What do *you* think has happened?' asked Mrs Todd.

'Some religious trouble, I expect. Hindus fighting Moslems or Sikhs fighting both. We are too kind to them, too soft, that's the trouble.'

'Indeed we are,' Mrs Todd agreed. 'Funny thing, none of my servants have arrived, either.'

She said this to show Mrs MacDonald that, although she and her husband might inhabit a lower social level, they also had servants; and in the plural, not just one.

'Now, that tea,' she went on. It was the only gesture of hospitality she could think of, and they would all feel better after some warm sweet tea. It also introduced a comforting routine of safe and familiar things into a morning that somehow seemed all wrong, as though it was going to fragment into chips of fear.

She led them into the kitchen, and filled a kettle from a stone water jar. The grate had gone out overnight. She pushed some pieces of firewood wrapped in an old copy of the *Delhi Gazette* between the black bars, and lit a lucifer.

'It'll take a minute or two,' she said.

At that moment, they heard a knock on the back door.

'It's George,' Mrs Todd announced thankfully. 'He kept forgetting his key so often that he doesn't even take one now. I let him in at the back door.'

She slid the bolt and opened the door, delighted that her husband should be home. He could take charge of things now; he would know what was happening and what to do.

Mrs Todd's smile of welcome froze on her face. Outside, framed in the doorway, stood three soldiers in the grey uniforms of Meerut. One held a whisky bottle in his hand. He had been drinking, and the spirit had slobbered down his chin and his tunic, washing away the dust of the journey.

As he saw Mrs Todd, he smashed the empty bottle against the lintel, and, holding the neck, thrust the jagged brown edges towards her face. She drew back. The other two men moved forward with him. They had swords in their hands. They were all grinning, mouths red as blood with betel nut.

Between them, the three women could see other soldiers vaulting easily over the whitewashed compound wall and running across the dry garden towards them. Some carried incongruous trinkets they had looted; a mirror, a child's doll, a carriage clock.

Mrs Todd tried to shut the door, but they were through it now, coming towards them, grinning. One of the swordsmen flicked a blue glass vase off a shelf with the end of his sword. It smashed on the stone floor and the splintering of the glass broke the paralysing spell of horror.

Mrs Todd swung round to the nearest shelf, picked up a frying pan and threw it sideways, like a discus. Its edge caught the first man in the throat. He dropped to his knees, choking for breath, and rolled over on his side, just outside the door.

Arabella seized a chair, and threw it, legs forward, into the second man's face.

Mrs MacDonald grabbed a burning stick of wood from the grate and trust its smoking, flaming end into the eyes of the third man. He screamed, and staggered back.

Arabella slammed the door on them, slipped the bolt and stood for a second, her back against it, sobbing with reaction.

'Quick!' said Mrs Todd. 'The shutters. And then up on the roof.'

All the windows had heavy wooden shutters, now pegged back against the walls. They ran from room to room, closing them, slamming bolts, dropping hooks in place.

'Have you a gun?' asked Mrs MacDonald.

'A shotgun.'

'Bring it.'

Mrs Todd rummaged for the gun in the cupboard, and then for a box of cartridges, and gathering up their skirts, they all ran up the stairs to the flat roof.

'Have you ever fired it?' asked Mrs MacDonald.

Mrs Todd shook her head. She was beyond speech now. What *could* have happened to George?

She handed over the gun to Mrs MacDonald. After all, she was the colonel's lady, and as such, should naturally be their leader. Mrs MacDonald broke the gun, slipped in two cartridges, snapped the gun closed and took general aim at the crowd of sepoys milling about in the yard. She squeezed the triggers and fired both barrels. The butt slammed her shoulder and the noise of the two explosions made her ears ring like bells.

Down in the yard, all was chaos. She had blown off one man's head. Others staggered about, screaming, holding wounded chests, scarred arms and faces. Two barrels of twelve-bore at that range were devastating.

She reloaded and again fired both barrels.

The sepoys started to run in different directions, scrambling over walls: anywhere to escape from these volleys. Mrs MacDonald lowered the gun.

'You see,' she said calmly. 'They only want showing who's in charge. General Hewitt's men will be here soon. Then we'll all be safe. Thank God, General Hewitt's so near.'

13

At that particular moment, General Hewitt, bloated as a corpse that had been drowned for days, lay in his flannel nightgown on his bed, while one orderly held his shoulders and another a glass of brandy and soda water to his lips.

The room was full of officers. The senior ones—like Brigadier Wilson and Colonel Carmichael Smythe—showed some compassion in their faces. After all, Hewitt was an old man, and the events of the previous afternoon and night had unnerved them all.

The younger officers, their uniforms blackened by fire and stained by blood, with sleeves ripped out and trousers slashed by sepoys' swords, watched this tableau with barely concealed anger and contempt. None of them had any clear idea of what would happen or what they should do. They only knew what had happened already, and this was bad enough. The hospital was empty, and all the prisoners gone. The armoury had been systematically looted. Pack mules, elephants to draw cannon, transport camels and dozens of newly arrived Australian chargers, had all been seized. The trail the mutineers had left, marked by dung droppings and loot thrown away because it was too heavy to carry, stretched fifty yards wide into the shimmering infinity towards Delhi.

One cavalry officer, Captain Charles Rosser of the Dragoons, had begged for permission to take two squadrons of his regiment and three horse artillery guns and race the head of the column to the nearest bridge and force them back.

Wilson said, 'No.'

He was afraid that the mutineers might double back when they saw the dragoons, and attack the garrison again.

'I cannot divide the force,' he explained unconvincingly.

'With respect, sir,' replied Rosser, 'the force is *already* divided. Worse, it is fragmented. I *beg* for your permission to follow my plan.'

He appealed to the general, but the general replied weakly from his bed: 'I can give no orders without Brigadier Wilson's approval.'

'But, sir,' protested Gough, 'Brigadier Wilson says *he* cannot give orders, under Section Seventeen of the Bengal Army Regulations, unless *you* agree.'

'Then we stay as we are,' said Hewitt. So Rosser and his men, guns unlimbered, had stood uselessly by, as the tide of men and beasts streamed out and away, towards Delhi.

The general finished the brandy and the first orderly wiped his brow with a linen square. Brigadier Wilson coughed discreetly.

'General,' he said, 'at least we must warn Delhi what has happened.'

'We have already sent a telegraph message, sir,' said Lang.

'Then we *have* warned Delhi,' the general said thankfully. 'We have done all we can do.'

'Not quite, sir,' said Carmichael Smythe. 'We should inform General Anson at Army Headquarters of the insurrection. There is no direct telegraph from here to Amballa. We will have to send an officer.'

'Well, send one,' said the general peevishly. His liver burned in his body like a fiery coal. Every joint ached. His head throbbed as though smiths had been hammering hot horseshoes inside it. 'Why keep asking my permission to do these obvious things?'

'As you say, sir.'

Smythe turned and looked in Lang's eyes. This new arrival would do as well as anyone else. He had come from a cavalry regiment—why, he was *still* wearing these wrong buttons! The insolence of the whippersnapper! And after he had personally told him to change them! Smythe stiffened with irritation.

'You, Mr Lang,' he said. 'Report to General Anson's Headquarters in Amballa. Take your own horse and a spare in case he goes lame. Explain the whole situation to him.'

'Can I have your written appreciation, sir?'

'There's not time for written appreciations,' retorted the colonel quickly. 'Give him your verbal report.'

Smythe had no intention of committing to paper the fact that, as Orderly Field Officer, he had done nothing to prevent the rebels from freeing the prisoners, seizing all the arms they could possible carry, and heading off towards Delhi. He had, however, comfortingly rationalized his inaction. He had ridden hither and yon in search of British commanding officers, but owing to the chaos and confusion and the dark, he could not find them.

'And one other thing, Mr Lang,' he added coldly. 'Those buttons. I do not expect to have to repeat an order to a junior officer.'

'No, sir.'

Lang clicked his heels together, bowed stiffly to the general, and left the room. He walked down the steps of the portico, mounted his horse which he had tethered outside, and rode across the *maidan*.

The horse was tired, and so was he. He had not been to bed all night and the prospect of riding for nearly eighty miles, through possibly hostile country depressed him.

He crossed the *maidan*, littered with corpses. Crows and vultures gouged curved and reddened beaks into the bloodied rags that half-covered burst bodies. Soon these would swell with the heat and the stench would become unbearable, but now some were still recognizable as men.

His horse snorted at the sight and the smell; vultures spread their wings and arched their fouled necks as he passed, but they did not fly away.

His bungalow had some thatch singed, but the fire had not spread. His bearer crouched on the veranda, polishing the pale brown boots. He stood up and salaamed, the brush still in his hand, as Lang approached.

'*Gussel tyara,*' he said. 'Your bath is ready.'

'Thank you,' said Lang. It seemed incredible that, after

all the shambles and madness of only hours before, his bearer should still be there, uninvolved with treachery, still keeping water hot in the tin bath, his boots polished.

He felt an enormous rush of warmth towards the man, and the loyalty he represented.

'Were there any letters?' he asked.

'Only one for Mr Gough, sahib.'

'*Nothing* for me?'

'No, sahib.'

Lang looked at his face in the mirror, hardly recognizing himself with his stubble, his hair matted and caked with dust, his eyes ringed with the violet shadows of fatigue.

How different he would have felt, how totally different, if only there had been a letter from Arabella; even one letter.

Simon Fraser, the British Commissioner in Delhi, stood on the flat roof of his house, listening to the shouts and chants of the crowd that swarmed through the narrow streets.

What the devil could be happening? There was no religious procession due, so far as he knew. No leader had died, for his body to be borne through the streets on the shoulders of his sons, sprinkled with vermilion dust and a retinue of drums and buglers leading the mourners. So why all this commotion?

Fraser was a stocky man with a black beard. In his career, he had frequently faced shouting mobs of hundreds, alone, and grasping nothing more lethal than a thorn stick. He saw nothing unusual in this behaviour; he was only doing his job. It had never occurred to him that anyone might attack him. After all, they knew who he was. They would never attack the Commissioner. What could they possibly gain from such folly?

He ran down the stone steps to the ground floor, called for his buggy and set off with his driver towards the King's palace. Bahadur Shah, the cunning old fellow, would know what was happening.

The streets around the Fort seemed unusually crowded, and as they passed through them at less than walking pace, his driver shouting and cracking his whip over the heads of the crowd to force them to give way, people shouted and waved their fists at them. What insulting and disgraceful behaviour, thought Fraser to himself. And, also, so unusual.

Ahead of them lay the cantonment. To his astonishment, he saw that roofs were on fire. Flames, forty feet high, stretched scorching fingers towards the sky. A British rider came up alongside him and leaned in under the canopy. His face was streaked with burning ash and sweat.

'Captain!' cried Fraser with delight, recognizing Captain James Douglas, Colonel MacDonald's second-in-command. 'What on earth is going on?'

'God knows, Commissioner. I can't find the colonel anywhere. The roads round the palace are blocked. Hundreds of sepoys with muskets are streaming in over the bridge from Meerut. They've got elephants, cannon and gharries piled high with ammunition.'

Fraser picked up a portable telescope he carried in one of the door pockets and looked out through it over the river, towards the swirling clouds of dust on the far bank. Douglas was right; half a dozen elephants were ponderously pulling cannon over the dipping, heaving barges. He moved his telescope to the head of the column, but no English officers rode on their chargers, leading their men. He lowered his telescope, his face furrowed with bewilderment.

'Look out!' shouted Douglas suddenly, and jumped from his horse into the ditch.

Five Indian troopers came galloping down the street towards them, muskets in the air, firing wildly. They gave a roar of rage as they saw the two Europeans, and charged.

Fraser's horses reared. Their driver fell backwards from his box to the ground and broke his neck. Fraser jumped into the ditch beside Douglas, who was aiming his American Colt. He fired. A trooper threw up both hands, let go his musket and slid from his horse. One foot caught in the stirrup. His face and shoulder dragged along the rough surface of the road.

'Get a gun!' shouted Douglas desperately.

On the side of the bank was a sentry box, guarding the back door of the palace. Fraser jumped out of the ditch

and into the box as the other four troopers wheeled
around.

The Indian sentry was still inside, unsure whether to
join the mutineers or stay loyal. Fraser punched him on
the jaw, seized his musket and fired from the shoulder at
the nearest trooper. The direct hit blew a hole through his
chest. He slithered backwards to the ground. His riderless
horse careered off wildly, stirrups flying. The other three
disappeared up the street. Douglas scrambled up out of
the ditch, limping. He had been hit in the foot. Fraser
handed back the rifle to the sentry. He was always a polite
man; also he had neither powder nor ball to recharge it.

'What do you make of that?' he asked.

'Madness,' gasped Douglas, wincing in pain. 'Madness.'

'We've got to reach the King,' said Fraser. 'You can't
ride with that foot. Come in the buggy with me.'

'Your driver's dead.'

'I'll drive the thing myself.' Fraser jumped on the box
and whipped up his two jades. They galloped through the
streets to his special entrance to the palace. His horses
were tiring, lathered with sweat, foaming with fear. A
handful of Indians watched his arrival from the shelter of
sweetmeat stalls.

'Wait here,' he told Douglas. It would have been impossible for him to climb the interminable stone stairs to the
King's chambers with his wounded foot. Douglas sat in
the back seat, revolver on his knee.

Fraser opened the door with his private key and went
inside and ran up the stairs, two at a time, and into the
King's room. The old man sat cross-legged on a satin
quilt, surrounded by a pile of cushions. He was smoking a
hookah, his wet, soft lips holding the mouthpiece loosely.

'Your Majesty,' said Fraser bluntly, without any of the
usual polite perambulations. 'Delhi seems to have gone
mad. Sepoys are pouring in from Meerut with artillery
and muskets. I was fired at coming here, and Captain
Douglas has been wounded. I can only assume that the
troops have mutinied. Do *you* know what's happening?'

The King stood up, a long silvery rope of saliva trailing
from his toothless gums to the ivory mouthpiece.

'I only know what I have seen. Hundreds of men coming over the bridge just before dawn. But Colonel Mac-

Donald left here to report to you.'

'I have not seen him, your Majesty. I ask you to turn out your guard immediately, and order your ceremonial artillery to fire over the bridge of boats, and stop any more of this rabble reaching the city.'

'I cannot fire at my own people.'

'I am not asking you to, your Majesty. Only to fire *over* their heads as a warning to come no farther. No one will be injured.'

'The Guard Commander is in his room, Commissioner,' said the King, and turned back to his hookah; air bubbled through the cooling water.

Fraser felt irritation pump with every beat of his heart. He opened the door and bellowed down the stairs in Hindusthani: 'Royal Guard Commander!'

An Indian officer came out from a room below and stood looking up at them.

The King called down to him in a tremulous voice: 'The Commissioner thinks you should fire cannon above the bridge of boats.'

'Your Majesty,' replied the officer smoothly. 'Your wish is naturally my decree. But we have no ammunition. It has been withdrawn. Therefore, we cannot fire.'

'You see?' said the King.

'I see nothing,' Fraser shouted, 'except insolence from this officer, and revolution if you don't act!'

'We each see what we see,' mumbled the King, but he was also alarmed. Only days previously he had received two unexpected visitors, who had crossed the bridge of boats in closed carriages at dusk. And nothing that Nana Sahib or Azi Mullah had told him had decreased either his suspicion of their motives or his unease about his own situation.

The King sensed the delicate hairline between treachery and expediency; if he conspired against the British, and failed, they would have no mercy with him, just as his own ancestors had not wasted mercy on the Persians who had attempted to overthrow them. Danger lay in failure— and who could guarantee success?

Patiently, he had reasoned with his visitors. Once started, how could they hope to control, or contain, a revolt against the British? It was known that British troops were

on the seas, bound for a minor war in Burma. Fast ships,
with new engines that needed no sail, could overtake them
and bring them back to quell any revolt in India. And
even assuming that the projected revolt *should* succeed,
was it not possible that the revolt itself might throw up
new leaders as a volcano spews out white-hot lava? And
who could be sure that these new leaders would not seize
their chance—as others had done in the past—to turn victory to their personal advantage?

Nana Sahib had agreed with what the King said, but
Azi Mullah disputed every point. He craved power, and
was it not written that the craving of a thoughtless man
grows like a vine? He runs from life to life, like a monkey
seeking fruit in the forest. And, like monkeys, these men
might find little fruit and much anguish in their plan.

They had left an hour before dawn, when even the sentries slept and the river ran sluggish and low, but with no
assurances from the King. Equally, he had sworn by the
faith not to reveal to the English what they had planned.
Now, as he faced Fraser, uneasiness lay like a stone in his
stomach.

Fraser, knowing nothing of this, looked at the old man
angrily, contemptuously. It was useless arguing any longer
with him, so he ran down the steps and out into the street.

Douglas still sat in the buggy, revolver in one hand,
sword in the other, warily watching a crowd which had
gathered round him.

Fraser heard a rattle of musket bolts from the guard
and jumped from the doorway to the buggy. As he hung,
half on, half off, and Douglas lashed the horses, three
Indians who neither had seen, but who had been
crouching on the top of the wall, jumped down on the
buggy.

Their swords flashed like quicksilver. A great spout of
blood gushed from Fraser's trunk, spraying the seats scarlet, as one blow severed his head. Then one of the Indians
impaled his head, eyes still open, on his sword and held
it high, a symbol of toppled and dead authority. All three
Indians leapt down into the street, and Douglas was suddenly on his own, dizzy with reaction, firing wildly after
them, and missing with each shot. The crowd followed for
fifty yards, and then fell back. The horses' traces had been

almost severed, and now they snapped and the animals galloped away out of the shafts. The buggy stopped. Douglas climbed down into the road and began to limp towards his home, sword in one hand, empty revolver in the other.

He reached it somehow and leaned weakly against the wall, beating on the door with his revolver.

'What's happened?' his wife asked, shocked at his appearance.

'Mutiny!' he gasped. 'Lock all the doors and the shutters. Bring my shotgun. We may be attacked at any moment.'

As a servant slid home the heavy bolts behind the door, someone else shouted outside in English: 'Let us in! Let us in!'

Douglas motioned to the servant to open the door.

The new chaplain, the Reverend Geraint Ponsonby, came in with his daughter.

'They have overrun our house, and burned everything—even my Bible!' he cried.

'The Sixtieth from Meerut will soon sort them out,' said Douglas grimly. 'They murdered poor Fraser, right next to me. Cut off his head.'

He shuddered at the memory, feeling again Fraser's warm blood soaking him, the sudden dead weight of his headless body against him on the buggy seat.

'May God have mercy on his soul,' said the parson. 'And on theirs outside. They know not what they do.'

'They seem to have a pretty good idea to me,' retorted Douglas, cramming cartridges into his pockets.

'You are a man of war,' said Ponsonby gently. 'These people are inflamed, for some reason I do not know. I am a man of peace. Let me talk to them. Let me find out their grievance.'

'Don't open that door!' shouted Douglas, shotgun in his hand.

'I cannot speak to them if the door is shut.'

'They do not want to hear you!'

'Even so, sooner or later, we *must* speak with them. Let it be sooner. We may not have a chance later.'

Before Douglas could stop him, the parson pulled back the bolts and opened the door.

The street was packed with Indians holding clubs, hammers, knives, even branches ripped from trees; all watching them. The chaplain held up both hands as a sign of peace.

'My friends,' he began, 'I do not know what your grievances are, but I give you my word they will be dealt with, if you will only . . .'

He had no chance to finish. He did not realize the violent, unreasoning hatred that the sight of his clerical collar aroused. Here was one of those who wished to convert them from the faith of their fathers to this Christian faith from Jerusalem.

'Maro! *Maro!* Kill! *Kill!*'

The crowd roared with rage, and poured through the narrow door into the house, sweeping aside Ponsonby and his daughter and Douglas and his wife and the servants before they could slam the door. Swords and knives hacked at their arms, their legs, their throats. Douglas went down first; then his wife. His daughter and Miss Ponsonby fled upstairs to hide in a cupboard, but the Indians chased after them, dragged them out and killed them.

Ponsonby seized an ornamental sword from the wall, leapt on to a table and fought bravely until someone cut his legs from under him. Then the murderers went through the house, smashing the glass in pictures, spitting, tearing sheets off the beds, pulling books from the shelves. Then they fled, barefoot, to St James's Church. With hammers and axes they smashed the monumental slabs on the walls, then seized the brass sacramental plate and the communion cups, and made off with them, believing the base metal to be gold.

Three even toiled up the three hundred steps to the belfry to ring a peal, and cut the ropes so that the bells crashed down on the stones beneath—a knell to all Europeans, and a peal of triumph to the shouting, screaming Indians who now crammed every street in the city.

From his superb house, set in a park of a thousand acres, overlooking the river, Sir Theophilius Metcalfe, the joint Magistrate of Delhi, one of the two English lawyers who judged the most serious cases, watched with mounting amazement as Indian cavalry detachments, pennants flying, artillery elephants and camels streamed across the bridge of boats—and no one challenged their right to do so.

How could the military allow this rabble to march into the city?

Metcalfe galloped out to the Magazine, six hundred yards from the Kashmir Gate in the city wall. He knew the young lieutenant, George Willoughby, who commanded the eight British soldiers on duty there.

'What are your orders if they attack the Magazine—as they will if they seize the city?' he asked.

'I have no orders, sir,' said Willoughby. 'Such a situation has never been imagined, but I will do my duty.'

'What if this place is over-run?'

Willoughby said nothing. The question answered itself.

'Why don't *you* escape sir?' Willoughby suggested. 'You are well known in Delhi. You must have sentenced hundreds of these knaves who are now running the streets. They'll murder you on sight.'

'Possibly,' agreed Metcalfe. 'But I feel my place is here in Delhi. And my duty also.'

'Not so, sir. We will need magistrates to judge them after all this.'

'I accept your point,' said Metcalfe carefully. 'I had not considered it in that light. May God sustain you in your task.'

Metcalfe spurred his horse away and turned south through alleys until the houses fell away and gave place to shacks, and the shacks to black skin tents and then the tents to rough spiky grass and anthills, that stretched unbroken, trembling with heat, to a range of hills some miles away.

Metcalfe was not a coward. He felt that leaving Delhi smacked of desertion, of saving his own skin, when he should have stayed, if only to share whatever fate awaited his countrymen. And the farther away from Delhi he rode, the greater grew the feeling that he should return. So, at last, he turned around and began to ride back.

Almost immediately, his horse stumbled on a sharp stone and almost fell. The stone had bruised the frog under the animal's left front hoof, and immediately it went lame. Metcalfe was marooned on the plain, miles from anywhere, with a horse he could not ride.

Heat beat down on him like a physical weight. He closed his eyes wearily, and the sun bored redly through the lids. He opened them again, and to his horror saw a cloud of dust rapidly approaching him from the direction of Delhi.

Some of the mutineers must have seen him go. They would kill him where he stood, at their pleasure, and taking their time. He glanced around desperately for some high ground where he could stand and fight.

The nearest was a small hillock about two hundred yards away, pocked with caves and bear holes. He left his horse to graze and ran towards it, drawing his sword. Outside one of the caves, an Indian was squatting, cross-legged. His body was naked, save for a strip of cloth about his lean loins, his shoulders smeared with grey wood ash and dung, his hair long and matted. He wore half a dozen strings of beads round his neck, and he was hunched up, contemplating his wrinkled navel, in the familiar Yoga position. He did not even look up as Metcalfe approached; he was a fakir, a holy man.

'I am English,' Metcalfe explained. 'There has been a rebellion in Delhi. I am being chased. I will be killed if I am caught. Can I hide in this cave?'

The fakir gave an almost imperceptible nod.

'The cave is long and deep,' he said. 'Go to the back and wait.' It was an order, not an invitation.

Metcalfe bent his head down and went inside. The cave felt dark and damp and uninviting, hung with crystallized fingers of rock salt. For a second, panic fluttered wings in his heart. Was this a trap? He set his teeth and walked on. If he had to die, he would die as an Englishman.

He crouched down on the earth and watched the bright sun through the opening over the shoulders of the holy man.

Hooves clattered on the hard ground. He could see the legs of horses, hear them blow, and the rattle of their bridles.

'Old man,' called one of the riders. 'We are following an English dog. Is he in this cave?'

'There is no English dog here,' replied the fakir.

'You lie, you dog. That's his horse. I think he's hiding in this cave. If I find him I will kill you as well.'

The holy man stirred.

'If you enter this cave, you will kill no one but your-self,' he said quietly, as though the matter was of supreme unconcern to him. 'There lives inside a dragon who eats the heads of all who enter. Keep ye far off.'

'Out of my way,' said the sepoy roughly, 'or I'll run you through.'

Metcalfe saw the sepoy silhouetted against the burning day, sword in his hand, eyes narrowed against the darkness.

He let him take three paces in, and then his own sword sang through the air.

'Aaaah!' roared Metcalfe, as his blade bit through bone and sinew and artery.

Aaaah . . . 'aah . . . 'aah . . . ! The sound beat back from the tunnelled walls, echoing and re-echoing as though he was shouting down a well.

The sepoy's head rolled at his feet. Metcalfe kicked it straight out through the mouth of the cave. The horses reared up in alarm.

'It is as I said,' remarked the holy man calmly. 'The dragon is angered. Go ye from hence speedily, lest he fall upon you all.'

A rattle of bits, the pad of hoofs, murmurs of horror and fear, and the horsemen rode away.

Metcalfe gave them ten minutes, and then came out thankfully.

'You have saved my life,' he said. 'Do you know who I am?'

'I know well,' replied the holy man. 'You are Sir Theo-philius Metcalfe, the magistrate. I have appeared before you.'

Metcalfe smiled.

'Did you win your case?'

The holy man looked up for the first time. He was also smiling.

'No, sahib. I lost.'

'Then why did you save my life now?'

'Because you were a fair judge, sahib. When I appeared before you in court, I lied. You heard words on my tongue, but you read the lie in my mind. So you gave judgment against me. As was right. It is good to help a just man.

'As the Lord Buddha says, "Just as kinsmen, friends

and lovers salute a man who has been long away and returns safe from afar, in like manner good works receive him who has done good."

'Now sit down and rest, and I will give you honey and milk, and then you can proceed on your way.'

Inside the forty-foot-high walls that ringed the Magazine, Willoughby and his deputy, George Forrest, both in their early twenties, faced each other across a small table in their mess hut. The fact that so senior a dignitary as Sir Theophilius Metcalfe should be concerned about the situation worried them.

As Willoughby had told him, he would do his duty. In the last extremity, this would mean destroying the Magazine, and to do this would be to destroy themselves, for they had no means of escape. It seemed strange and unreal to be drinking India Pale Ale and contemplating the prospect of eternity, perhaps only minutes away.

Willoughby's unit consisted of Forrest, a British Warrant Officer, Conductor John Buckley, and seven British private soldiers, with a number of sepoys who now stood in a sullen group about fifty yards away, watching the Englishmen resentfully.

'Let's run through the orders again,' said Willoughby; anything was better than inaction.

Forrest shouted, 'Fall in the Magazine party!'

Nine men doubled in. The ninth was a civilian.

'Who are you, sir?' asked Willoughby coldly. So many strange things seemed to be happening that he could not trust anyone he did not know.

'My name's Ryley, sir. I am a clerk in the Judge's office.'

'Then what are you doing here? Your place is with Sir Theophilius Metcalfe.'

'I was carrying some papers to the office, and I was chased by a bunch of niggers. I thought I'd be safer inside than out, so I ran in here for safety.'

The irony of this amused Forrest. Here were a handful of Englishmen reluctantly preparing to blow up the greatest concentration of explosives in the world, and this man had joined them—for safety!

Willoughby and he exchanged glances.

'We hope you will be safe here, Mr Ryley,' he said.

'Thank you, sir.'

'Right,' said Willoughby. 'Have you laid powder trails, Conductor?'

'Yes, sir,' replied Buckley. 'Laid and ready to be lit.'

Sooty paths of powder led from a withered lemon tree in the middle of the yard to the inner doors of the Magazine. A burning torch set to the end of this trail, would reach the Magazine in seconds. This was the last remedy, for after this trail was alight, only God in His mercy could save them.

Their armaments consisted of two six-pounder guns, double charged with grapeshot, facing the huge wooden gates, and one seventy-four-pound howitzer in front of their office building. The first mutineers through those gates would face a fearful reception.

'You, Conductor, stand to one side of the gates, out of our firing line. If the gates give, raise your hat in the air. We'll fire the guns, and if that doesn't stop them, Mr Forrest, you will light the powder trails. Any questions?'

'No, sir.'

'Right. Then all we have to do is wait and see. And may God help all of us.'

'Amen, sir,' said Buckley.

The men doubled away. They had enough ammunition in the Magazine to fire their guns until the barrels melted, but Willoughby calculated they would probably only be able to discharge a few barrages before they were physically overwhelmed. That would be the moment to light the powder trails.

Willoughby climbed up the watch-tower; sepoys outside were placing ladders against the walls. Within seconds, arms and shoulders and heads appeared on top of the walls. He shouted to two of his men, who raised their muskets and fired. Two sepoys were hit, others ducked down, but more and more were climbing now, and it was impossible to head them off because the old-fashioned muskets needed reloading and charging after each shot.

Over the wall, like a javelin, came a bamboo ladder. It crashed to the ground, and immediately the sepoys inside the Magazine seized it and rushed up the rungs and over the wall to join their cheering comrades. Within seconds, the Englishmen were alone.

The huge gates began to heave and creak on their gigantic iron hinges with the weight of the crowds outside. Beams a foot thick bent and cracked with a noise like cannons firing. The wood splintered; bolts snapped under the enormous pressure.

Up went the Conductor's hat.

'*Fire!*' bellowed Forrest.

The portfire flickered, its blue flame near the howitzer barrel. Then the gun bellowed and bucked on its wheels, digging in its iron trail. The charge flattened the shoddy buildings outside for half a mile down the street.

'Reload!' shouted Willoughby. 'Fire the six-pounders!'

The men sponged out the howitzer and rammed a new charge and wadding and shot down its smoking muzzle, as the six-pounders boomed, one after another.

'Keep firing all guns!'

Again the howitzer thundered. Dust as fine as flour from shattered buildings now coated everyone, turning Indians white, covering the wounded so that they writhed in pain like tormented wraiths.

The Magazine was also clouded with the choking dust, thick as London fog, rough on throats and eyes as sandpaper. The six-pounders boomed through the haze, orange tongues of flame flickering at their muzzles, but the nine defenders could only deal with the sepoys coming over the walls behind them by swinging round their clumsy guns. The yard was thick with swarming figures. Within seconds, they would all be annihilated.

This was the moment when Willoughby did his duty.

He turned towards Buckley and shouted: '*Now,* if you please!'

Again, Buckley raised his hat. A soldier held a burning taper to the end of the black powder path. The trail began to crackle and sparkle, and suddenly seemed to die.

Then the Magazine exploded.

The gigantic roar was heard in towns and villages a hundred miles away (where people, knowing nothing of events in Meerut or Delhi, assumed it must be pre-monsoon thunder). In Delhi, it blew out every glass window within a mile radius, and brought down the forty-foot walls around the Magazine like a child's set of bricks.

Willoughby, blown flat on his back, lay gasping like a

newly-hooked fish while masonry rained around him. But he was alive, and he still held his sword. He rolled over on to his stomach and began to crawl on all fours towards where the gates had been.

Others were staggering and stumbling, too: Forrest, his face blackened, uniform almost blown from his body; and Buckley and three more, all with eyes wide and hair singed, moving slowly like men in a nightmare.

Where seconds before houses had stood, and shops and stalls, nothing remained but splintered beams sticking jagged ends out of mounds of bricks and dust.

It was impossible to say how many had died, how many more were blinded, deafened, or mutilated by the force of the blast.

It was enough to know that, as Willoughby counted his survivors, and they shook each other's hands dazedly, eyes white in their sooty faces, eyebrows burned off, lips cracked with heat and exhaustion, they were alive.

'We've done it!' cried Willoughby in astonishment. Then, as he saw Ryley, he grinned.

'You were right, Mr Ryley. You *were* safer in here than outside . . .'

Mrs MacDonald broke the shotgun and slipped in her two last cartridges.

'I'll get some more,' said Mrs Todd.

'No, don't,' said Mrs MacDonald. 'It's not safe to go downstairs. They may be in the house already.'

As she spoke, they heard glass tinkle like tiny temple bells.

'They are,' said Arabella dully.

'The only way up here is through the stair door,' said Mrs MacDonald. 'I can shoot the first two. After that I can only club them.'

They stood very close together against the far parapet, the sun beating down, unnoticed now, on their uncovered heads. Mrs MacDonald raised the shotgun and looked along the sights between the two blued barrels, at the roof entrance. They heard a shout in the room beneath and a crash of furniture overturning and then bare feet drummed on the ladder rungs, coming up to the roof.

A head, shoulders, two brown hands, appeared at the

door entrance. Another man pushed out the first and a third man jumped out behind him.

Mrs MacDonald fired the left barrel.

To Arabella's horrified gaze the three men appeared to disintegrate, exploding in a roaring red flash of blood and splintered bone that spread over the far walls of the parapet and the rooftop. Three corpses, grotesquely mutilated, sank down.

A fourth man peered cautiously round the entrance with a pistol in his hand.

Mrs MacDonald fired the right barrel. Shot peppered the trap-door, but too late. He had ducked back inside. Now he came out, knowing she had spent both barrels, and fired at her. The bullet hit her in the stomach with the soft padding sound of someone beating a carpet. Mrs MacDonald dropped the shotgun and went down on her knees and rolled over slowly, hands clawing at her terrible wound, thick bright blood oozing between her fingers.

'Mama! *Mama!*' cried Arabella, kneeling by her side. A dribble of blood ran out of the side of her mouth, then her body went loose, and her hands opened.

'You have killed her!' shouted Arabella, standing up. She seized the shotgun and flung it at the man. It missed him.

'She has killed three of us,' he replied in English.

'Three of *you?*' shouted Arabella. 'Shoot me, too, if you have a mind to. Shoot!'

She threw out her arms hysterically, and stood, eyes closed.

'I do not wish to do so,' said the man simply, slipping his pistol into a fold of his dhoti. He was about thirty, short and shaven-headed, except for the characteristic Hindu tuft of hair.

'Come downstairs,' he told them. 'I can give you safe conduct.'

'Who are you?' asked Mrs Todd.

'Hazara Lal. I will guarantee your safety.'

'Why?' asked Arabella. 'You have just killed my mother.'

'It was self-defence, memsahib.'

Hazara Lal owned a leather shop, making chaplis and belts and shoes. His brother, the Naik from Meerut, had

ridden in the previous evening with the exciting forecast
that soon Indians would be in control of their own country. Hazara Lal was not so sure. The British would be
harder to beat than his brother realized; and what better
guarantee of his own safety—and possibly even a reward—than to have saved the lives of these two memsahibs? Like many men of commerce, Hazara Lal was also a
man of caution.

Other Indians were crowding past him on the parapet,
peering into the street beneath, shouting down to friends.

'Come with me,' Hazara Lal said urgently. 'I cannot answer for the temper of these men.'

'Do as he says,' said Mrs Todd. 'If only for a few hours
until the British troops arrive.'

He stood to one side and the two women went downstairs, past the shattered bodies of Mrs MacDonald and
the three Indians, out into the street.

'I'll lead you to the palace. You will be safe there,' said
Hazara Lal.

'Safe?' repeated Mrs Todd incredulously. Yet what else
could they do but obey him? If they stayed where they
were, they would be murdered, without doubt.

Huddled together, miserable and terrified, the two
women followed Hazara Lal through the teeming streets,
walking with heads down, bodies bent forward, like people in a dream: as though the shouting and the sweat of
hundreds of milling, unwashed bodies, their foul breath
and scented hair, their bloodied hands, had nothing whatever to do with them; as though they would soon wake up
and the sun would be shining, and early morning tea
would be waiting by their bedsides, in fancy china cups.

Outside the offices of the Delhi Bank, a crowd of Indians were beating on the double oak doors with clubs.
They did not want to cash cheques or deposit money, but
to loot the vaults, believing that a fortune in gold lay literally beneath their feet.

The recently appointed manager, George Beresford,
with his wife and family, lived in a flat above the banking
hall. From their front room windows, they had watched
with astonishment and alarm as the streets outside had
filled with shouting, wild-eyed men of the roughest sort,
waving clubs and stakes of wood.

Beresford ran downstairs, double-locked the huge old-fashioned safes, and the vaults themselves, and wrapped the keys in his handkerchief. Holding them against his body, he buckled his cummerbund over them. Now, if anyone wanted to seize his keys, they would have to kill him first. It never entered his head that they would do just that.

All this while, the commotion outside increased. Window shutters began to splinter, and he saw widening cracks of daylight as men levered iron bars between them to try and force the catches. Within minutes, they would be split open.

'Up on the roof!' he shouted to his wife and family, looking round frantically for a weapon. There was only an ornamental spear on one wall, and a locally made tulwar above the mantelpiece.

He tossed the spear to his wife and grabbed the sword himself, and then marshalled his children up the wooden staircase to the roof. They went through a trap-door, which he slammed shut.

The bolts were inside, so they all stood on it.

'Papa,' asked his eight-year-old son, Christopher, 'do you think Joey will be all right? I forgot him.'

'Yes. He will be safe,' Beresford assured the boy. Joey was a wooden doll with hinged arms and legs that a local Indian carpenter had made for Christopher's birthday.

'Let us pray that we will *all* be saved,' said Mrs Beresford. She went down on her knees on the dusty flat roof.

'Oh, God, Thou who see'est everything. Who knowest the innermost thoughts of all our hearts, save us this day, we beseech Thee. Amen.'

'Amen,' echoed Christopher. 'And please look after Joey, too.'

Suddenly, the trap-door buckled beneath them. The green-painted wood splintered white as bone, and a sword blade came through, moving like a metal finger. This was something Beresford had not anticipated. The children screamed and jumped away. Another blade pierced the wood. Beresford pulled his wife back and crouched down by the side of the door. Immediately it sprang open and an Indian leaped out.

Beresford ran him through the chest with his sword and

the man fell back, screaming. Others behind him lost their footing and fell.

Then, almost inexplicably, the Indians retreated. The family was safe. They all went down on their knees and thanked God for their deliverance.

As Beresford stood up, something made him glance at the only building that overlooked them, fifty yards away. To his horror, he saw Indian marksmen up on the roof with muskets, aiming at them.

'Down!' he shouted.

But they only presented prone targets instead of standing ones. The first volley killed them all.

Then Indians, who had been hiding in the room beneath, swarmed up and hacked their bodies to pieces. Someone found a tin of kerosene in the kitchen and emptied it over the floor of the flat and threw a lucifer on to the carpet. Within seconds, the bank was ablaze. The last man out carried Beresford's keys. He would let the building burn itself down, and then he would return. He was a bank clerk, Gopal Singh, and of all the mob, he knew exactly which key would open the vaults.

The telegraph office in Delhi, like most buildings with no direct profitability, either to the government or the East India Company, was an obscure building on the edge of the bazaar. It was sparsely furnished: two chairs, a wooden trestle table for the keys and the volt-meters and message pads, with pencils attached by small chains.

This office was also the main relay station between Meerut and Lahore, where the British Commissioner, John Lawrence, had his office, and Amballa, fifty miles away, where the general commanding the Bengal Army, the Hon. George Anson, maintained his permanent headquarters, with several British infantry and artillery regiments.

For months, there had been talk of laying a direct line from Delhi to Simla, seventy-six miles away, where the government moved from Calcutta in the hot weather, but nothing had been done about it.

Senior officials did not regard the electric telegraph very seriously, and, more important, the government had no wish to be disturbed by telegraph messages during the three months they spent in the cool Simla hills each year.

Their journey involved twelve thousand staff and servants from Calcutta, who needed eight hundred and fifty camels and one hundred and forty elephants to move all their belongings. This required so much planning and effort that everyone felt they were entitled to more agreeable relaxation than being at the whim of a chattering telegraph key.

In any case, no one could recall when an urgent message had needed to be sent to Simla. In general, military messages only referred to cases of wine lost in transit, or changed arrangements for regimental polo matches or foxhunts, that could equally well be delivered by ordinary mail: and if any matters were urgent, they could be dealt with by the military directly at Amballa where the telegraph line ended. And, in any case, General Sir Henry Barnard, the Amballa garrison commander, sent his son, who was also his A.D.C., out to Simla several times a week to deliver any messages.

The Delhi telegraph office was staffed by three men who were sometimes on duty together, sometimes separately. Mr Todd was the superintendent; William Brendish was his chief signaller, and a young man with a withered leg, John Pilkington, was relief signaller.

Messages were few, but the signallers would 'talk' to their opposite numbers in Amballa and Meerut to keep the line open and test it, and also to pass on any local news or gossip.

Early on Sunday morning, Brendish, 'talking' by Morse to his colleague in Meerut, had heard an absurd rumour that eighty-odd sepoys were to be blown from guns. He thought the man was joking, and did not think it worth while staying on duty any longer to hear whether the rumour was true or not.

On Sunday evening, when the station re-opened, he had tried to contact Meerut, but could not raise an answer. The instruments indicated a break in the circuit, no doubt a cut line, which could be dealt with on Monday. But throughout Monday morning, crowds were pouring through the streets, and on every side shutters were going up on shops as though the owners expected trouble. People were shouting excitedly, and Brendish saw hundreds of sepoys either running or galloping on horseback through the streets.

'What do you make of it?' he asked Mr Todd.

'Some religious festival probably,' Todd replied, without any interest. 'Is the line clear yet to Meerut?'

'No, sir.'

There had been trouble before where the line crossed the River Jumna over the bridge of boats. Sometimes it broke under the movement of the boats, and sometimes water ruined the insulation.

'I'll go and have a look myself,' he said. 'Keep trying for contact.'

The telegraph office maintained a gharry with two ponies. Todd climbed into this and gave the driver his instructions, and set off towards the bridge of boats.

Brendish and Pilkington sat on in their office with the windows and shutters closed. The air smelled bitter from the sulphuric acid in the rows of glass electric cells.

The shouting was increasing outside, and now they heard the crack of musketry and screams, and people crying out, not in Hindusthani, but in English.

They looked at each other uneasily. Mr Todd was wrong; this was obviously no religious festival. This was rebellion.

The clock on the wall ticked away. Fifty minutes. One hour. An hour and a half. The line was still broken. And there was no sign of Mr Todd. Suddenly, Brendish saw a British soldier running towards them. His face was cut and gashed by blows from knives and staves, and he appeared crazed with pain and fear. He beat frantically on the door with his fists. Brendish shot the bolts to let him in.

As the door moved, the mob started to shout and half a dozen men charged the door.

'For God's sake,' the soldier gasped, realizing what would happen. 'Close the door! They'll kill you otherwise. Stay inside. They've killed nine so far. And your Mr Todd. I saw it. Pulled him out of the gharry.'

'What's happening?' shouted Pilkington nervously, but the man was seized by a dozen hands before he could answer, and tossed into the centre of the crowd and clubbed down.

'We must get out,' said Brendish. 'But first we must send a warning.'

He sat down at the key, threw over the switches and tested the lines to find one that was still working. He could send a message to Lahore or to Amballa. He chose Lahore. He was a civilian and he believed John Lawrence was more likely to act on the message than some anonymous military officer. In any event, the Lahore office would relay it on to Amballa.

'We must leave office,' he tapped out. 'All the bungalows are being burned down by the sepoys of Meerut. We are off. Mr Todd is dead, we think. He went out this morning and is not yet returned. We learnt that nine Europeans were killed. Good-bye.'

'Shall we smash the equipment?' asked Pilkington as Brendish pulled down the main switch.

'No. The Indians think it's magic, anyhow. With luck, they'll leave it alone. It's us they're after.'

They went out through the back door into an alley a yard wide where tradesmen threw their refuse.

'Where shall we go?' asked Pilkington nervously.

'High ground,' said Brendish. 'Out of Delhi.'

'Flagstaff Tower?'

'Yes.'

This was one of the highest buildings in Delhi, four storeys tall and on the Ridge, a mound varying between forty and eighty feet high, that stretched for nearly two miles to the north-west of Delhi, a traditional place for Europeans to admire the view it commanded.

They set off at a run along the back alleys, behind the shops, Pilkington's surgical boot creaking with every step.

The tower was already packed with Europeans: wives searching anxiously for husbands, children crying, everyone without servants, and not coping very well on their own.

An English brigadier, George Graves, was marshalling a group of grim-faced men with what shotguns and fowling pieces they had managed to bring. Brendish reported to him at once.

'What news from Meerut?' asked the brigadier.

'The line's dead, sir. We can't get through.'

'My God,' said Graves. This was worse than he had

imagined. What if the sepoys had killed all the British troops in Meerut? The idea seemed preposterous, but then the whole morning was preposterous, with thousands of sepoys, armed and accoutred, streaming into Delhi and swarming everywhere, looting and burning, and no one to stop them.

'Where else are you in contact, lad?' he asked.

'I have alerted Lahore and the line is still open to Amballa.'

The brigadier took out a notebook and scribbled a message to General Anson.

'Can you send this message to Headquarters? Mark it to be passed to the general at once.'

'I'll never get back to the office alive,' said Brendish.

'You will,' said Graves. He called to half a dozen men with fowling-pieces.

'Escort this gentleman to the telegraph office through the back alleys. Shoot if attacked. And shoot to kill.'

They set off at the double. Pilkington watched them go, grateful for the first time in his life that he was a cripple, and so excused the terrible risk of returning.

14

General the Hon. George Anson was giving a dinner party in Simla for twenty-five guests.

Anson was a big, bluff man, sitting at the head of the table under his coat of arms engraved with the family motto: *Nil Desperandum.*

He was a very good hand at whist, a devoted escort to pretty women, and a considerable authority on horses. One of his relatives had inherited an estate with an annual income of £70,000, and had squandered the lot on racing within a few years; and while Anson did not openly condone this extravagance, he sympathized with it.

He had been commander-in-chief of the Bengal Army for two years, and before that had been a Member of Parliament for nearly thirty. He and his staff were now on a leisurely tour of inspection of units under his command—which stretched from Calcutta in the east to Madras in the south, an area nearly a hundred thousand square miles. This excuse allowed him to stay for as long as he liked in any place he fancied. He had been in Simla for nearly three weeks. His wife and their three daughters were in England, and a most delightful lady, the wife of a local officer, was acting as his *mem* or hostess in his official residence, Barnes Court, a huge house, decorated with mock Tudor beams, and upper storeys that jutted out over the ground floor. It had been used by commanders-in-chief for the previous twenty-five years, and took its name from the first one to live there, Sir Edward Barnes.

The evening was cool, and in the sentry boxes on either

side of the stone gates, above which oil lamps flickered inside circular glasses, the *chowkidars* stood shivering in their thin uniforms. They kept warm by wrapping themselves in army blankets, beneath which they hugged small metal braziers packed with glowing charcoal embers. The fumes made them cough and choke, but at least they produced some warmth.

Anson, as host, was conscious of his own rank as the most senior officer present, and he liked to repeat how he had served as an Ensign at Waterloo. He did not add that he had seen no action since. As he sat now, while the *khitmagars* in their long white tunics and wide belts in the Headquarters' colours of scarlet and gold expertly removed the dishes, he leaned back in his chair and allowed his right knee to move out gently past the leg of the table until it contacted the knee of the officer's wife, which moved just perceptibly against his.

How ridiculous that a woman of such charm and beauty and understanding could ever have been bedded by a dull slug like her husband! How ironic and wasteful that her feminine talents should be squandered on such a stupid man, whose only merit was that he had inherited whole acres of London slums producing an income so huge that money had literally no meaning for him!

The chatter down the table, tinkling like tinsel, provided a happy background to Anson's thoughts; it was part of the whole scintillating atmosphere of colour and elegance he appreciated so deeply. Gold and silver plate on the table; the glitter of reflected light on crystal; claret, red as blood; the pale amber of hock; bubbles rising gaily in champagne.

Outside, a sergeant came riding through the gates. His horse's shoes sparked on the gravel as he galloped up between the rhododendron hedges. A servant tethered his horse outside the back door, and he ran inside the rabbit warren of corridors.

'Urgent telegraph for the commander-in-chief,' he told the English butler. In the kitchen, he saw with astonishment the huge wood-burning cooking ranges supporting pots so large that two actually had Indian children crouched inside, burnishing them. Near by, a dozen helpers washed silver plate and Spode china in steaming

sinks. The left-overs of ham and chicken, and oysters, lob-
sters and salmon from hermetically sealed stone jars la-
belled Fortnum and Mason, stood on one side for the staff
to finish when dinner was over.

'It's from Amballa. Captain Barnard brought it over.'

The sergeant unbuckled his message pouch and handed
the blue envelope to the butler, who pulled on his white
gloves, picked up a silver salver, placed the telegraph on it
and walked down the corridor, the sergeant a few paces
behind. He entered one of the double doors and stood behind the general's place. During a lull in the conversation,
he coughed discreetly, one gloved hand to his mouth. The
general looked up inquiringly.

'A sergeant from Headquarters, sir,' whispered the butler, bending down. 'He has delivered this telegraph.'

Anson put out his hand, picked the envelope off the silver plate, and nodded dismissal. What could conceivably
be urgent at eleven o'clock on a Monday evening in May?

He pushed the envelope, without opening it, beneath his
plate and turned to his mem.

'If I may pay you a compliment, ma'am, as an old man,
let me say how beautifully your jewels complement your
eyes.'

She smiled at the general, put out her hand and brushed
his wrist, soft as the gossamer touch of a butterfly's wing.

'*Old?*' she repeated incredulously. 'How *absurd* you are,
George. I was reading the American writer, Emerson, today. He said that a man only counts his years when he
has nothing else to count—and look at all you have
achieved.'

Her hand now rested on his wrist . . .

The dinner continued, and finally, chairs scraped on the
tessellated floor as the gentlemen stood up and bowed, and
the ladies left the room.

Port and brandy were passed round and the butler offered boxes of Havana cigars, each as thick as a child's
wrist. Anson had forgotten all about the message. He only
remembered it two hours later when, with his *mem* at his
right hand, he stood beneath the portico and waved good-
bye to the guests, each one departing in rigid order of seniority and importance. The butler was waiting with a
folded paper on a salver.

'The telegraph, sir.'

'Oh! Yes,' said Anson. He opened it, cigar in his mouth, expecting some routine information about arrangements for his trip or his own comfort on the next stage of the journey.

Instead, under the giant oil lamps that swung gently in the wind from the portico roof, he read the incredible message that William Brendish had sent from Delhi.

'You have heard the news, sahib?'

Rajib Ali rolled his one eye lugubriously as he stood in Hodson's little office in the headquarters building at Amballa.

'A telegraph was delivered to the general sahib yesterday in Simla. Sepoys in Meerut have mutinied.'

'How do you know?'

'The third son of my second sister works in the general sahib's kitchen. The butler told him and his brother-in-law told me.'

Hodson walked across the room to the large-scale map he kept pinned on the wall. For weeks, he had been sending regular Intelligence reports to the Staff, informing them of localized acts of unrest and indiscipline across the sub-continent. The logical site for any blow against British authority was obviously Meerut, the garrison nearest to Delhi. Whoever commanded Delhi, commanded India, for although the English might have made Calcutta their commercial capital, Delhi, the home of the old Moguls, the heart of all ancient Indian culture, would always remain the real capital of the country.

'When is the general sahib coming back?' he asked Rajib Ali.

'I hear within two days.'

'Two *days*,' repeated Hodson in astonishment. It seemed incredible that such sloth should be countenanced. But he was only a lieutenant. He could do nothing with higher authority. He put on his tinted spectacles: his headache was returning.

As Hodson stood poised on his toes, in his characteristic fashion, as though eager to be away, Birdwash opened the door without knocking and came in.

'That cheque, Hodson,' he said, without either introduction or preamble. 'The one you gave me in the mess. There seems to be some difficulty with the bank over it.'

He glanced at Rajib Ali with contempt. God! Fancy Hodson, hob-nobbing with a nigger who had only one eye, and worse, dirty clothes. He really *must* be a bounder. The bank manager had intimated as much, but discreetly, of course, because, after all, Hodson was an officer.

'I am sorry,' said Hodson. 'I was expecting some money out from home, but the mail's delayed.'

'Well?' Damn it, the way this fellow Hodson prevaricated.

'I said I'm sorry,' said Hodson quietly. 'As soon as I receive the money I am expecting, I'll pay you.'

'The mails arrived yesterday.'

'The letter wasn't among them.'

'Oh! Well, I'll just have to wait, I suppose. But what's *this* feller doing in your office?'

He jabbed a finger at Rajib Ali.

'*This* feller,' said Hodson, 'has just informed me that the sepoys have mutinied in Meerut.'

'How the devil does he know?'

'General Anson had a telegraph from Delhi.'

'Good God! Well, we'll soon show those niggers a thing or two.'

'Meanwhile, they may show us a thing or two.'

'What do you mean by that?'

'Exactly what I say. You haven't read the Intelligence reports I have been circulating?'

'Good God, no. Got something better to do than read that rubbish. Damned spies will tell you anything you want to hear. Sell you a lie for a chip, a damned lie for two. What's that got to do with it?'

'Everything,' said Hodson. 'I am thinking of seeing the brigadier and telling him.'

'He's out shooting today,' said Birdwash. 'Won't be back until after dusk. And then he's got a dinner party. You take my advice, Hodson. Do nothing hasty. There's still a good deal of feeling about you here, you know, after that business with the Guides.'

'I was cleared,' said Hodson, his throat suddenly tight.

'Of course you were. I am not suggesting you weren't. But lots of people say there's no smoke without fire.'

Hodson crossed the room and took off his glasses, put them in the top left-hand pocket of his tunic.

'Are you suggesting anything, Captain Birdwash?' he said, his voice barely a whisper.

Birdwash took a step back and glanced towards Rajib Ali. These fellows were mad, both of them; mad as bloody hatters.

'I'm just stating the truth. There *is* resentment about you, and you know it. And part of the resentment stems from the fact that you owe too much money to too many people.'

He went out, banging the door noisily behind him.

Hodson looked at Rajib Ali and shrugged his shoulders and smiled, it was either that or weep. Two hundred chips. The bank manager was neutral, neither for him, nor against him, only concerned with keeping his own books in order. After all, he could not lend money indefinitely without security, and the only security Hodson had provided was a small insurance policy. And even this was dubious, for some premiums had not been paid. What profound irony, to be concerned with such a petty matter, when the whole country trembled on the edge of anarchy and darkness!

A knock came at the door.

'Come in,' he called.

A young man entered, a second-lieutenant, who saluted, looking uncertainly from one to the other.

'Mr Hodson?' he asked hesitantly.

'Yes. Who are you?'

'Lang, sir. Richard Lang. I have ridden from Meerut with a report on the situation.'

'Come in, my boy. Come in. What made you report to me?'

'I asked the sentry, sir. He said you ran the Intelligence Department.'

'Don't call me sir,' said Hodson. 'I am only a full lieutenant, you know.'

He held out his hand.

'What *is* the situation in Meerut? Let's see your Appreciation.'

'Colonel Carmichael Smythe told me to give you a verbal report.'

'He would,' said Hodson dryly. If you never put your opinion in writing, you never were wrong. Only the wind held a record of spoken words.

'Well, what is the situation in Meerut?'

Lang told him of the events on the Sunday afternoon and evening.

'What did General Hewitt do?'

'Nothing, sir.'

'Don't call me sir.'

'I am sorry—Mr Hodson. Nothing.'

'I see. What was he doing when you left?'

'He was lying on his bed, sir—I mean Mr Hodson. He is an old man, of course.'

'Then he should make way for someone younger. If not in years, then in ideas. Have you been quartered yet?'

'No, Mr Hodson.'

'Come with me. I know a spare bungalow. You have a bearer?'

'Yes, outside.'

'Rajib Ali!'

Hodson turned to the Moslem.

'See that Mr Lang's bearer and their horses are looked after. Then report back to me.'

'Salaamaji.'

'I have a letter for you, Mr Hodson,' said Lang.

'From somebody in Meerut?'

'No, sir—sorry, Mr Hodson. From a clergyman who knows your brother.'

He unbuttoned his pouch and handed over the envelope Colonel MacDonald had given him so many months ago in the library at Five Mile Place. Hodson ripped it open, read the note, put it in his pocket.

'Have you met my brother?' he asked.

'No. Never.'

'Very good fellow,' said Hodson. 'As a parson, I'd say he is a first-class soldier.'

They laughed.

'I am glad to meet you, Lang, but I must make it quite clear that at this present stage in my fortunes I can't be of much help to you.'

'Colonel MacDonald told me that in the army you needed influence, and if you haven't influence, you needed money. I suppose he was joking, really?' said Lang.

'Not at all,' said Hodson. 'That's the tragedy. If he were joking, none of this mess would have happened in Meerut. Come over and I'll show you the bungalow. You speak Hindusthani?'

'A little.'

'Learn it,' advised Hodson. 'It is a beautiful language. And you will never know your men unless you can speak to them in their own tongue. Yet far too few British officers can say more than a few words in it.'

'That's what Kalyan Singh says.'

'Who is he?'

'Some relation of Nana Sahib. He joined the ship at Bombay. He had been over in England trying to persuade the directors to give Nana Sahib a pension. He said he had to bribe people.'

'Of course,' said Hodson.

'You are *not* surprised, then?'

'No. But I might have been when I was your age. For then I believed people were good or bad, black or white—I don't mean their colour, but their natures. But now—no.'

They were walking across the parade ground, ringed with thatched buildings. An orderly came out from one and saluted Hodson.

'Excuse me, sir,' he said. 'A message from Simla. All staff officers will attend a conference tomorrow night at eighteen hundred hours in the billiard-room. General's orders.'

'Very good,' said Hodson.

The man saluted. They walked on.

'Why the delay?' asked Lang.

'Because the general is in Simla. It will take him nearly two days to get here with all his entourage.'

'Can't we send any reinforcements to Meerut before then, or at least orders that the Sixtieth Rifles *must* pursue the mutineers?'

'Impossible,' said Hodson.

'But Meerut is a shambles. The prisoners have been freed, the armoury emptied. There is hardly a house in the cantonment that has not been looted and burned. Are they to get away with this?'

'Presumably we'll learn that tomorrow night at six o'clock,' said Hodson blandly, and opened the bungalow door.

The billiard-room was the largest room in headquarters for, next to the mess, it was the one the officers used most. Sets of cues stood in their rests on the walls, like rows of tapering lances. A small dais, approached by three steps, gave spectators an uninterrupted view of play. Dotted round the room were a number of wicker chairs with holes in the arm rests for glasses.

At five minutes to six on the following evening, it was packed with staff officers, middle-aged and old; most with swimming watery eyes glazed by years of gin, stroking their moustaches and wondering how long it would be before they could clasp their right hands round a reassuring glass.

As the garrison church clock began to whirr before striking the hour, the door, with its sign *Do not enter on the stroke,* swung open, and General Anson came in.

He strode up to the dais and stood for a moment looking down at their upturned faces, like row after row of huge pink eggs on which a child had drawn human features.

'Gentlemen,' he began. 'I expect you all know the serious news we have received from Meerut. It is impossible to assess the situation clearly from this distance.

'We cannot tell yet when or whether we will have to march to Meerut, or maybe on to Delhi, but we must be ready, and the purpose of this meeting, gentlemen, is to establish the earliest timetable for our movements.

'First, the commissariat. How long would you require, colonel, for all the baggage wagons to be ready, the elephants, the camels and so on?'

Heads swivelled on wrinkled necks towards a short, stout colonel in the middle of the group, his soft stomach pressed against the polished mahogany rim of a billiard-table.

'It is impossible to say, general,' he replied frankly.

'It may be *difficult,* colonel. It cannot be impossible. We must have a date.'

The colonel swallowed, bit his lip with rabbity front

teeth and looked down at the smooth green surface of the table. Everyone knew that, eleven years earlier, in 1846, after the First Sikh War had proved prohibitively expensive to the East India Company, the directors had cut down drastically on their army transport.

They had thus avoided the gigantic cost of maintaining hundreds of elephants—for one elephant could easily eat a ton of hay a day—and thousands of camels and bullocks and mules, when they were scarcely ever needed.

Some ingenious accountant had proposed that, instead of maintaining these ravenous animals, they should sell them. Then, in any emergency, they could commandeer from local contractors and farmers elephants for the heavy guns, camels for baggage, and mules and bullocks to pull the carts of food and ammunition. This proposal saved the Company thousands of rupees and completely emasculated the striking power of both their armies, in Bombay and Bengal.

That morning, the commissariat colonel had ridden round the district to try to find enough animals for the convoy—known as a 'train'—but without any success at all. They had all been marched away through the night to stockades up in the hills where their owners would keep them until the emergency was over.

'How long would you need then, colonel?' asked Anson.

'Say a week, sir.'

General Anson's A.D.C., using a card-table as a desk, began to write on a sheet of paper bearing the Bengal Army's crest.

'Ammunition?'

A tall major to the left of the room replied.

'The warlike stores are all on the Frontier, sir, nine hundred miles away.'

A murmur of dismay rustled through the room. The army kept their reserve stocks of ammunition in the Delhi Magazine, or near the North-West Frontier. They feared a surprise invasion by Russian troops through Afghanistan, and stood prepared for that contingency.

As the questions rattled on, the answers became more and more depressing. The special wagons heavy enough to carry the ammunition to Delhi when it arrived, if it arrived, were seven days' march away.

No tents were stored in Simla, because the troops there were quartered in barracks.

The heaviest guns available were six-pounders and nine-pounders, useful against some mountain fortress made of mud, but barely capable of splintering the walls of the Red Fort.

Some British regiments had twenty rounds per man; others, only five; others, none at all. There were no carriages for the staff officers, no litters to carry the wounded, no hospital supplies of any kind. Everything for a mobile fighting force was missing.

In addition, they would have to round up camp followers, such as civilian grooms, men to cut down acres of grass for the elephants and camels and horses at every night stop, *bhistis* to carry water, sweepers to dig latrines, and make arrangements for their families to follow them. An army of ten thousand fighting men needed as many as thirty thousand camp followers, plus their women and children, trudging on behind, with all the problems of health and feeding that this entailed.

'So what is your estimate, gentlemen, for the earliest which we can be on the march?' asked Anson.

'At least three weeks, sir, to be ready in all respects, a proper fighting force,' said the adjutant-general.

Three weeks, thought Lang in dismay. That would take them into June. He was to be married in June. *Oh! Arabella, where are you? Are you safe? Have you written? And do you love me?*

'The monsoon, sir,' said Hodson. 'It will break in five weeks.'.

'What of that, Mr Hodson?' asked Captain Birdwash.

'It *could* be important,' said Hodson. 'It will be impossible to move in the monsoon.'

'You are always a pessimist,' snorted Birdwash. 'A few rounds over their heads and we'll show these niggers a thing or two.'

'That may well be so. But if we cannot get within range of these niggers, then we can show them nothing.

'The present basis of three weeks before the men are ready to move, and one week on the march, will give us one more week to deal with the matter before the monsoon breaks—and stops all further action for five months.'

Some of the other officers nodded agreement. When the heavens opened and the rains fell, the few tracks along which they could march would become roaring, streaming rivers. Paddy fields, now hard as rock after months of sun, would become porous bogs and slippery morasses buried beneath feet of water. Horses would stumble on hills, and carriages would slither and slide and turn right over. Men would have to be harnessed to the guns to drag them up slopes that had become mountains of slime.

'Right, gentlemen,' said Anson, not committing himself. 'Any questions?'

'Yes, sir,' said Hodson. 'I would suggest sending a reconnaissance patrol to Meerut to find out exactly what the situation is there. Both with regards to Indian intentions, and our own.'

More murmurs of agreement.

'I'll go myself, willingly,' added Hodson.

'Very well,' said Anson. 'You shall.'

'I would like to take Mr Lang, since he has just come from Meerut and knows the people and the place.'

'When would you leave?' asked the adjutant-general.

'At dusk. Tonight.'

'You have my permission,' said the general magnanimously. This poor devil Hodson might find some sort of glorious death in Meerut, and that could solve a lot of problems. On the other hand, he might even bring back a few nuggets of information, and this could solve others. Either way, Anson could only benefit.

'I'll appoint you assistant quartermaster-general, Mr Hodson,' Anson announced grandly, 'and I suggest you increase your Intelligence Department by one hundred horsemen, who can scour the country for news, and fifty infantry sepoys for general duties.'

'Very good, sir,' said Hodson.

Anson nodded, well content. The appointment cost him nothing, and no one could ever accuse him of not doing his utmost to make a rapid appreciation of the situation. By his decision, he had foiled all possible future criticism.

After the conference, Hodson sought out Lang.

'Sorry to involve you in another long ride, but I would value your company and your introductions. We'll set off in an hour. See you have a fresh horse, and we'll each take a spare. On the way I'll call on the Maharajah of Jhind and raise the hundred horsemen from him. He knows which side his bread is buttered. Then we should be in Meerut in time for breakfast. Travel light. I need not tell you how long seventy-odd miles can seem in the saddle.'

'I know already,' said Lang wryly.

At eight o'clock, the grooms had eight horses ready, four saddled, the others running light on leading reins. If one horse went lame they would simply turn it loose and ride on without it. They vaulted into their saddles. Hodson looked ungainly on his huge grey horse, his hair bleached like flax, his blue eyes narrow as he mentally calculated their chances of reaching Meerut.

'Ready?' he asked.

'Yes.'

'Then—here we go.'

They set off at an easy canter, Hodson in front leading his second horse, Lang behind him, because the road was not wide enough for four horses to go abreast, then his bearer and then Rajib Ali.

Lang kept twenty yards to the rear, just clear of the dust cloud thrown up from the hooves ahead. Soon dust settled on his uniform and his face, clogging the pores like a heavy mask, drying his lips, forcing its flour-like way up his sleeves and under his collar, to rasp against his sweating arms and neck.

Ten miles up the road, the clatter of hooves ahead dwindled to a trot, and then stopped.

'The maharajah's palace,' said Hodson.

They turned off the track, along a path several feet above the dried-up paddy fields on either side. A lamp glimmered in the window of a guard-house. An old man came out with a stake, to inquire into their presence.

'Two British officers to see His Highness urgently,' Hodson hold him in Hindusthani.

The man shambled away on his bare flat feet. They rode after him, up to a single-storey house with a square pillared porch. A storm lantern was hanging in it from a piece of wire. A middle-aged man, stocky, with broad shoulders and a springy tread, came out and peered up at them in the dim light. Lang could smell the jasmin oil in his hair. He had a smooth, soft, well-fed face.

'Is it Hodson sahib?' he asked.

'It is, Your Highness,' said Hodson. 'We are riding to Meerut. You have heard of the trouble there?'

The Maharajah laid his head on his left shoulder, signifying he had heard but did not wish to comment.

'I need a hundred horsemen,' said Hodson.

'One hundred men and one hundred horses,' said the Maharajah musingly. 'It is a bad time to diminish one's own forces.'

'If you delay,' said Hodson bluntly, 'they may be diminished for you. It may be that the sepoys who have revolted in Meerut will also revolt against the landlords who keep their families poor.'

'You speak wisdom,' said the Maharajah. 'It is as the Lord Buddha says, "Even though a poem be a thousand words, if they are senseless words, one word of sense is better, which, if a man hears, he becomes quiet." '

'You have heard my words of sense,' said Hodson. 'I will assume you will send the men to Amballa at dawn tomorrow?'

'You have my hand.' Hodson gripped it.

'God go with you,' said the Maharajah.

They wheeled their horses back on to the track. The night was thick; the stars had not yet come through the clouds, and Hodson rode by compass bearing. The only sounds were the creak of the horses' bridles, the rattle of bit chains, the occasional grunt of a horse breaking wind. Now and then one of the spare horses on the outside would whinny and neigh and try to rear up.

'Wild animals,' explained Hodson laconically. 'This is tiger country. We're all right if we don't stop.'

The road entered a narrow gorge, with a cluster of mud huts with glimmering lights in window-holes. Then a shout and the crack of a musket, and their horses were rearing up.

'Charge!' roared Hodson, and whipped out his sword. A handful of men with staves and muskets fled away to escape their thundering hooves. A scream of pain from one, a cry of alarm from another, and they were through the ambush.

'Do you think they were mutineers?' asked Lang.

Hodson shrugged.

'More likely to be thuggees. They lie in wait for travellers, like our highwaymen fifty-odd years ago.'

The moon was coming up the sky now. Lang relaxed his tense muscles so that he sat easily like Hodson, letting the horse do the work. His eyes were pricked with dust, the inside of his nostrils so dry he had to breathe through his mouth—and then the dust made him choke and cough.

They were coming to familiar landmarks; a well by the roadside; a black flag marking the grave of a holy man; a garland of flowers in a secret shrine. Then they were in the outskirts of Meerut, going faster because they were almost safe.

They reached the officers' mess and dismounted. There was a new roof on the mess now, Lang noted. And great efforts had clearly been made to tidy up the building. A bearer in mess uniform lay asleep on the floor behind the bar. Hodson shook him awake.

'Two baths,' he told him. 'And then two breakfasts. Then tell the adjutant sahib Mr Lang and Mr Hodson are here.'

After their baths, they sat down at a long mess-table, and ate a breakfast of coffee and toast, with bacon and eggs. Other officers, including Brigadier Wilson, crowded round them.

'Now, sir,' said Hodson to Brigadier Wilson, pushing away his empty plate. 'What message can I take back to General Anson?'

'The Sixtieth Rifles are setting out today,' said Wilson.

'Why the delay, sir? General Anson will want to know.'

'We have had to draw ammunition and extra kit. Then a lot of our horses and mules were stolen. We had to find others. It has not been easy.'

Gradually, the whole pitiful story of delay and indecision filtered out.

'The Lord made the world in six days,' said Hodson dryly, 'and rested on the seventh. We have lost our world in six hours—and we are still resting.'

Wilson did not reply.

'What do you propose to do now?' he asked, changing the subject diplomatically.

'Make my own appraisal of the situation and ride back with Mr Lang tonight—if I have your permission. I could use him in the Intelligence Department. General Anson has ordered that it is to be increased immediately.'

'By all means. He was only posted here because his own regiment was disbanded.'

'Riding a hundred and fifty-odd miles in two nights!' Gough exclaimed in amazement.

'Your arithmetic does you credit,' Hodson told him. 'What else do you suggest? That we stay here indefinitely?'

'I wasn't suggesting anything,' said Gough. 'I was just surprised.'

'I am surprised, too, that it should be necessary,' said Hodson sadly. 'For months, I have been collecting Intelligence reports from agents throughout India about the possibility of some such insurrection as this. So that we could prepare for it. But no one paid any attention. . . .'

'I will make out a report for you to take back to General Anson,' said Wilson, standing up.

'Well,' said Hodson, smiling for the first time as he looked around him after Wilson had left. 'Here we all are. The telegraph wires cut, north, south, east and west. Not a soul can interfere with us. We have the cracking of the nut in our own way, and we are as jolly as a bug in a rug!'

The others looked at him in amazement and then at each other. They did not realize that, for the first time in many months, Hodson was experiencing an inner peace within himself, as all his frustrations dissolved in the elixir of action.

It was four o'clock by the watch on Lang's bedside table when he awoke. Hodson was still asleep. Lang could hear his bearer and Rajib Ali talking in low tones on the veranda.

'What sort of man is your master?' asked the bearer, 'who is still a lieutenant and so old? Why do you stay with him?'

'Because I admire Hodson sahib, not for what he has done, but for what he will do.'

'You could get greater riches elsewhere,' persisted the bearer.

'The pursuit of great riches is not the main goal in life,' answered Rajib Ali. 'Let me remind you of the day when the Prophet Mohammed, with only three hundred men, met an infidel army ten times the size at the foot of the Uhud Mountain outside Medina.

'The Prophet ordered his few archers to stand high up the hill, and they poured down such a rain of deadly arrows that the heathen were on the point of flight. And they *would* have fled and been defeated, had not the archers suddenly left their posts and come down the hill.

'They deserted their duty because they feared they might not have their share of the bounty after victory. So there was no victory—and no bounty to share. That is a lesson to learn, my friend. Blessed is the man who stays at his post. Rich is his reward. In this world and the next.'

'You speak wisely,' said the bearer, with respect.

'I speak truth,' said Rajib Ali, smiling. 'And truth is always wisdom. Even for infidels.'

Lang shook Hodson gently.

'It is almost time to leave,' he said.

Hodson was instantly awake, and swung himself out of bed. The bearer brought in two china teapots of tea with the familiar thick cups emblazoned with John Company's crest.

'Any *dak* for me?' Lang asked him.

'No, sahib. Not even one letter.'

'You are *sure?*'

'Certain, sahib. Not for you. But for Gough sahib, two letters came from Delhi last night.'

Lang took a drink of tea to hide his disappointment, but it was too hot and made his eyes water. Not a letter from Arabella, and the post was still functioning. The only explanation was the one he did not wish to admit; that she had not written. A patch of sadness began to spread through him. He tried to shrug it away, and busied himself with telling his bearer what kit he needed, but it stayed.

The heat had already left the day and the sun was falling behind St John's Church when they saddled up. Brigadier Wilson handed Hodson his report in an envelope sealed and stamped with his signet ring. Hodson buttoned it into his message pouch, and saluted.

'See you in Delhi,' called Gough.

'In Delhi,' repeated Lang.

'Soon,' added Hodson, and with a backward wave they were off.

The little crowd stood watching them until the blue dusk swallowed them up.

15

Six o'clock in the morning, nine hundred miles south and east, Calcutta sprawled untidily on the banks of the Hoogly River.

The *ricksha* wallahs trotted with empty *rickshas* from the huts and hovels where they slept on straw, ready for their first customers. Such was the humidity that offices opened almost as soon as the sun came up. Within hours, the effort of crossing the street would bring a European's body out in a rash of sweat. Ladies would rest in shuttered rooms under creaking flapping punkahs, and only venture to drive in their splendid carriages along the Strand in late afternoon, when most of the heat had drained from the day.

A bugle brayed outside the whitewashed guard-house near Government House. Sepoys in scarlet uniforms, with pipe-clayed belts and gaiters, sprang to attention as Lord Canning, the Governor-General, a slightly built man, thin and ascetic, walked from his private quarters along the marble corridor to his office.

He nodded a salute to them as they stamped their feet, unlocked the door of his office with his own key and sat down on the high-backed blackwood chair behind his mahogany desk. Another day of bad news; of reports of unrest among Indians and indecision among his own countrymen. His face wrinkled with distaste at the prospect as he tinkled a hand-bell for his personal clerk.

The room was cool now, but through the horizontal slits in the wooden shutters the light outside was brighten-

ing steadily, lighting up the dark red dispatch cases, the
piles of papers on side tables. Parakeets were calling from
their nests in the colonnades round the courtyard. The
Governor-General's personal bearer nodded to the punkah
wallah who put one foot in the loop that made the tapestried punkah move above the head of the most important
Englishman in the east.

An A.D.C., incongruously wearing a frock coat, salt
and pepper trousers with loops under the insteps of his
patent leather boots, came in and bowed.

'What is the latest situation?' asked Lord Canning.

'Very grave, sir.'

The news of insurrection at Meerut had not surprised
Canning; what did surprise him was the astonishment of
the military at it, because for several months he had been
reading Intelligence reports of drums beating their urgent
messages along the Grank Trunk Road, of dyed chappa
ties, blazing arrows and the fears of the sepoys that their
religions were being threatened.

He knew the strength of Indian superstition. When he
had arrived in Calcutta to take up the post of Governor-
General, he had tripped on a step and nearly fallen. He
could hear the sigh of alarm; this, so many watchers felt,
was an omen of ill to come, a weakening of British
resolve, a sign of approaching trouble. And, judging from
what had happened since, they had all been right.

He walked round his desk, until he faced the map of
India that almost completely covered one wall of the
room. A scale hung at one side and a pencil was suspended from a long black cord so that he could make rapid
calculations about distances.

Days earlier, Canning had been awakened by an orderly
bringing him a telegraph message with news that the
sepoys had mutinied in Meerut, set free the prisoners, and
then marched to Delhi, which apparently they now controlled. He did not know whether they occupied the Magazine with its prodigious store of ammunition, and in the
absence of definite knowledge to the contrary, he had to
assume they did. It was always prudent to presume the
worst; then any good news came as an unexpected bonus.

His sharp eyes under their puckered brows moved from
one familiar name to another; Delhi, Agra, Dinapore,
Lucknow, Cawnpore. None held any comfort for him.

They were almost all without British troops or with totally insufficient numbers. In the seven hundred miles that separated Calcutta from Agra, there was only one British regiment—less than a thousand men, many of whom had been in India for ten to fifteen years, and having seen no action in this time, had no stomach for it now.

Cawnpore had a garrison under old General Sir Hugh Wheeler, known to be a gay dog on the dance floor, with a love of the polka and the lancers—but what would he be like in action? In any case, he was relying on the local maharajah's friendliness towards the British; or, at worst, his neutrality. And, in the event of trouble, would Nana Sahib be either friendly to the British or even neutral?

Another single British regiment was supposed to control the twelve hundred miles between Dinapore and Meerut, where the insurrection had started. They could be massacred in a single night; and perhaps they already had been.

Canning suffered from migraine, and as the bright morning sunshine drove burning spears of light at him through the shuttered slats, he could feel the hated pain and nausea returning.

If only he could call on young men with drive and initiative who would act before it was too late! Everyone in command in India seemed elderly and affected by heat, claret or a generation of inertia, and sometimes by all three.

'Everything depends on Anson,' he told the A.D.C., thinking aloud. 'What's the latest message from him?'

'He needs three weeks to move, sir.'

'Three *weeks!* But that's ridiculous! There may be no English left alive in India in three more weeks, unless we act. What possesses the man pray?'

'His dispatch is here, sir. He says he has no tents. No litters. No ammunition. No carts to move them when he has ammunition, which incidentally is being fetched from the frontier, nine hundred miles away.'

'My God!' said Canning. 'All negative replies. Is the telegraph line still open to Amballa?'

'Yes, sir.'

'Then pray send him a most immediate signal to move *at once*. Sign my name to it.'

'I understand, sir, that Sir Henry Lawrence is also urging General Anson to march to Delhi.'

'Delhi is the whole key to this insurrection. Capture Delhi speedily and I wager resistance will disintegrate. Can't these military men understand this basic principle of history?'

'It has been explained to them sir, in your earlier messages.'

'What about the disposition of other British troops?'

'We have already sent telegraphs, sir, to Bombay and Madras and to Ceylon, urging them to release all available British troops immediately for Delhi. Then there's Lord Elgin, who is leading the China Force. He's on the high seas.'

The Chinese had unwisely seized some members of the crew of a British merchant vessel in the Canton River and inexplicably refused to release them. Lord Elgin was on his way with troops to teach the Chinese the basic lesson that British subjects, however humble, could not be treated in this way without inviting retribution. Sound as this intention was, Lord Elgin's men could now be better employed in India. But how to get in contact with them?

'Are they under sail, or in steamships?' he asked.

'Both, sir.'

'Then they should stop at Singapore to take on coal?'

'It is possible, sir.'

'I will draft a message to Lord Elgin today, ordering him to return. You commission the fastest light steamship you can find in the Hoogly River. Give the captain the course and bid him overhaul his lordship. What is the situation elsewhere?'

'In Calcutta, sir, as you know, nearly all the men are wearing pistols when they go to their offices each day. We have already disarmed the sepoy regiments without any trouble. It is now just a question of wait and see. The mass of the Indian people, I suggest, sir, will want to be on the winning side.'

'Of course,' said Lord Canning. 'If I were one of the mass of the people, Indian or otherwise, I would entirely share those views. But will there be a winning side in this dispute? Perhaps there are rights and wrongs on both sides? We must never lose our sense of proportion. Remember, we are dealing with people who believe we have deliberately offended their religious susceptibilities. Imagine our own feelings in England, if some black race from over the sea descended upon us and demanded we change our ways immediately.'

The A.D.C. said nothing. The idea was so far-fetched that he could think of no reply. He did not altogether approve of Lord Canning's liberal views, for which his lordship was already being nicknamed Clemency Canning in the local newspapers. Like the mass of the people, the A.D.C. also wanted to be on the winning side.

'A number of Europeans have already left the city. They've locked up their houses, dismissed their staffs and taken ship to Madras or Ceylon, or even Rangoon.'

'I'm not surprised, either,' said Lord Canning. 'But our duty is here, Percival. We shall stay. And we shall prevail.'

'Yes, sir.'

The young man bowed, picked up the sheaf of papers and left the room. The old boy was in good form today, but were they all living an illusion?

How could a few thousand British troops put out the flames of rebellion in a country covering one and a half million square miles, and containing at least a hundred million people?

'Ram Gupta has arrived,' announced Nana Sahib's butler, bowing low before his master.

'Let him enter,' said Nana, picking a crystallized date from a silver tray.

As Ram Gupta stood to attention before the Maharajah, the uncomfortable thought crossed his mind that he was growing so used to violence and evil deeds that they were beginning to mean as little to him as the luxury of this palace, which had awed him when he had seen it first, but which now he took for granted.

'What news do you bring?' Nana asked him, licking sugar off his fingers.

'I have been to Delhi as you requested, Your Highness. The sepoys have seized the Red Fort and the Palace. The telegraph operators have disappeared. The type in the *Delhi Gazette* was broken up. The bank has been burned down.'

'So. And what are the British doing meanwhile?'

'They appear to be like a chicken with its head cut off, wandering about bewildered, hither and yon.'

'That is unlike them,' said Nana thoughtfully. 'They are a cunning people. I have offered General Wheeler, who commands the troops here in Cawnpore, security for all women and children, and I have even placed some of my own men at his disposal. I wish to appear above conflict, and only interested in securing peace.'

'And, of course, your rights,' said Azi Mullah, who had entered, silently as ever, in his soft sambur skin shoes. 'You are surprised by the inaction of the British, Your Highness? I am not. Individuals, like nations, act as they have always acted. That is the main lesson of history. And, apart from a handful of positive characters, their national characteristics are inefficiency, sloth and indecision.'

'I would not entirely agree,' Nana replied. 'Crises in their past have thrown up new leaders. That is also a lesson from their history. Afterwards, these men may wither in obscurity. But only after they have served their purpose.'

'General Wheeler is certainly serving *our* purpose,' said Azi Mullah scornfully. 'He has a perfect fortification in Cawnpore. But instead of using it, he is now frantically having a new one made, which he has sited in an indefensible position. It is nothing more than an earth wall a few feet high and thick, like the beginnings of a mass grave.'

'I have promised that he and all the English community here will be safe,' interrupted Nana Sahib sharply.

'I know, Your Highness. But sometimes, as you truly say, events throw up new leaders. Perhaps if this fever spreads, other leaders may not honour that promise. They may not even know of it.'

Nana felt uneasy. At first, Azi Mullah's plea for judiciously fermenting some controllable disturbance and then suggesting to the Company that he could subdue it, if his own wish for a pension was granted, had seemed ingenious and impossible to fault. But now he doubted its wisdom; nor was he so convinced that it would be successful.

His main hope now was to steer events into a course that could help him by keeping Cawnpore calm. Then, should Azi Mullah's scheme fail, his apparent steadfastness to the British must surely bring him some reward.

* * *

Outside Delhi, the Ridge was as crowded as Epsom Downs on Derby day.

Ladies filled the honeycomb of tiny rooms in the Flagstaff Tower, which had never been intended to house more than a handful of visitors, and then only temporarily.

Wearing unlikely clothes—cotton shifts, long evening dresses, sometimes even only nightgowns with shawls about their shoulders for the sake of modesty, anything they could find in a hurry—they had crowded into the Tower, desperate for shelter and news of their families, all social differences temporarily forgotten in their anguish.

Mothers, whose children had been in the care of Indian ayahs, begged others for news. Women, whose husbands had been away from home on Monday morning, waited in the hot, foetid rooms, not knowing whether they were wives or widows.

Brigadier Graves, with a handful of British officers, kept urging calmness in a situation which he assured them was already all but over.

'General Hewitt's men will be here before dusk,' he told them. But dusk came, and then night, but there was still no sign of General Hewitt's men.

They shivered through the hours of darkness, too cold to sleep, except fitfully, starting up uneasily at the incessant whine of mosquitoes and the croak of bullfrogs.

Where *were* the British troops? What had happened to the messages telegraphed to Lahore and Amballa?

As dawn came up on the desolate scene, many people asked the questions, but no one cared to give an answer.

South of the Ridge, in the Red Fort, the King of Delhi had also experienced an uneasy night. That morning, he needed two opium pills to calm his nerves, and even then the breakfast pilaff lay heavy on his stomach.

It was one thing being King when the British were in control, and he could blame any inaction or dilatoriness on them. It was another entirely to be on his own in this vast, ancient and uncomfortable palace, with not one person near him on whose integrity he could completely rely.

To Bahadur Shah's astonishment, sepoys who only hours before had approached him with such awe that they were tongue-tied in his presence, had grown so accustomed to being close to their King, that they treated him as an equal. Some even tapped him on the shoulder as though he were a buffoon. Because they were younger and stronger and taller than him, their friendly pats rocked the old man on his withered heels, so that he stumbled and often would have fallen had not others held him upright.

Finally, since he could not keep them out of his palace, he kept himself in his own room, and would only allow courtiers to enter when he could personally identify them from their voices.

The palace possessed no lavatories, and dozens of sepoys always seemed to be squatting to defecate on staircases and in corridors, and the stench of their dung and urine, with the everlasting buzz of flies, made the Royal apartments smell like a sewer.

Now his Chamberlain came to see him in a great state of alarm.

'Your Majesty,' he explained. 'Your palace is virtually taken over by sepoys. They are demanding to see you.'

'We have nothing to say to them,' said the King, using the Royal plural because he was angry.

'They ask how are they going to be paid? They have been used to regular pay under the British authorities.'

'Then they should have stayed under the British authorities. We have insufficient money in our treasury for our own needs, let alone for them. What sort of folly is this, that we are expected to *pay* this rabble?'

'I have told them of the depleted state of your treasury. They reply that, with you as their leader, they will bring the revenue of the whole British Empire into your treasury.'

'Madness,' said the King. 'They talk with the tongues of fools.'

'I fear that their present mood may grow ugly if you do not humour them.'

'We are old,' said the King. 'What would you have us do?'

'I have a royal elephant outside with its mahout and a howdah. I suggest that you make a progress around the Fort. They like a show of royalty. If you continue to sit in your apartment, some disaffected persons may say that you fear to go abroad.'

'Then we will make a progress,' said the King. 'In the meantime, where are my sons?'

'They have taken over command of regiments, Your Majesty.'

The King gave a wry smile. This was the first work these young men had ever done. He wondered how they would cope, how long they would hold their new commands.

'We will go forth,' he said.

Two royal trumpeters, who had been waiting outside Bahadur Shah's apartment, sounded a fanfare as he walked slowly down the steps. Other trumpeters, standing on either side of the main gate, wheeled into line and repeated the call. A royal elephant, tusks sawn short and tipped with gold, toenails painted with gold lacquer, bearing a crimson and gold howdah on its back, knelt humbly before him as he approached.

The crowd roared excitedly: 'Zindabad! Zindabad!' This was how they imagined a King should be. Not a little old person shuffling about, to be physically looked down on, but a man riding high on a Royal elephant, towering above them, superior and unapproachable.

Secretly the old man hoped that the British would not be too long in reasserting their authority. As with many old men, he found the sheer exuberance and health and vitality of younger people both frightening and depressing. He had been old before they had been born; he would die before any of them grew old.

Servants in uniforms of scarlet and gold, their turbans aglitter with jewels, ran forward in step, carrying a small ivory ladder, the rungs bound with scarlet leather lest the royal foot should slip.

'Oh King, live for ever!' intoned the Rhapsodist. 'May your shadow ever stay tall, and your power remain as the sun at noon.'

The King climbed into the howdah and seated himself on the cushions. Then, carefully holding the rails of the howdah as the elephant stood up, he bowed stiffly (because he suffered severely with arthritis) and the animal moved forward behind the trumpeters and men beating drums.

He hated elephants; their swaying motion, the sweaty

dungy smell of the huge uncomplaining beast, and all the voices of the crowd braying at him.

The progress moved slowly around the walls of the Fort, and then, suddenly, the shouting died. Blocking their road was a crowd of fifty English men and women. Their clothes were torn, and some were barefoot. The women's hair was unpinned, and streamed down over their shoulders. The hems of their long hot skirts were brown with dust, their blouses ripped to shreds, some stained with dried blood. Around them all, ringing them in like a giant lasso, was a tight hemp rope.

The men were unshaven, their lips cracked and dry, but they bore themselves defiantly enough, shoulders back, looking the old King in the eye. The shimmering sun beat down on their bare heads.

'Look at the sahibs now!' called a havildar exultantly. The King looked, but uneasily. The English had long memories. They would not forget this humiliation, and was it really necessary to have the women tied like bullocks?

'How long have they been here?' asked the King, not addressing the captors directly.

'We have kept them in cellars,' a guard explained. 'We have just now let them out for air.'

'What harm have we done to be bound like beasts here, huddled in cellars for a day and a night, with no water, and then tied up like animals for sale in a market?' asked one of the men. 'I appeal to Your Majesty to set us free.'

'Be silent!' shouted another sepoy, and hit the Englishman across the face with a pistol. He staggered back at the unexpected ferocity of the blow, and the whole group moved a pace and almost fell.

'There was no need for that!' called another Englishman angrily.

This time, the sepoy fired and hit the second man in the chest. The bullet passed through his body and hit an Indian standing near him. Both men staggered and fell dead.

'Stop!' shouted a woman. 'For God's sake, stop! We've done you no harm!'

But the crack of the pistol, the smell of the sweat of fear, the Englishman and the Indian falling, compounded a catalyst of anger. Other sepoys drew pistols or raised carbines and fired into the mass of captives without even taking aim. The rope held as men and women crumpled to their knees or folded forward over it.

Forty-nine corpses were bound together by a rope.

Only one woman was still alive, frantically tearing herself out of the rope and the dead embrace of those about her. She flung herself on the ground in front of the King's elephant.

'I will become a Moslem! Anything!' she shouted. 'Only do not kill me!'

'Take her away,' ordered the King. 'See that she has instruction in the faith and that she keeps her vow.'

He felt physically sick at the sight of the massacre. Their screams kept echoing and re-echoing down the tired tunnels of his mind.

'We will proceed,' he said hoarsely. The mahout dug in his sharpened goad, and the elephant lumbered forward.

The King shut his eyes. The sun was so hot now that it burned redly through the lids, and he saw again the bodies falling, the blood running. There was no one in whom he could confide. Captain Douglas was gone; so was Colonel MacDonald, both no doubt dead. He was an old man, and alone, left at the centre of events he could not control, and with which he had no wish to identify.

Fear tightened its fingers round his heart. How long could he survive, a puppet prisoner in his own palace, controlled by his own people?

16

Peshawar.

Nicholson let the two Indian agents into his office and locked the door behind them.

'You have done what I told you?' he asked the first man. The question was purely rhetoric. Everyone did what Nicholson told them.

'Yes, sir. We have examined all the letters going to our troops at the sorting office at Attock, and all the incoming mail from the regiments to their families here.'

'You have copied any relevant passages, with the names of the sepoys involved?'

'Yes, sir.'

'Give me the copies.'

They handed over a leather case.

'Thank you for your help,' Nicholson said, dropping it into a drawer in his desk. 'You will be rewarded.'

They bowed, he unlocked the door and let them out. He glanced at his watch; ten minutes to six in the morning.

He called his adjutant to him.

'Please give all the commanding officers my compliments and ask them to see me here. Now.'

'Some may be taking company orders, sir.'

'They can take company orders *after* I have seen them.'

He sat down in a cane chair behind his desk, tapping his finger tips on the blotting pad, and waited impatiently for the colonels to arrive.

'What is the meaning of this summons?' asked the first commanding officer, a man of sixty-five, bald, with a huge walrus moustache and white sideburns down to his collar. He did not like Nicholson; why, the man was thirty years his junior. Also, he was taller.

'I regret its urgency, gentlemen,' Nicholson replied, ignoring the question. 'And I would not have you think me discourteous in asking you to see me at such short notice. The fact is, the gravity of our situation increases hourly.'

'What exactly do you mean by that?'

'As you know, Delhi is in the hands of the insurgents. I mean, bluntly, that if we do not act here immediately, we will also be overwhelmed by the sepoys in your regiments.'

'Then you must be either singularly ill-advised or medically insane, sir,' retorted the colonel. 'I have served with these men for forty years. They are as loyal as you or I.'

'I would agree with that,' said another colonel.

'So would I,' agreed a third.

'Then I must disagree with you, gentlemen.'

Nicholson opened a drawer and the brief case, and dropped the sheaf of letters on the desk before them.

'This correspondence is from your troops to and from others in their villages. It was intercepted on my instructions. I have had extracts copied, with the names of the sender or recipient attached to the copies. Read them for yourselves.'

He pushed them over the desk and sat back in his chair.

'My God,' said the first colonel in amazement. 'Here are all the details, and the *date* on which they aim to take over my regiment.'

'*All* your regiments, gentlemen,' corrected Nicholson.

He looked at the officers' faces, wrinkled with distaste, as they pushed the letters back to him.

'I do not like your methods, sir,' said the colonel.

'Desperate situations demand methods we would normally abhor,' agreed Nicholson. 'As Commissioner, I must ask you to disarm your regiments at the earliest possible hour.'

'I cannot do that,' said the colonel. 'They are soldiers. It is too great a dishonour for them to be disarmed.'

Nicholson looked from one to the next. All looked back at him, stony-eyed.

'No more discussion, gentlemen,' he said. 'The troops *will* be disarmed. Those are my orders, and I must have them obeyed.'

Silence, save for the heavy breathing of the colonels, the creak of their belts as they turned round to look at each other in horror and disbelief.

'When do you propose to inflict this—indignity, sir?'

'In one hour,' said Nicholson. 'I will have British troops out on either side of the parade ground, in case there is trouble. I will also make arrangements for the news to be passed on to every surrounding village. All the tribal leaders are waiting to see which side is going to win. As a result of this action, they'll come out for us.'

And as Nicholson rode out to watch the parade an hour later, it was as he had forecast. Grey-bearded chieftains, with crafty faces and cunning eyes, rode up to salaam him.

'You have only to speak, sahib. To ask is to receive,' one assured him unctuously.

'I asked for your support yesterday,' Nicholson replied shortly. 'You did not promise it then!'

'Ah, yes, sahib,' the chief replied, grinning. 'But yesterday was—*yesterday*. Today, things are—*different*.'

Nicholson smiled to himself and rode on.

The disarming parade passed without incident, but some of the British officers felt so ashamed at being forced to disarm sepoys with whom they had served for so long that they threw their own swords into the artillery wagons along with the firelocks and carbines. Others tore off their spurs and threw those in, too.

Nicholson rode back to his office. Such displays of emotion did not touch him. He felt just as deeply as they did, but his mind, like a camera obscura, saw the whole picture of anarchy that could develop, while they only saw part of it, and that but dimly. As he dismounted, an orderly ran up and faced him excitedly.

'Colonel Spotteswoode's killed himself!' he said.

'Come into the office,' said Nicholson curtly. 'Never let the natives see you feel any alarm.

'*How* has he killed himself?' he demanded when the door was closed.

Colonel Spotteswoode had commanded the Fifty-fifth Regiment at the Fort of Multan, forty miles away. Only a few evenings previously, he had dined with Nicholson, and thumped the table in his vehemence, stressing the loyalty of his troops.

'His regiment mutinied, sir. The colonel felt that he was somehow to blame. He had given you his word they were loyal. So he took his own life.'

Again, this was an action that Spotteswoode's brother officers would view with sympathy and respect; he had died as he had lived, a gentleman. But to Nicholson, suicide was a mark of ultimate defeat and failure. By killing himself, Spotteswoode had solved nothing. By staying alive, by facing his problems, he could have overcome them—and been an example to others.

'Where are the mutineers?'

'They've taken all the money and the ammunition from the Fort and have fled towards Multan into the hills.'

'Right,' said Nicholson. 'I want a new horse and whatever British troops you can get—quickly.'

'It will be very difficult to find more than a company.'

'Well, find a company. And always remember this. Difficulties argue for themselves. They need no advocate in you.'

Nicholson ate breakfast while his bearer folded a few spare clothes in a bedding roll, and the groom saddled up his grey charger. It was half past seven, and the sun was moving up the sky. A British colonel arrived as he was finishing his coffee.

'I have information, sir, that you wish to advance on Multan?'

Although Nicholson had only reached the rank of lieutenant in the army, there was something about his physical presence, his hard piercing eyes, the impressive hypnosis of his personality, that made his seniors call him sir. He never argued with them or dissuaded them from this mark of respect.

'That is true,' he agreed; for it was.

'It is a long march.'

'That is also true, colonel. But if we let these mutineers escape, they will spread rebellion throughout the whole Punjab. We have to break them while we can.'

'My men will be ready in an hour, sir.'

'I'll see you in thirty minutes,' Nicholson told him. And in that time the colonel's company of infantry waited outside, the colonel at their head. Two majors, irritable at what appeared to be a wild ramble through the heat of the day, fumed about on their horses. Nicholson nodded in salute, jumped on his charger and led the march.

At ten minutes to each hour they halted, and the troops lay down in whatever shade they could find, took off their packs and put them under their feet, sweating in the baking heat. The officers dismounted and walked about stiffly, trying to restore circulation to their limbs.

During these halts Nicholson stayed on his charger, shoulders hunched, mind miles away up in the burning hills with the mutineers, consumed with irritation at what he considered totally unnecessary delay.

He knew quite well how unfit the British troops were; how used they had become to bearers carrying their equipment, and he held no sympathy for this soft attitude of mind and body. They were soldiers, and as such their task was to march hard and to fight hard; just as his was to subdue these mutineers speedily, and before the cancer of disaffection could spread uncontrollably.

At dusk they camped in a dried-up nullah, lit their fires and cooked some beans and brewed pannikins of tea, and slept in their uniforms, while sweat dried on their bodies and mosquitoes buzzed around their necks and wrists, and red ants crept into the laceholes in their boots, and up under their sleeves, biting their sweat-softened, salty flesh.

An hour before dawn, Nicholson had them all awake. A breakfast of tea and hard biscuit, and they were on their way again. By afternoon, they had reached the foothills, dried brown volcanic earth devoid of shade and vegetation, naked like the bared backbone of the world. The rasping rock cut the infantrymen's boots, and those unfortunates in charge of the six-pounder guns, drawn by horses, cursed as the iron-tyred wheels struck sparks from stones, and the guns reeled dangerously from side to side.

The men were weary now, sobbing for breath, uniforms open at the throat, red coats dark with sweat. One or two had developed stomach trouble through dropping out of the line of march to drink from a polluted well or tank. Diarrhoea ran down inside their trousers. Their companions cursed them, for they stank, and blue-bellied flies buzzed greedily around the fouled cloth.

'How long, do you think, before we see the mutineers?' asked the colonel.

'I would say by tomorrow. Why?'

'My men are tired, sir.'

'Then your men are in bad shape. Why is it that in all these years of peace you have had no manoeuvres and forced marches, no living off the land to toughen them up, to prepare for action like this?'

The colonel had no answer.

The men were beginning to mutter and grumble among themselves now. Nicholson. That big bastard. All right for him, riding his bloody great horse, while they were slogging along. What he wanted was a bullet up his arse. He heard the mutterings and ignored them. This scum was as much a danger to its own side as to the enemy. He despised them as much as they disliked him. He was not, therefore, unprepared when, on the following morning, the colonel sought him out.

'I am sorry, sir, but we have a number of cases of sickness, and the sergeant-major reports that the men are unwilling to go further.'

'So they are mutinying, too?'

'I wouldn't say that, sir.'

'I *am* saying it. Your men are not only sick in body, colonel, they are sick in mind. Well, if they won't come on with us willingly, I will not take them at all.'

'You mean, you'll go yourself, sir?'

'I'll certainly not ask for their unwilling company, colonel. You had better lead your sick men home.'

'Well, then,' said the colonel awkwardly, 'I will bid you farewell, sir.'

'I will bid you *good-bye*,' said Nicholson, and rode off on his own. The thought that he had already lost unknown hours on the journey through their halts, infuriated him. The fact that he was now on his own in hostile country did not enter his calculations. On the outskirts of a village he saw a native policeman on horseback, and called out: 'How many men have you got in your force here?'

'Twenty-five, sahib.'

'Are they loyal?'

'Of course.'

The man appeared surprised.

Nicholson was relieved. He had arrived before rumours of mutiny had reached this remote spot. The mutineers must have fled past without stopping, desperate to reach a defensible position before any pursuers could overtake them.

'Any other troops in the area?'

'A squadron of Multani Horse under an English officer, sahib.'

'Please be so kind as to give your own commandant and this officer my compliments. And ask them to meet me here as soon as possible.'

'And *you* are, sir?'

'John Nicholson.'

'Of course.' The man's voice dropped in respect. 'I have heard of you.'

He spurred his horse away. Within minutes, he was back with his commandant and a British captain.

Nicholson explained the situation.

'Are you with me?' he asked.

'Absolutely, sir.'

'Then we'll ride as soon as you are ready.'

That night they camped half-way up the mountain. They were awake before dawn, and in their saddles while the sun was still trembling on the rim of the horizon.

At eight o'clock, they saw the rearguard of the mutineers toiling up the hill ahead of them.

'Charge!' shouted Nicholson, waving his sword at the head of his force.

The horsemen and police galloped behind him over the iron rocks. The sepoys turned and saw them and dropped to the ground to take up firing positions, but before they could press their triggers, Nicholson's men were on them, their blades flickering like windmill sails in a summer sun. The mutineers had no time to fire. They were killed as they lay, facing downhill, musket stocks tight against their shoulders.

Nicholson's men dismounted, cut the ammunition pouches from the corpses, seized their muskets and pistols, tied them on their horses, and rode on up the hill after the others.

The main body of mutineers had split into three groups, each waiting in a separate nullah. In the centre nullah, the mutineers had planted the regimental colours. The flag flew stiff as a board in the morning breeze.

'You take the left, captain,' said Nicholson. 'I'll take the centre with ten men, and you, commandant, handle the right.'

The Multani Horse and the policemen wheeled away.

'Charge!' shouted Nicholson again, and laid his bloodied sword over the right shoulder of his horse.

The sight of his huge charger, foaming at the mouth, the drum of its flashing iron-edged hooves, leading ten swordsmen, was too much for the mutineers. They broke and ran.

Those on the left and right saw that the colours had been deserted. They also turned and fled, stumbling on huge boulders, slipping on loose stones, frantic to escape. They were ridden down, pounded to pulp under the thundering hooves. A few went down on their knees, threw away their weapons and, with hands in the air, begged for mercy.

Down and up, down and up, went the avenging sword blades. The ground burned hot as an oven grill. Blood dried on the baking rock as soon as it was spilled.

By late afternoon, apart from some who had flung away their arms and fled, all were dead, dying or had surrendered. Nicholson formed them up in four ranks with a colour party to carry the regimental flag. Then he set off back to Peshawar.

'How many do you think we killed, sir?' asked the police commandant.

'I have counted one hundred and fifty bodies,' Nicholson told him dispassionately. 'I would think that as many more have escaped or crawled away to die. And we have taken a hundred and twenty prisoners. We shall reach Peshawar tomorrow.'

'But that's seventy miles away.'

'I know,' said Nicholson. 'We'll have to make them march quickly, won't we?'

Crowds were out in the dusty streets to watch the strange procession return. The prisoners, hands bound behind their backs, some barefoot and in rags, others still in

full uniform, stained with sweat and blood, shuffled along
wearily like a slave gang, heads down, jaws hollow, chins
unshaven.

Brigadier Cotton, the senior British officer, was waiting
for Nicholson.

'I never thought you'd do it,' he said admiringly.

'Neither did they,' said Nicholson laconically, meaning
the mutineers and the other British officers.

'What will the punishment be for these men?'

'Death,' said Nicholson. 'We'll blow the lot away from
guns.'

'Good God!' said Brigadier Cotton. '*All?*'

'No, not *all*,' said Nicholson, thinking again. 'Some of
them are very young and easily led, and the Sikhs, so I
understand, were loyal until the very last moment. I therefore suggest we temper stern justice with mercy, and spare
the Sikhs and the younger groups.'

A message to this effect was sent to John Lawrence,
who entirely agreed with its sentiments.

'I would not put them all to death,' he replied. 'I do not
think we should be justified in the eyes of the Almighty in
doing so. I suggest we destroy a third to a quarter of
them.'

So, the next day, forty men, the unfortunate third, were
bound across the mouths of cannons, pointing out over
the empty waste towards the hills where they had fled.

The entire garrison was drawn up on three sides of the
square in full drill order, and thousands of spectators rode
in from outlying hamlets to see forty men launched into
eternity at a single word of artillery command.

'A terrible day,' said Cotton in Nicholson's office that
night. He had aged years in days. His voice was hoarse.
His skin had yellowed like parchment.

'To think that all my years of work in this country and
the years of service these men have given us should end
like this—bound double across a cannon mouth and
blown into whatever heaven or hell they believe in.'

'I take your point,' agreed Nicholson. 'But our concern
now is not what has happened, but what more we must
prevent from happening—worse massacres, worse mutinies.

'Thousands of villagers rode in today simply to see

whether we would punish these men severely—or whether
we would just talk about doing so. Now they'll ride back
to their villages with one answer. And what they have
seen will not lose in their telling.

'We have killed forty men, agreed. But these forty
deaths will save hundreds, possibly even thousands of
other people who will think twice now before they rebel.
Before this they would not have thought at all.'

Cotton said nothing. What Nicholson said was true; but
the truth had been bought at a terrible price.

Calcutta.
Lord Canning sat on his desk in Government House.

The punkah creaked above his head and moths fluttered
their trembling wings blindly into the pale globes of the
oil lamps.

Why wouldn't Anson *move?* How could he *still* be
stuck in Amballa, sending his absurd excuses to Lawrence,
that he had no transport, no litters, that his guns were too
small? General Sir Henry Barnard was also supposed to
be gathering a force at Amballa. But he was another old
officer who had served without any distinction in such
diverse places as Canada, Jamaica, Corfu and in the Crimea. And having only arrived in India less than two
weeks previously, he had no knowledge whatever of the
country or its problems.

Across India, from shore to shore, little pockets of
revolt were flickering like phosphorous flames in the forests of the dark. Only decisive action could put them out
for ever. Action like that taken by Nicholson in Peshawar;
and, in Lucknow, by Sir Henry Lawrence, from whom he
had just received a report.

Lawrence had placed a guard of one native officer and
sixty sepoys on the Residency, and when he heard a rattle
of muskets from mutineers in the cantonment, he ordered
his men to load.

'Now,' he told them, 'I am going to drive those scoun-
drels out. Take care while I am away that you all remain
at your posts, and allow no one to do any damage here,
or enter my house, *else when I return I will hang you!'*

Such was the strength of Lawrence's character and the
effect of his words that the Residency was the only house

not pillaged or burned that night.

But what use were one or two men of resolve among hundreds of officers who were feeble and supine? Oh, for a young man to lead the march on Delhi, for whoever held Delhi, ruled India. The mutineers controlled Delhi, and every day that passed, every hour lost through British indecision and inertia, strengthened their hold on the city—and, therefore, on the country.

Oh, for leaders who would *lead,* instead of finding soft, self-convincing excuses for inaction! Lord Canning pushed the papers away from him with almost physical distaste. The river of time was racing past them; and all they could do was stand on its banks and watch the tide go out.

General Anson put down his morning cup of chocolate and wiped his mouth with his silk handkerchief. His A.D.C. stood at his right hand, holding a sheaf of telegraph forms in a folder.

'Well?' asked Anson resignedly.

'They are from Lord Canning, sir, and Sir Henry Lawrence. All are marked "Most Immediate." '

'Pray read them to me. I do not have my glasses.'

'From Lord Canning, sir. He urges you, and I quote, "to make as short work as possible of the rebels who have set themselves up in Delhi." He says, "Allahabad and Benares will continue to be a source of anxiety until Delhi is disposed of." '

'I concur,' said General Anson, swirling his cup to spread the sugar more evenly. 'The only question that worries me, which does not seem to worry his lordship, is *how* are we "to make as short work as possible" of them? We have no transport, little musket ammunition, almost nothing for the guns. And still no litters for the wounded. No matter. What is the next signal?'

'It is from Sir Henry, sir. I quote. "Delhi would open its gates at the approach of our troops," he says. "Pray only reflect on the whole history of India. Where have we failed when we acted vigorously? Where have we succeeded when guided by timid counsels?" '

'Again, I entirely agree,' said Anson enthusiastically. 'But it is one thing to talk, and another to act. What is the spirit among the civilians here, in Amballa, and in Simla?'

'There's been some panic in Simla. The Gurkhas were said to be disaffected and their colonel ran from bungalow to bungalow, shouting, "Fly for your lives! The Gurkhas are upon us!" '

'Silly fellow,' said Anson. 'They have been loyal for thirty-nine years, these Gurkhas. Why should they attack us now?'

'The same could be said for the Indian regiments, sir.'

'Possibly. But the Gurkhas? Never! What is our present state of readiness to march?'

'Another two weeks, sir.'

'That means we will have been three weeks preparing to move, as was forecast. Twenty-one days. Slightly over half the time Our Lord spent in the wilderness. Well, we cannot just wave a wand and send men marching to Delhi simply because telegraph messages urge us to do so. We are doing the best we can. Reply along those lines. But show me the messages before you send them.'

'Yes, sir.'

'Anything else?'

'Your chief of staff would like to see you, sir.'

'Pray show him in.'

Colonel Whitehead entered the room, tall and lean, suffering as usual from his stomach. He had joined the staff from Barrackpore; he had an idea to put to the general concerning that outsider Hodson.

'There is some feeling in the mess among certain junior officers regarding Mr Hodson, sir. They feel that his ride to Meerut was, shall I say, rather theatrical. Especially Captain Birdwash. I believe there is some personal animosity between these two officers.'

'Well, what of it?'

'Hodson did well in the Guides, when they travelled light. You have already authorized him to increase his Intelligence Department considerably. I would like to suggest, sir, that you authorize him to raise a band of irregulars—a light regiment, if you like.

'We will be two weeks yet *at least* before we can march. But they could go as soon as they are ready. It would show initiative and be a great example to the other commanders. It would also rid us of Hodson.'

'You do not like him, colonel?'

'Nothing personal, sir. He is simply not my sort of person.'

'I can believe that. Possibly he feels the same way about you—or me, for that matter. I like your idea. I think it is capital. If this regiment of his comes to nothing, well, at least we have tried, and that will count in our favour. Now, what about General Barnard's problems?'

'A rather difficult situation, sir,' admitted the colonel. 'We have brought in a regiment from the hills with all the camels and mules for their immediate requirements. But now the beasts have had to go back to fetch their guns and ammunition. I remember, at Barrackpore . . .'

'Never mind that. How long before they return?'

'Possibly a week, sir.'

'And *then* Barnard will be able to move?'

'Yes. So long as fresh ammunition has arrived from the Frontier. Otherwise, he will have to march with only twenty rounds a man. An afternoon's firing and his men are disarmed.'

'Then we must wait,' said Anson. 'And when all is ready, *I* will lead the column to Delhi. And send Mr Hodson to me immediately.'

'Very good, sir.'

Anson sat back in his chair and pared his nails with an ivory letter opener. It was wonderful how a cup of chocolate pulled one together, for he had not been feeling too well recently. All these ridiculous requests to hurry, as though he was not fully aware of the need for speed, had ruffled him. He had also been suffering from headaches, and his water had a strange odour. Perhaps he was sickening for something? He would have a word with the sawbones.

Mr Hodson was announced.

'I am impressed by your clear assessment of events in Meerut, Hodson,' Anson told him, in his smooth way. 'It seems to me that we need to apply new and possibly even unorthodox methods to deal with a totally new military situation.

'Accordingly, I am empowering you to raise a body of men—all good riders, to travel light, as I understand you travelled in the Guides. Then you will ride to Delhi with them and put them at the disposal of the British Commander, Brigadier Wilson, from Meerut.'

'How many men am I to engage, sir?'

'As many as you need.'

Anson did not want to give an exact figure. The Treasury would no doubt quibble about the cost, and it was always wiser to delegate an awkward decision to a junior, who could not avoid the responsibility.

'In that case, sir, I will form a regiment. My own regiment of horse.'

'Hodson's Horse, in fact!' said Anson with a smile.

'Thank you, sir. Now, what about weapons?'

'You know the position there as well as I do, Hodson. You will have to do the best you can. As for money, I will give you an advance from the imprest account. You can take it in cash at your own responsibility. But I ask one thing. You must be ready to move at the earliest possible moment.'

'I can give you my word on that,' said Hodson. They shook hands across the desk, and Hodson went out in a daze of astonishment and delight.

He galloped back to his bungalow, hoping that Susan would be sitting on the veranda crocheting, or reading the latest copy of *The Times*, which was only three months old; but the veranda was empty.

He clapped his hands, and the bearer came out through the bead curtain.

'Where's *mem?*' he asked.

'She is not well, sahib. She is in her room. I have made her some lemon tea. Will you have your tea with her, or outside? Alone?'

'Alone,' said Hodson.

He went into the sitting-room, took off his cap, loosened his jacket and tiptoed into the bedroom. Susan lay face turned towards the wall, away from the window, even though the curtains were drawn.

'Are you awake?' he asked gently.

'Yes, Willie.'

'I have some news,' said Hodson, picking up one of the wicker chairs and turning it round and sitting down with his elbows on the back. 'They've asked me to raise a regiment, my own regiment, to march to Delhi. The chance I have waited for ever since—the Guides—ever since—before . . .'

'Before Olivia's death,' she said, finding the words he

had not wished to utter. 'I am very pleased for you, Willie.'

'We will be all right at last. They are advancing me money. I will settle up all our debts before I go. You will be able to afford another doctor now.'

'I don't want another doctor. There is nothing wrong with me.'

Nothing, he thought, that another child could not cure. But there would never be another child. No medical aid could help his wife, because doctors only treated the body and not the mind; and yet he sometimes felt that the mind might have some bearing on physical ailments. Perhaps, one day, doctors would also specialize in its diseases? He stood up.

'You have the pain again?' he asked.

'Yes,' she said. 'It's the sun. I'll be all right later on.'

'Would you like a Seidlitz powder, or some soda water?'

'Nothing,' she said. 'You have tea and I'll join you at sundown. And I'm glad for you about this appointment, Willie, I really am.'

He stood up, and put a hand on her bare shoulder. The skin felt chill to his touch; cold, like a dead child; like Olivia.

He went out again on tiptoe so as to make as little sound as possible, and sat down and poured himself a cup of tea, pondering on their life together. Marriage should be like a mirror, he thought. Each partner should reflect the other's moods, magnifying the joys, minimizing the discord.

Instead, he felt like someone sending urgent light signals through the darkness, but no one answered from the other side.

'We've had a hundred volunteers already, Mr Hodson,' said Lang.

'And I've told *no one* about it, but you,' said Hodson delightedly. And, of course, Susan, he thought. But then she didn't count. 'Let's have a look at them.'

They came out of the mess, down the steps. The men, who were squatting in the scanty shade of the trees, stood up and bowed.

'Salaamaji,' they murmured.

They were of all ages, from adolescents to old wizened fellows with faces gnarled like roots, and hair white as duck-down. Sikhs with black beards and turbans; Moslems in pantaloons and pointed slippers with turned-over toes; shaven Hindus with curved swords in their belts. Some had brought their own horses and others had arrived on foot. Hodson stood on the bottom step, his arms folded, head and shoulders above the men, surveying them.

'I am empowered to raise a regiment of horse to travel light and fast to Delhi,' he told them. 'You know already that some of your countrymen's regiments have mutinied at Meerut and elsewhere against their British officers. These mutineers—loyal soldiers one day, heads turned by false and lying rumours the next—have marched to Delhi.

'Mutiny, as you know, is the gravest offence in any army, and deserves but one punishment—death. But to combine mutiny with the murder of helpless civilians, of women and children, is too terrible to talk of, so I need not speak more of these things.

'I tell you now that the regiment I raise has but one aim—to seize Delhi, and to punish these mutineers and murderers. I tell you this now so that those who are not with me can be against me. But no one rides with me who does not have this cause as his. So let anyone who is in any doubt, depart from hence. We wish him no ill.'

Hodson paused. One or two men on the edge of the crowd bowed, touched their foreheads in salute and moved slowly away across the burning *maidan*.

'Don't you think they will tell the other side what we are up to?' Lang asked Hodson in an urgent whisper.

'Of course,' replied Hodson. 'And the more rumours they spread the better. They will lose nothing in the spreading.'

'Well,' he went on, 'are your minds made up?'

'What are the terms of service?' asked a man in the front rank. He was about thirty-five, with gold rings in his ears, and white teeth and flashing eyes.

'In money, ten rupees a month, payable at the end of each month. If you die in action, your family will receive a pension.

'All horses will be valued, and if your horse is killed, we will pay its value to you. But we can offer more than money. We offer you the chance to join a mission of right and justice.'

'Will there be any loot, sahib?' the man asked to an approving murmur and a vigorous nodding of heads.

'That is not for me to say,' said Hodson. 'Remember that the things you call loot were once the possessions of ordinary people like yourselves. I promise you nothing, but a hard ride and a chance of action. Are you with me?'

'We are with you, sahib.'

'So it is agreed. Mr. Lang sahib and I will test your horsemanship. If you pass our test, wait on the right of the *maidan*, and we will send a clerk to take your name, and form you into squadrons.'

He turned to Lang.

'I have asked for two of the jungliest horses in the lines. I'll take one. You have the other. Then we'll divide these recruits between us. Let them ride to that tree and back. And accept no one who has not ridden before.'

An orderly brought out two unsaddled, frisky grey mares, each fifteen-three. One he walked over to Hodson, and the other he brought over to Lang, and stood, holding the reins.

Lang nodded to the nearest recruit. He came up, patted the horse on the back, and then leapt astride. The mare stood for a moment not moving, and then bucked left and right. She kicked up her rear legs and arched her neck, whinnying with rage at being ridden. The man catapulted off into a thorn bush. He picked himself up, and dusted his robes ruefully.

'Have you ever ridden before?' asked Lang sympathetically.

'No, sahib, but I need ten rupees a month.'

'Then you will have to apply to the infantry. Next one.'

The search went on all afternoon. By evening, they had eighty recruits. But next morning, instead of only a hundred potential recruits, the *maidan* was thick with men, and most of them were able to ride.

As Lang tested the last twenty recruits out of the thousand they needed, a man walked out from the shade of the trees and salaamed him. He was of medium height, with hennaed hair and beard, showing that he had made the holy pilgrimage to the sacred city of Mecca. He had a strong, hard face, a beak nose and carried an air of authority like a sword.

'Can you ride?' Lang asked him.

'I can, sahib.'

'What's your name?'

'Kadir Ali.'

'Prove your worth then, Kadir Ali.'

The man walked slowly and stiffly to the mare. The groom threw him the reins, smirking, expecting to see this stranger on his back in the dust within seconds. Kadir Ali brushed the mare's nose with the palm of his hand, patted her neck, and then vaulted on to her back. The animal reared and bucked, but Kadir Ali rode her as though he were a centaur, a physical extention of the horse. He cantered round in a wide circle, pulled up, turned the mare in her own length, then rode up to Lang, and stopped.

'You see, sahib?' he asked.

'I see, Kadir Ali. Can you write your name?'

'I will make my mark.'

Lang took out the notebook in which he had written the details of the recruits he had accepted.

Kadir Ali dismounted, waved the mare away to the groom, put a cross against his name, and took the single silver rupee, token of one day's service for the Company.

'Tell me,' said Lang, a sudden suspicion crossing his mind. 'Have you seen Mr Hodson?'

'Ah, yes, sahib,' admitted Kadir Ali. 'I saw Hodson sahib. But he would not accept me.'

'Why not?' Was the man a spy or a trouble-maker?

'You have a knife, sahib?' asked Kadir Ali.

'Yes.'

Lang took out his pocket knife and handed it to him. Kadir Ali opened the blade. With a swift, sudden stabbing motion, he dug the blade into his right leg, and then twisted it viciously.

'You're mad!' shouted Lang in horror.

'No, sahib. I have a wooden leg!'

And he roared with laughter, slapping his good leg.

'You have enlisted the only one-legged horseman in the army, sahib. But what need has a rider for two legs, when his horse has four?'

*   *   *

The sentries outside General Anson's house saluted, as Hodson rode in through the gates. He returned their salutes smartly, just as he punctiliously acknowledged the waves he now received from other officers who only days before had refused to bid him good-day.

Hodson dismounted, threw his reins to an orderly, and walked up the steps, his spurs clanking on the stone.

An A.D.C. hovered outside the double doors of the inner hall.

'General Anson is expecting you, sir,' he said.

'I know,' said Hodson, and brushed past him.

Anson was standing, back to the window, hands clasped behind him.

'You are ready to march, I hear?'

'Yes, sir,' said Hodson. 'My plan is to take the first day or so easily, and then to approach Delhi in a wide sweep, going through as many towns and villages as we can. That way we'll show the natives the strength of our forces, and the fact that we *are* on our way to Delhi.'

'Good,' said Anson approvingly. 'You have everything you need?'

'No, sir. We have little ammunition, and no fodder. But we have fifty grass-cutters with us, and we'll live off the land. With luck, we may meet some of the opposition.' (He liked India and the Indians; he could not yet bring himself to use the word 'enemy'.) 'And we'll take their arms and ammunition from them and use it ourselves.

'And there is one other thing, sir. The money you promised. To pay the men. And to buy information.'

'How much do you need?'

'Sixty thousand rupees,' said Hodson. 'In specie. I have two mules with panniers to carry it. It will be under my personal protection for the whole journey.'

Anson pulled a bell-rope. The A.D.C. entered.

'I want sixty thousand rupees in coin in sealed bags to be delivered to Mr Hodson immediately from the Government treasury. You will sign for it.'

'Very good, sir,' said the A.D.C., glancing sharply from one to the other. Sixty thousand rupees was a lot of money. And everyone knew about Hodson's debts.

'Then it only remains for me to wish you Godspeed and a successful journey. I will be following you down tomorrow with our, shall we say, more orthodox forces.'

Anson held out his hand. Hodson shook it. Anson's hand felt curiously warm and dry. Hodson looked at the older man closely. His eyes were dull and yellow, his face the colour of dried putty.

When he was alone, Anson turned towards the window. He felt oddly listless and heavy, and his clothes rasped against his flesh in a way he had never felt before. He must be sickening for something. The sawbones had prescribed pills of camphor and opium mixed with quinine and calomel, but they had not helped him. He did not put much faith in sawbones. In fact, the older he grew, the less faith he put in anyone, or anything.

Hodson rode out through the gates.

His horsemen waited on one side of the dusty track, half a mile up the road; a wild crowd of horse-thieves and horse-dealers, the younger sons of younger sons, eager to make money by the only trades they knew, riding and the sword.

They straddled mares, geldings, stallions. Some carried two swords by their saddles; others, muskets and huge pistols with elaborately carved stocks. Behind their saddles were rolled lengths of carpet containing a change of shirt, a pair of walking shoes, a strip of woollen rug to wrap up in when the nights were cold. Each saddle also had two thin leather straps or ropes coiled neatly on one side. These, Hodson knew, were to tie on whatever loot the riders could find.

They wore army caps or shanters, or woollen hats pulled down over their ears. Some of their horses had brasses that glittered like gold; on others, they were dull or even green with verdigris. They were a rough, bearded or unshaven lot, a regiment of freebooters, men without homes, names without addresses, drawn together by the common magnetism of adventure, and the prospect of riches.

Hodson rode up to the front of the column. Heads turned and nodded to each other as he went by; they trusted him; they would not ride south in vain.

'Are we ready?' Lang asked him.

'Five more minutes,' said Hodson. 'We are waiting for some money.'

'I should think that's the last thing we'd want, with all these ruffians.'

'No,' said Hodson. 'When you are as old as me you'll realize it's the first thing you ask for. If your superiors wish you to undertake a difficult task because they lack the character or ability to do so themselves, they'll pay *anything* to be relieved of their responsibility. It is not their money, after all. But once you are on your way, it is too late then to start asking for cash and conditions.

'We have a thousand men under our command. If any of them come to me and ask for an advance of pay and I have nothing to give him, what kind of commander will they think I am?

'And, for my part, Richard, I can pay my own debts. I think that is ironic.'

'I think it's wrong to pay your debts out of this money,' Lang told him.

'I would only borrow the money,' Hodson assured him. 'It's the custom of the country. You will have heard of Lord Combermere, who used to be commander-in-chief here?'

'Yes. He captured the fortress at Bharatpur a few years ago?'

'Correct. And, as a result, he and his men shared four hundred and eighty thousand pounds in prize money. The sepoys drew four pounds each. Lord Combermere took sixty thousand.'

'What did he do with so much money?' asked Lang in astonishment; he had never thought of soldiering in such commercial terms.

'He gave it to a banker,' said Hodson drily. 'And lost the lot. Moral, Richard, never trust bankers. If they *really* knew anything about money, they'd make their own. Trust yourself, and your own judgment, and seize your chances as they come.

'Now here comes the money. Let us seize it before these ruffians guess what is in these boxes, and then—to Delhi!'

17

Twenty-seven women huddled in the stone-walled room at the heart of the palace. One small window opened on to a corridor, and the room stank with the salty-sweet smell of too many women who have been crowded together for days.

Several women crouched on the filthy floor, skirts fouled with blood and faeces, hands pressed into their stomachs, retching and groaning with the paroxysms of dysentery. A space along one wall had been cleared, and six or seven children lay on dirty straw. They were all ill, eyes gummed with pus, their skins dry and feverish, lips cracked. Two or three women sponged the brows of the children from time to time, with a square of muslin dipped into a canvas bucket of yellowish water.

Three times a day, their Indian jailers slid back the double bolts on the door and allowed the women and children out to use the latrine. This was simply an open hole in the ground, buzzing with blue-bottles, encrusted with dung, and spattered with blood from menstrual flows. They had no paper or rags to wipe themselves and tore strips of linen petticoats or blouses.

Apart from the foul physical conditions, and the food—one bowl of rice and a tin mug of brackish water twice a day—they suffered from the crushing weight of defeat. One moment they had been in their houses with servants and *ayahs* for their children, and a whole, safe, predictable life stretching ahead—promotion for their hus-

240 JAMES LEASOR

bands, bridge parties, regimental dances, church-going, and now—what?

They hated the physical proximity of the Indian guards, with their black, oiled bodies stinking of jasmin, and their huge white teeth ringed red with betel nut juice. They did not realize that, with their pale sweaty skins, their drooping breasts under dirty bodices and their own stinking bodies and unbrushed teeth, they appeared equally unattractive to the guards.

Mrs Todd lay in a corner of the room, face turned away from the rest, knees drawn up, touching her elbows in a foetal position, her hands across her eyes. In this way she could blot out the sights and smells around her, the coughing and retching of the children, the complaints and groans of the ill.

She was thinking of her husband; wondering where he was. Somewhere on the way to his office, or leaving it, he must have been killed.

Now that she was on her own for the first time since she had left Lichfield—no longer surrounded and protected from reality by bowing servants, a cook who only needed to be given the menus for each day's meals—she could think. And she realized that she had not thought deeply since she was a girl. What was she doing in India? She had never really liked this strange, alien existence on the other side of the world from where her heart would always be, but she had adapted to it, accepting her role in a society with strata as rigid as rock formations. And now that it all was crumbling about her, she admitted for the first time that this was not her way of life, and it had never been, and never would be.

She had been pressurized into marriage by a widowed mother with five other children to support, and George Todd—dear George—had seemed so dependable, so loyal, so trustworthy, that she had escaped from poverty through him. These were excellent virtues for any man, but were they sufficient foundations for a marriage? To share your life physically and emotionally with a man with whom one had really nothing in common except basic humanity?

She was thirty-seven and they had had no children. That side of their life had never really been very satisfac-

tory. Of course, women had to submit; the rumours she
heard about Indian women enjoying the act of connection
were, no doubt, exaggerated. And yet. . . . Perhaps, with
someone else, someone more imaginative, not primarily
concerned with his batteries and cables and volt-meters,
even that secret unmentionable part of their life could
have been different; exciting, even stimulating.

She had a pain in her head that beat like a hammer,
and she was thirsty. When she looked at her face and her
tongue in a sliver of mirror someone had picked up on
the road to the Fort she saw her tongue was coated with
white mucus, and brown around the edges. She was ill;
she had some fever. But then they were all ill. Two
women had died and been carried out, and at least one of
the children, already in a coma, would never last the day.

Mrs Todd struggled up and leaned against the wall. Arabella dipped her handkerchief in the bucket and wiped
her forehead.

'You're very hot,' she said.

'I have a fever,' said Mrs Todd. 'You don't mind if I
call you Arabella?'

'Of course not.'

'Yet we've never really been introduced,' said Mrs
Todd, the rigidity of social customs binding her in like a
steel corset.

'I can't think of a better introduction than fighting together on a rooftop.'

'Perhaps you're right. What do *you* think is going to
happen, Arabella?'

It was a question they all asked each other every day,
over and over again; it always produced the same answer,
the only answer: 'I don't know.'

'If they keep us in here for another week, we'll all get
the fever and die.'

'I don't think they'll allow that. We are too useful to
them as hostages.'

'You are,' said Mrs Todd. 'You are young and pretty. I
am useful to no one.'

She began to sob, her thin shoulders shaking helplessly,
tears rolling down her yellow cheeks. Arabella smoothed
her hair. It felt brittle, like wire.

'I have been thinking,' Mrs Todd continued. 'About my

life. If I had it over again I wouldn't come out to this
stinking country. These foul black niggers, always out-
numbering us. This uprising was bound to happen. Like
sitting on Vesuvius. It had to blow up one day. Last Sunday was the day.'

'Nonsense,' said Arabella. 'British troops will be here
soon from Meerut. It's less than forty miles away.'

'Perhaps they are dead.'

'Nonsense. There are thousands of them.'

'And there are millions of Indians. If all the British
troops in the country fired every round they had, they
would kill thousands of Indians, agreed. But by sheer
weight of numbers they'd eventually be defeated. It's a
matter of arithmetic. Nothing else.'

'You're not well.'

'Of course I'm not well. I'm dying. And don't tell me
I'm not. I've never felt like this. I can hardly breathe.'

'I'll get you a drink.'

'No, thanks. I just want you to listen to me. You're
young, Arabella. Barely half my age. Don't waste your
life like me.'

'How can you possibly say that, Mrs Todd?'

'Because it's true. I only married George because my
mother thought he was *suitable*. What a word—*suitable*.
And there was no one else I'd met who wanted to marry
me. Not then, at least.

'Afterwards, I did meet someone, but that was too late.
I was already married.

'We've all only one life, no matter what the parsons
say. I've wasted my life with the wrong man in the wrong
country. Don't you do the same, Arabella. You're about
the age I was when I married George. It's so *easy* to make
a mistake. Don't, I beg of you, for you only regret it
once—always.'

'You need a doctor,' said Arabella, seeing Mrs Todd's
face glisten under a varnish of sweat. 'I'll get one.'

Arabella left her and began to beat on the door.

'Fetch a doctor! There's illness here. Fever! Pestilence!
You may catch it yourselves and die,' she shouted.

Bolts rattled on the other side of the door. It opened a
few inches. A sepoy, unshaven, thick lipped, thrust his
head inside the room.

'Less noise,' he ordered.

'Don't you talk to me like that. Fetch a doctor, I tell you.'

The man stared at her blankly, his eyes bloodshot and unfocused. He had been drinking for hours in the bazaar, and all he saw was a white face that receded and then approached him through a mist of hair.

'Get a *doctor!*' shouted Arabella again, pushing her face right into his to try and make him move.

'What is the trouble?' a man asked in English behind the sepoy.

A dark manicured hand came down on the sepoy's shoulder and moved him out of the way. Arabella was facing a man nearly six feet tall, beautifully dressed in white.

'*You!*' she breathed.

'Miss MacDonald. Arabella!'

'I did not expect to see *you* on the other side, Kalyan Singh,' said Arabella. 'You were so—friendly—before I left for England. And on the boat you were so eager to be friends again. You invited my parents and me to meet your relation, the Maharajah of Bithur. I am sorry to say that my mother will not be able to accept your invitation. She is dead. Murdered by your countrymen.

'I haven't seen my father since last Monday. I expect he is dead, too. As for me, I'd rather die here like all the rest than spend one minute under your roof.'

'I am sorry. Ugly things happen in the heat of passion, which are afterwards regretted by both sides.'

'If you are any better than a savage yourself, you'd find a doctor. Some of these women are dying.'

'I will try and find one,' said Kalyan Singh. 'But the palace here has been taken over by the troops. It is difficult to know who is in command.'

'Why? This *is* the King's palace, isn't it?'

'In name, yes. But in fact he is almost as much a prisoner here as you are. At present, we have something approaching anarchy. But that will change.'

'It will change when the British come from Meerut. They are on their way.'

'So I hear. But you must not overestimate the capabilities of your countrymen, considerable though they are.

JAMES LEASOR

We already have forty thousand Indian troops in the Red Fort and the city. We also have big guns that can pick off any attacking force when they are still miles away.'

'If only they had marched on Sunday, when this first started,' began Arabella bitterly.

'If only,' repeated Kalyan Singh. 'The two saddest words in every language. Yes, things could then have been different. But this is how things are now. We command the city, and soon we will command the whole country. And within months, maybe much sooner.'

The way he spoke, so sure, so certain, chilled Arabella. For the first time, she realized the extremity of her own danger. She swallowed, and felt her heart flutter like a bird's wings inside her.

'That doctor,' she said firmly. 'If he doesn't come soon, it will be too late.'

Kalyan Singh turned to the sepoy.

'Find a doctor,' he said. 'Quickly.'

'Ji, sahib.'

He was back within minutes with a fat Indian carrying a small black leather portmanteau.

'I want all these ladies and children examined and treated. And I want the sick ones moved.'

'Where to?' the Indian doctor asked.

'When you speak to me,' said Kalyan Singh coldly, 'you will call me sahib. Do not ask *me* where you will take them. *You* are the physician. *You* make your own arrangements. But they will be out of here within the hour. Or else you will be in a cell in their place. Do I make my meaning clear?'

'Perfectly, sahib.' The man ran into the room.

'You see,' said Kalyan Singh, turning to Arabella. 'We are not all savages, as you would seem to think.'

'I judge people by their actions,' she replied. 'But thank you for what you have done.'

'I will be here for two more days,' said Kalyan Singh. 'Shall I visit you tomorrow?'

'We have no alternative but to receive you. You are free to come when you please.'

'It would please me to see you tomorrow morning. Just to find out how the ill ones are faring, of course.'

'Of course.'

He bowed. The guard closed the door.

'Who was that Indian? A *friend* of yours?' a woman asked Arabella accusingly.

'Someone I used to know, and then met on the boat to Bombay.'

'What kind of doctor has he given us? More likely he'll murder us than cure us.'

'How can you say that? Just because he's an Indian?'

'It's just because these people *are* Indians that we are imprisoned here. You will be saying it is *our* fault soon.'

'Please do not be so absurd.'

'You would not call it absurd, Miss MacDonald, if your child had died like mine, in my arms, with nothing I could do to help him. *Nothing.* You would call that murder, and you would hate these black swine with their filthy habits and heathen ways.'

'I am very sorry about your child. I am also very sorry about my mother, and I expect my father, too. But *anything* we can do to help the living can only be good. Kalyan Singh has supplied a doctor for us. If he does nothing else, he has at least shown us some humanity.'

At that moment, Kalyan Singh was talking to the King. Bahadur Shah's personal servant had not brought him an opium pill that morning—he explained that his stock had been stolen—and the King's stomach was knotted with irritation at this obvious lie. He was trying hard not to listen to Kalyan Singh and succeeding tolerably well.

'Your Majesty, a number of Englishwomen and children are being held prisoner in one of your storerooms. Some have already died, others will die shortly unless they are moved. Their deaths do our cause no good. I seek your permission to move them to more commodious quarters.'

'You have our permission to do anything,' said Bahadur Shah irritably. 'Do whatever you think fit, Kalyan Singh, but leave us alone. We are old and we would seek peace.'

Kalyan Singh bowed his way out of the apartment, and went down the stairs and along the stinking corridors. Beggars were sleeping on straw palliasses or wrapped up in rags like corpses along the floor. Others were grilling strips of meat on skewers over small charcoal braziers. These hangers-on had crept in for shelter, and would be difficult and possibly dangerous to dislodge.

He picked his way over the sleepers until he reached

the cell door. Two sepoys stood outside with muskets.

'Open the door,' Kalyan Singh commanded.

The bolts slammed back. Kalyan Singh went inside the room. The smell of vomit and sweat and filth was appalling. He swallowed quickly to prevent himself retching, and held up both hands.

'Ladies,' he said in English. 'I have seen the King. You are being transferred to more commodious quarters.'

'When are we going?' asked Arabella.

'Within an hour. You have my word.'

'Thank you,' said Arabella. 'I speak on behalf of all of us here. We will remember this.'

He bowed and went out of the door. Then he paused and looked back at the squalor. But he did not see the dirt, the buckets of foul water, the blood-stained rags drying on a string stretched across the room. He only saw one girl looking at him.

Arabella.

'Are we ready to march yet?' asked General Anson peevishly. He had been feeling dizzy for days, and this had sharpened his temper. He also suffered from a stabbing pain in his stomach and spasms in his muscles. He was obviously sickening for something, but it would be nothing serious; he was sure of that.

This march to Delhi, then the attack on the capital, would be the crowning achievement of his military career. He would almost certainly be given a knighthood; it could easily be a peerage.

'The infantry are still falling in, sir,' reported Colonel Whitehead. 'I have given orders for the band to start as soon as the Fortieth Rifles are in position.'

'The sun will be up in two hours, and we have a five-hour march at least before we bivouac. Pray make the fall-in as swift as possible.'

It was the custom for British troops to march either through the night, or to start out before dawn and stop before noon. They thus avoided the pitiless heat of the sun which, burning down on them as they marched in heavy shakos and thick serge uniforms, with their furled greatcoats or capes rolled on top of their packs, caused collapse from heat stroke.

A bugle brayed through the dim mists of morning.

With a clatter of chains and bits and the grind of metal tyres on the long hill out of Amballa, the column moved forward. Gunners, riding the limbers, jumped down to wedge metal shoes beneath the wheels to give brake to the heavy gun-carriages. The shoes screamed on the stones, striking rows of sparks, and the horses pressed back into the shafts, arching their necks, veins like cords beneath their coats, as they strained to keep the limbers from running away with them.

Anson rode at the head of the column with his two aides. He felt as though he was watching the scene, not a part of it. He had never felt so ill before; his bowels burned with an agony within him. Occasionally, he winced and almost doubled up in the saddle, gasping with relief as the pain passed. His aides glanced at each other behind his back. What was wrong with the old man?

Back in the infantry columns, marching four abreast, rifles slung over their shoulders, heads down, minds switched off, the troops tramped through the dust. Officers rode at the head of each column; N.C.O.s marched behind, or to the left, everyone intent with their own problems, their own thoughts.

The rankers had spent the previous night drinking in toddy shops, and were nearly stupefied with liquor, many only held upright, as they staggered along in step, by the sheer closeness of their companions on either side. Very few were in condition for a hard march; almost none were alert enough to carry out an order quickly. They had grown so used to life in barracks and cantonments, to having servants—when, in England, they would have been the servants of servants themselves—that the prospect of hardship appalled them. Sullenly, sleepily, drunkenly, they reeled along.

Well to the rear came the long caravan of bearers, *bhistis,* cooks and grass-cutters, who at every halt would take their scythes and hack prickly grass for the elephants and horses and camels to eat. These camp followers, marching with their wives and children on donkeys or in carts, made no pretense of keeping in step, or even within the column, but dragged on behind, chattering among themselves, holding lanterns, more from fear of darkness than for the light they gave.

Down the hill, the column trudged to a sharp corner

that led over a bridge at the bottom. As the head of the
column slowed to turn and cross the bridge, the riding
sergeants shouted, 'Whoa!' but the infantry, half a hundred yards behind, half asleep, kept on marching. Orders
directed to camel leaders, elephant mahouts, and gunners,
meant nothing to them. They despised men who went to
war sitting astride gun barrels, resting their legs or travelling in carts and gharries.

Too late, an infantry officer saw the blockage ahead as
the leading limbers over the bridge had the brake shoes
pulled from under wheels, so that their horses could take
the strain of several tons of cannon and shells, and lean
into their harnesses to haul them up the other side.

'Halt there, I say!' called one aristocratic lieutenant. But
hardly anyone heard his voice over the tramp of feet
which had raised the dust so high that most of the column
was marching in a yellow fog through which the early sun
was only now beginning to burn.

Thus, the first four ranks of the infantry marched
straight into the back of the jammed limbers. Behind
them, hundreds of other men piled up, falling, cursing,
shouting. Other limbers, medical carts laden with bandages and drums of caustic, crowded behind them. One
turned over on its side, spilling carbolic acid across the
road.

Horses reared up at the commotion and confusion,
while those already pinned on the ground by the shafts of
overturned wagons, thrashed their legs furiously and
arched their necks in terror. Mahouts dug goads behind
their elephants' ears and charged off on either side, elephants trumpeting wildly, and pulling cannons that
lurched and crashed through bushes and saplings.

Anson, a hundred yards over the bridge and up the hill,
turned round in astonishment at the noise; the crash of
breaking shafts, snapping axles, the cries of men being
trodden underfoot. Hundreds of men milled about blindly
in the dust, not knowing exactly what had happened,
while riderless horses darted dangerously through the
crowds, and camels trod disdainfully over fallen bodies.

Colonel Whitehead galloped up to the general.

'We'll have to halt, sir. A limber was jammed on the
bridge, and those behind have gone into it.'

'Very good,' said Anson, as though it was. 'Get the matter sorted out.'

The sun was burning its way up the sky towards the dreaded hour of noon by the time the limbers had been freed, the elephants caught, and gharries and carts repaired. Fifty men had suffered broken legs or arms or cracked skulls, and they had to be carried ignominiously on makeshift litters to Amballa. The rest, suddenly sober, mouths dry, eyes pricked by the abrasive dust, skin sour and soft with sweat under their uniforms, marched on sullenly, Anson riding at their head.

Gradually, as the fever moved in his blood, the whole disgraceful affair appeared more comic than tragic. After all, no one of any consequence had seen the shambles. A few natives might have done, but they did not count.

They marched through the baking afternoon, to make up for time they had lost, and pitched camp thankfully at five o'clock. Anson dismounted wearily and stood while orderlies set up his two tents, one for work, the other as sleeping quarters with canvas chairs, a table, a bed, a wash bowl, and a metal bucket of water, warmed over a wood fire.

Usually, he would bathe and change and enjoy half a pint of claret, but now he was shivering; the thought of water touching his dry burning flesh made him shudder. He looked at his face in his metal shaving mirror; he appeared to be turning purple, like an over-ripe plum. His whole body was soaked in a foul-smelling clammy sweat. He pulled off his uniform and his shirt and drawers and crawled naked between the sheets of his camp bed. The sheets felt so rough that he might have been lying on sandpaper. He rang a handbell for an orderly.

'Give the surgeon my compliments,' he told him. 'Ask him to come here at once.'

Assistant Surgeon James Cartwright arrived at the double. He had never even spoken to Anson before. He was much awed and impressed by the size of the general's tent as he stood to attention in the doorway and saluted.

'Never mind that,' said Anson, speaking slowly as though the words did not want to leave his throat. 'I am ill. What is it?'

The surgeon had brought his bag of specifics: cinna-

mon, laudanum, tincture of soap, spirits of hartshorn, calomel, camphor and opium. He put the bag down on the
table and opened it before he examined the patient.

If he diagnosed correctly, and, more important, if he
could cure quickly, he might be promoted Surgeon of the
First Rank. Wild dreams fumed in his young ambitious
mind, and died instantly as he examined the general.
These were the symptoms of cholera: fingers drawn up
like hooks into the palms, eyeballs suffused with red lines,
the pulse low, and that fearful pain that came and went,
making Anson draw up his knees and press them in
against his stomach.

'What *is* it?' he asked, his voice already faint and far
away.

'It is the fever, sir. I will give you a tincture.'

He mixed a scruple of ammonia carbonate, half an
ounce of prepared chalk, one drachm of laudanum, two
of aromatic confection and seven ounces of cinnamon and
water.

'Drink that, sir.'

He motioned to an orderly to help him raise Anson up
on his bed, but the general was already so weak that he
could hardly swallow the scented mixture. It slobbered
down his chin, and he retched and vomited out some
whitish bile, and sank back groaning. The orderly looked
in alarm at the doctor, who did not meet his gaze.

'I am dying,' said Anson simply, as a statement of fact.
'Give General Barnard my compliments. Ask him to come
here.'

The orderly dashed away. Barnard was there within
minutes and took in the scene at once. He raised his eyebrows inquiringly at the surgeon. The surgeon nodded;
there was no need for words. They were all in the
presence of death.

'You sent for me, sir,' said Barnard softly.

Anson was lying back on the bed, the vomit still on his
sheets, his face pale, his breathing as heavy as though he
had been running uphill for a long weary way.

'Yes,' he said, not opening his eyes. 'I am dying, Barnard. You take command.'

'Very good, sir.'

Barnard drew back.

Anson moved his lips as though to say something else, then his jaw fell open loosely, and he died.

'What was it?' asked Barnard in an undertone.

'Cholera, sir.'

'Is it—catching?'

'Wash your hands in this carbolic, sir,' suggested Cartwright. He did not know the answer to this question. Some held it was contagious but not infectious; and this was no time to quibble on words.

'We'll have to send the body back,' said Barnard, rinsing his hands. His A.D.C. had appeared in the doorway. He turned to him.

'Unhitch a gun limber and get the carpenters to use some of the planks from one of the store wagons to make a coffin. Send the body back on the limber with a detachment. Be so good as to give my compliments to the Chief of Staff. Order him to arrange an escort with a field officer.'

The A.D.C. doubled away. The surgeon handed Barnard a towel.

'Cholera, you said?' the General asked musingly.

'Yes, sir.'

'Mm. You may put that down *officially* as the cause of death. But I don't think that was the *real* reason. General Anson was hounded from all sides to march on Delhi. What really killed him was a fatal attack of—John Lawrence!'

18

The British bugler sounded Reveille, and Gough, who had already dressed, came to the mouth of his tent, and turned his binoculars on Delhi.

The city slumbered barely five hundred yards away; mosques and minarets, the spire of St James's Church, small buildings with thatched or wooden roofs, and here and there, larger, square, white-washed houses on which black sooty streaks above open windows told their own story of arson.

The great city wall, thrown around the outskirts like a gigantic stone belt, seven miles in circumference, bristled with cannon, and as he watched, he saw more artillery being wheeled into position to repel an attack from any direction. A few fires were burning, as the mutineers cooked breakfast; the smoke rose straight as flag poles in the still, windless air.

Across the bridge of boats another company of Indian sepoys, wearing their best company uniforms of red jackets, with gaiters newly blancoed, buckles polished and winking in the sun like heliographs, were marching in by fours behind the brass band that went out to meet each new contingent. Incongruously, the band was playing, 'Cheer, boys, Cheer.'

Well might they cheer, thought Gough bitterly, for the so-called relieving force from Meerut had already been in position on the far (and safer) side of the Ridge for nearly three weeks. And in that time they had relieved no one and nothing. Worse, no senior commander had any plan, or even any feasible suggestions for recapturing the city.

Brigadier Wilson, in command of the Meerut contingent, had expressed his intention to wait for reinforcements.

His artillery commanders were reluctant to consume their meagre supply of cannon balls to pound fortifications so thick that they could only dislodge chips of granite or flake pieces of brick. They, therefore, gave it as their view that the recapture of Delhi was a technical matter for the engineers. The walls should be mined or the gates blown open by explosive charges. Tunnels could even be dug to come up inside the Red Fort so that the infantry could reach the enemy unseen.

But the Chief Engineer, a plump major in middle-age, married to a Persian girl of twenty, had other worries on his mind. So infatuated was he with this sulky, scented woman, that he had requisitioned thirty camels and fifteen mule carts to carry her belongings—mostly dresses, petticoats, boots, hats and silk parasols—from Meerut.

Her clothes, stored in racks his engineers had made from broken beams and rafters taken out of looted houses, filled several tents that ringed around the especially elaborate tent where she lived.

She was a sexually demanding woman and the major, old and enfeebled beyond his years, was incapable of satisfying her burning needs. Thus, even when he was not with her, she was in his thoughts, and any suggestions about burrowing mole-like beneath the fortifications to come out in the heart of the palace, received scant attention from him.

The infantry, of course, could not be expected to attack without cover of some sort, either of artillery or gunpowder bags to blow in the gates. So, everyone sat and waited; and every day the garrison they had come to subdue was strengthened by fresh reinforcements.

Although the British troops had brought what baggage mules, artillery elephants, chargers and camels the mutineers had in their haste left behind in Meerut, they had little forage for the animals, which died by the dozen. Now, as Gough scanned the scene of desolation and inertia, the bloated bodies of elephants and camels, grotesquely blown up by gas to three times their usual size, dotted the brown hillside. Here and there, they had burst. Foul, rotting entrails, thick as a man's thigh, spilled out to be fought over at night by packs of jackals, and picked over by vultures during the day, tearing with reddened beaks at the crawling mass of putrefaction.

The ground was too hard for anyone to dig graves to conceal these monstrous corpses—it was difficult enough to dig shallow graves to bury soldiers—so the smell of their giant decay hung in the air like poisoned fog.

Within an hour of sunrise, Gough knew, everyone would be plagued by swarms of blue flies buzzing from these corpses over their sweating bodies, settling on their necks and ears, even in their nostrils. By noon, when the mercury in the thermometers stood at a hundred and twelve degrees, and the ground baked and trembled in the heat, the troops would sit in their tents, for the Ridge had no shade. There they would wait until night, when, despite plagues of mosquitoes, the cooler air would not carry the stench of death so strongly.

Because of the hardness of the ground, no proper latrines could be dug and now, as he watched, troops in nightshirts or dirty vests and trousers, were squatting across the face of the hill. Indian sepoys did not use latrines in any case, but for the British, this crouching at stool was an unnecessary indignity, and the little pyramids of human excrement steaming in the sun added a further foul smell to the already corrupted air.

Gough went back into his tent. Every day they waited, more British troops died of illness. The causes of their deaths were variously ascribed to dysentery, heatstroke, or the all-embracing medical description: fever.

They died, for the most part, after days of agony, of retching until they had no liquid left in their bodies to expel; eyes sunken in their heads, flesh drawn over their ribs tight as parchment on a drum, skin turning blue. Many went blind or lost the power of speech, or became paralysed, unable to move hand or foot, and lay like living hulks until death released them. And with every death the force was diminished by a fighter, and the morale of those left died a little with him.

The Ridge itself was almost indefensible against any attack, but it was the nearest that the British could come to Delhi and still stay out of range of the mutineers' mus-

kets. The earth that covered it had been brought up by the
cartload years before to support a few ornamental shrubs
around the one large house it had boasted, belonging to a
local dignitary, Hindu Rao. The British now used this
house as an observation post.

The whole situation of besieged and besiegers seemed to
Gough as unreal as the day-to-day routine. Sir Theophilius Metcalfe's house, now looted and gutted, his priceless
library a mound of feathery black ash, with occasional
pages still blown past on the empty wind, had been surrounded by a thousand acres of parkland and orange
groves, all now stripped and derelict. His tennis courts
remained untouched, and some of the keener spirits among
the subalterns would enjoy an early morning or evening
game, with the risk of a splinter from an exploding shell
enlivening the set.

Between the river and the city, on a roughly triangular
plain of baked brown earth, cracked by ravines and
dried-up streams, choked with reeds and brushwood, stood
a handful of abandoned houses and burned-out bungalows. Nearer the city were the tombs of holy men,
mosques and other buildings and formal gardens, that had
once been lovingly tended, now nearly all destroyed.

Ludlow Castle, the home of Simon Fraser, the former
Commissioner of Delhi, was on a slight hill about half a
mile from the main Kashmir Gate into the city. The Kudsia Bagh, about three hundred yards from the wall of
Delhi, had been the imperial summer palace in the days
of the ancient Moguls. There, fountains had played and
tame cheetahs had been led on silver leashes, when nobles
gathered to enjoy the splendid luxuries of their time. Now
it was only an empty hollow shell; remnants of mosaic
glittered in gateways and arcades, and the long stone clois-
ters were framed with orange, lime and rose trees.

Between this ruin and Ludlow Castle, a hundred yards
from the city, Gough could see the Custom House, planted with as many European trees and shrubs as could be
found to give it as English an appearance as possible.
This, and all the other houses which only weeks earlier
had echoed with children's laughter, were now charred
and roofless shells, their walls calcined and blackened by
fire, and already covered with fronds of jungle creeper.

The roads that ran like wheel spokes between them

were littered with furnishings and toys and incongruous pieces of unknown homes, like music boxes, broken china jugs, smashed oil lamps. Many ornamental shrubs and small trees had either been torn down by the mutineers in a fury because they represented a civilization and a gentle way of life they hated, or those that remained had been eaten by hungry elephants.

He moved his glasses on towards the city. To the north-west, behind the Jhil Canal that bounded the cantonment, stretched steaming swamps, green with bamboo beds and jungle, bright yellow with poisonous reeds and rushes; then more ruins and empty buildings, and clusters of native huts.

The canal had been built to prevent flooding from a shallow depression in the ground, and extended for nearly thirty miles beyond Delhi. Usually it ran dry in summer, but because of heavy rains the previous year, it still contained drinkable water. This was most fortunate for the British, for the river was too foul even for natives to drink from with their stomachs hardened against bad water; and the mutineers had filled nearly all the wells in the cantonment with bodies to deny them to the British.

Because of the danger of pitching tents too near the top of the Ridge, the British had been forced to camp near this canal, which was the most unhealthy position they could have chosen. Mosquitoes swarmed everywhere, and each morning, officers and men alike, who had sweated out the night with their faces and hands wrapped in strips of cloth against their bites, still woke up with their flesh swollen and puffy. Those in the tents nearest to the canal suffered most heavily from fever and malaria, which no amount of enthusiastic head-shaving or blood-letting by medical orderlies could keep under control.

Every day, both sides fired artillery rounds at each other, and maybe there would be some skirmishing of patrols, but neither side was anxious to come too close. Near Hindu Rao's house stood a small Hindu shrine, known as the Sammy House, from the Indian word *swami*, meaning an idol, and by this was a rocky crag, The Crows' Nest. This commanded a view of the Subsi Mundi, the former vegetable market, which was the lowest point of the encampment, overlooking a gorge in which both the Grand Trunk Road and the Western Jumna Canal ran, side by side, towards the Kabul Gate in the city wall.

Observation patrols kept watch day and night from these outposts, but although they religiously reported what enemy movements they saw, no use was made of their information. To do so, would call for action, and no British commander wished to take responsibility for this or its consequences.

Behind Hindu Rao's house, about a hundred and eight yards to its left, was a dismal, dank building, constructed years before by a Rajput astronomer, basically only a masonry column sixty feet high, with an outside staircase leading to a few tiny rooms and an upper platform about five feet across. Beneath this, the artillery had mounted two field guns, and observers crouched uncomfortably on the platform, exposed to shot and shell, to give the gunners beneath them some indication where their fire was landing.

Another observation point was Flagstaff Tower, which, because of its sheltered position, became a meeting place for convalescents and off-duty officers who would climb up to the parapet to enjoy a smoke in the cooler air, and discuss the chances of an early attack on Delhi.

Every new officer, as he arrived, usually by mail cart, with his belongings piled behind him or, if on horseback, with an out-rider, and a couple of camels to carry his gear, would immediately climb the winding staircase to this parapet for his first panoramic view of the city, across the walls, topped by eight-foot parapets, with flanking bastions and martello towers, to the minarets, the Jumma Musjid mosque and the intricately pierced screens and domes of the Red Fort.

The riverbed here was nearly a mile wide, and now that the water was low, it presented a network of channels and sandbanks and shallow brackish lagoons, some bordered by cultivated terraces and orange groves, and some by jungle and more swamp and marsh. The whole scene possessed a strange iridescent beauty; the deep green of swamps, the brownish yellow dust of the desert, white domes and minarets, orange and red petals of the flowers, and the river green or blue or silver, according to the sun and the clouds.

Garroway came out of his tent and called to Gough. He lowered his binoculars.

'Good morning,' Gough said coldly. He did not like Garroway. No one did. Yet no one could produce any real reason for their feelings.

Garroway had kept Mrs Bolivar's five hundred rupees wrapped up under his shirts in his black metal trunk in his tent, with the key hanging from his belt.

It was a pity in many ways that the insurrection had cut short his association with her. In the meantime, until he knew whether she was alive or dead, he would keep the money, for all kinds of bargains were now becoming available.

Each time an officer died, more often from sickness than from wounds, his belongings were auctioned so the money would go to his family. At first, his richer colleagues had generously paid hundreds of rupees for worthless kit, such as a camp wash basin, or a pair of riding boots that did not fit, simply so that the families of the dead should have some money. But as more died, the bidding became less enthusiastic, except where personal stocks of wine or India Pale Ale were concerned.

So Garroway was biding his time. He knew the belongings of other officers that he wanted. Gough, for instance, had a very fine charger; another lieutenant owned a solid gold watch and chain; a third, a vest of chainmail, which could prove good insurance against a sword or bullet, but no protection at all against dysentery and fever.

With care, and a little luck, Garroway could assemble a whole list of accoutrements and equipment he would not normally have been able to afford.

'Think there will be any news this morning?' he asked.

Gough shrugged.

'We'll see,' he said shortly, not wishing to be drawn into conversation.

They went together to the mess, a huge canvas room the size of a circus tent. A green haircord carpet was pegged to the hard ground. Tables were set up with freshly laundered white cloths. *Khitmagars* in white uniforms with gold and red regimental belts, brought them plates of popaya and then fried eggs, a chapatti, and beakers of coffee. A few officers read months-old newspapers, propped up on silver stands on the tables; others ate morosely without conversation. Senior officers sat well apart from the juniors so that physically, as well as mentally, they had as little contact as possible. Between the young and the old' was an ever-widening gulf, not of years, but of attitude. The junior officers realized the terrible dangers of indefinite delay in assaulting Delhi, for each day brought new reinforcements for the mutineers and diminished their own forces through fever and wounds. Every day also entrenched the spirit of revolt more deeply in Indians, who otherwise had feared that such effrontery would meet with instant punishment from the British.

The older officers had no stomach for attack. The unexpected and revolting sight of mutilated bodies, of eyes blown big as onions bulging from sockets, torsos shattered, limbs separated from trunks, horrified them. This was a side of war they had never seen in their safe cantonments. Why should they now be forced to take decisions on which not only the lives of their troops could conceivably depend, but also the lives they held most dear—their own? If they waited, then maybe the whole situation might unexpectedly resolve itself.

After breakfast each morning, Wilson held a conference in his tent. All the officers filed in, sprang briefly to attention at the door, then sat down in order of seniority on canvas stools. The few chairs with backs and arms were reserved tacitly for the more senior among them.

Wilson, with two or three of his staff, sat at a trestle table covered with a grey army blanket. Usually, the conference was leisurely enough. Reports from patrols were read, news from spies discussed, but today the atmosphere was heavy with gloom.

'We have had news, gentlemen,' Wilson began gravely, 'of a disaster at Cawnpore, another example of Indian perfidy.

'As you know, Sir Hugh Wheeler, the commander, saw fit to take up his station with two hundred and forty fighting men and six hundred and thirty women and children and invalids in a special entrenchment he had ordered to be built.

'He did this because he felt it was safest for all the British to be in one place, and he had also received repeated assurances from the local maharajah, Nana Sahib, that no discourtesy or violence was intended towards any British subject.

'General Wheeler ordered local contractors to stock this

entrenchment with provisions so that, at the worst, they could exist there for a month, which he estimated was the longest it would take for reinforcements to reach him.

'Alas, events took a different turn. Almost from the first day in that entrenchment, these wretched people were under constant bombardment by Indians from guns of all kinds.

'General Wheeler's force possessed eight guns and fifty-nine gunners. But all were invalids, with hardly the strength to ram a shell into the breech.

'We may doubt whether it was wise to shelter behind these flimsy earth walls, but we are far from Cawnpore, gentlemen, and we should not presume to judge his decisions any more than he would have presumed to judge ours.'

The past tense struck his listeners like a blow. So Cawnpore had fallen. Wheeler was dead. What other bad news would Wilson have?

The Brigadier cleared his throat.

'Apparently, the mutinous sepoys sacked Cawnpore and then went in search of other targets. General Wheeler thought the worst was over, but it had not yet begun. For the mutineers returned and increased the violence of their attack.

'Their food ran short. Officers' horses were killed and eaten. They trapped stray dogs and boiled the bones to make soup for the children. The only source of water was one well. Every day, men died trying to drag a bucket of water back for the women and the children.

'Finally, after three weeks, with almost everyone ill and still no news of rescue, no news indeed of anything, with the thatch roofs blazing on the shelters, and the defenders almost too weak to stand, the general sent out emissaries to Nana Sahib. He sent them out, gentlemen, to a maharajah whose hospitality he had often enjoyed. Who had, on many occasions, expressed himself in terms of warmth and friendship towards the British.

'Now, Nana Sahib guaranteed safe conduct to these beleagured people. More than that, he would give them boats so that they could escape down the river to land on some more peaceful shore.

'He gave them boats, gentlemen. But as soon as they were in midstream, their boatmen leapt over the sides and swam for the shore. With no one at the helms, the boats veered and swung and became perfect targets for the mutineers who lined both banks. The British refugees then discovered that the boats had no spare oars—and all the rudders had been locked solid, so that they drifted around helplessly.

'At some command, the shooting ceased. Those still left alive believed they were about to be rescued. They saw men wading from the side in the mud towards them. They cried out for help.

'They got help, gentlemen, but it was help to a far distant shore. For these men had swords and knives concealed in their clothes, and as they boarded the boats, they hacked to pieces the defenceless women and children who crouched inside.

'Some escaped by swimming for miles, carried on the currents, and it is from these few escapers that this intelligence has been gathered. But I believe that there were no more than four or five Europeans, according to our information, who survived the massacre.

'I thought, gentlemen, as no doubt you have thought as well, that this mutiny was an isolated outbreak, some manifestation of local discontent and fears about native religions and customs.

'This news from Cawnpore makes it appear far more serious. I know I speak for everyone in this tent, and on the Ridge, when I say that we will not rest, nor shall our swords sleep, or our guns be silent, until we have avenged this most foul and bloody murder of hundreds of innocent, defenceless and harmless people.'

He paused, visibly moved.

Many of his listeners had parents or relations in Cawnpore. Nearly all had friends there. Had they escaped before this shambles? Or were they all dead? The news was so shocking that no one spoke. They sat in silence, just looking at each other.

Nana Sahib. A few had met him, had even been his guest, had shot on his estate from the backs of caparisoned elephants. They had also entertained him in return on numerous regimental occasions.

How could he suddenly have countenanced such an act of horror? Was it some change in his temper and character? Or had he always been like this underneath—like a man wearing a mask? Worse, were *all* Indians like this underneath? Had they always been secretly violent and ferocious, like the wild beasts in their jungles—and was what had been secret and concealed now exploding into the open?

As these fearful thoughts surged through their troubled minds like rivers at high flood, an A.D.C. entered the room and saluted Wilson.

'With your permission, sir. A body of mounted troops has been sighted, approaching from the north-west.'

The officers looked up with interest, glad of anything to take their minds from dwelling on tragedy.

'Who are they?' asked Wilson.

'We have sent an observer to the Flagstaff Tower with a glass, sir. He reports them to be irregulars, wearing all kinds of uniform. The outrider has a lance and a pennant. The officers appear English.'

'That must be Hodson's force,' said Wilson, standing up.

'Hodson!'

Others repeated the name. Some of the younger officers, remembering his achievements with the Guides, spoke in accents of admiration. Others, who thought him an upstart, a bounder, an officer who did not abide by the accepted traditions of the army, had rather less enthusiasm.

'We will go and see for ourselves,' announced Wilson, standing up and leading the way out of the tent.

Across the plain, like a moving dust cloud, stretched a long column of riders. Without glasses, it was difficult to make out individuals. Although those in the lead clearly had pale faces, the rest seemed dark-skinned.

As they drew nearer, they could see that some were bearded, with turbans; others, clean-shaven. All wore odd items of equipment, but all rode their horses as if they were part of the animals, extensions of them, born to the saddle.

'They look a rabble to me,' said one regular officer, whose only experience had been limited to the strict routine of the Lancers. British troops were coming out of their tents to see this strange contingent. A thousand men, with barely a hundred pack mules, no impedimenta of bearers and camp followers, and even the grasscutters armed with swords, riding across the burned earth at a steady jog trot, as though they were machines, tireless.

A few shells from the mutineers burst around them, but they rode through the puffs of dust and smoke unharmed and unconcerned, and something about them made the British soldiers cheer.

Up the Ridge they came, in perfect formation, their horses lathered with sweat on which yellow dust had dried. Their dark faces were also masks of dust, and they had an air about them of grim professionalism.

They had not ridden for miles across hard and hostile country to parley, or to wait for other orders. Every line of their tough, lean bodies stressed their fitness to fight. They were not about to wait for other reinforcements. They *were* the reinforcements.

Hodson jumped down from his horse, and a cloud of dust blew out from his uniform as he saluted Brigadier Wilson.

'We have arrived, sir,' he said simply. 'All we seek is your date for the attack on Delhi.'

19

Nana Sahib's servants had set up a splendid pavilion for him on the upper banks of the Ganges near Cawnpore, overlooking the Satichaura Ghat, where the British women and children had embarked in the boats for their last journey. Now he walked alone on the dried-up grass, hands clasped behind his back, looking across the sacred river that flowed by sluggishly.

It was impossible not to see the bloodstained dresses, the abandoned toys, the bonnets, the shredded Bibles and prayer books, their leaves turning handsprings in the wind.

Here and there lay the bloodied body of a child or a woman, full skirts billowing in the river breeze, while vultures stood insolently on their corpses and picked away at their entrails.

Several charred boats with rudders still locked bumped bows into the bank and then turned slightly in the current. Bodies hung over their sides, pale hands trailing in the water. It was difficult to say how many had died and who, if any, had escaped, but when the British came back he would take the blame, for he was the maharajah. And who would believe him then if he claimed that it was none of his doing? That he had genuinely wanted to give them safe conduct, and that the first he knew that others had usurped his order was when he heard the muskets fire?

After all, these English refugees were an embarrassment to him, crouched in Wheeler's ridiculous earth fortifications. He had wanted them out of his area, for if they did not die from bullets, then disease and fever would kill them, and he would be blamed in any case.

Azi Mullah watched him from the mouth of his tent, guessing his thoughts. The trouble with Nana was that he was weak and a fool, too willing to fall in with other people's ideas, without considering them enough, or weighing them against his own.

Now, if *he* had been the adopted son of the maharajah, he would never have gone begging to indifferent Englishmen for a pension. He would have forced a bargain from them years before.

He spat on the ground in his contempt for Nana. Then he smoothed back his oily hair with both hands and walked out into the sunshine to meet his master.

'We will have the place cleared up, Nana,' he assured him.

'You can clear up the bodies, no doubt,' said Nana. 'But you will never erase what has happened here. It will go down in history as a mark of infamy against us.

'I gave these people my word they would have safe conduct down the river. Instead, they have been murdered.'

'There seems to have been some confusion of orders among commanders on the banks,' began Azi Mullah.

'It was a fatal confusion,' Nana interrupted him. 'Fatal to all these women and their children. It will be fatal in the end, to us. What sort of reception will we have when the British return?'

'They will never come back,' replied Azi Mullah confidently.

'You delude yourself. You are like other Indians who think that all the British army is out here in our country. Who believe that no more than a hundred thousand Englishmen are left in their home islands. I have even heard some say that their army here is like a stage army, the same men being marched round and round. All that is foolishness. They *will* be back and we *will* suffer for this. And with all our possessions—possibly even with our lives.'

'Your Highness is taking an unnecessarily gloomy view of the situation.'

'I am taking a realistic view. The forests will have been full of eyes who saw this massacre. When the British return, they will be full of mouths to speak against us. I will swear I know nothing about this infamy. But who will believe that? I gave my word to the general. He accepted it. And now—this. Who will ever trust me again?'

'Trust goes with power, Your Highness. They *will* trust you, *and* make treaty with you. You now command an area of hundreds of square miles. British rule here—the Company's suzerainty—no longer exists.

'I will issue a *kotwal,* an order, that everyone must give allegiance to *your* rule, as they have done to John Company's rule.'

'What good will that do? These are only words and promises, empty as the air—like your scheme to start small rebellions which we could control and turn to our own advantage.'

'You accepted that idea, Your Highness.'

'To our great cost, I did.'

'I did not realize, when I made it, Your Highness, that the conditions for revolt were as ripe as they were.'

'We are like men who have lit a fire to cook food in the forest, and the wind has set all the trees aflame.'

'So there is only one thing we can do now, Your Highness—spread the flames farther.'

'Then all India will be in revolt. You must be mad.'

'Not so, for in the general conflagration, this will pass unnoticed. It is all or nothing now, Your Highness. There is no going back. We outnumber the British in our country—our *own* country, remember—by ten thousand to one, maybe more.

'Our hope is to defeat the British completely here. Then we can talk to their Government from a position of strength. *They* can propose, we will dispose.'

They walked on, Nana Sahib pondering on what Azi Mullah had said. It made sense; but then so had his earlier proposal, and violence was against his nature. In the silence of his mind he remembered the words of the Lord Buddha: 'Let a man avoid evil deeds, as a merchant, if he has few companions and carries much wealth, avoids a dangerous road; as a man who loves life avoids poison.'

Already he had taken too many steps down a dangerous road to retrace them. He stood committed to a journey through valleys of unknown violence which he shuddered to enter, but through which he had to pass, for there was no way back.

'What is your suggestion, then?' he asked Azi Mullah.

'You stay here, Your Highness, because if you leave, too many people will know. I will go to Delhi and urge Bahadur Shah to attack the British, who are encamped about the city. The sepoys outnumber them ten to one. Only sloth and fear and indolence allows them to be besieged inside their own capital.

'He is an old man, Bahadur Shah. His blood is thin for fighting. Yet he does not need to fight himself. He is a king. He can create generals from subedars, if need be. There are plenty of common sepoys who will fight because they are fools enough to believe they are fighting for something worth while.'

'Perhaps we are the fools?' said Nana Sahib. 'Every man must believe in something.'

'He should believe in himself. In the strength of his right arm. In the cunning of his own brain. I will take with me that old subedar, Ram Gupta. He will know many of his comrades, who have deserted from the army. The fact that he is there will give them confidence in me and in my mission.'

'I wish you well,' said Nana Sahib, but he felt neither goodwill towards the man, nor optimism for the future.

He was a man of peace. All this killing could only lead to more; for violence was a master that in the end would enslave them all.

'You have two visitors, Your Majesty,' the chamberlain told the King of Delhi. 'From Cawnpore.'

'Then let them return whence they came. They do not arrive at our invitation.'

'They come from the Maharajah of Bithur.'

The King swallowed. Nana was not a real maharajah, only a maharajah's adopted son. He could trace his ancestors no farther back than his own mother. Why, the man was not really sure who his natural father had been. How was it that people like this were now set on a level with himself, the last ruling descendant of the great Mogul, who could trace his line, father to son, for hundreds of years; whose ancestors had marched with Tamburlaine and Ghengis Khan? And yet he had to humour them just as he had to appear polite to these upstarts from Meerut and elsewhere, who had virtually taken over his palace.

He sipped a glass of warm water. Wind rumbled in his tired old stomach, and the pains of age speared him in his rusty joints.

'We will see them,' he said resignedly.

The chamberlain bowed. He had known the answer before he asked the question, but you had to humour the old fellow; after all, he was the King.

He opened the door. Azi Mullah and Ram Gupta came in. They had ridden with an escort of a hundred and fifty sowars, and spent the night elsewhere in Delhi, and now were bathed and in fresh clothes.

To Azi Mullah, the King was only a symbol, an aged totem, who lived and breathed, and could be turned to his own advantage.

To Ram Gupta, meeting Bahadur Shah was the highest honour of his life. He knelt reverently on the ground and kissed the carpet with open lips. And when he raised his eyes, the old King saw genuine adoration, almost worship, in them.

'You bring a message?' asked the King, holding his hands round the beaker, drawing some comfort into his withered flesh from the warmth.

'We bring you news of victory, Your Majesty. We have entirely defeated the British garrison at Cawnpore. A few stragglers may have escaped, but they are like chaff when the wheat is gathered in. General Wheeler's force no longer exists.'

The King put down his beaker and looked at Azi Mullah, his eyes sharp under their grey brows.

'You have killed all the dependants, the women and children, too?'

'It is as you say, Your Majesty.'

'Why do you bring me this news?'

'Because, when the British hear it, great will be their fear. Not since the disaster at Kabul—when four and a half thousand of their troops—and three times as many camp followers—died, for no purpose whatever, have they suffered such a defeat.

'We came here, Your Majesty, to suggest that this was the moment for your forces to attack them. To sally out from this fortress with all your thousands of men, under a gigantic barrage of cannon, and cut down the British on the Ridge before their buglers can even sound the alarm.'

'It would not be possible,' said the King sharply. 'They watch the gates through glasses all the day, every day.'

'Then send out one body of men to the south as a diversion, with fireworks and rockets and cannon. To-night. While their attention is taken, attack them in the centre and in the north from behind. You *can* do it, Your Majesty, even as we did it in Cawnpore.'

'It is a thought,' agreed the King.

'It is more than a thought, Your Majesty,' pressed Azi Mullah earnestly. 'It is *essential*. Break their power now, and, like the broken back of a wrestler, it will never be the same. But miss this moment, and they will receive re-inforcements from Burma, from Ceylon, and eventually from England itself. Their shame in the defeat at Cawnpore will never let them rest. You must attack *now*, Your Majesty.'

The King walked over to his window and stood looking out across the river. What Azi Mullah said was true, but to carry out his counsel meant that he was cast irrevocably on the side of revolt. And, deep down in his old man's heart, wavering as a weathercock, he feared this course; it had no way out.

On the other hand, if he did not agree, then Azi Mullah would doubtless address himself to his subordinates. They might act without him, and then he would be in an even worse state.

Standing there, he made his decision; he would do as Azi Mullah proposed. What had he got to lose but his life? And of this at best only a few weary painful years remained.

'We will attack,' he said.

'Good. The maharajah thought this would be Your Majesty's decision.'

'Call the commanders,' said the King. 'We will give them their orders.'

Private Dougan crouched, defecating in a nullah, his head bent below the level of the Ridge.

He hated performing this intimate act in public, under the bright hard sun, when flies crawled over the exposed

parts of his body, so he would slink out after dark when
no one could see him.

The guard rested on the muzzles of their carbines and
muskets, looking out towards the flickering firefly lights
around Delhi. The sluggish river slid yellow under the
moon. Mosquitoes whined like distant saws and cicadas
and bullfrogs rattled and croaked incessantly. Above all
these familiar noises of the night, Dougan heard another
sound, and was instantly on his feet, wiping his backside
on a handful of grass, pulling up his serge trousers.

He had heard the clank of a bridle chain, the clop of a
muffled hoof on a rock.

None of the British mules or chargers were out; they
were kept in a kind of corral on the other side of camp.
He ran to the guard tent.

'Someone's coming up the hill,' he told the sergeant.

'What sort of someone?' asked the sergeant.

'How can I see in the bloody dark? They've got horses.'

One of the guard now ran in.

'A body of men, sarge, approaching from the east in
single file. Leading mules or horses.'

'How many?'

'Hundreds of the boogers.'

'Bugler, sound Stand-to.'

The bugler boy ran to the mouth of the tent and blew
the familiar call. As the first notes brought the troops out
of their tents, buckling on equipment and cursing the interruption, the Indians charged. They had not meant to
charge so soon, but now they were discovered, they could
only go forward or back.

As they charged, shouting to keep up their courage, artillery began to fire from the Fort. Each explosion lit up
the rough ground, now dotted with figures on foot and
horseback, like a frieze suddenly come frenziedly to life.

The British artillery fired back in reply, and the ground
trembled with the iron argument of the guns.

In the flickering darkness, horsemen tripped over tent
guy-ropes. Cooks rushed out of field kitchens carrying
carving knives and huge ladles. Private soldiers, lacking
time to reload their muskets, swung them like clubs from
the muzzles, smashing in the skulls of their attackers.

On the outskirts, Hodson's men raced for their horses,

leapt up into their saddles, and riding round the camp to
avoid the treacherous guy-ropes and scurrying figures, fell
upon the Indians with a Biblical fury.

Hodson, with Lang at his side, then led his men on in a
wide sweeping curve to attack reinforcements riding out
from the Fort. One moment, Indian sowars were trotting
to the scene of battle; the next, a whirlwind had taken
them unawares. Swords flickered like quicksilver. Heads
and riders rolled; horses galloped off, riderless, or trailing
dead men by the stirrups.

The sepoys broke and fled into the darkness, anywhere
to escape those flaying swords.

From the ramparts of the Red Fort, the old King
watched the battle, only an occasional twitch on his face
showing his feelings as the mutineers scattered under
Hodson's attack. He turned to Azi Mullah.

'It seems that the British still have fight in them.'

'They must have heard what we planned, Your Majesty.'

'Not necessarily. In a sense, they are in the same position as ourselves. They have nothing to lose but their
lives. Such a situation, I find, tends to compose one's
thoughts remarkably.'

'You will order other attacks, Your Majesty?'

'We shall see.'

As the King led the way back to his apartments, he
wondered what they would see, and when. Eventual
peace, with victory for one side or the other; or a stale-
mate of attack, retreat and counter-attack, stretching
ahead into an infinity of inconclusion?

When Lang dismounted, and walked into his tent, Hodson was sitting in a canvas chair. Lang poured out two
glasses; one of *nimbu pani*, lemon juice and water for
Hodson, who did not drink spirits, and one of Martell for
himself.

'Well?' asked Hodson. 'How do you feel after your first
action?'

'It was worse at Meerut. I killed a man there.'

'For a soldier, the first kill is like a first kiss for a girl.
After that, none is ever quite the same.'

Hodson crossed to the mouth of the tent. The spires
and minarets and domes of the Red Fort, and the mosques

and other buildings, lay pale under the moon. The plain was dotted with bodies. Bearers moved slowly among them, looking for signs of life.

'Are you married?' asked Hodson.

'No,' said Lang. 'Engaged, though. To be married in St James's Church.'

'Where is your fiancée?'

'I don't know. She is Colonel MacDonald's daughter, Arabella. He is in charge of the special detachment in the Fort. Or he was.'

'You haven't heard anything?'

'Nothing.'

'A strange place, this Red Fort,' said Hodson. 'I can never look at it under the moon, just as I can never look at the Taj Mahal, without thinking of Shah Jehan, the man who built them both.

'He was in love with one woman, Muntaz Mahal, his wife, and she died. It's an odd thing, Richard, but in love stories, one of the partners *always* dies. Love seems like a precious flame that burns and glows and warms the lives of two people, and then it grows dim and, finally, it goes out. But if one dies while the flame is still bright, it never goes out in their partner's heart.

'Anyhow, Muntaz Mahal died, and Shah Jehan built the Taj Mahal as a mark of his love for her.

'It took twenty thousand craftsmen twenty-two years to finish. They brought jewels from Persia, sandstone from Fatehpur Sikri, marble from Jaipur and Makrana.

'When he had finished it, he decided he would build one where he could be buried himself. But his son grew tired of all this living in the past. Young people do, very easily. They have no past, only their future. But when you grow older, the past seems much more important. There's also more of it.

'So the son imprisoned his father right here in the Red Fort for the last seven years of his life. When he died, he was buried as he wished. He had been alone for thirty-six years, and was still in love with his wife's memory. On her tomb, he had these words carved: "Help us, oh Lord, bear that which we cannot bear!" '

'Of course,' said Lang, 'He didn't mean Our Lord— Jesus?'

'Certainly not,' agreed Hodson. 'But we Christians cannot claim monopoly on religion, or even on eternal life. I've had so many talks with gurus and fakirs and other holy men—Sikhs, Moslems, Hindus—that it seems to me all religions have much in common. As Christ said Himself, "In my father's house are many mansions." There will be room for all.

'Much of our trouble here in India stems from the fact that we are trying to Christianize these people. We take away their own religions and give them one that a lot of us find difficult to believe ourselves.'

'Don't you believe in God, then?' asked Lang, surprised.

'I ought to,' said Hodson. 'My father is a parson. So is my brother. I believe there must be another world after this, or life here is all a terrible charade. And that is possibly the greatest strength of all religions, the comfort they give. But enough of this philosophizing. Tell me, Richard, what are your plans after this is over?'

'To marry, I suppose. Then to make a career here. Like my father. And yours?'

'Well, I am already married,' said Hodson and paused, thinking of Susan in their bungalow, reading out-of-date newspapers, smoothing out her dead daughter's tiny clothes in drawers with dried lavender.

He suddenly saw a vision of his own future; passed over again for promotion, sneered at by officers with long family pedigrees and private means, yet what could he achieve if only he could find a way out of the maze of frustration that surrounded him! And at the heart of the maze was Susan, cold, enigmatic, remote.

How different his life could be, shared with someone warm and compassionate, a woman interested in his interests. He sighed and let fall the flap of the tent. This was a dangerous cul-de-sac; and his thoughts had already travelled along it too often, for it led nowhere, nowhere at all.

'Well,' he said, as brightly as he could, finishing the *nimbu pani*. 'I'd better go back to my tent, and get some sleep. Tomorrow should be busy. We *must* plan the attack on Delhi. For if we don't act soon, we never will.'

'Don't you think that is rather pessimistic?'

'No. Realistic. The rains break soon, and then we'll be bogged down here for five months at least. Can you imagine the mosquitoes and the cholera and plague we'll have here then? Thousands of men under canvas. Everything streaming with water like a riverbed. We'll have to retreat then, but where to—back to Meerut to start all over again? No, Richard. We have brought a thousand men here, and if no one else will help us, we'll take the Red Fort on our own.'

Of the original twenty-seven women and children whom Kalyan Singh had moved to upper rooms in the Fort, Mrs Todd and four other women and two children had died.

None of those remaining owned a watch or a clock, but they all remembered they had been captured on a Monday, and Arabella scratched a calendar of lines, one for each day, on the sandstone wall of the room.

One woman had a sliver of mirror. She passed this round every day, and they combed their hair.

'Nearly four weeks we've been here,' she said. 'How long do you think it will be before we are rescued? Do you think they even know anyone is in here as prisoners?'

Arabella pulled a stool under the high-grilled window and stood on it. By holding on to the bars and standing on tiptoe she could see across the red parapets of the Fort to the Ridge.

'Give me that mirror,' she said. 'I can signal.'

'Do you know Morse?'

'A little. S.O.S. at least.'

Holding the grille with her left hand, Arabella fitted the mirror into her right palm, and moved it until she caught the sun, reflecting a tiny triangle of light, first on the parapet, then on the distant Ridge.

A patrol of twelve British infantrymen moved diagonally across the ground. She flicked the mirror. The light shone like a sunbeam around their feet. She moved it carefully until it caught the leading soldier in the eyes. He put up his hand and shook his head and stopped. The patrol stopped behind him. Then they all looked towards the Fort.

Keeping the light on his eyes, Arabella flicked the three dots, three dashes and three dots. The leader raised a pair of binoculars and focused them on their window.

Arabella waved. It was doubtful whether he could see her, so she repeated the signal, and was about to repeat it again when she heard the warning rattle of a bolt as the guard unlocked the door. She jumped down, pushed away the stool, and was combing her hair unconcernedly, when the guard came in, carrying two buckets of fresh water.

Hodson sat in his own tent on the right of the Ridge. The patrol commander, a full corporal, stood to attention in front of him.

'I was leading the patrol down the west nullah, sir,' he said, 'when I saw a light flashing from a window of the Fort. I put up my glasses but I couldn't make out anybody because the windows are very small. There is no doubt though, sir, someone in there is a prisoner. They signalled S.O.S. twice.'

'Can you show me the window?'

'Yes, sir.'

Hodson called an orderly.

'Get me my horse.'

He rode out with the corporal down the Ridge and both focused their glasses.

'That one there, sir. The small one on the left under the dome.'

Hodson strained his eyes to catch any movement behind the window, but there was nothing.

'Thank you, corporal,' he said. 'I'll give instructions for our agents to report who is being kept prisoners there.'

He summoned Rajib Ali.

'A job for you,' he said. 'I want you to go into the Fort. Say where you have come from—Amballa. The place will be full of mutineers and it's easier to remember a true story than a false one.

'The corporal saw someone signaling from a window. It could be an Englishman—or woman. I want you to find out how many are prisoners there. And when you're in the Fort, you might pass the word round that we pay well for information. No questions asked. No names taken. Half of an agreed sum down on presentation of the news. The other half when we check it's accurate. Any questions?'

'No, sahib. I will make ready immediately.'

'Good,' said Hodson. He turned to Lang.

'Now for this morning's conference.'

Another report of inactivity. They had been there a week and Hodson, as one of the most junior officers on the Ridge, yet in command of a regiment, was beginning to despair at the paradoxical situation.

Here he was, with his thousand men especially raised on General Anson's express command to march on Delhi; and here were General Barnard and Brigadier Wilson and half a dozen other senior officers, each with their circles of sycophants who revolved around them like planets around stars—and without whose permission he could undertake no more than patrols and minor skirmishes.

'Any questions?' asked General Barnard, as he ended the morning's resumé of inaction.

'Yes, sir,' said Hodson.

Some senior officers groaned and turned their eyes in exasperation to the roof of the tent.

'Well, Mr Hodson?' asked Barnard patiently. He had no intention of being carried away by some madcap plan that could decimate his force. Far better to wait until further reinforcements arrived; numbers held a comforting safety for an old man.

'I would suggest, sir, that we mount an immediate attack from two different directions under a covering fire from guns laid so that their shells land in the centre of the Fort.'

'You have made this proposition almost every morning since your arrival, Mr Hodson,' pointed out Wilson sharply.

'I submit that this does not render the proposition any less feasible, sir, or any less urgent.'

'I'll tell you what we'll do,' said Barnard. 'You and two or three other young officers, Mr Lang here and Mr Gough, and you, Mr Jackson'—he pointed to an engineer subaltern—'draw up your plan and submit it to me in writing. If it is at all practical, I assure you it will have our most earnest consideration. Now, any other questions, gentlemen?'

They all shook their heads. Camp chairs scraped on the dry ground as the officers stood up.

'Oh, there *is* one thing, Mr Hodson,' said General Barnard, before Hodson could reach the door. 'Stay behind, if you will.'

The others filed out. Hodson faced the old man.

'I want to congratulate you, Mr Hodson,' said Barnard. 'You have just been promoted to captain. It is not right for a lieutenant to take your responsibility.'

'Thank you, sir.'

'And good luck with your plan.'

Barnard turned back to the papers on the table. Hodson came out into the bright sunlight. Garroway was waiting for him. The two men had disliked each other on sight. Hodson, because he saw through Garroway's thin veneer of sophistication and breeding to the shabby, third-rate spirit which carefully sheltered behind fine words. Garroway, because he sensed Hodson had no use for him. Well, he would soon put a spoke in Hodson's wheel. This fellow was too autocratic altogether. Putting up his ideas every day at conference. Now being told to prepare a plan. Whoever heard of such a thing? A general asking four subalterns to work out a plan of attack for him!

'I wanted to see you,' said Garroway. 'I've had a complaint from some of your men.'

'If they are *my* men, why should they complain to you?' asked Hodson.

'They told my bearer. He told me.'

'You listen to native gossip, then?'

'When it affects the well-being of the troops, yes.'

'And how does what you have heard from your bearer affect the well-being of any troops, either yours or mine?'

'I don't like to say this, Hodson,' said Garroway, with such relish that he obviously enjoyed saying it very much, 'but, apparently, some of your men haven't been paid.'

'Go on.'

'And some are worried that the relations of comrades who have been killed haven't been paid, either.'

'How do you expect us to get money to their families hundreds of miles off in the hills, when there is no safe *dak* service, even for ordinary letters?'

'That is your problem,' retorted Garroway. 'I just thought you should know. One or two other officers also think it's a bit odd.'

'And what is their sources of information, or the yardstick by which they judge an oddity? Is this also from your bearer's lips, or from yours?'

'You can talk round the problem as much as you like, Hodson, but some of these officers here remember what happened in the Guides. All that business of regimental money vanishing, the fact you kept no proper accounts.'

'What are you suggesting?' asked Hodson.

It seemed he would never escape from this unquiet ghost of the past. First, Birdwash; now, this creature.

'I am not suggesting anything, but for your own good name I think these men should be paid.'

'Your concern for my good name does you great credit,' said Hodson. 'But what do my men need cash *for?* They hold their credits with me. They can have their money whenever they want—*now* if they ask for it. But they want it after this is over, when it will be of some use. There is no bank here, so it is under lock and key in my tent. I am the only one with the key. I assure you, Garroway, they know the money is being well taken care of.'

'I am sure it is,' agreed Garroway insolently.

Hodson seized him by the arm.

'I don't know whether you are being deliberately offensive, or whether this is your normal behaviour, Garroway, but I'll tell you this now. If ever you speak to me like this again, I'll either challenge you to a duel, or I'll break your jaw. Now, get out of my sight.'

He turned away so he would not hit the man's grinning, arrogant face.

'Do you think they'll report your signal?' asked the woman with the mirror.

Arabella nodded.

'I'm sure.'

'What about your Indian friend? Haven't seen him lately, have you?'

'If I did see him,' said Arabella, 'you'd sneer at him— or me. At least he got us out of that awful room.'

'He did it for *you,* not for us. You should be ashamed of yourself, consorting with a nigger.'

This came from a bitter middle-aged woman with a lined face, and hair lank like voles' tails, fingernails bitten to the quick, a nervous twitch to her mouth.

'You should be ashamed of *your*self,' said Arabella. 'How many times have you been delighted—honoured—to dance with a maharajah at a regimental ball? His colour didn't mean anything to you, then.'

'It wouldn't mean anything to me now, if he were a maharajah, for he would know how to behave, and would help us. But these filthy niggers, with their disgusting habits, squatting everywhere, wiping their bodies with their bare hands, stinking of scent, ugh! *I'*d be ashamed, if I were you.'

'Fortunately, she is not you,' said a voice from the judas hole in the door. Kalyan Singh's face was framed by the wood. He was smiling. A rattle of a bolt and the door opened. Kalyan Singh came in; behind him, the guards carefully locked the door.

'I have been away in Cawnpore,' he explained. 'Otherwise I would have visited you before. Have you any points of criticism, apart from being incarcerated here, about which I regret I can, at this moment, do nothing?'

'We need some new clothes. We have been wearing these nearly a month. And some vegetables or fruit.'

'I will do what I can,' promised Kalyan Singh. 'You'll have to wear native clothes, as we have no European ones. But fruit should be possible, and perhaps some more goats' milk for the children.'

'Thank you,' said a mother. 'You are doing your best, even though you are an Indian.'

'The God we worship under different names teaches the same code of behaviour,' said Kalyan Singh. 'I am sure you would all do your best for me if the situation were reversed. I have to leave Delhi myself tonight, but I will be back.'

He turned towards the door.

'What is the news from Cawnpore?' asked Arabella. She suddenly wanted to keep him there, to hear his voice, to have him near her. There was a calmness about him that appealed to her.

'All news, in the context of war, is only good or bad, according to which side you are on,' said Kalyan Singh carefully.

'What about General Wheeler?'

'General Wheeler's misguided resistance in Cawnpore has ended. He asked leave to surrender.'

'But what's happened to all the people with him?' asked a woman suckling a child. 'My brother and his wife and three daughters are up there.'

'Owing to a confusion of orders, madam, not all the Indian troops realized that the British had safe conduct. I regret to have to tell you that a number were killed.'

'*Murdered,* you mean! They were murdered! You and your kind led them out under some promise of safe conduct, I'll be bound, and then you shot them down. And now you come in here offering us milk and fruit and vegetables! My God, when the British take Delhi we will remember this!'

'I am sorry,' said Kalyan Singh quietly. 'I know what you must feel, how you must feel.'

He tapped on the door. It was opened instantly and he went out.

Arabella put an eye to the judas hole. She could see a small stretch of corridor, with two Indian guards lounging against the wall talking to each other, and then Kalyan Singh.

He turned and looked back at the door and saw her and paused, and they looked into each other's eyes, seeing the person within the mind. Arabella felt her throat constrict, and blood colour her face, and she lowered her eyes and turned away, leaning for a moment against the door, heart pounding as though she had been running a long way, and had only just stopped.

She had been away from Richard for months now and she hardly missed him. To be honest, she rarely thought of him. And yet here was an Indian, of all people, a nigger, whom she had only met a few times, but already it was as though he had been in her life, in her mind, timelessly.

And she knew, and was ashamed, that she wanted him also in her body: and nothing more than to submit to him, time and time again.

Three floors above, the old King pulled irritably on his tasselled bell-rope. No one answered. He pulled again and again, listening to the bell peal faintly at the end of the long corridor outside his room.

He had endured a most exhausting morning. His chamberlain had begged him to make an inspection of the cannon, and once more, against all his own wishes, he had allowed the royal elephant to be brought to the gates. Then he had ascended the golden ladder, into the gold and crimson howdah, as he had done so soon after the arrival of the sepoys. But this time, instead of cheering him, they jeered him, shaking their fists and spitting at him. The elephant's legs were spattered with red juice from their mouths.

'Give us our pay!' they chanted.

The King bowed and nodded in the accepted way of royalty, as though he were acknowledging loyal salutes, while his heart raced with terror. Why should he be subjected to these humiliations? They *knew* he had no money to pay them.

Somehow, the elephant had threaded his lumbering way through them, and now he was back in his room, but no one answered the bell. He sat down feebly on his silk cushions, too weary to tug the tassel any more. Tears filled his weak old eyes, tears of frustration and self-pity. He was a prisoner in his own palace, and there was no one in all the world who genuinely cared whether he lived or died.

20

'We have a new commander,' said Lang.

Hodson looked up from the plan he was drafting.

'Who is he?'

'General Reed.'

'My God. He's over seventy if he's a day.'

'Seventy-one. I looked him up. He's been chosen because he is the most senior military officer in the Punjab. That means the oldest.'

'What does Barnard think about this?'

'From my information, he is a bit put out. Thinks it's a slur on his own military capability.'

'Possibly he's right,' said Hodson musingly. 'Barnard's a kind old man, but he is just not up to this task. Anyone with an ounce of initiative and a drachm of energy would have blown in the gates of Delhi weeks ago. Where is our new commander?'

'In bed.'

'But it is only afternoon . . . ?'

'He is fatigued from his journey.'

'If he is fatigued riding in a cart for a few days, how on earth is he going to lead an assault?'

'I don't think he ever will,' said a voice from the door.

They both turned. The surgeon-lieutenant stood watching them.

'I have just visited him. I know, under the Hippocratic Oath, doctors do not discuss their patients, but General Reed is a very special patient.'

'Is he ill, then?'

'Diarrhoea. Old age. Worry. He's too weak to stand. I have him in a darkened tent. But he should be better in a week or two.'

'A week or *two!*' exploded Hodson. 'The rains will be here any day. We haven't *got* a week or two.'

'You'd better tell General Barnard that.'

'I will,' said Hodson. 'I am taking him this plan.' He stood up, buttoned his jacket, buckled on his pistol, and walked over to General Barnard's tent. Barnard was sitting at his table, reading another telegraph message from Lord Canning in Calcutta. Why had no attack yet been mounted on Delhi? What were they waiting for? It was imperative, repeat *imperative,* that an early assault was made.

Now old General Reed had arrived to take over from him and had immediately succumbed to illness. He groaned. How easy it was to urge an attack, how incredibly difficult to make an attack successfully. He had never made one in all his military career, and he was too old to start now.

'Yes?' he asked irritably as Hodson saluted in the doorway.

'My plan, sir. I have drawn this up with the help of the engineers and the artillery.'

He handed it to Barnard, who read aloud: 'Project of Attack on the City of Delhi, prepared for Submission to Major-General Sir H. Barnard, K.C.B. Camp Delhi Cantonment.'

'If I could tell you the basic plan first, sir, it might help?'

'Pray begin.'

'First, the essence of success is complete surprise. As a feint, we withdraw all picquets before the attack and saddle up mules, and load camels and elephants as though we are going to withdraw before the rains come.

'This, I wager, will have the effect of lulling the enemy into a false sense of security.

'The engineers then blow in the gates with gunpowder charges. Immediately the gates are open, storming parties go through and fan out into the city. At the same time, other detachments with bamboo scaling ladders climb up over the walls at selected places.'

'It sounds all right as you say it, captain, but there is

often a great difference between words and deeds.'

'Precisely, sir. My submission is that unless we attack now, before the monsoon, we will be here outside Delhi for months.'

'What is your deadline?'

'Before dawn, the day after tomorrow.'

'That does not leave much time for preparations.'

'There have been four weeks for preparations. The longer we postpone this attack the more chance we give spies of discovering our intentions.'

'On the basis of what you tell me, then, captain, and subject to my perusing your plan, you have my permission to carry it out.'

'Thank you, sir. I would ask that only officers directly concerned shall be informed of this report.'

'You have my word.'

They shook hands.

Back in his own tent, Hodson called the engineer officers together, with Lang, Gough, Jackson, and a handful of other lieutenants.

'I have his promise to attack,' he said, excitement showing in his face and his voice. 'You all know your roles. Keep strict security on our plan, and only inform the picquet officers tomorrow afternoon that their men are to be withdrawn.

'If we do this earlier, the Indians may send out spies and see they are all only waiting on the other side of the Ridge. As it is now, they will assume we are withdrawing, under cover of night. And, of course, we are—away from the Ridge and into Delhi . . .'

At half past four the following afternoon, Lang rode out along the side of the Ridge facing the city. His stomach felt hard as a stone inside him, his muscles taut, as though this could in some way minimize the size of target he presented to the enemy.

The men on picquet duty crouched behind outcrops and in ravines, watching him without interest. Officers riding about were no concern of theirs. A captain in charge of one detachment nodded to him. Lang dismounted and saluted.

'Captain Hodson's compliments, sir. You are to withdraw your picquets from the Ridge.'

'You mean take them all away?' asked the captain incredulously.

'Yes, sir.'

'But we have been in position barely half an hour. I can't withdraw without written orders.'

'There are no written orders. You have only my word for it.'

'Sorry, young 'un. You'd better see Brigadier Graves. He's field officer of the day.'

'Where is he, then?'

'Farther over there.'

He waved towards the river. Lang remounted and rode on. Brigadier Graves, with a small escort, came riding towards him. Lang saluted. Graves nodded to him.

'With your permission, sir,' said Lang rather nervously, 'I have to ask that all the picquets must be withdrawn from the Ridge.'

'Withdrawn? Who says so?'

'It's with the general's knowledge, sir. For a special reason. The order comes from Captain Hodson.'

'Hodson! That madman with all those ruffians and horse-thieves in cast-off uniforms? The ring-tailed roarers, I call 'em. Are you serious?'

'Perfectly, sir.'

'For what special reason are they to be withdrawn?'

'An assault on Delhi, sir. This is part of the plan.'

'I've heard of no plan for this. Whose plan is it?'

'Captain Hodson's, sir.'

'I might have known it. This is some ill-thought-out, harum-scarum idea of his, no doubt? Otherwise, we would have had proper orders of the day. Written, not verbal. You seriously ask me, as a brigadier, Mr Lang, to remove hundreds of men from this Ridge and leave it naked for any attack? Certainly not.'

'I beg you, sir, to reconsider your decision. This plan has General Barnard's authority.'

'But General Reed is now commanding, boy, *not* General Barnard,' said the brigadier triumphantly.

He turned to his escorts; they rode off. Lang watched them, despair rising within him like a bitter tide. He galloped back to Hodson. Already, the sun was losing its heat and some of its light. The picquets would have to move immediately, or it would be too dark for the mutineers to see them, and the whole object of the feint would be lost.

'Brigadier Graves refuses to move without written orders,' explained Lang breathlessly.

'Damn him,' said Hodson. He ran over to Barnard's tent. The general lay asleep on his camp bed. Hodson stood coughing in the doorway until he woke up.

'My apologies, sir, but Brigadier Graves refuses to move his men.'

'Why?' asked Barnard stupidly, half awake.

'Because he has no written orders. Could I ask, sir, that you reassure him? It is essential.'

'Bless my soul,' said Barnard, levering himself reluctantly off the mattress. 'Bearer! Bring me my boots! Of course I will see him, Hodson. If I can find him, that is. God knows where he may be.'

By the time they found the brigadier, the air was already blue with dusk, and although the picquets were instructed to make as much noise as possible, Hodson knew his stratagem had lost much of its value. But now he had begun, he had to go on.

On the far side of the Ridge, the British troops who were to attack, formed up, but none of their officers had told them what was intended; so far as they were concerned, this was another of a dozen earlier and abortive alarms, that had led to nothing. The Sixtieth Rifles, however, were already running through the gloom down towards the gates of Delhi—and there they waited, crouched down in what cover they could find, for the engineers to arrive with charges to blow in the gates. They waited all night, but no engineers appeared.

Gradually, the shadows thinned, the sky grew pale and the sun trembled on the horizon. Inside the Fort, the muezzin called the faithful to prayer, and it was light enough to see sentries moving on the ramparts. To stay where they were was suicide, so back they ran up the Ridge, sentries' bullets pinging around them. The whole scheme had been a fiasco, a bitter, useless, pointless failure.

Hodson admitted this at that morning's conference. He

looked at the smirking faces of his brother officers, and heard Birdwash's open laughter and saw Garroway's face aglow with glee, and realized with astonishment that they had deliberately not co-operated, so that he should be made to seem a fool. It was pointless accusing them of this for they would all produce unarguable reasons for not doing what they had promised to do.

The messenger had not reached the engineers at the agreed time. The artillery were awaiting the bugle call to fire, but somehow it had not sounded. The infantry officers had not informed their troops, because they had been ordered to tell no one of their intentions.

What depressed Hodson most—what he found almost impossible to bear—was the blunt fact that these officers, entrusted with the task of assaulting Delhi, had deliberately misinterpreted the plan—simply to humiliate him.

As he sat afterwards in his tent, writing his daily letter to his wife, the pettiness of their action almost overwhelmed him. What had he done to be so disliked? He wanted desperately to succeed in his chosen profession. And this, he now realized, was what his colleagues could not stomach. You played the game for the sake of the game, not just to win. To succeed was somehow not compatible with being an officer and a gentleman. He might be one, but in their eyes he would never be the other.

Lang came in, sat down on a camp chair, and poured out two glasses of *nimbu pani*. Its sourness accorded with their thoughts.

'They deliberately sabotaged you, Hodson,' he said at last. 'I thought the army was above such things.'

'Then you know very little about the army,' replied Hodson. 'When I was with the Guides, a brigadier arrived once to inspect us. He was so blind, I had to lead his horse by the bridle until his nose touched the bayonet, and then he asked me, "Pray, which way are the men facing, Mr Hodson?" He should have been retired years before, but he is no doubt still serving.

'I served on the frontier under General Roberts, whose colleagues think he is too young for command. And *he* is sixty-nine! Blindness, age, foolishness, these are no drawbacks in the army, provided you have important friends or private means.

'Officers, you see, Richard, are like clerics in the Anglican Church. In the job until death relieves them. They bought their commissions and they feel their investment entitles them to a life of ease. Most of the officers here in the British service are not even the ones supposed to be with their regiments.'

'What do you mean?'

'This. Say a British regiment is being posted to India. Its officers are rich and fashionable, and do not wish to be marooned here for five, ten or twenty years in what, to them, is a social and cultural desert. So they deliberately go on half pay to avoid the draft.

'If the men do that, it's called desertion, and they face death. But not so with officers. They simply find *other* officers, who are short of money, and pay them to take their place.

'On paper, therefore, the first set of officers may have served for thirty years, in all sorts of overseas stations. In fact, the only action they have seen is inspecting the guard at St James's Palace or Brighton Pavilion.

'They are not professionals, Richard. They are play-actors. The army is an amusement for them, a gentlemanly way to spend a fortune someone else has left them. And a career of arms should be a career of honour.'

He banged down his glass angrily.

'Come on,' he said, smiling suddenly at his own irritation. 'Let us purge this out of our system. One of my spies says some mutineers have arrived in Khurkund, a village a few miles away. Let us pay them a visit.'

'How many men do you need, and when?'

'Fifty horsemen in ten minutes.'

Lang went out, and Hodson studied the map. Khurkund. Where had he heard that name? It seemed to burn out from the shaded contour lines, the grid references and the squares. And then he remembered. Bisharat Ali, the Indian money-lender, had been going to Khurkund.

Of course. With his wealth, he would be as invaluable to impoverished mutineers as they would prove to him. He could advance them pay at a rate of interest that would put them and their families in his debt for years.

How many other rich Indians like him, ever greedy for

gold, were now laying the foundations of even greater fortunes? A shadow fell across his map. Rajib Ali was standing in the mouth of the tent.

'Salaamaji.'

'What news from the Fort?' asked Hodson.

'I have found some friends of former days, sahib. I have given them a password—"Checkmate" from your English game of chess—should they wish to bring information direct to you.'

'Good. What else?'

'The King fears for his own safety more than for the success of the revolution. He never wished for this, I am sure.'

'What about the sepoys from Meerut and elsewhere?'

'They are bewildered, sahib. They were under the impression the King was going to pay them, but he has no money. So they have looted most of the shops. They exist on a system of barter. They have great stores of grain and rice in the city, of course, so they do not starve. And the British have, so far, done nothing to frighten them. So they think it is only a matter of time before they control all India.'

'At the rate we are progressing, they may be right,' said Hodson grimly. 'What about hostages?'

'That is more difficult, sahib. I could wander at will in much of the palace, but not in the part where the guards were strongest. I believe there are a number of *memsahibs* and children being held there.'

Hodson turned to Gough, who had arrived to tell him the troop was ready.

'Give my compliments to the officer commanding the artillery, and pray inform him to keep all shells away from the area of the palace where the S.O.S. was seen. There are British hostages there, wives, and children. Then join me with the horses. And you, Rajib Ali—we are taking a ride. We have a horse for you.'

'Thank you, sahib.'

Hodson strapped on his revolver, buttoned his uniform, mounted his horse, and led the troop out down the Ridge and across the plain.

The sun blazed like a sullen comet in the sky. He put on his tinted glasses. Oddly, now he had been more active, his headaches had almost left him, but the fiasco of the early morning attack had set off those half-forgotten hammers in his brain. A hard ride out and a frisk through the village would, he hoped, exorcize his headache and his frustration.

'Is the mail service still running?' asked Gough suddenly. 'I have had no letters at all from anyone since I've been on the Ridge.'

'*Dak* carts arrive and leave Delhi every day. But what happens to the letters, I do not know.'

Lang had seen the little two-wheeled vehicles pulled by two sturdy ponies, able to keep up a jog-trot for hours, and he knew that the mail routes across India were divided up into stages, as for stage coaches in England. But here each stage was only about six miles long because of the fierce heat and the roughness of the roads. Then the horses would be changed for the next part of their journey.

'It is odd,' said Gough musingly, 'but we have had no reports of any of these mail carts being ambushed.'

'Of course not,' replied Hodson. 'Because they don't contain any mail.'

'No *mail?*' his companions repeated. 'No. Their drivers are too crafty. They tip the lot into a shellhole or a ravine and go on empty. Better to save their lives than the post. Sometimes some letters *do* arrive, but the post office clerks are mostly drunk, and if you want to find a letter you have to go down to the postal tent and rummage through thousands for it. I have been talking to Harvey Greathed, the senior civil servant here, and his tent is next to the post office tent. He says his pillow is stuffed with official letters no postman has bothered to deliver. He calls it "futile Agra correspondence".

'God knows what messages have been lost. Or how many appeals for help and what urgent reports are lying all around us, thrown away. When I send instructions out to my spies and ask for their reports, I use messengers. I write the messages on thin paper and fold them up in bamboo cylinders which they conceal in their orifices. And in case they are captured, I usually write in French or Greek—about the best advantage of a classical education I have discovered so far. Trouble is, one has to have a classics man at the other end to decipher them!'

They were approaching Khurkund now. A rash of mud buildings with palm trees leaning away from the walls; a bright green swamp near a water-hole with a bucket on a beam. Some children stood watching them, thumbs in their mouths. One ran away; to warn someone inside, Lang thought.

'Prepare for attack,' shouted Hodson. The horsemen spread out into a single line, with twenty feet between each rider. A musket cracked from one of the huts, and then another, and a third; the bullets went wide, spouting up little fountains of dust.

Hodson raised his sword and his troop charged. Within seconds, they were behind the hut, horses panting, chickens squawking and a tethered goat with bursting udder under their feet.

The rear wall had no windows, only an open doorway, leading into an earth floor. Hodson called out in Hindusthani: 'Come out, with your hands above your heads.'

Half a dozen sepoys filed out, holding muskets up over their heads.

'Throw them on the ground.'.

They did so. Hodson turned to a file of his men.

'Seize them,' he ordered.

They dismounted, picked up the muskets and jumped back on their horses.

'What regiment are you from?' asked Hodson.

'Nineteenth Cavalry, sahib.'

'How many are in this village?'

'Only us, sahib. The rest have gone on to Delhi.'

'Why are you staying here?'

The man paused. Hodson put the point of his sword to his throat.

'Answer me or die.'

'There is a rich man here, sahib. He has paid money to our comrades and to us. We are his guards.'

'Is his name Bisharat Ali?'

'That is so.'

'Where is he?'

'In his house, sahib. He is unwell.'

'Then we will visit him,' said Hodson. 'A visitation of the sick, as my father would say. You lead us.'

The sepoy ran ahead, holding his dhoti up out of the dust, until they reached a house with a mud wall. Women in purdah fluttered off a veranda into the shadows as they approached.

Hodson dismounted, threw his reins to Lang, and walked into the compound of trodden earth. Chickens fluttered around his feet.

'Are you coming out to see me, Bisharat Ali, or do I come in to see you?' he asked, waiting, sword in hand, feet apart, watching the veranda. A curtain moved behind a window. A fat man walked out slowly, hands outstretched in greeting.

'Mr Hodson sahib,' said Bisharat Ali, trying to smile. 'How good of you to visit my humble home.'

'You have often waited hours outside mine,' replied Hodson. 'I thought the least I could do was to repay the compliment. Especially since I hear you are not well. You remember, the other week in Kurnaul, you were going to tell my brother officers about my debts?'

'Ah! That was only talk, Hodson sahib. You must not believe all we businessmen say.'

'I believe nothing you say, Bisharat Ali. But I believe some things about you. That, for instance, you have many I.O.U.s in your house. Deeds for plots of land that poor persons have given you in return for a few rupees to buy a share in a wooden plough or an ox. By so doing, they have mortgaged themselves to you for ever. If they lived a thousand years they could never pay off your compound interest.'

'Oh, sahib, that is not so! I myself have many poor relations. I help them. I am a man with a large family.'

'You are a rogue and a traitor. I also believe you have paid many deserters and mutineers who have marched to Delhi. What did they give you in return? Promises of a share in their loot? Or protection when you finally feel it is safe to come out and declare yourself?'

'That is not true, sahib. Whoever said that is an enemy. I have many enemies.'

'While I live, you need no more. Bisharat Ali, I have come to pay my debt. Do you remember what it was at your last accounting?'

'I have forgotten, sahib.'

'I have not. It was two thousand, four hundred and fifty rupees.'

'I do not want it. *Please*, sahib!'

'You were going to denounce me to my brother officers,' Hodson went on remorselessly. 'Denounce me.'

'No, sahib. You misunderstood me.'

Hodson took out a wad of notes tied with a string and threw the bundle on the ground. He saw sweat run down Bisharat Ali's fat trembling jowls, the conflict of fear and greed flickering like flames in his evil old eyes. He brought up the sword slowly and pressed it against the money-lender's stomach. The flesh moved like a soft balloon.

'Go into your house, Bisharat Ali. Bring out all your receipts for your debts.'

'I have none here, sahib. They are all in Kurnaul.'

Hodson's sword moved forward a fraction of an inch. Bisharat Ali felt the tiny nick it made in his puffy flesh. A bead of his blood reddened his shirt and grew damp against his body, and he trembled with alarm.

'Bring me these papers, or I'll kill you here and then go in and take them.'

'I will see what I can find, sahib.'

Bisharat Ali turned and fled up the wooden steps. He was back within minutes, carrying a tin chest. He placed it on the ground.

'It is locked, sahib,' he said triumphantly. 'And I have no key.'

Hodson drew his revolver and fired twice. The lock shattered. Papers and receipts for money lent had been crammed in so tightly that they burst out with an elasticity of their own as the lid leapt open.

'So you have no papers? You see, you lie again.'

Hodson threw him a box of lucifers.

'Set fire to them,' he said.

'No, sahib, I beg you. They are not mine. They belong to friends. To the bank.'

'Either you light them or I will,' said Hodson, and stirred them with the point of his sword.

Bisharat Ali, trembling, drops of sweat falling like tears on the papers, knelt down and struck the match. The papers burned reluctantly at first, then with a swift fierceness; pages fluttered like huge black leaves over the roof of the house.

'That settles a number of debts,' said Hodson with satisfaction. 'Now, take my money.'

Bisharat Ali stood up, counting the notes mechanically, but his eyes could not leave the flames. A fortune was being destroyed in front of him. He trembled at the unspeakable sight.

Hodson cocked his revolver and took a pace back.

'Say your prayers, Bisharat Ali,' he said. 'If there is any God in whom you believe except the god of money.'

'No, sahib, I beg of you. Do not kill me. I will give you anything. Anything you ask. All I have is yours. I am not a poor man.'

'You are poor in every worthwhile virtue. And you keep poor, everyone who falls into your clutches. You are a *very* poor man.'

Bisharat Ali opened his mouth to speak, and Hodson fired.

For a second, the money-lender stood, hands outstretched beseechingly, mouth still open. Then he sank slowly, like a huge white sack collapsing, and fell forward at Hodson's feet.

Hodson broke his revolver, blew down the barrel, extracted the spent shell, replaced it with another, snapped the revolver shut and put it back in its holster.

'You have killed him,' said Lang, horrified.

Hodson did not reply. He walked out of the compound, leaving his money behind. He had paid his debt. Who took the new notes was not his concern. Crowds who had gathered at the gate parted silently to let him go through. No one spoke. Hodson jumped on his horse, turned out across the plain and led his men back towards Delhi at a smart canter.

'That was murder,' said Lang.

'When I was reading law at Cambridge,' replied Hodson, 'the definition of murder, as I remember, was "to kill unlawfully with malice aforethought, to kill wickedly or inhumanly." None of those conditions applies in this case. Bisharat Ali financed hundreds of rebels against us. He was one of the bankers of the revolution.'

'But you killed him because you once owed him money. Because he hounded you for it,' said Lang.

'Rubbish,' said Hodson. 'I don't know what you're talking about.'

'I do,' said Lang. 'That is the reason why people will say you shot him, anyhow.'

' "They say," ' quoted Hodson. ' "What say they? Let them say." They can say what they like, pass on what rumours they like. But *I* say that in killing that parasite I've done as good a deed today as any in this whole campaign.'

They rode on in silence. Lang kept glancing at Hodson. What an astonishingly complicated character the man was! He could not have shot anyone, no matter how corrupt, when he stood defenceless, beseeching mercy. But then, of course, Bisharat Ali *had* financed the rebels. He had deserved to die. It was probably only the manner of his death that seemed so distasteful.

Then Lang remembered the first man he had killed, the man who had rushed with a flaming torch outside his bungalow in Meerut. That shot had been a reflex action. Perhaps, in a sense, Hodson had fired for the same reason, a delayed reflex action?

'Do you ever read Shakespeare?' Hodson asked him suddenly.

'Only when I was at school. Why do you ask?'

Hodson shrugged. He had been thinking of Susan; wondering whether she was still in her darkened room. The one-sidedness of their relationship nagged him, the long gnawing dissatisfaction of being in love with someone who was not in love with him; the light shining into the unreflecting mirror.

'I like his sonnets,' he said, almost talking to himself now. 'The dark lady. The woman Shakespeare loved. The woman whose name no one knows. I was thinking about men who love women who don't love them.'

Lang thought immediately of Arabella; a quick kiss at their engagement party, turning her face away from him. Always elusive, just out of his reach.

'Does that often happen, do you think?' he asked.

'Often,' said Hodson. 'Too often.'

Lang was surprised. Somehow he had always assumed that when people fell in love, as in a kind of arithmetical equation, they loved each other equally. But, of course, there was no reason why that should be so. Could that be

the reason why he had received no letters from Arabella?
Maybe he loved her more than she loved him? Maybe she
did not love him at all?

'Shakespeare,' Hodson went on. 'In one sonnet he wrote
words that are applicable to Bisharat Ali—and to all of us
out here—"the fools of time . . . which die for goodness
who have lived for crime."

'What are we really living and perhaps even dying for
out here? To subdue a great country and a proud people?
No. To make a fortune for ourselves? Not so far as I'm
concerned. To convert the heathen to a religion not all of
us find easy to believe? Is *that* our purpose? Or do we just
do these things because we are driven on by some imperious power within ourselves? Like the badger who has to
keep on digging or his nails grow into his own flesh?'

They rode on, silence shrouding their thoughts.

Garroway sat on a stool on the shady side of his tent,
while his bearer shaved him. When the man finished, Garroway stood up, patted his face on a towel that had been
warming on a stone in the sun, pulled on his jacket, and
went slowly down the hill. He did not thank the bearer,
who bent down slowly to pick up the towel his master had
thrown on the ground.

The camp on the Ridge had changed since Garroway
had first arrived; he felt pleased that he had helped to in-
stigate some of the more important changes, and even
more gratified that he had profited from them.

When Garroway realized that the siege would be long,
he had sent back a special messenger to Meerut with a
note which he signed indecipherably 'on behalf of the general commanding,' demanding that machinery for making
soda water and ice should be sent to Delhi forthwith.

When this eventually arrived, dismantled and on the
backs of six camels, no one knew where it should be delivered, and Garroway's brother officers were therefore
pleasantly surprised when he unexpectedly suggested that
he would take it.

None guessed that the money charged for bottles of
soda water served in their mess tent, which he claimed
was needed to pay Indian servants who worked the machinery, actually went into the black metal chest he kept

locked in his tent. For his bearer operated the machinery
for no extra money at all.

Garroway next persuaded two English traders from
Meerut, Mr Peak and Mr Allen, to set up shop on the
Ridge, where officers could buy delicacies such as
preserved oysters in stone jars, and pots of Oxford mar-
malade.

He organized Indian marksmen to shoot wild geese,
which he sold to officers' messes. For, having little work
to do, the officers lived surprisingly well. Each mess boasted some culinary specialty.

Infantry officers dined regularly on roast goose, with
rice pudding and stewed guavas, drinking bottles of India
Pale Ale and claret by the pint. The artillery enjoyed six-
course dinners every night, with fish and mutton, and
elaborate pastries. Yet, while the officers dined formally in
full mess dress, waited on by *khitmagars* in white uniforms, the stench of rotting bodies outside—elephants,
mules, camels and human corpses in shallow graves—was
so foul that open bottles of eau-de-Cologne stood on the
tables to drown the smell of death.

Garroway also promoted impromptu pony races, taking
bets through an orderly, and games of cricket and quoits
in the lines of the Sixtieth Rifles.

He was determined never to be poor again. He took his
percentages in so many ways and from so many enterprises that, so far as he was concerned, the siege of Delhi
could never last too long. His greatest worry was the quite
unexpected enterprise of Hodson and other officers like
him, not cast in the traditional army mould of caution
and procrastination. For them and for a dozen other
junior officers, the siege had already lasted far too long
and had degenerated into a conundrum: Who are the besiegers, and who the besieged?

General Reed, still in bed, sent a telegraph to John
Lawrence urging him to appoint a brigadier in whom he
personally had confidence, Neville Chamberlain, as adjutant-general, and to send John Nicholson to Delhi with
what he called 'a movable column' of troops.

The new chief engineer, Colonel Richard Baird Smith,
who had succeeded the elderly major, although ill with
dysentery, camp scurvy, trench mouth, and wounds that

persistently refused to heal, threw in the weight of his authority with Hodson's appeals for an early attack, for the
logistics of the situation appalled him.

They were losing at least thirty men a day through
mortal wounds or illness; and on some days as many as a
hundred. They had barely enough powder for one day's
active firing of the siege guns, and only thirteen thousand
rounds of musket ammunition, with eight hundred rounds
of shot for the heavy guns.

Every day they fired so many rounds and lobbed so
many shells over the city. And every day their force was
diminished by death and disease; so the longer they
delayed, the weaker they became, both in men and muni-
tions.

Then General Barnard fell ill with cholera one morning. The attack was so severe that by afternoon his problems resolved themselves, for he was dead. After his funeral, his effects were put up for auction, with those of
General Anson, which by some military mischance, had
been misdirected from Amballa to Delhi. The mess of the
Ninth Lancers paid £400 for General Anson's stock of
wines and beer, and rather less for General Barnard's.

Left now in total command of a dwindling force of dubious morale, General Reed made his only decision of the
campaign. He sent an urgent telegraph to Lord Canning
in Calcutta: 'MY SHATTERED STATE OF HEALTH HAS COM-
PELLED MY MEDICAL ADVISERS TO URGE MY IMMEDIATE
REMOVAL TO THE HILLS AND I ACCORDINGLY LEAVE CAMP
FOR SIMLA TONIGHT.'

Before Canning received this information, which was
not entirely accurate, and lest he should have other instructions, General Reed and his entourage of officers, servants, camels, mules and baggage carts were a hundred
miles away from the scene of action, and heading north at
a sprightly rate for one recently so ill.

An hour before he abandoned camp, Reed promoted
Archdale Wilson to the rank of general; he was, therefore,
in command. Reed did this to scotch any ugly allegations
that he had deserted his force and left them leaderless.

Wilson was not the most senior brigadier, but he had
made himself agreeable to the general, inquiring solici-
tously after his health every morning; this was his reward.

Wilson viewed his new appointment with a mixture of

alarm and horror. He could no longer quote the comforting Article Seventeen of the Bengal Army Regulations as an excuse for inaction, but he did the next best thing. He immediately sent a long message to Lord Canning as an insurance against what he felt would be almost certain failure.

'Our force comprises two thousand two hundred Europeans and fifteen hundred Punjabis,' he wrote. 'The enemy is without number, having been reinforced from all points, well equipped and strongly entrenched. The siege is on their part, not on ours. They attack us day after day, and are always repulsed, but not without considerable loss to us.'

That evening an old Indian beggar, dressed in rags, limped into the camp. Thin, bowed, gripping the traditional staff of his profession, he made his way to Rajib Ali's tent, and crouched outside in its shade until Rajib Ali emerged. Then he stood up and they had a short discussion. Rajib Ali took him on to Hodson's tent.

Hodson sat at his table, writing to his wife. He wrote nearly every day, sometimes letting the letter run on over several pages, describing what had happened or not happened; his hopes for an early attack, his best wishes for her welfare. Some of the letters, he knew, would be thrown away by the *dak* carrier. But surely one or two would reach her, and tell her of his love? And perhaps, one day, she might even reply with a letter of warmth. He frowned at the interruption.

'What do you want?' he asked Rajib Ali.

'A messenger wishes to see you, sahib. He says he has saved the life of Sir Theophilius Metcalfe.'

'Show him in.'

Hodson laid down his pen and wiped the ink off the nib so that the dust would not clog. He had heard about Sir Theo's experience; he looked with interest at the man who came in.

'I thought you were a holy man,' he said.

'Checkmate,' replied the fakir, giving Rajib Ali's password. 'The sahib does me much honour. Sometimes, in these troubled days, it is safer to travel as a beggar. Poor I may be in worldly goods, but now I speak for one who has riches in this world.'

'Be seated.'

Rajib Ali closed the tent flap. They all sat down on stools. The little hurricane butti cast a gentle yellow light around them, throwing up their shadows, larger than life, on the grey canvas walls.

'I have come from Mirza Mogul, one of the King of Delhi's sons,' the fakir continued. 'I bring you a message from him. A prayer that when this unfortunate time is ended, he may have safe conduct and still retain his position and his title.'

'That is impossible for me or anyone else to promise. When we recapture Delhi, Bahadur Shah and the princes will have a fair trial—if they survive, that is, and do not die before then at our hands, or their own, or at the hands of the mutineers.'

'The prince is a rich man, sahib.'

'All the riches in the world cannot give life and freedom, when life and freedom are priceless.'

'Sahib speaks wisely, and the truth. But can I return to the prince and say that at least you are not ill-disposed towards him?'

'I do not know the man. Only the foul deeds that have been done in his name. They do not dispose me to show friendship or mercy towards him.'

'He would be willing to pay for what evil he has done.'

'You mean—a bribe?'

'I would not use that word, sahib. A business transaction.'

'Go back to your prince, holy man,' said Hodson. 'Tell him he will get a fair trial. No more, no less. If he lives.'

He stood up; the other two men rose with him.

'I will do as the sahib says,' said the fakir. 'In the meantime, to show the prince's friendly intentions, I have brought a list of English *mems* who are hostages within the palace. If the sahib could guarantee safe conduct for the prince, he in turn would guarantee their lives.'

'I will consider what you say,' said Hodson.

The fakir passed over the piece of paper, folded half a dozen times, which he had been carrying in the palm of his left hand. Hodson bowed to show the interview was at an end. As Rajib Ali and the fakir went out, they passed Lang, coming in.

'I heard the mail had arrived,' he said. 'Anything for me?'

Hodson shook his head sadly; he had been hoping, too.

'We are unlucky,' he said. 'However, news from another source. One of the princes would like to buy safe conduct. And he has sent out a list of hostages to prove that underneath it all he is really an Englishman at heart.'

Hodson laughed grimly and unfolded the paper. Lang leaned over his shoulder and held up the lamp. Together, they went through the names.

'Arabella!' exclaimed Lang. 'Thank God she's alive. To think she is only a few hundred yards from where we are now. If I shouted, she might hear me. My God, Hodson, we *must* attack! *Soon!*'

'I am going to keep negotiations with this prince open, for he offers to guarantee the safety of these hostages.'

'You mean you would treat with the enemy?'

'I would treat with the devil himself if it would help the situation—and these wretched people, including your fiancée.'

At that moment, a great shout came from outside the tent. They both dashed to the door. Up the Ridge came a group of horses, and behind them, stretching it seemed to infinity, marching men, their feet stirring dust in the moonlight like mist from the ground.

'It's Nicholson!' cried Hodson excitedly. '*Now* we'll march on Delhi!'

Other tents were opening to show triangles of light, and officers and men peered out, giving a great cheer at the sight of the tall man who rode at the head of the column. Nicholson raised his right hand to acknowledge the reception, and rode past them to Wilson's tent.

He had set out as soon as he had received Reed's instructions. They had marched and ridden solidly, with only a few hours' break each night for sleep, for his experience at Multan had made him impatient of delays with British troops. Knowing their custom to march by night, when the air was cool, and to rest in what shade they could find during the burning heat of day, he had set off at dusk. By dawn, as the sun came shimmering over the rim of the earth, he had halted his column in a grove of trees.

Thankfully, they loosened their equipment and threw themselves down on the hard earth to rest. He let them lie for ten minutes, then issued a strange order: every man

was to cut off a branch big enough to give him shade.
What an ingenious idea, thought the troops, and far better
than having to move every few minutes to keep beneath
the shade as the sun travelled across the sky.

But when they had hacked the branches down, Nicholson gave another and altogether unwelcome command:
'Fall in, in four ranks. Prepare to move off!'

They had marched through the night. Now they were to
continue in the heat of the day. The branches they had
cut they were to carry as sunshades. When weariness and
heatstroke overcame some men they were lifted on to baggage carts. When elephants pulling guns wilted in the
heat, trumpeting, red-eyed, for water that was not there,
and sank down exhausted on the burning ground, unable
to drag the oak and iron limbers another foot, Nicholson
harnessed men to the guns instead; and so the column still
moved forward. Nothing had delayed him; and everyone
in the column knew that nothing would.

Up on the ramparts of the Red Fort, under the bright
moon, three soothsayers were burning the disembowelled
body of a goat to determine, by the direction in which the
wind blew the smoke, when the British would attack; if
they would attack.

Ram Gupta squatted on his haunches watching them.
They were not of his religion, but he was open-minded
enough to believe that good men could follow gods other
than his own. Yet somehow he doubted whether these
three *moaulvies*, who had the ear of the King, were more
than charlatans.

To Ram Gupta, the idea of burning a goat on the ramparts to discover an enemy's intentions seemed absurd. If
you desired to know such things, you sent out patrols and
scouts and spies, and you built up a mosaic from isolated
facts they uncovered. That the man he had revered as
King could believe this superstition disturbed him—like
the endless inconclusive discussions between Nana Sahib
and Azi Mullah. He had treasured illusions about them
all, and they had shattered like broken mirrors.

These men no longer reflected reality; and reality was
that the legendary Nicholson had arrived on the Ridge
with a column of men. Hodson was already there, with at

least a thousand more and he heard rumours of a siege
train and giant guns, only a few days' march away. These
were facts, and he need burn no goats to find them.

And what else was happening in the Fort meanwhile?
The sepoys had not been paid since the beginning of May,
so they had looted the shops of everything they could lift
to barter for food.

Groups of them, carrying a loaf of bread and a bottle
of rum, would beat on the front doors of the larger
houses and inform each terrified owner that they knew he
was harbouring sympathizers with the English. When he
protested his innocence, they would look at him knowingly—and produce the bread and rum.

'Then how is it that we find these here?' they would
ask, and seize him. In most instances, he would bribe
them to set him free. If he did not, they would simply loot
his house and go on to the house next door.

Other sepoys, drunk with toddy on empty stomachs,
rode their starved ponies in mad races down the streets.
Passers-by had been trodden underfoot and fearfully injured, but neither discipline nor punishment prevailed.

Pyramids of garbage, and human and animal excrement, steamed and stank in every street, picked over by
rats and vultures; all the chickens had long ago been
killed and eaten. Wells were fouled, and the smell of pol-
lution, corruption and decay hung like an evil miasma
over what he remembered as a city of splendour.

As Ram Gupta squatted on his haunches, he recalled a
conversation earlier in the day with the bank clerk, Gopal
Singh, who had looted George Beresford's vaults of all
they contained. He had buried five hundred thousand rupees, more than either of them would earn in nearly a
thousand years at the rates the British had paid, and the
sheer size of the sum had terrified him.

'What shall I do with it, subedar sahib?' Gopal Singh
had asked. 'Every day sepoys dig in some garden, knowing that frightened people have hidden silver or jewels or
gold. It must only be a matter of time before my secret is
discovered. Could it not be put to some good use?'

'I will think about it,' said Ram Gupta, and he had
thought. And in thinking again as he squatted, wrinkling
his nose at the unsavoury smell of burning flesh, he

reached his decision and drew himself up to his full height. As he did so, something cold touched the back of one hand; and then the other, and then his face. He looked up at the sky; drops of rains were falling. This meant that within days the monsoon would begin, the Jumna would swell to a roaring torrent, and the ground all around the city would become a quagmire, a morass which neither man nor beast could cross. This rain was a sign from the heavens that he had decided wisely, and he felt content.

He walked down from the ramparts, through the long, draughty corridors of the Fort, where beggar couples copulated, half covered by rags, and abandoned babies cried in the dirt, crawling on hands and knees like stinking turtles, covered in flies. How horrible, how unbelievable to think that all this could happen in the King's palace!

He reached the door of the King's room and knocked on it sharply.

'Who is it?' called the King.

'Subedar Ram Gupta, Your Majesty.'

'Enter, subedar.'

Bahadar Shah was squatting on his cushions, puffing his hubble-bubble pipe. The room felt cold and cheerless, the air stale and used-up.

'Your Majesty,' began Ram Gupta. 'I present myself to you with a proposition.'

'Not a request?' interrupted the old King, narrowing his eyes.

'No, Your Majesty. It will be my privilege to give, and not to take.'

'Speak on.'

'Already some of your commanders have sent emissaries to the English to ask what terms they might expect—if they surrendered. And since your troops have not been paid, their interest dwindles in our cause. This is understandable, for they have no money whatever. I can remedy that.'

'How?'

'If you make me commander-in-chief, Your Majesty— and I submit that with my years of service in every rank from a sepoy, I know how to command men—I will change this whole situation. I also know the whereabouts of half a million rupees.

'If I were a dishonest man, I would take them for my-self and vanish, as hundreds have already done with what loot and treasure they can find. Instead, if I am honoured with Your Majesty's trust and authority, I will pay the men a week's wages from this money. The rest I will keep in reserve for their needs.

'I will drill them, as the British drilled us and as every army needs to be drilled. I will demand obedience from everyone, the princes included, and I will punish wrong-doers in the ways of our ancestors. For insolence, I will cut off their noses or their ears. For theft, I will cut off their right hands, and I will bring you victory. This I can promise, if any man can.'

The King put aside his hubble-bubble pipe and stood up, looking Ram Gupta in the eyes.

'You speak as an honest man, and the voice of honesty is not often heard in our court. It is as the Lord Buddha said, "If a man make himself as he teaches others to be, then, being himself well subdued, he may subdue others; for one's own self is difficult to subdue."

'You have subdued any wish to personal riches. You are thus qualified to subdue greed and envy in others. You have our full authority to take command. Do whatever seems good to you.'

He held out his hand.

'So I am now a general, Your Majesty?'

'Yes. Our general.'

The King went across the room to a lacquered cup-board, opened it, took out a small ceremonial shield and a silver sword, the coveted badges of a general in the old Mogul army and handed them to Ram Gupta.

'I will pay the men, Your Majesty. Then we will attack at the earliest auspicious hour.'

Ram Gupta bowed and saluted with his sword, and backed out of the room. He had no illusions about the difficulty of his task. He had seen the princes humiliated by the sepoys, for they could not speak or even under-stand the low class dialects the soldiers used, and had to give orders through interpreters.

Some sepoys had even jeered and spat at them. And lacking authority and the will to dominate, the princes had pretended not to notice. Other sepoys, uneager for ac-tion, had dipped old rags in the blood of cats and dogs, and wrapped them round their legs, pretending they were wounded, to escape the dangers of a patrol.

Ram Gupta ordered the buglers to sound Assembly, and addressed the sepoys as they paraded in the courtyard of the Fort.

'I am your general now,' he told them. 'Here are my sword and shield of rank. I have the King's authority. Moreoever, I have money. Everyone will receive ten rupees at nine hundred hours tomorrow morning. This is the first instalment of your pay.'

He joined in their enthusiastic cheers, feeling himself to be with them but not of them. He would never be of them again; for now he was in command.

From an upper window, the King watched the scene, and was unmoved by it. But then the night air was chill and his blood ran thin, and he distrusted the people when they cheered; they had cheered him once, and that but recently.

He closed the shutter and turned back into his lonely room. He was old and almost done. He felt the bitter taste of gall in his mouth; the worms were already all but in his body.

21

The big headquarters' mess tent was packed with officers, called there urgently for an evening meeting by an order pinned to the camp notice board and signed by Colonel Geoffrey Goatherd, a senior officer holding the Queen's commission in the regular British Army—as opposed to officers commissioned in the East India Company's Army.

Goatherd was a fussy little man in his mid-sixties. His family controlled a brewery in the Midlands, and he had paid for each step of his promotion out of its profits.

Despite his willingness to invest in himself, promotion had not been swift, for even among contemporaries not noted for quick perception or sharpened wits, Goatherd was unusually slow to understand even simple matters. Hodson quoted Crabbe whenever he thought of him: 'Habit for him had all the weight of truth; it must be right, I've done it from my youth.'

'Gentlemen,' Goatherd announced gravely, standing on a table so that he could command the attention of those a foot taller than himself, 'I have called you here together urgently to discuss a most serious situation which, if unchallenged, could establish a dangerous precedent which we might never reverse.'

His audience waited without much interest. What might appear most serious to Goatherd would not necessarily impress them to the same extent. Only his seniority had assured him of their presence.

'With the arrival of Mr Nicholson, who does not hold the *Queen's* commission, but the *Company's* commission, an extraordinary state of affairs has arisen, quite unauthorized in my understanding by the terms of the Queen's warrant.

'Although only a *lieutenant,* he will, in fact, rank as a *brigadier,* promoted in the field.

'This means that other officers, colonels who have served for years—like myself, although I do not put myself forward for any honour or promotion—they—we—have been passed over for a man, who, however brave, lacks both their experience and their years.

'Some commanding officers feel so strongly about this that they threaten to refuse to serve under this gentleman. Accordingly, to prevent embarrassment, it has been agreed by the general that two Queen's regiments, the Queen's Fifty-Second Foot and the Ninth Lancers, will not serve under him at all, but will be transferred to another brigade.

'These two regiments will physically change positions on the Ridge with the First Fusiliers. Now while many senior officers holding the Queen's commission are agreeable to this, other officers, who hold the Company's commission, think it is entirely unnecessary.

'They point out that the tents of all these regiments are in a deplorable state and will not stand striking and pitching again. But if tradition is to be maintained—and I put it to you that the roots of our regimental strength are their traditions—we *must* do this.'

'Are we to understand then, sir,' asked Gough, 'that this has been agreed, and that you have called this meeting to hear views on it?'

'That is so.'

'Then this seems to me to be an unnecessary waste of everyone's time, when we are on the eve—or so we all hope—of a general assault on Delhi.

'This decision will mean, sir, that thousands of men, and officers, too, will have to sleep by night and live by day, under the open sky. The rains are due within days. I submit that their situation will then be intolerable.'

'Hear, hear!' came other voices.

'I second that,' called Hodson. For some days, he had been confined to his bed with dysentery, and he had only come to this meeting because he assumed that it must have some connection with the assault on Delhi. So far as he was concerned, this was the paramount aim of all officers and men, that took priority over every other consideration.

'We have all accepted what many consider to be needless privations on this baking Ridge for weeks already,' he went on, 'although many of us feel that if we had attacked earlier, we would now be inside Delhi in proper quarters. I submit, sir, that senior officers holding the queen's commission should think again.'

'I take it, Captain Hodson,' said Goatherd frostily, 'that you hold the Company's commission?'

'You take it correctly. And although you may feel it is socially inferior to the commission you hold, colonel, and I do not argue the point, this to me does not seem a time when we should busy ourselves unnecessarily with trivia of this kind.'

'Trivia!' repeated Goatherd in astonishment. 'Are you suggesting, Captain Hodson, that I have called this meeting together to discuss *trivia?*'

He had no answer. At that moment, a shell, screaming like an express steam train, whistled through the top of the tent, tearing two gaping holes, and exploded behind the Ridge. Immediately, they heard the bugler and rushed out to action stations.

Goatherd sat down on the table and slid off; he did not care to jump from such a height on his short legs. Really, the type of man who now accepted a commission! It was intolerable to think that one had to share the mess with them, and still maintain a semblance of cordiality.

Galvanized by Ram Gupta's exhortations, the Indians were charging across the Ridge outside. Ram Gupta, realizing the physical difficulty of running uphill and then engaging an enemy he believed would be entrenched in nullahs and ravines, had swept his forces over to the right, heading out towards the village of Nujufghur, sixteen miles away. This had an abandoned fort with thick walls and parapets, and a well.

He guessed that the British would be at first bemused by these tactics and then, realizing their destination—Nujufghur was the only village in that direction for thirty or forty miles—they would follow.

Their roles would then be reversed. Instead of defending prepared positions, the British would have to attack a fort devoid of cover for several hundred yards all round. His men would be inside its walls with cannon. They could decimate the British if they approached closer than a quarter of a mile—and at almost no risk to themselves.

Elephants carrying artillery secured to their bodies by giant girths crashed, trumpeting, through prickly grass. Limbers rattled, and sowars shouted threats and curses as they rode, breakneck, swords glittering under the moon.

By the time the Sixtieth Rifles had loaded and adopted firing positions, the mutineers were out of range. The artillery lobbed a few shells hastily in the general direction of the column, but they weaved to the right and left more quickly than the gunners could traverse their guns. Within seconds, it seemed, they were no more than a moving cloud of dust disappearing into the distance.

Nicholson walked into Wilson's tent, and saluted.

'I am going after them, sir,' he announced.

'But you will never see your way,' Wilson protested petulantly.

'There is a moon,' replied Nicholson dryly. 'I will need sixteen hundred infantry, say four hundred and fifty cavalry, and as many horse artillery as you can spare— say, fifteen or sixteen. The officers don't know me yet, sir, so I would appreciate it if you could form this force for me.'

'That is a large contingent,' said Wilson doubtfully.

'I agree,' said Nicholson. 'But if they hurry they can be ready within thirty minutes. However, they will be travelling light. So let us set that as our outside time—and aim to be ready to move off in fifteen.'

He saluted and left the tent.

'My goodness,' said Wilson, impressed despite himself. 'Fifteen *minutes*.'

Why, a day, or even two, was not considered too long to make sure all limbers were packed with ammunition, axles greased and rations issued. Now he wanted them ready in minutes! This fellow Nicholson was certainly a goer!

Outside, Sir Theophilius Metcalfe approached Nicholson and introduced himself.

'I know this area well,' he said. 'Can I accompany you as guide?'

'I would be honoured,' replied Nicholson. 'We leave in fifteen minutes.'

Lang reported to Nicholson, who was tightening the girth of his saddle, while the syce stood by, holding his sword.

'Captain Hodson's compliments, sir. He is ill with dysentery and asked if I could accompany you.'

'And you are?'

'Richard Lang, sir.'

'Lang,' said Nicholson. 'Ah, yes. I had a letter from my mother mentioning you. At least, I assume it's you? Apparently your mother lives near mine in Torquay?'

'That's right, sir.'

'Come along, by all means. Anything is better than staying in this stinking camp waiting for something to happen. For, in this life, and presumably in the next, if you want something to happen, you are best advised to start it yourself. As we are now.'

He swung himself up into the saddle. Columns of men were appearing in the gloom; infantry, with packs on their backs; artillery horses pulling guns; cavalry with lances. Officers rode out to report to Nicholson.

'Ready in all respects to move off, sir.'

'Very well, then. Proceed.'

Soon the cavalry, riding at an easy canter, had outdistanced the infantry, who trudged along, first in their own dust, and then across a plain which, even under the little rain that had already fallen, had unexpectedly become a bog.

They sank in to their knees. Leeches half an inch long slid through laceholes in their boots, battened on their flesh and swelled up on blood to the size of slugs. The swamps gave way to brackish water, so that the soldiers had to unbutton their ammunition pouches and hold them on their heads to keep them dry. Just when it seemed they would have to turn back, for by now the water reached their waists, the ground grew firmer, and then they were out on the other side.

Nicholson sent riders far ahead to make sure the mutineers did not turn back towards them unexpectedly, as behind them the gun limbers sank up to their axles in mud, and the infantry were called to heave with the horses. Men and beasts struggled in the marsh until the wheels were on hard ground and they could all go forward.

They stopped to brew up a quick breakfast of tea and chapatties, scraped away the worst of the mud from their uniforms with the sharp edges of their bayonets, and then they were off again.

At four o'clock in the afternoon, almost exhausted, they came in sight of Nujufghur and halted in a grove of mango trees. The men threw themselves down on the ground to rest, unbuttoning their jackets, lying, eyes closed, sobbing for breath, while Nicholson, still on his horse, and apparently not tired, scanned the village through his glasses. He could see the fort with its thick mud walls and the snouts of thirteen guns poking out between the turrets.

To attack directly, with his own troops weary, would be suicidal. These guns could blow them to pieces; and yet there was no other way. As he sat pondering the bleak situation, rain began to fall, heavy drops at first and then long spears of it, turning the ground to mud, soaking everyone within seconds.

At first they welcomed its coolness. Then, as rough serge chafed their tired, sweaty bodies, and they wrapped strips of shirt tail round the actions of their muskets to keep them dry, they cursed it. Even with glasses, Nicholson could only make out the fort and the village as dim shadowy shapes. Equally, therefore, the watchers behind the loaded cannon could not see them clearly. This would give them some protection.

He formed up his men, and rode slowly down the line explaining his plan quietly.

'We are going to attack,' he announced simply. 'Cavalry to the right. Infantry, straight ahead. At my command, the artillery behind will open fire.

'Infantry will advance in extended order, but hold your fire until you are within twenty yards. Then fire—and charge.

'And I promise you, the fortress will be ours.'

There was something about this huge, confident officer on his gigantic charger, unwearying and seemingly impervious to heat and rain and danger, riding slowly along the ranks, repeating these commands, that the men found immensely refreshing.

Someone gave a cheer, and then, suddenly, they were all cheering and waving their shakos in the air, shouting their approval of an officer who spoke a language they understood, who bore the mark of the born warrior.

'We'll get the boogers . . . ! We'll hang their balls on their own bayonets . . . !' they shouted, oblivious of the rain and their own weariness.

'Save your energies for the charge,' reproved Nicholson.

He rode over to the artillery.

'Have you your range?'

'Yes, sir. Four hundred and fifty yards it is.'

'Right. When I draw my sword and hold it above my head—Fire! Reload immediately and fire three more rounds.

'At the first volley, gentlemen, you go forward,' he told the infantry and the cavalry. 'Any questions?'

'Yes, sir,' called Private Dougan from the back. 'Do we take any prisoners?'

'None,' said Nicholson shortly. 'But if there is any prize in that fort, if there is any treasure *whatever,* it will be yours equally.'

Behind the infantry, the gunners stood away from their pieces, portfires already lit, sheltering the flames with their caps.

Nicholson drew his sword and held it high. Immediately, the earth shook and thundered with the guns and a cacophony of orders and counter-orders.

'Sixtieth, prepare to advance! . . . Ad-*vance!* Number three gun, reload. Number two gun, *Fire!* . . . Sixtieth— *Charge!*'

He heard the sudden accelerated clatter as the cavalry went forward, lances horizontal with the ground, horse hooves drumming on the steaming earth.

Through a shining screen of rain, the infantry began to run forward, each holding his rifle in his right hand, muzzle steadied by his left, until the officers riding slowly ahead of them whipped out their swords and gave the command: 'Fire!'

Sixteen hundred muskets cracked as one. The men ran on, through their own sharp grey cloud of gunpowder

smoke, while cannonballs whistled and trundled above
their heads, crashing into the Fort, sending up great red
gouts of mud.

Up the slope to the walls, the soldiers ran, soaked,
wretched, hungry, filthy, Nicholson at their head, ignoring
the crackle of fire that poured down on them. Now and
then, a man stumbled and fell, and the ranks closed up as
though he had never been there.

Close to, the walls were lower than they had anticipated. They jumped on each other's shoulders and leaped
down on the other side. Mutineer gunners went on firing
their cannon until they were bayoneted or clubbed to
death, and their bodies fell across the reeking, steaming
barrels.

Others fled. The artillery saw ragged stragglers pelting
across the desert and swung round their guns to blow
them to pieces. Within minutes, the fight was over, and
the battle won.

The muddy compound streamed with water; bodies lay
face down in puddles like sodden bundles of rags. The
fort contained several small buildings with locked doors,
soon smashed open by musket butts. Inside, lay treasures
hidden for safety, no one knew by whom; gold ornaments
and lockets, jewels, rings. British soldiers, reeling with
weariness, grabbed handfuls of jewels and crammed them
into their jacket pockets. It was too wet to sleep, or to
light a fire to cook any food, but they found some rum,
and passed the brown bottles from mouth to mouth,
chewing dry chapatties, unable to think beyond the moment. And that was enough. They had triumphed.

Then they moved the bodies of the dead, and spread
out their capes and lay down in inches of water, too
weary to seek shelter elsewhere. Some time during the
night, the rain eased and then stopped; and by morning all
the water had drained into the ever-thirsty earth.

They marched back towards Delhi, dragging behind
them the thirteen guns they had captured. Camp followers
rode ponies laden with loot. One man carried a live
peacock under his arm.

Limping, sodden, exhausted, but triumphant, they
reached the Ridge at sunset, and Wilson, with unexpected
imagination—having seen them when they were still a

long way off—ordered two regimental bands to play them in for the last few hundred yards.

This victory was an omen of others to come. It proved to everyone on the Ridge that, under vigorous leadership, they could attack seemingly insuperable odds—and overcome them.

John Lawrence, receiving the news by telegraph in the Punjab, cabled to Nicholson delightedly: 'I wish I had the power of knighting you on the spot.'

Only Colonel Goatherd disapproved. Why could not such a victory have been won by a *gentleman*, holding the Queen's commission, instead of some upstart in the Company's army?

22

At first, Arabella thought that the scratching outside the door was only the cautious scraping of rats' claws; the Fort was over-run by rats. She stirred uneasily. Weeks ago, the sight of a rat would have made her scream; now she accepted them as part of living, something to be endured.

She sat up and listened. Kalyan Singh had provided four rooms for the women and children, each smaller than their original cell, but higher up in the Fort, with windows through which they could look out across the bridge of boats.

The five women in the room slept like corpses, The macabre impression heightened by the old white saris that Kalyan Singh had procured for them, which they had put over their faces as protection against mosquitoes.

The scratching continued. Arabella suddenly realized that there was someone outside the door.

'What is it?' she asked in a whisper, so as not to awake the others.

'I am opening the door,' replied Kalyan Singh in a soft voice. 'Come outside, and say nothing.'

Arabella tiptoed on bare feet over the stone flags. The door opened a few inches as she reached it, and closed again and the key turned in the lock. Kalyan Singh motioned to her to move a few paces down the corridor in case any of the women in the rooms overheard them.

'I have news for you,' he said softly.

They were so close she could smell the oil of crushed

Kashmir petals he used on his hair. She had never liked
this scent before; it seemed too wholly Indian. Now, in
the darkness, it smelled fresh and clean, and altogether
different.

'I am leaving for Cawnpore in the morning.'

'Well?'

'I may not come back.'

'Oh. In that case, thank you very much for what you
have done to help us.'

'I did not ask you out for that. I wanted to see you
alone to tell you what is likely to happen here. A former
subedar in the Company's army has been made commander-in-chief. He has just been defeated in his first battle sixteen miles from here, by a new general on the British side, someone more energetic than the others. John
Nicholson.'

'Good for him,' said Arabella.

'Now that your countrymen have had this victory after
so long, they are almost certain to attack the Fort within
days. First, because their spirits are up. Secondly, because
the monsoon will break very soon, and after that it will be
too late.'

'So we will be rescued?'

'Not necessarily. Many of my countrymen resent your
being here at all. They may take you as hostages to bargain for their own safety. Or they may simply decide to
do away with you all as being dangerous witnesses against
them.'

'Why do you tell me this? To frighten me?'

'No. Because I don't want you to be hurt. I want you to
come away with me.'

'But I couldn't possibly do that. I could not abandon all
these other women and children. And you are . . .' She
paused, not wanting to say the word, suddenly not wanting to hurt him.

'An Indian,' he supplied quietly. 'But *why* can't you
come with me? *They* would leave you in the same circumstances.'

'I don't think so. Anyhow, that is not the point. They
are my people.'

'Listen, Arabella,' he said gently. 'This is a battle for
survival. Nothing less. I don't know whether I will survive
myself. But at least, if you come with me, I would know I

had done everything I could to save you.'

'Why do you want to do so?' she asked.

'Because I—like you.'

'I like you, too, Kalyan Singh. But what hope have I of surviving in Cawnpore if I did come with you? They have killed all my countrywomen there.'

'You will have my protection. You can trust me. I have done my best to help all of you here.'

'I would reproach myself always if I escaped and my friends did not, without my even telling them what may happen.'

Kalyan Singh put out his hands and took hers. He smoothed the backs of her hands gently with his thumbs. His touch was very gentle.

'So I will say good-bye,' he said.

'Yes. But maybe we will meet again. And when my countrymen do come back, I will speak for you. I will tell them what you have done for us here. That you are not like the rest.'

He bowed his head, and lifting her left hand up, he kissed it lightly.

'That is your English custom, is it not?'

'Only when you hope to meet again,' she said, and suddenly she knew she did want to meet him again, that she could not think of life as a prisoner without his visits. And when he had gone, she might never see him again. She would be on her own.

'What a terribly senseless thing all this is,' she said sadly, meaning not just the fighting between her race and his, but the difference between the colour of their skins, the fact that he was leaving her and she felt that a part of herself was going with him.

'I pray we may meet again,' he said.

He took her by the hand and led her back to the door.

'Your mind is finally made up?'

She nodded. Somehow, she could not bear to speak in case she broke down, in case she lost her will, and against all her upbringing, all her beliefs, she went with him to Cawnpore, and from Cawnpore to who knew where—with a stranger, an Indian, a *nigger!*

She took a deep breath as he turned the key and opened the door. She went into the room and then leaned against the wood, listening to his footsteps fade away. Everyone still seemed asleep and she tiptoed to her own bed and lay down, but someone was awake; Mrs Bartram, the widow of a surgeon.

'What's wrong?' she asked urgently.

'Nothing. Kalyan Singh came to say good-bye. He is going to Cawnpore. He believes the British are going to attack the Fort soon.'

'Trust him to run away,' said Mrs Bartram bitterly. Her husband and seven-year-old son had been hacked to pieces as they sat at breakfast on that terrible Monday morning.

'I *would* trust him,' agreed Arabella. 'But not to run away. He has done all he could to help us.'

'When the British come back we'll soon sort out these black swine.'

'These black swine, as you call them, may sort us out first,' said Arabella.

'What do you mean?'

'They could take us as hostages, Mrs Bartram, or even kill us, rather than let us live to say how we have been treated.'

'To have endured all this for so many weeks, to have lost my husband and son, only to be killed on the eve of rescue! Why? Oh, God, why?'

She looked out of the window, her face pale as marble under the moon. The two women lay in silence, thinking, all sleep banished until the sky turned pink, and sunlight began to cauterize the room, and the others awoke.

Nicholson stirred in his bed, and was instantly alert. Rain drummed with a thousand fingers on the roof of his tent so loudly that the noise had woken him up. The monsoon was almost here. He sat up, listening to the water gush and swirl down the tent walls, streaming off the rocks outside. Soon, their boots and leather equipment would be coated with green mildew overnight. It would be impossible to move guns or carts, or even to march, for tracks became roaring rivers, and the desert ground a treacherous quicksand into which frantic horses would sink to their stomachs.

They would have to take Delhi within days or abandon the whole attempt.

Despite the early hour, Nicholson got out of bed, washed and shaved in cold water by the light of a hurricane *butti*, and dressed. He had made up his mind what he would do.

He looked out of his tent. The sun was coming up; soon the ground would begin to steam. He saw Hodson walking through the lines, hands behind his back, and called to him. Hodson turned and crossed over to his tent.

'I have made up my mind,' Nicholson told him. 'It is absolutely essential that we attack at once. And if Wilson does not move, I intend to propose at today's meeting that he is superseded. Are you with me?'

'Yes,' said Hodson. 'Wholeheartedly.'

'This is mutiny, you know,' said Nicholson with a wry smile. 'If we oust Wilson and take command and *fail*, then we stand to be court-martialled. We will be just as guilty as those poor devils we have blown from guns. What I am proposing, Hodson, is a kind of treason.'

' "Treason doth never prosper; what's the reason? For if it prosper, none dare call it treason," ' quoted Hodson dryly. 'Who do you propose should take command?'

'Neville Chamberlain is ill, or I would put forward his name,' said Nicholson. 'And, under the circumstances, I cannot very well suggest myself. The last thing I am after is self-advancement. I will put forward the name of Colonel Campbell of the Fifty-Second. No one else is senior enough. Frankly, I do not care who leads so long as we break the siege before it breaks us. And, by us, I mean the whole British Empire. Because, if India goes, everything goes.'

The two men were silent. Clearly, Campbell would only be a figurehead; Nicholson would be in actual command, in every sense but title. Then they shook hands.

After the conference that morning, Nicholson waited behind when the other officers had left.

'I would like to speak to you privately, sir,' he told Wilson, who was fussing with papers on his table, patting them sideways, until they were all neatly laid together, one on top of the other.

'About the assault on Delhi.'

'What about it? You know my views. We need to wait for reinforcements. Also, the rains are starting. It is very doubtful whether we will receive reinforcements in time. Conditions up-country for moving columns of troops and horses and elephants will soon become impossible.'

'Exactly, sir. The whole situation is becoming impossible. I have brought a movable column to Delhi for the sole purpose of helping to capture the city quickly.

'Captain Hodson is here with his Horse, with the same special purpose in mind. In addition, according to the latest Parade State, we have a total rank and file, including everyone—lascars on the guns, *classies* to pitch the tents, cart drivers, and recruits—of eight thousand seven hundred and forty-eight men.

'Of these, two thousand nine hundred and seventy-seven are off duty, ill or unable to fight through wounds. Of the Europeans, in whom I place my greatest trust, we have only two thousand two hundred and ninety-four infantry in a physical condition to fight, though what their mental state for attack is after all these weeks of needless waiting, I am not competent to judge.

'We have five hundred and eighty European artillerymen and four hundred and forty-three cavalry. A grand total of nine thousand and eighty-eight men to tackle maybe ten times their number.'

'I know all that, Nicholson,' said Wilson irritably. 'We just have not enough men for the task.'

'Yet every day we delay, sir, our numbers dwindle dramatically and desperately. Out of the six hundred men I brought here three weeks ago, I have today only two hundred and forty-two in fighting condition. More than half have died or are in the hospital without spending a single day in action.

'My reason for seeing you privately now, is to inform you that I intend taking a very serious step. Unless you give the order to assault Delhi, I will suggest to the other officers that another commander be selected.'

'I assume you intend to put yourself forward for this position?'

'No, sir. I do not. I seek no self-advancement. I would suggest Colonel Campbell. He is a cavalry officer, and also possesses the inestimable social advantage over me of holding the Queen's commission.'

'You realize the gravity of your proposal?' asked Wilson coldly, stroking his thin, cone-shaped beard.

'To the full, sir. I also realize the far greater gravity of our situation if we do *not* attack. If the rains catch us on this Ridge, we will lose the majority of our men through fever, dysentery, cholera, and God knows what other disease. We will also lose Delhi for ever, and probably India.'

'What are you trying to tell me, Nicholson, that I do not already know?'

'I am trying to tell you, sir, in the simplest, most direct way at my command, that we will be defeated ignominiously—without even going into battle.

'There is no possible reason for delaying our assault, whether of logistics or strategy. If we continue to do so, you, sir, will be blamed for not putting our cause to the test. I need not dwell on the calumny that will result from this.'

'You need not, indeed,' said Wilson acidly. 'But no doubt you will. Since you are so convincing I give my permission—but reluctantly. Delhi will be attacked as soon as the men are ready.'

'Within days,' pressed Nicholson.

'As you say. Now, please leave me.'

Wilson sat, fists clenched, after Nicholson had gone. The tent was hot and he was sweating so much that his hands stuck to the pages. He called an A.D.C.

'Fetch the surgeon,' he ordered him.

'I am ill,' Wilson told the Assistant Surgeon when he arrived. 'I have not slept for weeks, despite your doses of laudanum.'

'There is nothing physically wrong with you, sir, apart from nervous exhaustion.'

'That is surely unusual for a general to suffer from?'

'Not in this command, sir,' replied Cartwright, remembering General Anson and General Reed.

'I cannot think properly,' said Wilson. 'I have headaches. I do not eat. When I drink brandy, it burns in my stomach. And I am continually pestered by other officers who do not have the responsibilities of command, who seem unable to appreciate the realities of our situation. Attack! They say, Assault! At once! *Now!* They are fools, Mr Cartwright, *fools!*'

Wilson stood up. His hands were trembling; streaks of sweat coursed down his face. He stared at the young man with wild, unhappy eyes.

'And I will tell you something else, as a doctor, and for your ears only. This whole business of waiting here is unhinging my mind. I'll tell you a secret—two secrets. One, I have given these fools permission to attack, against all my training and my judgement. The second secret is this. *I am going mad.* Do you hear me? Mad! *Mad!*'

And he beat the table with his clenched fists, until the inkwells danced and the papers fluttered. Then, suddenly, he collapsed, face in his elbows, sobbing uncontrollably.

'Well?' called out Hodson impatiently as Nicholson passed his tent.

'We are going in,' said Nicholson. 'Ask Colonel Baird Smith and the rest to meet in my tent immediately.'

Officers crowded in. News that action seemed imminent flickered like flames through the camp.

'I have called you here, gentlemen,' he said, 'to tell you that General Wilson has given permission for us to assault Delhi.'

'Hear! Hear!' called a colonel enthusiastically. 'If we wait any longer, there will be only me and my batman to make the charge. Most of my fellows are down with dysentery and fever.'

'No doubt,' said Nicholson, 'but if I know them they will rise from their beds, like souls from the grave at the last trump, when the time to attack arrives.'

He turned to Baird Smith.

'You, sir, have probably the most important role, because you have to site the guns and provide them with defences.'

'In the last ten days,' Baird Smith replied dryly, 'I have received no less than sixty letters from the general, arguing the difficulties of the situation, so I have plans for most eventualities.

'We have already surveyed the Ridge for the best places to dig in the guns. After all, we have spent the whole summer here, and some of us have been occupied with more serious matters than pony racing and quoits. I have sixteen thousand sandbags waiting to be filled—if you can

detail the men to fill them. We will carry the sandbags by
camels to our new gun positions. We should start work at
dusk tonight—and continue for several nights.

'I will put out working parties to cut down trees on the
rear of the Ridge, to bring them over for more cover. I
have also already detailed teams, with mules and camels
and bullock carts to carry the shot. We will dismantle the
guns and move them as near as possible to the Fort. The
artillery have some new twenty-four-pounders, which have
just arrived, and these should do some damage, provided
we get them close enough.

'Then a volunteer party will carry bags of gunpowder
down under cover of night and place them against the
wooden gates to explode just before the infantry attack.'

'Excellent,' said Nicholson. 'What about the artillery?'

Another colonel brought out a folder of papers.

'So far as the gunners are concerned, sir, I suggest we
start spasmodic fire this afternoon, just to make the Pandies keep their heads below the parapet in case they see
we're bringing up new guns and changing positions generally.

'At the hour of assault we will open up with every piece
we have on the Ridge—new and old.'

'Then *we*'ll take over,' said Nicholson, glancing at Hodson. 'We'll charge the gates. Since my arrival I have had
men making scaling ladders of bamboo poles. We will
throw these up against the walls, and those who cannot
enter Delhi through the gates will climb up and over.

'The whole enterprise depends on speed and audacity. It
is my belief, gentlemen, that this force has both.'

'Hear! Hear!'

'In the meantime,' Nicholson went on, 'we will continue
our patrolling activities as before. Any break could arouse
suspicion.'

'My information,' said Hodson, 'is that there is already
dismay and discontent within the Fort, and that many mutineers have actually left. They have been paid for one
week, apparently from funds some former subedar, Ram
Gupta, has acquired. He is now commanding the sepoys
and calls himself general.'

'I knew him,' said Colonel Whitehead. 'We were together at Barrackpore. A very loyal fellow. I am surprised

he has gone over to the other side.'

'Perhaps he was surprised at the way we treated him,' suggested Hodson gently.

'Right, gentlemen,' continued Nicholson. 'We will have another meeting at eighteen hundred hours tomorrow. We fight vastly superior numbers, but, under God, we will be victorious.'

He bowed to signify that the conference was at an end. The officers filed out into the noon-day heat.

Three hours later the guns began to fire on Delhi, and Hodson called Rajib Ali to him.

'We are almost certain to run short of shells, for this barrage may go on for days. Tell all the bearers and *bhistis* and *khitmagars* to collect for the artillery all the cannonballs they can find that the enemy has fired at us. I will pay a rupee for each one. There are hundreds lying about. We may as well lob them back as lose them.'

'It shall be done, sahib,' said Rajib Ali. 'In the meantime, while you are at your meeting, I have had another visitor in disguise, Munshi Jeewan Lal. He is in charge of various financial matters concerning the King. An important man, sahib.'

'What does he want?'

'He has been providing information to our agents. He trusts that this will be taken into account should we be victorious.'

'Is that all?'

'Not entirely, sahib. He proposes a gift of fifty thousand rupees to you.'

'Why?'

'To make sure you do not forget this, sahib.'

Rajib Ali handed him a letter, sealed with red wax. Hodson opened it. The proposition was there in writing.

'Anything else?'

'He brought another request. From the Begum.'

'A dangerous woman,' said Hodson, wrinkling his face in dislike. 'What does she want of me?'

'Your assurance of safe conduct, sahib. She asks that you accept for your lady wife a gift of some of the royal jewels.'

He handed over a second letter. Hodson put it in his pocket, unopened.

'Altogether, Rajib Ali,' he said cheerfully, 'we *could* make a fortune, you and I.'

'Not could, sahib. I hope we *will!*'

Hodson laughed.

'What shall I tell Munshi, sahib?'

'Tell him what the Lord Buddha said about money,' replied Hodson. ' "Riches destroy the foolish; not those who seek the other shore. The foolish by his thirst for riches destroys himself." '

Arabella was asleep, and when the door of her room was suddenly ripped open, she started up, half awake, terrified, clutching a strip of sheet to her.

All afternoon, the Red Fort had trembled under the thunder of British guns. Plaster had crumbled and small stones fallen from the ceilings of their cells. Sometimes, walls themselves had shaken, as though in terror. The bombardment was the heaviest they had heard, and fear spread roots in their thoughts as to what it presaged, and how they would fare when the British finally attacked.

'You have visitors,' announced the guard, holding up a hurricane butti. Half a dozen plump men filed in. A strong scent from their oiled hair filled the room with perfume. The women sat up, watching them warily.

One man spoke to them in English.

'As the eldest son of the King of Delhi, I regret that you are not being afforded the comforts which it is our wish to extend to you.'

'You have waited long enough then, you black swine,' one woman shouted from the safe anonymity of the darkness. 'Why come to us now?'

'As you have heard for yourselves, heavy artillery has been firing this afternoon. It may be that your countrymen will be misguided enough to attempt an assault on this impregnable citadel.

'They will, of course, be driven back in defeat and ignominy, and no doubt the fact that the rains are due has galvanized their cowardly leaders into this reluctant and unwise action.

'If this *were* to happen we would, nevertheless, like to be sure that you did not become instruments of revenge from the thousands of sepoys who hate your race and your religion.'

'In other words,' said Arabella, 'you want to keep us alive as hostages to try to barter your skins for ours?'

'You misconstrue the kindness of our hearts,' protested the second of the scented men.

'I see right into your hearts,' retorted Arabella. 'I see no kindness there. Only fear of what will happen to you when this attack is launched.'

'We are not here to talk, but to help you,' said the first prince. Then, quickly turning to the guard: 'Take them out. See the children are kept with their mothers. Move them into the rooms I have already shown you.'

Other guards now came in, carrying more lamps. In their shadowy glittering glow, the women packed up their few belongings and filed out in silence into the corridor. The smell of dung and sweat from the beggars, who crowded the corridors to shelter from the shells, was so strong that some of the smaller children began to cry, and the women choked and retched with the stench.

In silence, they were led past sleeping, huddled bodies, until they reached a stone staircase lit by oil lamps hanging from the walls. A cold sour wind blew down it. They shuddered in their thin clothes, terrified and dispirited.

A hand plucked Arabella's sleeve as she began to climb. Kalyan Singh was standing in the shadows. He pulled her to one side. The column shuffled on without her.

'I thought you were in Cawnpore?' she whispered to him.

'My horse went lame,' he said unconvincingly. 'I felt that it was an omen, so I decided to delay my departure. I am taking you to Cawnpore. Now.'

'What about my friends here?'

'I cannot take you all. You will come?'

His voice sounded anxious, as though she might suddenly refuse, as she had done before.

'Yes,' she said. 'I will come with you.' And it was as though a weight was lifted off her heart; not simply that she was escaping, but that she was escaping with a man who somehow meant more to her than any other man she had ever met. The feeling was absurd and illogical; but it was also true and would not be denied.

'Follow me.'

Kalyan Singh led her down a side corridor, completely dark, like a sewer. The rattle of a bolt in the darkness, and they were in a courtyard outside the Fort. A horse, already saddled, stood tethered to a hitching ring. Some clothes were thrown over its back.

'A sari,' he said, handing her one of them. 'Put it on.'

Arabella took off her shabby clothes and stood naked for a moment, except for the spine pad all Englishwomen wore against the heat of the sun, until she slipped on a white silk bodice. Then she wound the sari around her, as her ayah had shown her so many times when she was a little girl.

'You ride and I will walk, until we are across the bridge of boats,' he told her. 'Then we will both ride.'

'Why are you doing this for me?' asked Arabella, facing him.

'Because I wish to,' he said shortly, and busied himself untying the horse's rope. She put her hand on his arm. For a moment he pretended not to notice it; then he turned to her, holding the reins in his other hand.

'Is that the only reason?' Arabella asked softly, seeing his face as though for the first time, his hair curled and dark against his forehead. For a moment he did not answer, and they stood looking at each other in the dimness, the horse snorting behind them, and then his other hand went out and gripped hers.

'No,' he admitted. 'It is not the only reason. But you talk too much, Arabella. There is a time for words, and a time for deeds. Mount up.'

She hitched up her sari, and swung her leg over the saddle. He took the bridle, and, picking up a staff from the ground, led the way out into the streets. They did not speak until they reached the sentry at the edge of the river.

'Salaamaji,' Kalyan Singh called out. The man grunted a reply and spat into the mud. Then they were out on the bridge of boats that tipped and creaked and moved alarmingly like a living thing under the horses' hooves.

Half-way across, Arabella glanced back at the Fort. It crouched, bristling with armaments. Here and there a light flickered faintly in a high window. Which one would be the window of her friends' room?

She looked across at the Ridge, under the moon, dotted with tents, with guns pointing long fingers at the sky.

Then she looked down at Kalyan Singh, walking silently in his chaplis at her side.

He smiled up at her. She smiled back, and instinctively dropped one hand on his shoulder. He reached up and gripped it in his own; and they went on together.

A British sentry on the far side of the Ridge heard the creak of an ungreased wooden axle and the blowing of oxen as they strained forward under the whip.

'Halt!' he called. 'Who goes there?'

'Friend. An Englishwoman.'

The sentry advanced cautiously to the cart, through the dusk. An Indian was squatting on the centre shaft, his face shrouded against the vapours of the night. Behind him, on straw, a woman in her late thirties sat sideways in the cart, with a shawl around her shoulders, and her feet pressed out against a trunk to keep it from rattling.

'Who are you?' he asked.

'Mrs Rosemary Bolivar,' she replied. 'Wife of Major Bolivar of the First Ninth Dragoons.'

A corporal, hearing the voices, came running out and thrust a hurricane butti in her face. She *was* English, brown from the sun, but still with that aloof and imperious look he associated with officers' wives.

'Who do you want here?' he asked stupidly.

'Who do you think, man? I have been wandering in the hills for weeks, going from village to village. I want somewhere to sleep, a bath, food, protection.'

The corporal led the cart in through the lines, where the men dug in darkness, filling sandbags, their spades striking sparks from hidden flints, to the nearest officers' mess. Gough, the orderly officer, came out rather irritably to see what the trouble was.

'Good *God*,' he said in amazement. 'Mrs Bolivar, ma'am. I haven't seen you since Meerut. Where is your husband?'

'I haven't seen him since then, either,' she replied. 'He went on detachment. My bearer helped me to escape, and then I hid in a village which had, of all people, a German headman, who was friendly. He passed me on to another village, where I stayed for a few more weeks, and finally I

came south, for I heard thousands of British troops were
encamped outside Delhi.'

'I'll have a tent cleared for you,' Gough said. 'One of
the bearers' wives will look after you. In the meantime,
ma'am, would you accept a drink?'

'Gladly. A sherry, if you have one.'

An orderly, who had been listening behind the çanvas
of the tent, came out with a decanter and two glasses and
poured the sherry, one for Mrs Bolivar, the other for
Gough. They drank.

'What regiment is this?' she asked.

'A mixture,' he replied. 'Dragoons. Lancers. Rifles. We
are a motley lot.'

'I don't like to mention this,' she went on. 'But I am
without funds, except for a few rupees.'

'We will gladly advance you some money, ma'am, from
the regimental account.'

An Indian woman materialized in the darkness.

'Here is your servant. She will take you to your tent,
and make arrangements for you to bathe. Dinner will be
served there within an hour, if that is agreeable to you. I
must add, without appearing to be inhospitable, that you
have arrived almost on the eve of our assault on Delhi.'

'Then perhaps I'll bring you good luck,' said Mrs Bolivar, handing back the empty glass. She followed the
bearer's wife, and Gough went back into the mess.

Various half-caste women had trickled into the camp
from time to time during the siege, and had been found
jobs as unpaid nurses or mending shirts. Some had even
stitched up rents in the tent canvas. But an officer's wife
was rather different. After all, she was a lady; one could
not expect her to work.

Gough mentioned her arrival to a handful of subalterns
standing at the makeshift bar, drinking whisky and Garroway's soda water, cooled by Garroway's ice. Garroway
put down his drink.

'I met her once or twice,' he said musingly. 'She seemed
a charming person. I'll go and pay my respects to her.'

'She is having a bath now,' said Gough.

'Naturally I will wait until she has finished her ablutions,' said Garroway coldly.

Half an hour later, he was outside her tent.

'Mrs Bolivar!' he called through the canvas.

'Come in,' she said. 'I am dressed and refreshed now.'

Already, she had given personality to the impersonal tent. Two wooden chests were covered by a blanket to make a dressing-table, with a mirror and an oil lamp; various glass bottles of face and hand lotions were spread out on a box by the bed. Mrs Bolivar sat on a stool, brushing out her long hair.

'You!' she said in surprise. 'This *is* a lucky chance.'

Garroway bowed.

'The good fortune is mine, ma'am,' he said.

'Not entirely,' she said lightly. 'You have five hundred rupees of *my* fortune, for which I would trouble you.'

Garroway hated to be reminded of it; anyway, what proof had she?

'That was a gift, ma'am.'

'A loan,' she said firmly. 'An earnest, as I understood it, of further favours to come. From each of us to the other.'

He swallowed. If he could keep the money he could multiply it many times. But somehow his nature would not allow himself to explain this; he found it easier to claim that the money was a gift.

Mrs Bolivar went on brushing her hair, watching him through the mirror. Her blouse stretched tightly across her full breasts with each upward movement of her arms.

'So what you are saying is that what I thought was a loan, you regarded as a gift?'

'Naturally, ma'am, I would be pleased to help you in any way I can . . .'

'But that apparently does not extend to returning to me that which was my own—or rather my husband's?'

Garroway said nothing.

'Mr Garroway,' she said calmly. 'When we last met, our relationship was, shall we say, rather less formal and more intimate than our discussion now. To be blunt and unlady-like, you took your pleasure with me four times in my husband's house, in my husband's bed.

'Perhaps because you are what you are I allowed you to gratify yourself in this way, and also *loaned* you five hundred rupees. I am asking you now, as a gentleman, to repay this loan. I have only a few rupees with me. I must pay my servants and will have to be accommodated by a loan from the regimental account, unless you honour your obligation.'

Garroway fidgeted. What a bitch she was! He *would* give her back the money, eventually, of course, but only after he had trebled or quadrupled it. Anyhow, how could she prove what she said?

'Madam,' he replied with dignity. 'I am distressed to hear this astonishing allegation from your lips. I freely admit that, wearing the fancy dress I proposed to use at the Meerut Ball, I rode out to your bungalow as a jape to see your husband's face when he realized his visitor was *not* an Indian.

'But as for your other accusation, I am deeply shocked that you would think I would take advantage of a brother officer's absence in this way. There is really nothing more to say.'

Mrs Bolivar stood up now, hairbrush in her hand, and faced him.

'There is a great deal more to say, Mr Garroway, and I am sorry you force me to say it. Unless I have that money—and some other concessions, which I will come to later—I will inform your commanding officer of your attitude.

'You know what the result will be. You will be court-martialled for conduct unbecoming an officer and a gentleman. And you will be found guilty. Without private means, your only resource will be to re-enlist in the ranks as a private soldier. There are many former officers serving in these conditions, as gentlemen rankers, as you know well. Like them, you will be ostracized socially and professionally.'

'Mrs Bolivar, I came here to offer you what help I could, and you have made the most serious allegations, which I most resolutely refute. Now you make threats which I do not understand. Accordingly, with your permission, I will withdraw.'

'Very well then, since you are adamant, I will press this charge.'

Garroway looked at her, colour slowly leaving his face as horror clutched his heart with cold fingers. She meant what she said. But who would believe it? The answer came immediately: almost everyone. He was unpopular, without friends. And now he would need every friend he could find.

'How can you prove it?' he asked hoarsely.

'Ahhh! Now we talk!' she said, smilingly. 'So you admit it?'

'I admit nothing.'

'You asked me how I can prove you seduced me. Very easily. I was not entirely speaking the truth when I told you on that Sunday so long ago that the house was empty. My house was *never* empty. A bearer was in the next room.'

'What about it?'

'He saw you. He heard you. He will bear out my statement.'

'But he is not here.'

'He *is* here. He drove the bullock cart.'

They stood looking at each other.

'Five hundred rupees,' she said, holding out her hand. Garroway took out his wallet, counted out five one-hundred-rupee notes, gave them to her.

'I never want to see you again,' he said.

'Understandably. I reciprocate those feelings. But, in fact, we will see a lot of each other because there are the other concessions I mentioned.

'The bearer's wife tells me that you have organized a soda water plant, and ice-making machinery, and other profitable enterprises. You must not be greedy, Mr Garroway. We women are the weaker sex, and if you follow the Good Book, as I know you do, you would appreciate that it is more blessed to give than to receive.

'You will, therefore, give me, for a start, fifty per cent of what you have made from all these enterprises of yours, these trading concessions which go so strangely with the profession of arms.'

'Fifty?' repeated Garroway in a thin, high, disbelieving voice.

'Yes. Until we can agree figures, I will therefore take another thousand rupees from you. Now.'

'I haven't got that much,' he said.

'Well, you had better get it. You should remember, Mr Garroway, that, while we may not be married to each other in the eyes of the law, we are as good as married in the eyes of the Lord. From now on, we will have a partnership.'

Garroway seemed to shrink. He swallowed as though he was going to say something, and then he slunk out of the tent.

For a moment after he had gone, Mrs Bolivar stood looking at her reflection in the mirror, admiring her profile, her jutting breasts beneath her blouse. And then, suddenly, she burst out laughing, threw her hairbrush across the tent and ran her fingers through her hair.

Men! What fools! What pathetic feeble idiots they all were!

If Garroway had been half the man he imagined he was, nay, a quarter, he would have seized her, ripped off her clothes, and had her there and then on the camp bed. Instead, he was like her husband, like them all; weak and wanting her, while she was strong and wanted no one, no one at all.

'We'll stop here,' said Kalyan Singh, and reached up to help Arabella down from the saddle. The rutted road along which they had ridden from Delhi faded into thick grass. Half a mile ahead, she could see a village with mud huts; minarets stood white against the blue afternoon sky, like gigantic chessmen.

Kalyan Singh hobbled their horse with a length of rope, untied a small bag and took out a beaten metal container. Inside, was some rice, and, in a second compartment, a little vegetable curry. He handed down a *chagal* of water, the skin slightly porous to keep the contents cool, and filled a metal tumbler.

'Drink and eat,' he told her. He stood and watched Arabella as she sat on the ground.

'Are we going to stay the night there?' she asked.

'I don't know if it is safe. I must go into the village and see.'

'And leave me here?'

'You will be screened by the grass. So long as you don't stand up, no one will notice you.'

'Don't be long,' Arabella said, suddenly afraid, for the horizon stretched to infinity in every direction; empty, unfamiliar and therefore unfriendly.

'I will be as quick as I can,' Kalyan Singh promised and set off on horseback towards the village. The sun was well down the sky before she heard the swish of grass as Kalyan Singh returned. He dismounted and squatted by her side. He looked worried.

'This is a Moslem village,' he began slowly.

'What is the significance of that?'

'I have had to say I'm a Moslem, as they might kill me if they know I am Hindu. It means you will have to say you are a Moslem, too.'

'But I am a Christian.'

He took one of her hands in both of his.

'Listen, Arabella. The one true God has many names, and as many children as there are nations of men.

'If you wish to survive, you will have to trust me, and do what I tell you. First, you will become a Moslem, at least in name. Then you will have to go through a marriage ceremony with me.'

'But I am already bespoken,' protested Arabella. 'I cannot possibly marry you. You're . . .'

'I know. An Indian. But that did not prevent us making love last year, many times, until your father heard the rumours and sent you home. *Before* you were bespoken.'

'That was different,' said Arabella. 'Marriage is for life.'

'That is what I am offering you—life. The only other alternative is death—after I know not how many men will have pleasured themselves with you. If we go in as we are, you a Christian, me a Hindu, they will kill us both. That is not a threat, it is a fact. I know these people.'

Arabella sat thinking; feeling, rather than seeing the day die and dusk deepen round her. And with the gathering darkness, her sense of loneliness and fear increased. She felt naked to unnumbered enemies, and desperately afraid. The only friend she had, the only person she could trust at all, was sitting by her side. What he said was no doubt true. It seemed unbelievable, but then everything that had happened since that Monday in May had been unbelievable; the incredible became instantly credible after what she had experienced. And she also knew that she needed Kalyan Singh; not only as a companion, but sexually, as a man. Everything about him aroused her, and his colour heightened the attraction. She would marry him and the future would look after itself. What happened here and now was more important, more compelling than what might or might not happen in ten years' time. Was not this as Mrs Todd had also advised her as she lay close to death?

'Let us go into the village,' she said. 'I will do as you suggest.'

'You walk and I'll ride. In Moslem communities, the male is always superior!'

Thus Arabella came into the village on foot; a squalid square of mud huts with a tent pitched incongruously in a far corner. It had obviously been looted from some British camp. She saw with nostalgia the three-pronged arrow of the British War Department stamped on the open flap.

People appeared at the doors of huts, watching them, their eyes hard and hostile. Some of the men carried sticks. A dog barked at her heels and she was too afraid to kick it away. Two men in white robes, both carrying swords, came out of the tent towards them. Arabella recognized their robes; they were *maulvies*, Moslem priests. They halted. Kalyan Singh dismounted and faced them.

'I am Kalyan Mohammed Khan,' he announced formally. 'This is my bride, Arabella MacDonald. She wishes to embrace the one true faith. Great is Allah, the one true God, and Mohammed his Prophet.'

He tethered his horse to a tree and then, taking Arabella by the hand, led her into the tent. The mud floor was covered with half a dozen looted Persian carpets. On these stood several leather armchairs, one with an antimacassar.

'Why is it that you seek an unbeliever, an infidel, as your bride?' asked one of the *maulvies*.

'Each heart has its reasons,' replied Kalyan Singh rhetorically. 'The arrows of attraction fall on believer and unbeliever alike. But she wishes to embrace the faith of our fathers.'

The *maulvi* turned to Arabella.

'Is this so?'

'It is so, father.'

'You know that you will worship five times a day?'

'I know.'

'You will bow down, face towards Mecca, to worship the one true God? You will abhor the unclean flesh of pork and the wicked spirits of wine? You will observe the

Feasts of Islam, for you will be a bride of Islam?'

'Answer "yes," ' advised Kalyan Singh in English.

'Yes.'

'So that, at the end of your life, with the other faithful departed, you will cross Al Sirat, the bridge as narrow as a razor's edge, to drink the waters of Al Cawthar, which are whiter than milk, more perfumed than musk, and then you will walk in Paradise, your thirst quenched for ever, under the throne of God in the Seventh Heaven.'

Arabella bowed her head in assent.

The *maulvi* picked up a pomegranate from a table and handed it to Kalyan Singh with a silver knife and plate. Kalyan Singh cut the fruit in two, kept one part himself, and gave the other half to Arabella.

'As this fruit is one, so will you two also become as two halves of one person, at one with the oneness,' intoned the *maulvi*.

Arabella bit into the soft pink flesh of the pomegranate and handed it back to the *maulvi*. He placed it on the table, and gave them each a glass of sherbet. They sipped the sweet liquid, symbolic of the sweetness of life and love, while the *maulvi*, raising both hands to the roof of the tent, recited the words of the Moslem wedding ceremony.

Arabella felt a hand touch her elbow and a woman who had entered the tent silently behind them, took her to one side. Behind a canvas screen was a tin bath half-filled with muddy well-water. The woman motioned her to undress. Arabella stripped off her bodice and spine pad and sari and climbed into the bath thankfully, feeling the water warm and welcome on her tired body. She submerged herself in it luxuriously.

The woman handed her a towel. She climbed out and dried herself. Her clothes had disappeared. In their place was a *coorta*, a white linen jacket that reached almost to her knees, with long wide sleeves, a white muslin shawl for her head and shoulders, and loose-fitting cotton pyjama trousers. She put them on, and the woman led her into the main tent.

'You are now a Moslem,' explained Kalyan Singh. 'That was the ceremony of purification. Now you must repeat these words after the *maulvi*.'

Facing him, she repeated: ' "In the name of God, the

Compassionate, the Merciful, I betake me for refuge to
the Lord of Daybreak, against the mischiefs of his
creation; against the mischiefs of the night when it over-
taketh me . . ." '

'Now we are married,' said Kalyan Singh.

Arabella nodded and tried to smile. Suddenly, she began to cry. How different this wedding was to the one she
had anticipated in St James's Church with bridesmaids
and a choir, then a reception afterwards in her father's
house, and a honeymoon in the hills!

She had lost her father. She had seen her mother murdered. She had endured suffering, witnessed the needless
deaths of friends and their children, and all these experiences had changed her character, moulded her into someone altogether more mature, more gentle.

Now, instead of being married to a British officer, she
was married to an Indian. She could imagine what her
friends would say, what she would have said herself, only
a few months ago. But—now?

She looked at Kalyan Singh, and he looked back at her.

Her eyes softened; he was kind and he had saved her
life and she knew he loved her, although he had not spoken one word of endearment. She had lain with him already; and she knew now, as they stood in the darkening
tent, that she would lie with him again, and that night,
and for every night thereafter so long as he needed her.
For she needed him, and in that need, in the love he had
shown her, in his kindness, his protection, lay not only her
future, but theirs.

23

The King of Delhi sat in the throne-room of his palace, a
red Bokhara carpet under his feet, facing the angry crowd
who had crammed in for audience. They were all shouting
so much that he could not hear what any of them said;
and he did not greatly care.

Then Ram Gupta stood up and waved his hands for
silence.

'Your Majesty,' he began. 'The British are now about to
launch their long-awaited attack on our capital—or they
will be forced to delay it for months because of the rains.

'I must tell Your Majesty that rumours, possibly put
about by spies in the payment of the British, say that
many in high places here have already made contact with
the British and have offered them great bribes for their
own safety when this attack develops.

'As you are aware, I have promised payment to the
sepoys, Your Majesty. But I now find that your sons, the
princes, have appropriated money that was set aside for
this purpose.'

'You bring us much bad news, Ram Gupta,' the old
man interrupted him. 'And yet, only days ago, when you
took command, you assured us of victory. But at the first
battle, your men slunk away in defeat and disgrace. Your
words were braver than your deeds.

'Why do you all crowd into this room, like mendicants,
seeking comfort we cannot give? There is nothing more
we can do to help. Nothing!'

At these words, the sepoys leapt to their feet and

rushed at the dais, shouting, beating their fists on its wooden floor to show their loyalty and the extent of their feelings.

The King put his hands over his ears and then, with a sudden unexpected movement, jumped to his feet, and bending down, picked up the carpet, and flung it into the faces of the nearest sepoys.

'Get back, you dogs!' he cried. 'You mutinous curs, who come slinking in here for comfort and for money. If you want victory—deserve it!'

They stopped shouting and slowly they filed out in the baking sun, leaving the old man on his own, holding on to the arms of his throne, trembling with age and reaction.

He had been up on the ramparts to consult the *maulvies,* and they had told him gravely that the smoke from the sacrificial goats had blown back over the roof of his palace.

They did not add what he already knew; this meant that, just as he had committed evil deeds, so these deeds were now coming back to him. His treachery had begotten treachery. Like that smoke in the evening sky, it would darken his future and cloud his happiness for ever.

Knowing this fearful truth, how could he concern himself over such minor and totally unimportant matters as the pay of traitorous sepoys?

Night clouds, thin as torn silk, drifted before the moon. At one moment the Ridge was bathed in pale light, and then the scene dimmed, pricked only by a few oil lamps that flickered like captive glow-worms.

No attack would start tonight, as none had started on any other night since the British had first encamped there sixteen weeks before.

In his tent, Wilson was writing a report, one of half a dozen he wrote every day now, to send by special messenger to Lord Canning. Some gave more reasons for his delay in attacking; others, like the one he was finishing, excuses for the defeat he was now convinced that he and his troops would face.

'It is evident to me that the results of the proposed operations will be thrown on the hazard of a die,' he wrote wearily. 'But under the circumstances in which I am placed I am willing to try this hazard, the more so as I cannot suggest any other plan to meet our difficulties. The chances of success under such a heavy fire as the working parties will be exposed to are anything but favourable. I yield, however, to the judgement of the chief engineer.'

Earlier that day he had written an order of the day, on the suggestion of Baird Smith, his chief engineer, which troops were at that moment reading by candlelight on the camp notice board:

'The Major General feels assured that British pluck and determination will carry everything before them, and that the bloodthirsty and murderous mutineers will be driven headlong out of their stronghold or be exterminated.'

This bold intention was far from Wilson's mind as he sat, wearily pressing his trembling hands to his eyes. By this time on the morrow, he thought, we will know the best or the worst. We will either be safely inside Delhi, or we will be scattered like leaves in the wind.

On the far side of the hill, away from Delhi, in contrast to Wilson's silent tent, all was action, as fatigue parties loaded mules and camels with sandbags and cut trees for cover. They worked under strict orders of silence. The only sounds were the rattle of spades, the thud of axes into trees, and the crack as a trunk came down.

Now and then a camel would groan and roar, and to the hundreds of diggers, sweating and tense, it seemed impossible that these noises would not alert the sentries in the Fort. They had forgotten, in their tension, that camels made these noises every night.

Cloud thickened before the moon like a cataract before an eye, and the beasts went forward over the hill, where other men were already waiting to pack the bags around the new gun positions.

The guns themselves had been dismantled, and teams of men were carrying the giant barrels with tree trunks underneath them, while others struggled with wheels and the trails.

More men carried cannonballs, and bags of gunpowder and fuses, and placed them where the engineers had driven marked stakes in the ground, so there could be no confusion in the dark. Like an army of ants, they worked through the humid, sweaty night. *Bhisties* carrying hog-skins of water, slightly porous, so that they glistened like swollen black corpses under their arms, moved endlessly among them, filling their pannikins.

Hodson surveyed the frantic activity with a mixture of impatience and dread; everything had been left too late. They were now attempting to build six new gun emplace-ments on the right, and five on the left in hours, when they could have done all this at their leisure in weeks, in-stead of killing time with quoits or cricket or pony races.

As he stood, he saw flashes of flame from two of the Fort's guns and a shower of grapeshot came rattling down, ploughing up the ground near one of the new em-placements. Some of the sappers and pioneers fell writh-ing in agony, rolling on their bare backs, madly trying to dig themselves into the earth to escape the fearful pain of mutilated arms and legs.

Those uninjured waited for five minutes in silence, chests heaving, sweat streaming down their bodies, mos-quitoes whining in their ears, but there were no more shots. Then they carried off their dead and wounded, and started work again.

An hour before dawn, all the soldiers filed back to their tents, gulped down mugs of hot, sweet tea, and a meal, and fell thankfully on their beds.

When the dawn came up, the gunners filed into the new positions. As the sun strengthened and the call to prayer was heard from the muezzin in Delhi, the artillery colonel stood up behind the main battery, where all could see him. He raised his right hand above his head, and then brought it down smartly, and jumped down behind the parapet. This was the order to begin the barrage.

For a second, the whole Ridge lay silent save for the wavering call to prayer. Then the ground rocked as a mile of cannon spoke.

In the Kudsia Bagh, mortars cracked like whips in the sky. Their shells, trailing lighted fuses through the morn-ing like comets, burst in bright smoke clouds behind the wall between the Kashmir Gate and the Water Bastion.

Deeper than their sharp hollow bark, came the bass booms of the howitzers, squat barrels recoiling as though shocked by their own strength, digging iron-riveted trails back into the earth.

Higher up on the Ridge, a battery of rockets sent up their huge fireworks, hissing like flying serpents, to explode in showers of orange sparks over the wall.

From the ramparts, Indian guns fired back. Hodson, through his glasses, could see these rebel gunners, stripped to the waist, muscles rippling beneath their oiled ebony flesh, as they sponged out the reeking barrels, rammed down more shot, and stood to one side as their guns replied. Trees split like matchsticks, and rocks disintegrated into dust under direct hits. A yellow fog of powder smoke and dust blotted out everything, so that wounded men cried out unseen in the mist that shrouded the Ridge.

Cannonballs fell short and trundled across the earth like red-hot bowls. Artillery elephants trumpeted as the gunners, crouched up in their special howdahs, their swivelling guns able to traverse in a circle, fired until the barrels glowed red. The animals reeled as they bore recoil after recoil, eyes reddened with terror, ears out like grey wings, trunks upturned against the stench of burning flesh and cordite. From the far side of the Ridge, men ran, leading camels and mules weighed down with more shells and powder and wadding.

All through that day the guns fired until their barrels trembled with heat, and *bhistis*, running in relays with hogskins of water, to cool the guns now as much as the gunners, collapsed exhausted. When the barrels grew too hot for safety, the gun teams urinated in buckets, and poured their own water over the barrels.

As the sun burned up the sky, its scorching heat boring through the fog of smoke and dust, the gunners stripped off their jackets. Their faces and bodies were blackened with powder and back blast from the muzzles, so that it was impossible to know which guns were being manned by British, and which by loyal Indians. Through the barrage bearers ran quietly at the steady jog-trot of the trained Indian servant, carrying huge cauldrons of tea and chapatties, and between servicing the guns, men snatched a bite and a drink.

Late in the afternoon, a bugle blew for a brief ceasefire, and as the smoke cleared away, the British commanders could see for the first time the new breaches they had blown in the walls, the parapets carried away, the guns displaced.

Wilson, exhausted by the bellowing cacophony of the guns, bemused by his own responsibility, suddenly lost his nerve. He scratched out a note to the chief engineer: 'I should say the assault on the Water Bastion is *hopeless*. There is no approach to it, apparently. What do *you* propose? You are determined I shall not have a moment's sleep tonight. Please reply quickly to this, as it may change all our plans.'

But nothing could change the plans now. The chief engineer only showed his note to Nicholson who handed it back to him without a word. Baird Smith did not reply. Silence was their answer, so Wilson retired to his bed, lying on it fully dressed, a glass of soda water by his side, waiting for the worst.

The sentries were in position. More guns were being assembled behind sandbag screens, ramrods going down giant barrels, gunners checking pyramids of cannonballs, stocks of grape and sacks of powder, wadding and portfires.

Lang, who had been in charge of the right battery emplacement, went back thankfully to his tent. His bearer came in silently with a jug of tea, very sweet and hot. Lang loosened his uniform and sat down wearily behind his little table.

Images flashed and flickered through his mind like snowflakes in a child's kaleidoscope. His mother telling him that his father had died; Arabella on the front at Torquay; the sea viewed through her hair when her hat blew away; Colonel MacDonald talking to him in the library at Five Mile Place, warning him that the heat of India could change Arabella's nature.

Arabella. All his thoughts led back eventually to her. She must be somewhere in that dark monstrous pile of red stones, physically only a few hundred yards away, and yet in fact as far away as the Americas.

He wondered whether she was watching the night sky through her window, thinking of him as he thought of her.

He unscrewed the top from his inkwell, took another mouthful of tea, and began to write a letter to his mother. He had no idea if it would ever be posted, but composing a letter, assuring her of his love, made him feel he might also compose his mind during what could easily be his own last night alive.

Over behind the left emplacement, the Sixtieth Rifles were resting in a nullah, dark as a coalmine, drinking pannikins of tea, gritty with dust from the sandbags.

Private Dougan was thinking about a dream he had experienced the night before. He had been with his elder brother, Tom, who had been transported to Australia fifteen years earlier, for stealing two sheep from a farmer, and from whom none of the family had heard since he sailed.

Tom was not as he must be now, in early middle age, but as he had been then, young, cheerful, whistling, always ready to tickle a trout or poach a pheasant.

They were walking along a country lane, and the banks on either side were bright with bluebells and the sun was shining, and Tom held a blade of grass to his mouth and was blowing between his hands, as though it was a trumpet. They were not hungry and barefoot in ragged clothes, living in an earth-floored hovel. They were warm and well-fed and birds were singing. He had never felt so happy and relaxed. Then he had awoken in his tent, to the snores of his companions, and the furtive movements of the sleepless.

Now, sipping his scalding bitter tea, Dougan remembered the dream, and his brother, and he had an absurd overpowering wish to see him again, to talk to him. But he was probably dead long since.

Gough was down in the Kudsia Bagh, where the bittersweet smell of ravished orange and lemon groves rinsed the air. A few shells whistled harmlessly over his head as he stood on the overgrown terrace at the end of the garden, listening to the axes crash through the undergrowth where the fatigue party were enlarging the site for the mortar battery.

All around him lay British soldiers, fully clothed and asleep, rifles chained to their right wrists, snatching what rest they could, until it was time for them to awake and take their turn to hew more trees.

Gough had never been in any major attack and did not

know what to expect. He was afraid, and most of all he
feared to show his fear. He stood bare-headed in the soft
darkness, praying that he would survive; or that if it was
God's will that he should die, then at least that the death
would be swift.

He could not bear to lie out there in the heat, mutilated
and in agony, as he had seen so many of his comrades lie
for hours before stretcher parties dared to dash out to
bring them in.

As he prayed, he remembered from school Greek
lessons, Cicero's theory that men should always be ready
to leave life as if it were an inn and not a home, 'for
nature has given us a hostelry in which to sojourn, not to
reside.'

At nineteen, Hugh Gough found it painfully difficult to
view the possibility of a move from life's hotel with
Cicero's detachment. And he hoped desperately that this
was not some kind of omen about his own future.

As the sudden Indian dusk deepened over the valley,
and the guns stopped firing because their muzzle flames
gave away their positions, Nicholson called together the
commanders. They met in a tent on the far side of the
Ridge; he rolled up the canvas walls and posted sentries
around so no one else could hear his final commands.

'Gentlemen,' he said, head and shoulders above them
all. 'We attack Delhi at oh-three-thirty hours tomorrow
morning.

'I will lead the first column of a thousand men, and we
will storm the breach the artillery has made near the
Kashmir bastion. The second column will be led by Colonel William Jones of Her Majesty's 61st, and you, colonel, will take your eight hundred and fifty men in by the
Water Bastion.

'Colonel George Campbell commands the third column,
nine hundred and fifty strong, through the Kashmir Gate
when the engineers' special party has blown it open.

'Next, Major Charles Reid, you will lead your fourth
column of eight hundred and sixty, plus twelve hundred
Sikhs from the Maharajah of Kashmir's contingent in
through the Kabul Gate. My column will open this for
you from the inside. You will then go through the eastern
suburbs.

'All other troops to be in reserve, but ready to move instantly.

'There will be no looting, no plunder, no prisoners. No wounded of any rank whatever will be picked up. They will be left where they fall. Bearers will come behind with *doolies* for them. It is imperative to obey this last order, or the whole impetus of the advance will be slowed down.

'All prizes will be put in a central place—I suggest one of the dungeons of the Fort—to be distributed out fairly among everyone afterwards.

'All women and children are to be spared, whether they are fighting against us or not. Do you understand these orders?'

'We do, sir,' replied the senior colonel.

'Draw your swords, gentlemen.'

A rattle of steel from scabbards.

'Swear by your swords that you will obey these orders.'

'We swear.'

'Right, gentlemen. You will repeat these orders to the soldiers. They will swear they understand them, by taking their oath. If I find anyone going back on his word, I will kill him myself—whoever he is. Is that quite clear?'

The other officers nodded.

'Nothing more then, gentlemen, until we parade at two o'clock in the morning. May God be on our side. We fight for the right, and if we fail no one else will take up our cause.'

Midnight. Two hours to go to assembly.

Smiths were sharpening bayonets and swords and lances with files and whetstones. Some soldiers were oiling their muskets, and checking their supplies of powder and ball. Others wrote pathetic letters to wives or mothers. Those who could not write, dictated letters to those who could.

Hodson walked from tent to tent, wondering how many who sharpened their blades so zealously would be alive to carry them when the sun went down.

He heard the regional accents of Somerset, Cheshire, and Dorset; the brogue of the Irish, the broad vowels of Scots and Welshmen; the Cockney slang of Londoners, and he felt that a whole microcosm of Britain was encamped on this hill.

Thousands of miles away, in hamlets and towns and vil-

lages, their relations went about their daily tasks, unknow-
ing, some possibly even uncaring, what tomorrow would
bring to their representatives on the Ridge before Delhi.
Apart from national pride, it mattered little to them personally whether Delhi was captured, or left in the mutineers' control; whether Indian trade was taken by other
rich nations or held by their own.

But these men would fight, and many would die, and
many more bear wounds for the rest of their lives. They
would have stories to tell until memory dimmed the outlines in their minds; and that was all.

Hodson found it impossible not to feel moved by the
profound irony of the situation.

These soldiers would die willingly to keep their country
rich, yet they had no share in its prosperity themselves,
only a deep pride in its achievements, in its influence and
the Empire they had helped to form.

They did not see their role as being in any way ironic;
they were Queen's men and Company's men. They had
taken the Queen's shilling, or the Company's shilling. Now
they prepared, as a matter of honour, to give full value
for these twelve pennies, unmindful that this could well
cost them their lives. They had followed the drum, and it
had led them here to Delhi.

At half past one in the morning, the white-haired Roman Catholic Chaplain, Father Bertrand, came out from
his tent, robed in his vestments, carrying his Bible. All
around him, infantry were falling in, bayonets fixed, packs
on their backs, water bottles filled. He went up to the
colonel in charge.

'We may differ, some of us, in matters of religion,' he
said simply. 'But the presence of an old man and a clergyman can do nothing but good. Can I have your permission to ask for God's favour on this night's work?'

'By all means, chaplain,' replied the colonel gladly.

The old man raised his hands to heaven, and making
the sign of the cross, he said: 'Oh, Lord God Almighty,
who knowest the secrets of all men's hearts, look down in
mercy on us here at this hour.

'Grant us the blessing of victory. And for those of us
who do not live to see its fruits, we ask thy mercy and
forgiveness. We ask this through the intercession of thine

only Son, Jesus Christ, Our Lord, Who died that all might live, and be gathered up for eternity on the distant sunlit shore. Amen.'

'Amen,' came back the response.

The priest's sincerity touched the hearts of all who heard him. Many prayed for the first time in their lives as they stood, heads down, gripping their muskets with both hands.

Lang stood to one side, sword sharpened, pistol buckled in his belt. With a handful of others he was to run down the hill, carrying a charge to blow in the enormously strong main gates, which had withstood the tremendous barrage of the last twelve hours.

Behind him waited pioneers and dragoons, three to each scaling ladder. They were to follow the demolition parties, and place the ladders against the wall, for the infantry to swarm up and over the walls.

All officers' messes had been stripped of rum and whisky and brandy and bearers moved from group to group, pouring spirits into pannikins and mugs. The men drank the tots greedily; false fire ran through their bodies.

Three o'clock, and the morning sun was already hovering impatiently on the edge of the earth.

Every ill soldier able to stand had crawled from his hospital bed to be on parade. Some were so weak that they had to be helped into their equipment. Now they leaned wearily against trees, or lay full length on the ground, moaning with fever, faces contorted by the griping agonies of dysentery.

Hodson scanned the Fort with his glasses. During the night, the sepoys had plugged the worst breaches in the walls with sandbags and tree trunks and rocks. Once more, therefore, the order went to the artillery for a further barrage.

General Wilson and his staff watched from the safety of the roof of Ludlow Castle. Other officers, not actively engaged, crowded the top rooms of Hindu Rao's house. They shared a strange unrealistic feeling that what they were about to see was only a planned military manoeuvre, not one of the decisive battles in European and Asian history.

The sun was already far too high up the sky for Nicholson's peace of mind when the barrage ended. Colonel William Jones, commanding the second column, approached him.

'Is everything in order?' Nicholson asked.

'Yes, sir.'

All talking was done; only action remained. The two men looked at each other; one tall, reserved, saturnine, heavily bearded; the other shorter, Welsh and volatile.

'Right,' said Nicholson, and in a spontaneous uncharacteristic gesture of friendship, he put his arm round Jones's shoulders for a moment, then hurried back to his own post.

A few guns still grumbled. Then, as the smoke blew away, a strange silence lay over the Ridge. The first sound to break it was a bugle, as Nicholson ordered the advance. The next was a tremendous cheer of relief from the troops that at last the waiting was over.

The firing parties, carrying sacks of gunpowder, fuses and boxes of lucifers in their pouches, began to run downhill with the infantry and ladder-carriers close behind them. Lang felt the ground hard under his feet. The distance to the Fort walls seemed to stretch like elastic. The bag of powder grew heavier with each step he took. Bullets whined around him like hornets, as he ran, chest bursting, sweat running down into his eyes.

Up in the Fort's ramparts now, sentries were firing wildly and sepoy buglers sounded the alarm. Indian gunners, some only in loincloths, leaped to their guns, but the firing parties were already half-way down the Ridge before they opened fire.

Fifty more yards to go, and Lang could see the cracks and splintered holes in the huge oak gates, thick as the trunks of mighty trees. Above them, the mutineer gunners were desperately trying to lower the muzzles of their cannon so that they could engage the troops before they reached the walls, but the cannon were jammed high with sandbags and rocks, and the gunners back on the Ridge were spraying them with grapeshot so heavily that the wicker gabions that masked the batteries were smouldering. Gangs of men tore at the coverings frantically and others flung jars of water over the gabions before they caught fire.

The ground near the walls was far rougher than Lang had imagined from the Ridge, with thick green sprouting plants and cluttered by heaps of rubble and debris thrown from the walls. Several times he staggered and almost fell.

Finally, as he reached the wall, he saw with dismay that a wicketgate within the huge main gate was open and a forest of muskets pointed out directly at them.

'Scatter!' he shouted to the men behind as the sepoys fired. Lang flung himself flat on the hard earth.

Half a dozen men rolled over behind him, wounded or dead. Above their heads he could hear the crack of muskets. Sepoys were firing down furiously at them, at almost point blank range. Then he was up again and under the wall and the sepoys could not reach him.

He dropped down by the gate, to one side of the wicket, sobbing for breath, and jammed the bag of gunpowder against the wood. Other men were doing the same on the ofher side. Sergeants groped in their pockets for lucifers to light the fuses. From the ramparts came confused orders, in English and Hindusthani, urging the sepoys to hold their fire until the main advance was nearer.

To those on the Ridge, watching the desperate mission of the explosion parties through the glasses, they seemed to be like men in slow motion, moving deliberately from gate to gate as though they had all the time in the world. Then they saw the phosphorous flare of lucifers and prayed that the fuses had caught. Lang watched until the sparks on the fuse were within inches of the bag and then he started to run back up the hill. He heard a cry of anguish behind him, and paused.

'It won't go off, sir,' shouted his sergeant. *'It's bloody gone out, sir!'*

He turned and saw his sergeant, back pressed against the wall, struggling to open a box of lucifers. Suddenly he slumped forward, shot vertically through the head by a sniper leaning out over the ramparts. Lang rushed back, picked up the box, already soaked with the sergeant's blood, grabbed a handful of lucifers, struck them and held them against the fuse until it flared. Then for the second time, he started to run.

The shock of the explosion threw him flat on his face. As he lay, the earth rocked with a second and a third as two more gates were blown open. Up went ladders against the walls. The first troops reached them and started to climb. Others poured through the gates, climbing over the pyramids of rubbish and bodies flung down by the explosions.

Some ladders were too short, so soldiers picked up the dead bodies of their friends and jammed the legs of the ladders on them. Thus even the dead helped the assault on Delhi that day.

Lang struggled to his feet and started to run back towards Delhi, sword in one hand, pistol in the other. Through the open gate he went into a courtyard shrouded by a yellow fog of masonry dust. Some mutineers had wheeled out a giant cannon and were ramming grapeshot down its mouth.

Lang experienced the extraordinary sensation that he was somehow not involved; that these half-naked sepoys swarming around, with powder and ramrod, holding flaming portfires, had nothing whatever to do with him. Then the cannon's black mouth swung down to gape at him and all illusion vanished.

He fired at the nearest Indian. The gunner rolled forward. A great fountain of blood gushed out of his mouth, drenching his comrades. Then the fusiliers came in behind Lang with bayonets fixed and speared the sepoys like frogs on forks, and Lang and his men were running past, sliding on stones suddenly slippery with blood.

A warren of alleyways led out from the main courtyard. Sepoys were leaning out of upper windows, firing down wildly at them.

Across the compound, Lang could see Gough with a group of soldiers, and behind them, over the walls, others were jumping down as they streamed up the ladders. He could safely leave them to deal with the rebel gunners. His task was to reach the Fort and pulverize the heart of the resistance. But he had never been inside Delhi before, and had only heard at second hand of these tortuous alleys, and the maze of backstreets with overhanging houses. The street map he had been shown briefly on the Ridge bore no relation to reality, with roads blocked by ruined houses and upturned carts and piles of rotting vegetables.

More by chance than plan he came out into a square, opposite the mosque. The sun was very hot now, beating back from the white stones with a glare that hurt their eyes. As they formed up in a hollow square, soldiers on the outside down on their right knees, those behind them standing, rifles at the ready, the great green doors of the mosque burst open and a crowd of sepoys in linen robes, waving glittering tulwars, rushed at them shouting, '*Allah deeu!*'

The kneeling men raised their rifles to their shoulders and fired. As they reloaded, those standing behind them fired a second volley. Where seconds before had been forty or fifty young men in white running with swords, now as many corpses lay wrapped in bloodied rags. Lang suddenly realized what a long way he had come on the road to maturity, since he had felt guilty at shooting one man in Meerut. Now he fired or ordered others to fire with as little concern or involvement as if he were shooting rats in a hayfield.

'We have won, sir,' shouted a sergeant exultantly, his face black with powder, streaked with sweat. 'We've won!'

'The first round, at least,' agreed Lang. 'Now for the next.'

The King's chamberlain faced Bahadur Shah, his eyes wide with terror.

'The British are inside Delhi, Your Majesty. And they appear to be gaining ground. General Ram Gupta has asked that you make a progress round the defences to cheer on our men.'

'That is useless,' replied the old man. 'What is needed now is leadership, courage, action—not a procession.'

'But you *will* do it?' queried the chamberlain.

'Have we any option?'

The chamberlain did not even bother to reply.

'I have a palanquin here, Your Majesty,' he said, and opened the door. Eight royal servants in crimson and gold crouched on the tiled floor supporting the gilded poles of the palanquin on their shoulders. The King climbed up into the stretcher-like conveyance and lay down on the taut leather hides covered with a crimson quilt.

Another man unfurled a silk umbrella, symbol of royalty, to keep the sun's harmful rays from a kingly face. Then, solemnly and in silence, the strange procession set off through the narrow streets. The King, holding on to one pole to avoid being rocked too violently by the motion, bowed and raised a withered hand to each group of sepoys as he passed. Hardly any of them bothered to salute in return. He was a totem from the past, part of a gamble that had already failed. What concerned them now was the present and the future; their present, their future.

Up on the Ridge, Wilson watched in silence as the second and third wave of troops ran down the hill towards the inferno inside the city. Colonel Whitehead, looking the other way, saw to his surprise that four hundred British troops were still squatting in what shade they could find, and leaning against trees near the Castle, uniforms unbuttoned, smoking.

'What are these men doing, sir?' he asked

'I have given them orders not to charge,' replied Wilson, lowering his glasses. 'They are to stay here and protect us in case we are attacked.'

'But, *sir!*' protested Whitehead, anger etching his stomach with pain, 'there is no risk of that whatever. And Brigadier Nicholson's whole strategy is based on throwing *everyone* in. If you keep these men back, we put the whole assault in jeopardy.'

'Are you in command, or am I?' asked Wilson coldly.

'You, sir, but . . .'

'There are no "buts." They—and you—will carry out my orders.'

In the centre of Delhi in Chandni Chauk, The Street of the Silversmiths, one of the deputy column commanders, Colonel Hope Grant, waited with eighty or ninety men who had so far survived the assault with him.

It was nearly noon, and heat burned like an open furnace. All shops were empty, their plaited bamboo screens burned away by earlier shell-fire. They saw no sign of life, either human or animal, save for a leper who lay legless and in his own excrement under the shade of a bamboo. Between the stumps of fingers, he gripped a wooden begging bowl. The flesh on his bare arms had turned yellow and was pocked with holes like cheese. Disease had eaten away his face, so that mouth and nose had run together into one great suppurating hole, green with mucus. He moaned and snuffled, a bubble of phlegm blowing in and out of the hole in his face with every breath. The men turned away from him in horror. It seemed ironic that so many fit young soldiers had died from fever or wounds—and yet this pitiful creature should so stubbornly survive them.

'Where are the reinforcements?' Hope Grant asked Gough.

'They should have arrived, sir. Four hundred men should have joined us here.'

'We are a sitting target while we wait. Go back to camp and find out what has happened.'

Only for a second did the young man pause. To return through one of the gaps in the wall, and ride up the Ridge under pitiless fire from the Fort, was an invitation to suicide.

'Very good, sir.' He saluted and turned his horse away.

Gough galloped up to Ludlow Castle and reported to Wilson.

'Message from Colonel Hope Grant, sir,' he said. 'We have barely ninety men and are held up. Our reinforcements have not arrived.'

Colonel Whitehead turned to Wilson, his stomach knotted with the tension.

'You will *have* to send those four hundred men down as reinforcements, sir,' he said.

'What about *our* position? We will be naked here without them.'

'It will be useless having four hundred men here, sir, if our whole force is decimated in Delhi.'

Without waiting for the brigadier's answer he called a major to him and gave him orders.

'Detach four hundred men immediately to follow Mr Gough to reinforce Colonel Hope Grant's column in the city.'

Inside the city, all was confusion on both sides. The British had forced their way through three of the four main gates, but once inside, the maze of alleys confused and perplexed them.

Towering walls beat back heat like hearth stones, and the constant thunder of the guns, the ground trembling beneath their feet under the impact of shells, and crashing arches and buildings, stunned their senses.

They were within the city, but what happened now? Where did they go, in which direction should they advance?

The mutineers, having recovered from the initial shock of seeing the redcoats of the British actually in streets they had considered their own for months past, were desperate to destroy them before reinforcements arrived. They did not realize there were no reinforcements.

Wilson grew more morose with every message he received. The attack had lost its impetus. This ancient, amorphous city had absorbed its force as though soaked up by a giant sponge. He would have to bring the troops out. They could regroup. Then they could try again tomorrow. The whole assault had been folly, and he was to blame for allowing it to begin.

His hands trembling at the thought of imminent defeat, Wilson began to compose an order to all commanders, to be delivered by riders: they must retire immediately.

Although the British troops inside the city were now physically spent, after hours of fighting, and were leaning wearily against walls in what shade they could find, exhausted after their months of waiting, up on the ramparts both sides were fighting fiercely.

Slowly, the mutineers fell back, and by late afternoon, the British commanded five out of the seven miles of wall that ringed the city. Suddenly, with a cheer from the men around the Kabul Gate, the Union Jack was run up on a pole to show that the Gate was in British hands. But, farther round the wall, at the Lahore Gate, Nicholson's column was still fighting.

The road was narrow, with high walls on either side, and at the far end, behind a barricade of rocks and rubble and sandbags, the sepoys had placed a cannon. One round from this would clear the road completely.

As the British troops saw them preparing to fire they jumped into doorways, and the charge of grape shrieked harmlessly past them down the suddenly empty street.

'Charge!' shouted the major in command, but they were dazed by the deafening thunder of the cannon, firing from such short range, plus the heat, thirst, and weariness. Only a handful staggered half-heartedly from the doorways and, with bayonets fixed, they began to run down the road, while the mutineers furiously reloaded the cannon. As the British charged, snipers ran after them along the flat roofs of the houses on both sides of the street, shooting down at them.

Again the portfire flared and again the soldiers jumped into the doorways, just before the cannon fired; but next time fewer came out to continue the advance.

Nicholson had given his word to the artillery that he would open the Gate from the inside, so there should be no risk of the road being blocked by fallen masonry, as had happened at the Kashmir Gate, where there was so little space that soldiers could only enter in single file.

Nicholson could imagine the gunners outside wilting under a pitiless fire from the ramparts. Only one horse in each limber had to be shot for that limber to be useless, and the thought that he had not been able to open the Gate tormented him. He did not know that the artillery had been delayed by crossfire; they were nowhere near the gate.

As Nicholson came round the corner to see what was holding up the advance, the weary haggard faces of troops peering from shattered windows and open doorways, the snipers running across the rooftops firing as they ran, while mutineer gunners rammed more powder down the muzzle of their cannon, instantly gave him the explanation. He had asked too much of too few for too long. One more round from that cannon, and the men would break and run.

'Officers to the front!' he shouted desperately, sword in hand, oblivious of the sepoys on the roof already drawing beads on him. 'I never thought Europeans would quail before *heathen!*'

A brigade major, the only other officer still unwounded, ran up and joined him. At the sight of them, soldiery began to come cautiously out of doorways. Snipers on the roof crouched down to take better aim.

Nicholson shouted, 'Charge!' and began to race down the alleyway towards the gunners. Twenty men ran with him, bayonets fixed, yelling.

On the roof, the Naik, down on his right knee, musket tight in his shoulder, held Nicholson's chest in his sights. He felt no hatred for the sahib; he had never served with him, although that morning he had seen Gough and Lang and remembered them from Meerut. He had almost called out to them and saluted. And then he had remembered, with an almost physical shock, that they were on different sides now; they would never serve together again.

That old sepoy in the brothel in Meerut had been quite right; they should have thought more about their plan to release the prisoners before they embarked on it. And what had happened since then to that sepoy, and the prisoners and his own friends? Mostly, they had deserted. Some had died, and a handful were up on the rooftops with him.

Nothing had turned out as they had planned, but that was the way of life, the will of Allah; to hope for something was not necessarily to have it.

He steadied his musket, swinging round slowly to keep his target in his sights. Then he squeezed the trigger. The bullet hit Nicholson under his right arm, held high above his head, with his sword in his hand. His arm dropped and his sword clattered to the ground. He reeled with the force of the bullet at such close range and fell down sideways against the wall.

'You're hit, sir,' panted the brigade major.

This was so obvious, with blood already staining the front and back of his jacket, that Nicholson only growled, 'Yes.'

Behind him now, other men were running; they overtook him and swept past him. The sepoy gunners had not time to reach their tulwars, before British bayonets cut them down. Then the troops dropped on their knees to fire back at the snipers on the roofs. Bodies pitched headlong into the alley, like divers, bouncing off the stones, and lay in the grotesque, undignified attitudes of death. A private soldier kicked them to see if any still lived. They were all dead; four sepoys and a Naik.

The brigade major stretched out Nicholson against the

wall, among the melon rinds and rotting mangoes. He uncorked a flask of brandy and held it to Nicholson's lips, but he seemed unable to swallow, and the spirit ran uselessly out of the corner of his mouth.

'We'll get you out of here, sir,' the brigade major promised hopefully. 'I'll have four men carry you back.'

'The men who would not follow me shall not lift me from the ground,' retorted Nicholson weakly. 'I will remain here until Delhi is taken.'

'You can't, sir. We'll *all* be killed.'

The major motioned to some bearers with a *dooli* hovering in a gate behind them. They came out reluctantly, and loaded Nicholson on to it, and carried him away.

'Take him up the Ridge to the hospital,' the brigade major ordered them. 'And stop for nothing, or no one, on pain of death.'

The *dooli* had a cloth screen, and the men held a handle at each corner. They trotted back through alleys ominously empty except for the dead, chattering to themselves. They had all lived in Delhi; they knew every lane and by-way, and so could keep clear of the fighting. They also knew who they were carrying, and they knew that Nikal Seyn sahib was dying. He was an important and powerful man, a legend in many parts of the land; but now he was in their control, and like any other wounded person. His importance could not help him now; nor could he harm them if they decided to stop on the way to the Ridge to loot a little for themselves, as they had decided to do before the major saw them.

As they ran, chewing betel nut, spitting out of the sides of their mouths, they passed a house where the front had been blown off. Inside, they could see tapestries still hanging on the walls, and brass ornaments, a mirror, carpets. They looked at each other and stopped running.

'Go on,' urged Nicholson, weakly. 'Go on. *Jaldi!*'

They paid him no heed. He was only a weak voice in a shattered body, his strength ebbing away with every laboured beat of his heart. They set down the *dooli* at the side of the road and ran into the house.

The numbness, that had frozen the right side of Nicholson's body immediately after the shot, was now fading. The agony of his wound grew, intensified by the frustration of knowing that now he could do nothing to help himself, or the advance on Delhi.

The bearers were joined by other camp followers, *bhistis* who threw away their hogskins of water, and sweepers, every kind of low caste person covetous for loot. Then, suddenly, Nicholson saw a British officer running along the road, sword in his hand. He called out weakly to him.

With a shock, the officer recognized Nicholson. His grey face, the sallow sweat on his forehead told their own story.

'I am dying,' said Nicholson simply. 'There is no chance for me.'

'We'll see about that, sir,' said the officer stoutly, and ran into the ruined building, sword in his hand. The first four bearers he met he prodded out at sword point. Then he saw a British sergeant farther down the road and shouted to him.

'Brigadier Nicholson is seriously wounded,' he told him. 'Escort him with these four bearers to the hospital. At the double.'

They set off at a jog-trot, the sergeant running alongside, shouting to the grumbling bearers to move faster.

They ran through a carnage of dead and dying, of disembowelled horses, dead elephants and artillery wagons, up under the pitiless sun, over the Ridge. Grass and bushes and the thin top-soil had all been blown away by shells. They were running on brown, burning rocks, hot as oven lids.

The field hospital had been set up in a house about half a mile from the walls of Delhi, near the boundary of Sir Theophilius Metcalfe's park. Within minutes of the first assault, *dooli* after *dooli* had set down their groaning, mutilated passengers, and within an hour every room was packed so close with charpoys of wounded that doctors and orderlies had to walk over them to tend new arrivals. Within two hours, orderlies were carrying out the dead to a little tiled house in the courtyard to await burial.

The charpoys, stained with blood and vomit, and sometimes even with pieces of flesh remaining from their previous occupants, were immediately filled by other wounded men. Soon the house was full; and then the courtyard and the landings and the hall; and then every space that could be found in every corridor and passage.

Surgeons sent fatigue parties to the elephant fodder stores to fetch bales of straw, and spread these out on the ground outside. By noon, the straw covered an area of a hundred yards square by the house and all was stained red, sodden with human blood.

On verandas and trestle tables other wounded soldiers lay, faces pale with shock, varnished with sweat, while orderlies cut off their uniforms, soaked in blood, caked in dust, to expose fearful wounds which crawled with blue flies, while surgeons and apothecaries moved from man to man to perform amputations.

They worked in teams of four. One wielded a crude tourniquet made from a bandage and a stick, to turn twice around the limb above the injury, and staunch the bleeding. Another threaded needles with silk, and a third sponged off the clotted blood, watching for the leaking ends of arteries and veins. The fourth attacked the shattered bone with a saw.

The shock killed many patients almost immediately. Those who survived were given a dram of martell, and when the brandy ran out, they had to make do with a whiff of sal volatile or a draught of water flavoured with lavender essence.

Bearers ran in and out of the house in relays, carrying away the shattered arms and legs as the surgeons sawed them off. They piled them in heaps on the ground behind the house where other patients would not see them.

Soon the earth all round the house, already damp from the rains, was trodden into mud, reddened by blood that stank and steamed as the sun warmed it.

Vultures and other carrion birds wheeled around the sky in wide cautious sweeps, settling on the roof of the house and then flying off again uneasily, distrusting the noise of battle, yet greedy for its terrible fruits.

The four chaplains, Mr Rotton from Meerut, the Catholic Father Bertrand, another Anglican, Mr Ellis, and an Italian priest somehow caught up in these events during a social visit to India, moved among the dying, making the sign of the cross, comforting those still able to comprehend their words.

Assistant Surgeon Cartwright, wearing a bloodstained

white apron, like a country butcher, came out of the house as Nicholson's *dooli* arrived.

'Brigadier Nicholson, sir,' explained the sergeant. 'He's badly wounded.'

Cartwright examined him. Nicholson was virtually the only senior officer he had not attended during the weeks of waiting, for complaints of ague and fever and sleeplessness. And now that he was treating him, he was clearly beyond all human aid.

Orderlies cut away Nicholson's jacket and shirt. As they did so, he began to cough blood, slightly at first, and then great clots trickled out of the side of his mouth, down his shoulder.

'John,' said a voice gently. Nicholson opened his eyes. His brother Charles lay on a charpoy near by; he had not even known he was serving outside Delhi.

'So they've got you?'

'Yes,' said Nicholson.

'I have lost my right arm,' said his brother. The stump was bound by bloodstained bandages to his chest.

Cartwright saw instantly that he could do nothing to stop Nicholson's internal haemorrhage; he was drowning in his own blood. All he could attempt was to make him as comfortable as possible.

'Put him in an officer's tent,' he told the orderlies. They carried him to an empty tent near by, and laid him on the bed, and took off his boots. Nicholson could hardly speak now. Every word had to be dredged out of him, at the cost of the most fearful pain.

The bearers, who had brought him up from the city, gathered outside chattering to others, telling them of the loot to be had, urging them to come to Delhi with them and share it. Their shrill excited voices tortured Nicholson's body like darts. He summoned up all his energy.

'Shut up!' he gasped. They took no notice. He tried to call again, but the blood was choking him. His hand went down to his revolver. He pulled it out of the holster and fired through the canvas over the men's heads. They fled away, squeaking like frightened parrots.

The adjutant-general, Brigadier Neville Chamberlain, heard that Nicholson was wounded and went to see him.

'What news from the column?' whispered Nicholson, blood bubbling in his throat.

'Almost half the city is ours,' Chamberlain told him.

'You are keeping something back,' said Nicholson. 'What is it?'

Chamberlain paused. 'Wilson intends to withdraw from the city tonight,' he said reluctantly. 'He says we can't hold it.'

'My God!' exclaimed Nicholson, suddenly rising up, waving his revolver in a reflex action. 'I have the strength yet to shoot him if necessary, and I will if he does that.'

Then he collapsed, sobbing for breath.

'Cannot the man understand? To retire now would be to lose all.'

Ram Gupta, with his general's ceremonial sword buckled on his belt, peered anxiously out of an upstairs window in a house on the far outskirts of Delhi. The British, and the Indians loyal to them, had done infinitely better than he had anticipated. He felt some pride in this. It was as though he were really two people; one, proud of the way his old comrades had fought; the other, equally determined to distinguish himself in his own new role as leader of their opposition.

He called four of his subordinates to him. 'How many toddy shops are there in the city?'

'Dozens, general,' came the answer.

'Detail as many men as you can find to smash open these shops, but to leave all the liquor untouched in the bottles. The British will drink them and go mad in this heat, and fall down. And we will slay them as they lie. Now—go.'

When Private Dougan's section came down an alley so narrow that by stretching their arms they could touch the slimy crumbling walls on either side, they were astonished to find a grog shop open, when every other shop was closed. And, although its shutters had been smashed away, apparently nothing inside it had been touched. Maybe the looters had been frightened off before they could seize the contents?

Its shelves were filled with brown and green bottles that had once contained London Gin and India Pale Ale, and which Indians had scavenged from rubbish tips and filled with their own toddy, brown and sweet as rum, and so strong that sometimes it would evaporate from the mug.

'Let's have a gander,' said the corporal, and knocked the neck off one bottle with his bayonet. The other men in the section sniffed. There was no doubt. This was the real stuff. The corporal handed each man a bottle.

'Don't drink it now,' he warned. 'Not in this heat. It will go straight to your head.'

'Booger that, corp,' said Dougan. 'I'm as dry as a lime kiln.'

He pulled out the paper stopper and clapped the mouth of the bottle to his lips and drank.

'That's good,' he said. 'By God, that's good. Now, where are those bloody Pandies?'

The rest started to drink, too. At first, the spirit ran like fire inside them, and then the fire reached their brains and clouded their actions so that they stumbled and slurred their words, almost instantly drunk in the heat.

'You bloody fools,' shouted the corporal, smashing the bottles from their hands. But it was too late. Half a dozen snipers up on the roof, listening to the English voices, had moved closer to the edge, muskets already at their shoulders. Each one took his own target. Six men in the section dropped dead.

Dougan and the corporal fired back, but before they could reload, two sepoys from roofs on the other side of the street shot them.

Dougan felt a pain, sharp as a spear, in his chest, and then nothing more. He was falling through a timeless darkness, into sunshine; into an English country morning. And his brother was by him; and he was smiling.

Gough led his platoon cautiously round a bend in an alleyway which opened into an unexpected courtyard. Thirty mutineers faced them, loading their muskets.

Gough fired twice with his revolver; his sergeant fired once. Three mutineers fell forward and the rest immediately threw away their muskets and held up their hands. Gough had not expected this sudden surrender.

'Keep them covered while we take their weapons,' he ordered, and started to walk forward with five men.

At that moment, he heard a great cry behind him. A British captain, holding a sword in his right hand, rushed past Gough and started to hack the defenceless mutineers. The soldiers stood astonished as his sword bit into black flesh, with a madness fearful in its ferocity.

'Hold hard!' shouted Gough. 'They've surrendered!'

He brought the flat of his own sword down on the captain's sword arm. Gough seized his arms and the sergeant pinioned him from behind; he was clearly out of his mind.

'You're mad!' said Gough. 'Have you been wounded in the head or something?'

'Wounded in the head, be damned,' retorted the officer. 'These swine killed my sister. I'll not rest until I have killed every one I meet. I've killed thirty-five so far and I'd have had all these but for you!'

They looked at him with horror. His uniform was soaked with blood, his sword arm completely red up to his shoulder.

'Take this officer to the hospital,' said Gough.

Shouting and screaming, he was led away.

Hodson rode into an outer courtyard of the Fort, Rajib Ali by his side. A plump person detached himself from a heap of rags, and cringed in front of him.

'Stand up like a man,' Hodson ordered him. 'Who are you?'

'Munshi Jeewan Lal, sahib. At your service.'

'You are at anyone's service who has money, Munshi. And I do not want your fifty thousand rupees. I cannot promise you safe conduct, and I would not if I could. If you want to surrender, my men will take you back to the Ridge.'

'I have done nothing of which I am ashamed, sahib.'

'Then you have nothing to fear.'

'My allegiance is with the British, sahib.'

'Your allegiance is where the most money is.'

Hodson turned to two of his men.

'I will interrogate him on my return.'

'A hundred thousand rupees, sahib, for your promise of safe conduct. It is my last price.'

'And these are my last words,' said Hodson. 'Get out.'

Wailing, and beating his head with his fists, the Munshi was led away by grinning sowars.

* * *

Sergeant-Major Black stood with twenty panting dishev-elled riflemen outside the mosque.

'If you boogers don't come out, we're coming in!' he shouted. Then, turning to his men: 'Prepare to fire. It's full of Pandies.'

'It's a woman's religious temple, sir,' protested a ser-geant. He remembered Meeta, and Black's children by her. Why was he so savage now, when he had lived with an Indian woman for so long? He did not know that she had left Black, and that he had not heard from her or his sons, and he had been unable to trace any of them.

'It's a bloody heathen temple,' he shouted now, and fired into the doorway. Women began to scream behind the barred windows.

'More like a knocking shop than a temple,' said a pri-vate gleefully.

Then the main doors opened unexpectedly, and a woman, dressed completely in black, her face covered, with only two holes for her eyes, came out of the door. She walked with a certain grace and dignity, and the men lowered their rifles to watch her pass by. Another woman followed her, and then a third and a fourth, and then a whole crowd went past, some running in their eagerness to be away.

'Stop!' shouted Black suddenly. 'Rokho!'

The women stopped, heads bowed, not daring to look back.

Black moved forward slowly and then, with a quick movement, he ripped up the skirt of one, a little stouter than the rest.

'You know the orders about attacking women!' shouted his sergeant anxiously.

'Women!' bellowed Black. 'These aren't women! Or if they are they're the first women I've ever seen with bol-locks on! They're mutineers, mate, disguised! *Kill 'em!*'

In an agony of indecision, Wilson gnawed his lower lip until blood came. The column commanders had ignored his order to withdraw back to the Ridge. This was tanta-mount to mutiny, but what could he do? He had been un-able to prevent their assaulting Delhi, and now he could not make them retire. Perhaps they had been victorious after all? But why couldn't someone *tell* him?

* * *

Neville Chamberlain stood with some other officers in the dimness of Nicholson's tent. Outside, the purple dusk rolled slowly up the hill, but no one inside the tent lit a lamp. A light was going out; a light of inspiration and audacity; and somehow it seemed more fitting that Nicholson's great spirit should depart in darkness.

An orderly tiptoed into the tent, saluted and handed a telegraph to Neville Chamberlain. It was from one of Nicholson's friends upcountry. The brigadier read in a low voice:

' "Give John Nicholson our love in time and eternity, and read him Acts XVI.31 and Romans X.8. God ever bless him." '

'A Bible,' said Chamberlain, and turned up the two verses. He read in a voice barely above a whisper: 'Believe in the Lord Jesus Christ and thou shalt be saved.'

He turned over the pages to the next reference.

'If thou shalt confess with thy mouth the Lord Jesus, and shalt believe in thine heart that God raised Him from the dead, thou shalt be saved.'

'Amen,' echoed other officers, who had crowded into the tent and stood, heads bowed, watching the figure on the bed.

'What is the news?' asked Nicholson painfully.

'Delhi is ours.'

'Good. My desire was that Delhi should be taken before I die.'

He fell silent for a moment and then added weakly: 'One more thing. One last thing.'

The only sound was their breathing and the bubbling of blood in Nicholson's throat as he groped for words.

'Send a message to my mother. Tell her that I do not think we shall be unhappy in the next world. God has visited her with a great affliction, but tell her she must not give way to grief.'

It was clear that he was sinking fast. As he died, a bugle sounded outside. All those in the darkened tent were struck by the symbolism of the distant call. The surgeon bent down and closed the dead man's eyes. In silence, the officers filed out into the dusk. No one spoke.

A rider galloped up to the party, dismounted and saluted.

'Captain Hodson's compliments, sir,' he said to Chamberlain. 'His column is staying in the city. He is attempting to locate the King.'

'Return my compliments to Captain Hodson,' said Chamberlain. 'And also tell him that Nicholson is dead.'

'*Not* the brigadier, sir?'

'Yes.'

The man saluted and instantly was off on his horse into the darkness.

'Where is General Wilson?' asked Chamberlain.

'In bed, sir.'

'*In bed!* Is he ill?'

'He is overcome with fatigue.'

'My God!'

Chamberlain turned away so that the others would not see the extent of his irritation. He had enough worries without the added ineptitude of the general. Messengers were now reporting the serious extent of drunkenness among the British troops. Although patrols had smashed bottles in many liquor shops, as many more had been missed, or reached too late. Others contained huge vats and tuns of liquor into which the men dipped their hats and filled them with brandy and raw spirit, and drank as though it were water. These men were lying at street corners, and in doorways, snoring and insensible.

Near by, one-third of the British troops who had assaulted Delhi were seriously wounded or dead; possibly as many more were drunk, and the rest, inside the city, watched the shadows deepen as they crouched in their sweaty uniforms, hungry, thirsty, unutterably weary, preparing to face a night of prowling snipers, a barefoot unseen enemy armed with throttling ropes or knives.

Hodson and Lang unsaddled their horses, tethered them and lay down, using the saddles as pillows. In the silence after the constant crackle of gunfire every little noise—the creak of a door swinging on rusty hinges, the moan of a drunken trooper, the sudden cry of another in the midst of nightmare—jarred their nerves like a swordpoint.

At dawn, they stood-to wearily, horses saddled, men with bayonets fixed, watching for any movement. Someone scrounged a cauldron and built a fire of sticks from a ruined house. Another trooper had looted a sack of tea, a third found a goat and milked it into a helmet; and so they brewed up and prepared for another day.

Resistance to the assault was dying, flaring up only in isolated places where a handful of mutineers were cornered in a house or a cul-de-sac. Everyone shot to kill. A wounded man, a prisoner, a hostage, only meant other mouths to feed, and food was short enough.

The King, the Begum and the Princes had fled; and with the Princes went the money-lenders and other fat, bubble-bellied merchants.

Teams still searched every house and hovel in case mutineers were hiding inside, but most were empty or contained the swollen body of someone who had crawled in to die alone, ravished by rats, crawling with worms. The smells were almost unbearable. Bodies in the streets had swelled so much that they burst buttons on uniforms. Sometimes, ten or a dozen bodies blocked a road. As fatigue parties, loth to touch them, pushed them out of the way with poles, legs and arms fell away, masses of crawling, stinking putrefaction.

Only the final assault remained; to capture the palace within the Fort. A cannon wheeled up to the first outer gate of the palace blew it to pieces. Then a battering ram made from a tree trunk smashed open the second gate, which was chained and barred. Ahead, stretched a long tiled passage with arched recesses on either side, and high screens of delicate and erotic carving.

The archways were not filled with defenders, but with women and men lying on bloodstained rags on the tiles, covered in flies. Beyond was the courtyard, where a few loyalists crouched in the sun, muskets at their shoulders, prepared to die for their King and their cause.

'Fifty-First! At your target! Fire!' shouted Lang.

A hundred carbines cracked, echoing and re-echoing down the vaulted corridors. When the smoke drifted away only one sepoy was still alive. He fired—and knocked the helmet off a second lieutenant's head. Then he charged, and fell at their feet, shredded by bullets.

'Now to find the King,' said Hodson, and with Lang and ten men, he crossed the yard to reach the inner rooms. Rope-mattressed charpoys lay scattered about, with piles of filthy rags, and heaps of warm charcoal where fires had been lit. Wounded mutineers had crawled into the shelter of the filthy corridors.

Here also lay beggars and lepers, too weak to crawl away; men without legs or arms; others with trunks swollen to grotesque proportions; one with testicles the size of pomegranates; another blind and dumb, his mouth opening and shutting like a fish for food.

The King's apartments had been looted. Paintings had been ripped down and tapestries torn from walls. The only thing to remind them of the royal presence was a smashed hookah.

'Where do you think he is?'

'Hiding,' Hodson replied. 'They'll send out a messenger asking for safe conduct soon. I have already been approached by the Begum. And the Princes. They offered me a fortune in jewels and money.'

They went down the stairs, spurs clattering on the stone. The place was like a scavenged skull; everything of value lifted, looted, burned.

Elsewhere in the Red Fort, British troops were enthusiastically seizing what trinkets the sepoys had left behind. They smashed open caskets concealed behind false panelling in the walls and crammed jewellery into their pockets with powder-blackened hands. Above their heads, the Union Jack stood proudly in the wind.

The streets crawled with wounded mutineers, some dragging broken bodies along on their elbows; others crying pitifully for help, unable to move, with spinal injuries. Roving parties of British soldiers put them out of their misery with a bayonet thrust, or a blow on the head from a musket butt. They could afford no mercy, and they could spare no medicine.

The rains began to fall heavily. Then they ceased for a few hours, and the sun made the stinking streets steam; then the rain started again.

Fatigue parties turned out with carts and rakes to clear the streets of rotting corpses, shovelling them into makeshift graves. At night, rooting hungry jackals uncovered them and grouted among putrefying intestines, and then ran in packs, horribly phosphorescent with decay, like phantasmagorical animals.

Every day, more Indian refugees who had endured months of siege, fled away from Delhi, fearing that the British might identify them with insurrection and kill them. Some had been rich. Now, their possessions were reduced to the clothes they wore. Many had never left their homes before, but now these houses were taken over by British troops as billets, or were simply burned-out roofless shells, filled with wet, charred ash.

Refugees died in their hundreds from fever. Those the fever spared died at the hands of tribesmen, who would cut off a woman's ear rather than bother to remove the tiny gold ear-ring that decorated it.

Up on the Ridge, preparations went ahead for Nicholson's funeral. Nicholson's column was now commanded by a colonel holding the Queen's commission, a man of little imagination. It never occurred to him that private soldiers might wish to be represented at Nicholson's funeral. Accordingly, he paraded the men to give orders that on the morning of the funeral they would march into Delhi as usual, to help clear the streets.

As he rode down the ranks, their numbers diminished by disease and death, a private soldier of the Fifty-Second Light Infantry broke ranks and faced the colonel's black charger.

'If you please, sir,' he began.

'Get back into the ranks,' shouted the colonel.

'If you please, sir,' repeated the private, not moving, although the charger's head was over his now and the animal was snorting in his face, 'I have a request to make. The men want to know if they have permission to go to the general's funeral?'

'Certainly not,' replied the colonel.

'Sir,' replied the private, trembling with emotion in the agony of the moment, 'I joined the regiment years before you did. You know the character I have had while I have served. I mean no disrespect, sir, but *we are going!*'

The colonel's face reddened with anger.

'The regiment shall not go!' he shouted. 'If necessary, I will use force to stop you.'

'And what force will you get, sir?' retorted the private, now equally angry. 'This regiment will march through any other regiment you put in their way.'

He turned to the ranks.

'Isn't that so?'

'Yes!' they shouted. 'We *will* be there!'

The colonel looked down from his horse at the faces of the men who had marched half across India to help save an Empire in which they had no share but a shilling a day, while he owned estates in Dorset and Lincolnshire so vast that he had often ridden for twelve hours across them and still not reached their limit.

He had never really looked closely at the men's faces before; he was surprised at the determination he saw. They owned nothing, yet they had fought as bravely as if they were defending their own possessions. Why? Had they a secret strength he could not share? He did not know the answers, so he said nothing and rode off.

Thus it came about that, as the body of John Nicholson was borne on a gun carriage to a burial ground that had been prepared near Ludlow Castle, the former headquarters opposite the Kashmir Gate, where he had been the first to cross into the city, his whole column were there to do him honour.

And with the British soldiers, some brown as walnuts, others with faces bleached by fever, or sallow with jaundice, many with legs and heads in bandages, stood the proud tribesmen who had also ridden in his column, the Multanis and Afghans, and the bearded Sikhs who had sworn that Nicholson was a kind of god.

Slowly, his body was lowered on loading ropes into the grave.

'Where is the general?' Chamberlain asked Whitehead. As the chaplain read the burial service, the most senior officer should salute and throw in the first handful of earth, symbolic that the Lord who had given life had taken it away, that the flesh was returning to the dust from whence it came.

'He is in bed, sir.'

'Again?'

'Yes. His hair has turned white with the strain. He is too fatigued to join in the service.'

'Probably it's just as well,' said Chamberlain. 'I hate hypocrisy.'

As private soldiers shovelled the earth in over the flag

that draped the coffin, the tribesmen threw themselves on the ground and beat the ground with their fists, crying out to their gods for courage to bear the unbearable; the death of a man who had been greater than them all.

Finally, the earth was patted down, and the British troops marched away; but the Indians of Nicholson's Column still stood fast, eyes on the grave.

Hodson, Lang and Gough saw with surprise that bearers and syces had silently brought out from the lines the horses of all Nicholson's native troops.

Without a word or a backward glance, without any farewell, these men now swung themselves up into their saddles, and rode away across the burned, brown earth.

There was nothing they wished for that any man could give them.

They had come down to the accursed plains to serve their leader, to breach the walls of Delhi and to gather what loot they could. All three aims had been achieved; so, farewell.

It was enough that they should see the great Nikal Seyn buried in the way of his religion. Now they rode out of his life for ever. But he stayed on in their minds and memories, and children then unborn would fall silent when their elders talked, and old men would end all argument with the words: 'But *I* was there on the day that Nikal Seyn died.'

'What about the prisoners?' asked Lang. 'Dozens of sepoys are giving themselves up.'

'They are to be shot,' said Hodson. 'Colonel Goatherd's orders. But extract any information you can before they die.'

Lang sought out Subedar Rao.

'We are keeping no prisoners, subedar sahib,' he said. 'Detail a firing party, and shoot those we have captured. But first interrogate them.'

'It is a long time since I warned you at Meerut of the uprising, sahib,' said the subedar. 'You acted quickly on that warning. I would that others more senior had done as much.'

The sepoys to be shot would stand, blindfolded if they wished, twenty yards in front of the firing squad, three at a time. He sent a havildar to bring the bedraggled prisoners out of the house where they were being kept, and waited for them under a tree a little way to one side. Each sepoy was marched up to him separately, and gave his name, his village and the name of his regiment.

Vultures wheeled above them in the sky, marking their targets when the riflemen would withdraw. These sepoys would have no graves. The vultures and the jackals would be their undertakers, picking clean their bones for the sun to bleach.

One of the last prisoners was brought up to the subedar.

'Your regiment?' he asked him.

'The Fifth Light Infantry.'

'I had a son serving in that regiment in Sind, years ago, but he died. His name was Rao. Did you know him?'

The man shook his head; it was a very common name.

'No. But my name is Rao. Darjan Rao, subedar sahib.'

'Where do you come from?'

'From Kalangaon village, sahib.'

'That was my home,' said the subedar. 'When did you join?'

'Seven years ago, sahib.'

'How many brothers and sisters do you have?'

'Three brothers and two sisters, sahib. And one sister, Indira, who died when she was seven.'

'Who was your father?'

'Pandit Rao. I have brought great dishonour on him, too. He was a Jemadar in the Company's army at Meerut.'

'You *have* brought great dishonour on him, agreed,' replied the subedar. 'For you are speaking to your father now. I was promoted to subedar two years ago.'

The sepoy's face, downcast, unshaven, contorted with surprise.

'You are my son,' said the subedar. 'How have you come to bring such shame on your family?'

'I was led, my father. We were told that our religion was being defiled, our privileges as soldiers withdrawn. We had to do as we did, or we would be undone as men. Not only in this life, but in the next.'

'And you believe this?'

'Everyone else seemed to, my father. I followed them.'

'Wait a minute,' said the subedar. 'Stand fast while I speak to the others.'

He drew the sepoy to his side under the tree. There were only ten more men to interview. Ten more men to kill.

'Continue firing,' he told the havildar. 'I wish to interrogate this prisoner further.

'How is it, my son, that you have not written in all these years? Either to your mother at home, or to me at Meerut?'

'I can neither read nor write, as you know. I dictated letters to a writer of letters in the bazaar. He must have taken my money and not sent my letters.'

'But we thought you were dead in Sind, of fever?'

'It would have been better that I had died there than lived to bring this shame on you.'

'I cannot shoot my own son,' said the subedar, 'even though you have been disloyal unto death. I will see Hodson sahib, or Lang sahib. Come with me.'

He took the prisoner back up the hill to Lang's tent.

'Where is Lang sahib?' he asked.

'He has gone with Captain Hodson to Delhi on patrol. They will not be back until dusk.'

Pandit Rao took his son across to Garroway's tent. Garroway came to the door.

'What do you want, subedar?' he asked shortly. He was not particularly concerned with military matters at that moment; he had just secured an option on a row of four shops in Chandni Chauk. He stood to make as much out of this deal as he would in ten years' soldiering.

'This is the last of the prisoners taken in the Fort. I have been commanding the firing party to shoot them.'

'Well, what about it? Got no more bullets?'

'We have plenty of bullets, sahib. But this man is my son.'

'Really?'

Garroway looked at the sepoy with more interest. What an extraordinary coincidence.

'You are asking a pardon for him?'

'I am asking nothing, sahib, except that I do not have to kill him. If he must die, then he should die at another man's hand.'

Subedar Rao fought back an almost overwhelming urge

to beg for mercy for his son, to ask that, in the balance of justice, his loyalty to the Company for over thirty years would stand in his favour. But the subedar's iron discipline kept the words locked in his mind. His lips might tremble, but he would not ask for mercy for his son. Subedar Rao had followed the drum and taken the Company's money; he was the Company's man.

'I'll tell you what I'll do,' said Garroway, with an air of one making a most magnanimous proposal. 'You fall out, subedar. I'll get someone else to shoot him. That takes care of the whole thing.'

'I had hoped to see Captain Hodson sahib.'

'Never mind him,' said Garroway sharply. 'I'm Orderly Officer today.'

He turned to a passing clerk.

'Detail another subedar to take this prisoner to the firing party and have him shot forthwith.'

'Very good, sahib.'

The man doubled away.

Subedar Rao turned to his son and, stretching out both hands, held him lightly by his shoulders. How tall he was, how strong and young, how firm his muscles! Here was the child he had watched grow up; the boy to whom he had told stories of service when he came home on leave; the young man who had adopted his father's career, who had also followed the drum.

'There is no more for me to say, my son. As a soldier, you have lived like a man. Now you must die like one. Bear yourself proudly.'

He took out a knife and cut the rope that bound his son's wrists. They stood looking at each other for a moment that was timeless, spanning the years from childhood to maturity. And then the other subedar marched Darjan Rao away.

His father watched him go up the Ridge, over the top of the hill. At the peak, the young man turned and waved to him.

Subedar Rao waved back, and then went into his tent and sat on the end of his charpoy, elbows on his knees, hands covering his ears, so that he would not have to hear the crack of the muskets. He remembered the words of Lord Buddha: 'Let no one forget his own duty for the sake of another's, however great; let a man, after he has discerned his own duty, be faithful to his duty.' He had done his duty, he had stayed true to his faith.

He was sitting thus, thinking, when Lang returned from Delhi.

'What is the matter?' he asked. Subedar Rao told him.

'I wish you had waited until I came back,' said Lang.

'I would not have asked you for mercy for him, sahib. He has been untrue to the master who fed his father and his family.'

'At times we are all untrue to someone or something,' said Lang. 'Is there anything I can do now to help?'

'Only to give me permission, sahib, to conduct the funeral ceremonies over him. He is—was—a Brahmin. It is important that certain things are done.'

'Go and do them now, subedar, before it grows too dark.'

'Thank you, sahib. And may good fortune attend your kind heart. Ill luck never overtakes the merciful.'

Ram Gupta stood on a small hill south of Delhi and looked back at the capital. All around him, sepoys lay on the ground exhausted, wounded, dispirited. Some had horses tethered to stakes. The animals rooted in the dust for any blade of grass, for they were hungry, too.

An old sepoy approached him and saluted.

'What is it?' asked Ram Gupta.

'What are your orders, sir? We are too weak to march far.'

'We will have to march on or die here,' said Ram Gupta. 'There is no other choice.'

'We have brought out what ammunition boxes and bags of powder we could carry, sir.'

'They are useless without guns. Blow them up here. We will travel light.'

'So we have come a full circle, sir.'

'What do you mean?'

'I was in Meerut bazaar in a brothel, when a Naik of the Nineteenth Native Infantry suggested we should free the prisoners who had refused to bite on those accursed cartridges. I told him then we had numbers and nothing else. It is now as it was then.'

'We have fought and lost a battle,' agreed Ram Gupta, 'but one battle is not a war. We have acquitted ourselves like men. And, like men, we must bear whatever lies ahead.

'We have not prevailed, but others have seen how *nearly* we prevailed. They will learn from our errors. And others still who come after them will not repeat them. I speak from the heart, old one. I speak the truth. Now, let us prepare to march.'

Hodson opened the sealed envelope the messenger had brought him from Brigadier Neville Chamberlain: 'I am pleased to inform you that, with effect from today's date, you have been promoted to brevet major.'

So he was back in the rank he had reached years before in the Guides. He folded up the letter, put it in his pocket, and sat down in the canvas chair in his tent. The promotion hardly interested him now. The rank seemed unimportant. Nicholson was dead, and there were too many other empty places in the mess. This was part of the price of his promotion, and the price was high.

Hodson caught sight of his face in the metal shaving mirror that hung from the tent pole. The skin was yellow and tight on his bones. He had never really recovered from the dysentery from which he had suffered early on. His bones ached and he felt weary with the aftermath of weeks of frustration and then days of sudden action. He only knew one antidote: more action, in this case to find the King of Delhi.

So long as he was at liberty, other insurgents could rally round him and the mutiny might flare up elsewhere. Hodson walked across to General Wilson's tent, his decision made.

Wilson was dressed and sipping a cup of hot beef tea.

Hodson saluted.

'I want your permission, sir, to take out a party of men and bring back the King of Delhi.'

'What is the use?' asked Wilson testily. 'Delhi has fallen. That is enough. I cannot spare a single European for such an escapade. We have suffered enormous casualties.'

'Then I will take fifty of my own natives, sir, with your permission. And Mr Lang.'

'I think it is a wild goose chase,' grumbled Wilson,

blowing on his beef tea. Why had his bearer made it so hot? 'But go on it, if you must.'

Hodson saluted and walked to Lang's tent to order him to saddle up. Rajib Ali met him as he was leaving.

'There have been explosions some way out of Delhi, sahib. Mutineers have blown up stocks of ammunition they carried away. Shall we follow them and put them to the sword?'

'No,' said Hodson. 'Let them go. They will be their own executioners. We have more important work—to capture the King of Delhi.'

'I hear he has retreated through the Ajmeer Gate to the tomb of his ancestor, Humayun.'

'Then we will extract him, living, from this tomb,' said Hodson. 'Follow me.'

Humayun's Tomb was five miles from Delhi. The road to it was strewn with old crumbling forts, abandoned palaces, roofless houses and tombs that had sunk into the earth. Black flapping flags marked the graves of holy men. On either side, stretched the jungle, dank and steaming after the rain. Now and then, in a clearing, they saw a huddle of men in rags who could march no farther. Some were still armed with muskets and swords, but they did no more than look at the party riding past. They might only be the advance guard of a far greater force coming to seek them out.

Within half an hour the riders saw a cluster of high domes, white as milk, round as a roc's eggs, soaring up from the bright green jungle. They reached the great gateway which led into a wide courtyard containing the tomb of Humayun, the son of a famous father, Baber; the father of an even more famous son, Akbar.

For ten years, Humayun, as the King of Delhi, had fought the Hindus and the Afghans, and they had driven him in retreat to Kabul. But he had refused to accept defeat. His attitude brought him new followers and new victories. Finally, he marched back to Delhi and was proclaimed King for a second time.

His tomb was of a size commensurate with his courage and achievement. Lang, who had vaguely expected something like the vault in an English cemetery, was astonished by its magnificence.

Built of red sandstone, the main white marble dome

soared a hundred feet above it from a double terraced plinth. The lower terrace was four hundred feet square, cloistered with rooms and other vaults, and surrounded by a quadrangle laid out with a formal garden. The whole tomb was ringed by a high white wall.

Their horses clattered in under the main archway into the empty courtyard. A few vultures flapped lazily away into the burnished sky. The place seemed entirely deserted, with no sight or sound of any other living thing.

Hodson turned to Lang.

'Post two sentries at the gate. If anyone approaches, or if they see any movement they must return to warn us immediately. Spread the rest out round the courtyard facing outwards, swords drawn, pistols charged. But shoot only on my command.'

'Now,' Hodson told Rajib Ali. 'Take one man and go inside this tomb and find the King. Explain you are my emissary. Tell him to come out and surrender, or we will go in and seize him.'

Rajib Ali dismounted, and called a sowar to him. They walked up the steps into the main entrance, and were instantly swallowed by the darkness.

An hour passed, with no sign of them, and no sound whatever from within the tomb.

'At least they must have met *someone*,' reasoned Hodson, 'or they would have returned.'

'If they have not been killed,' replied Lang.

Hodson shook his head.

'The old King has nothing to gain by killing them. He is no doubt trying to strike a bargain.'

Horses fidgeted in the intense heat, beating back from the white walls. Their riders sat with eyes half-closed against the blinding glare.

Two hours passed.

The strain of waiting was growing so that they started at every unexpected noise; the flap of a bird's wing, the bleat of a goat, the crash of a wild boar blundering through the jungle.

Then suddenly they heard movements within the tomb, and Rajib Ali and the sowar came out.

'The King will surrender, sahib, but only to you,' he reported. 'And you must promise that your Government will guarantee his safety, and the safety of the Begum, Zeenat Mahal and her son, Jamma Bakht.'

Hodson rode up to the gate.

'Hear me, oh, King,' he called in Hindusthani. 'I will give you my word, as an officer in the East India Company's Army, that I will personally guarantee your safety and the safety of the Begum and of her son, Jamma Bakht.'

His words echoed back from the dark mouth of the door, but no other voice answered his. Impatiently, he dismounted. As he did so, one of the horsemen rode in from the gate, his face tense with alarm.

'Sahib, we are surrounded. We have only just seen the crowds. They have been gathering in the jungle. Now they have approached the gate.'

'How many?'

'Hundreds, sahib. Armed with muskets and swords.'

'Go back to your post,' said Hodson. 'Do not fire, but stay on watch.'

'But what if they attack us, sahib?'

'They will not attack—yet. So have faith.'

As the man galloped back to the gate, Hodson walked up the steps and entered the tomb. When his eyes grew accustomed to its darkness, he saw a long corridor stretching on into the heart of the building, its walls streaming with damp. Two palanquins were coming slowly along it on the shoulders of palace servants. Hodson walked outside again, and let them pass.

The curtain of the first was pulled open cautiously, and the old King looked out, blinking in the sudden, fierce sunlight. In his hands he gripped a ceremonial sword in a shabby red leather scabbard.

'Are you Major Hodson?' he asked in Hindusthani. His voice quavered with age and weariness.

'Yes,' said Hodson.

'We surrender to you, Major. Here is my sword as a token of my word.'

As the second palanquin approached, a eunuch, a huge plump man with a soft face like a black capon, wearing a turban studded with jewels, with a curved dagger at his belt, ran out of the tomb, bowed obsequiously to Hodson, and lifted the curtain.

Enveloped in a strong, musky smell of scent, sat the Begum, gold ornaments in her nostrils, and long gold earrings that jingled, as she inclined her head in greeting. Opposite her, sat her favourite son, a sheathed ornamental dagger in his hand. He handed this to Hodson, a symbolic token of their surrender.

'Keep everyone here,' Hodson told Lang. 'I must address the crowd outside, otherwise they may cut us down as we go through.'

He jumped on his horse and spurred it out through the gates between the sentries with such force that he almost crushed the nearest rank of men who crowded round, peering into the courtyard.

Hodson was dismayed at the numbers who stretched from the courtyard walls to the jungle, a hundred yards away, and on either side, for almost as far as he could see. Some held muskets across their chests. Others carried swords or branches cut from trees. Their faces were hard and hostile.

Hodson spurred his horse again and then pulled the reins hard so that the animal reared up on its hind legs, and as it came down, foaming at the mouth, those men nearest to him instinctively backed away.

'I give you notice that we are escorting Bahadur Shah, his Begum and one son,' Hodson shouted. 'I have given my word they will have safe conduct.

'I will personally ride on one side of Bahadur Shah's palanquin, and my brother officer will ride on the other. And we will each hold a pistol to his head for the journey.

'If I hear one shot, whether by design or accident, from any of you—or if there is any threatening act, however misguided or misplaced—we will shoot your King. So there you have it. Now make way as we go through.'

He turned in the saddle and shouted back to Lang: 'March the men out!'

At this, the fifty horsemen, swords in their hands, rode out through the gateway. A great cry of dismay, a wail of almost unbearable grief, came from the crowd as they saw the two royal palanquins follow, curtains now tightly closed, the towering structures swaying above their heads.

Hodson waited until the first palanquin drew level with

him and then rode on the right side, his pistol drawn,
aimed at where he imagined the King's head would be.
Lang closed in the riders so that they surrounded both
palanquins, two deep, and he rode on the left, pistol in his
hand.

The heat was intense, the air so hot that it dried their
nostrils as they breathed. The horses frothed and fretted
at the slowness of the pace, because the bearers could
only keep up a jog-trot with the pressure of such a huge
crowd all round them. Those farthest away shouted and
waved their swords and muskets, but those nearest to the
heart of the procession kept silent.

Gradually, some of the sepoys on the outskirts of the
crowd, sensing that nothing dramatic would happen,
turned back into the jungle. Those nearest ran alongside
to within a few hundred yards of the city walls, and then
they paused, and the palanquins and their escort entered
Delhi by the Lahore Gate.

The officer of the guard, strolling out to see this procession, greeted Hodson.

'Who have you got in there?' he asked.

'Only the King of Delhi,' replied Hodson casually, and
they clattered up the deserted street to the jail house. The
bearers lowered the palanquins, and British soldiers
gathered round to see the descendant of the last Mogul,
toothless and trembling with age and apprehension, being
led into his room.

This contained a bed with a string mattress, a basin into
which he was promptly sick, and the broken hookah
which someone had brought from the palace. He fondled
it gladly, his dim old eyes lighting up for the first time.

The Begum was led into another room, in which a blanket had been hung like a curtain round her bed. As she
went in, she kicked off one of her gold slippers and left it
outside the door, the traditional sign from a royal Moslem
lady that she did not wish to be disturbed. The prince was
put in a third room on his own.

Then Hodson dismissed the guard and rode over to report his arrival to General Wilson.

'I am glad you have got him,' said the General grudg-
ingly, 'But I never expected to see either you or him
again.'

Hodson smiled. That would have solved so many problems for them all, professional and personal.

Garroway sipped a whisky and soda. He was contemptuous of all the talk about Hodson's courage in capturing the King. If Hodson had any sense, he would realize that this would do him no good. He was pushing himself too much, and in so doing making enemies who would turn his initiative against him like a curved sword blade.

Garroway would never make a mistake like that. He had very sensibly come to an agreeable working arrangement with Mrs Bolivar, promising her a share of treasure he knew was still buried in Delhi—if she could first obtain finance to bribe his informants, who realized that once the treasure was uncovered, they would receive nothing.

'What exactly are you suggesting?' she had asked him.

'A business proposition. You are one of the few English ladies in this camp. Yet here are dozens of young rich officers who have been devoid of feminine company for weeks. It might be that you, with your liking for male— ah—companionship, could come to some financial arrangement with them. It would be extremely discreet, of course. And with the money, I could secure properties and deeds and gold at a tenth of their proper value. We would share the profits equally.'

'How can you arrange this?'

'Very simply. All the natives are now afraid of us, and with cause. They think we cannot tell the innocent from the guilty, so we'll punish the lot, as we probably shall.

'The rich ones have most to lose and they reason that if they keep out of our way for six months or a year, our tempers will cool. Also, witnesses will forget or die. But they have to stay alive for this time. So they are virtually forced to sell their possessions and their houses at a fraction of their value. Your money and my business acumen will procure them for us.'

'In our joint names, I trust?'

'Of course,' said Garroway. 'What else would I suggest?'

'I hesitate to think,' smiled Mrs Bolivar, 'but since your proposition, in the crudest terms, is that I should become a harlot, and you will be my ponce to secure introductions, I must be certain at the outset how you propose to divide what I am going to earn so hardly.'

'I am sure, ma'am, you will find it a pleasure,' said Garroway, grinning. 'We will soon fix you up with a proper house.'

'How very thoughtful of you.'

'There is no risk,' continued Garroway, all irony lost on him. 'Half the officers here will be involved. The others will know nothing about it. The only one I'd watch is Hodson.'

'Why Hodson? He is one of the few I would like to bed me.'

'He wouldn't object to any proposition on moral grounds, I am sure, but on grounds of efficiency, or something like that. He is a man I loathe. And he is now a major, while I am still only a lieutenant. And yet I am senior to him.'

'At the rate you are going on, Mr Garroway, I have no doubt you will be so infinitely rich in a very short time, that you will be able to buy a colonelcy or even a complete regiment.'

And, laughing, she put her hot, wet, soft, open lips on his.

'One thing remains to be finished in Delhi,' said Hodson. 'The matter of the princes. With the number of murders our agents say they have been responsible for, and the tortures they have inflicted on innocent people, and the hostages who were abducted at their command, it would be infamous if we should shoot wretched sepoys who were only carrying out orders, while the men who gave the orders go scot free. I know where they are hiding. In Humayun's Tomb, like the old King.'

'Then I'll ride with you again,' said Lang instantly, and went out to call for his horse.

For a moment after Lang had gone, Hodson sat at his table, fingers clenched, thinking. An emissary had come in with Rajib Ali on the previous evening; the eunuch who had pulled open the curtain on the Begum's palanquin, and who had then discreetly and prudently disappeared.

'The princes wish to surrender, Hodson sahib,' he explained in his nervous, high-pitched voice. 'But they wish you to promise them safe conduct.'

'I cannot promise anything,' Hodson told him. 'You

know better than I the evil deeds they have done. Witnesses say one English mother was forced to watch while, on their orders, her child was murdered. And then she was given a cup of its blood to drink. Do men like that deserve safe conduct?'

'They feared this might be your reply, sahib, so they asked me to pass on another message, which I do with the utmost reluctance. They say, sahib, that the sahib, in his infinite wisdom and mercy, has already taken money for the safe conduct of the Begum. They say that royal jewels have also been passed to the sahib.'

'What else do they say?'

'They say, sahib—and the words stick in my throat like thorns—they say, that if the sahib cannot give them the guarantee they seek, they will produce this proof. The sahib, powerful as he is, a vigorous man in battle, is not without enemies.'

Hodson smiled.

'Go back to your masters and tell them I guarantee them nothing save that I personally will come and take them from their hiding place.'

'These are your last words, sahib?'

'They are the last words they will hear from me until I meet them face to face. Now go. And remember *how* you go. You have already lost your manhood. Make sure you keep your head.'

'This time we have double the number of men,' said Lang, as a hundred sowars rode out behind them towards Humayun's tomb.

'Yes,' said Hodson grimly. 'We may also have double the trouble.'

'What did General Wilson say when you asked him for permission to capture the princes?'

'His exact words were, "Don't let me be bothered with them." So I will not.'

They rode in silence down the familiar track, the clatter of hooves, the rattle of bit chains, and the occasional snort of a horse, the only sounds. While they were still a mile from the tomb, they saw that the whole area in front of the arched gateway swarmed with people, as though it were market day.

'Close up the ranks,' Lang called over his shoulder to
the sowars. 'Make sure all pistols are charged.'

The sun was already past its meridian, and the domes
threw elongated, egg-shaped shadows over the crowd, who
turned to face them, shouting abuse and waving swords
and sticks at the sight of red uniforms and turbans, and
their glittering sword blades.

'Make way!' called Hodson imperiously, and laid about
him with the flat of his sword. The crowd parted slightly
and then closed in around them, so that their horses trembled and snorted nervously and began to rear up.

'Who is the leader?' shouted Hodson.

A man taller than the rest raised a sword in his right
hand.

'I, sahib.'

'Then go in to the princes, and tell them they must give
themselves up unconditionally or take the consequences.'

'Which will be . . . ?'

'Death,' replied Hodson bluntly. 'They surrender now,
or they die. Make way!'

This time, the crowd opened for him, and they rode
into the courtyard. From the dark doorway that led to the
tomb, they heard shouts. Fanatics were begging the princes to be allowed to die for them, both for the honour of
their royal masters and for the Moslem certainty that all
the joys of paradise awaited those who died in battle.

Then the shouting faded away to a murmur of many
voices, and the eunuch came out.

'Hodson sahib, the princes are on their way.'

'Stand back,' Hodson shouted to the crowd, for they
pressed even closer. The troopers turned their horses to
face them, swords drawn, ready to cut down anyone who
tried to rush them.

'Richard,' said Hodson. 'Detail ten troopers to go into
the tomb to act as an escort, in case the crowd seizes the
princes as they come out.'

Iron-tyred wheels grated on a tiled floor, and a cart
drawn by two bullocks trundled slowly out of the mouth
of the tomb. In it sat three men; two were in middle age.
The third was younger. They wore silk coats and turbans.
Five of Hodson's horsemen rode on either side.

The three princes bowed solemnly to Hodson, who

bowed in return. Then a sudden uneasy thought struck him. What if these were not the princes, but imposters?

'Identify yourselves!' he called and held his sword to the throat of the first man.

'I am Mirza Mogul, nephew of the King of Delhi,' the man replied.

'And you?'

'Khizr Sultan.'

'Ah, yes,' said Hodson. 'The man who murdered so many of the English women and children. No one else would claim your identity. And you?'

He pointed his sword at the third.

'I am Abu Bukr, heir apparent, sahib.'

Hodson swung round on his horse and pointed his sword at the throat of the man who had spoken as leader of the crowd.

'Do they speak the truth, or do they lie?'

'They speak the truth, sahib,' he replied quietly. There was a sadness in his face that convinced Hodson. He turned to his troopers.

'Ride on!' he ordered.

The crowd encompassed them now on every side, swarming around them like a human sea. The stench of their sweat was overpowering, and they pummelled the horses roughly with their fists. The air grew tight with tension, as though before an electric storm. The horses were sweating with fear, and the riders looked nervously from left to right, expecting at any moment to feel a sword blade in their backs. Suddenly, Hodson halted the column.

'It is no good,' he told Lang in a whisper. 'There are too many of them and too few of us. We must rid them of their arms.'

'But how?'

'By collecting them, here and now.'

He turned and shouted to the crowd: 'Lay down your arms in one single pile!'

'And if we do not?' asked the leader.

'If you do not, you will die.'

'You speak bravely, sahib, with so few men.'

'Thousands more wait in Delhi, only seeking an excuse to put you to the sword, as you have put so many other innocent people. Do not fence with words. Throw down your arms.'

Indecision hung like a tent over the whole plain. Then one man threw his sword in the dust; then another, and a third, and then dozens more.

Hodson sat still as a statue. Only his eyes, narrowed against the dying glare of the sun, flickered from side to side, until he was convinced that the majority had carried out his order.

'Fetch more carts,' he told the leader of the crowd. 'Load up these arms and then follow us.'

He spurred his horse and the column moved forward again.

'You stay behind,' he told Lang. 'See they do as I have said.'

A number of bullock carts and ruths, the covered wagons used to move ladies of the court with their attendants and eunuchs, lumbered out of hiding places in the forest. Silently, the sepoys filled them with the swords and muskets and then followed the procession. The heat had gone out of their hostility now, just as it was going out of the sun.

Lang rode ahead to catch up with Hodson. He was astonished how one man of iron will had bent the softer collective will of thousands. There was no doubt, the British must be a superior race. If they weren't, how could such a victory of one mind over so many be explained?

Half a mile from Delhi, Hodson heard a cry behind him. The eunuch had suddenly dragged a rider off his horse, by flinging a lasso around him from the rear. As the sowar struggled on the ground, the eunuch leaped into his saddle and galloped away.

Instantly, Hodson raised his pistol, took aim, steadying the barrel against his left forearm, and fired. For a second, the eunuch stayed crouched over the animal's mane, then his grip relaxed, and he rolled to one side and fell on his back, arms and legs outstretched. The horse galloped on, then turned slowly and stood, snorting and pawing the ground.

The crack of Hodson's pistol broke the spell of acquiescence. Unarmed as they were, the sepoys now began to jostle the princes' bullock cart, punching the flanks of the troopers' horses, shouting hoarse threats.

'Clear a way!' shouted Hodson, waving his reeking pistol. His sowars turned to face the crowd, beating them about the heads with the flats of their swords.

Hodson turned back to the three princes.

'Stand up,' he commanded them.

'But why, sahib? We are not yet in Delhi. We have not yet finished the journey.'

'Your journey has finished,' said Hodson, and jumped down on to the hard earth.

The three men stood up in the swaying cart, incongruous figures in brocaded jackets, white pantaloons and golden slippers with pointed, rolled-up toes.

'To the front of the cart,' he commanded them. 'Take off your clothes.'

'What are you going to do to them?' asked Lang.

Hodson did not answer. The three men stripped down reluctantly to their loincloths, and stood barefoot on the unsteady floor of the cart, feet apart to keep their balance.

Hodson turned to the crowd.

'These men are not princes,' he said. 'They are butchers. They have murdered and brutally used helpless women and children. Now they meet their punishment.'

He reached out a hand for a carbine from one of his sowars, put it to his shoulder, and shot the King's nephew. Then he reloaded and shot Khizr Sultan, and then the heir apparent.

The range was point blank. They dropped where they had stood, blood and brains and hair streaming down the sides of the cart, great gouts of red, raw flesh embedded with chips of bone, dropping on to the earth.

Hodson handed back the carbine. No one spoke. Then from the crowd one voice cried: 'God is great! God giveth and God taketh away! Blessed be his name!'

This was taken up and repeated, so that it seemed to echo and re-echo, stretching out to the farthest corners of the crowd, as a dying whisper. And then, unexpectedly, unbelievably, the crowd began to move away. They went singly, or in pairs, or in small groups, heads down, shoulders hunched with dejection.

Soon the shadows of the Indian dusk swallowed them up, as it mercifully swallowed the sight of the three corpses, the other carts loaded with arms, and the hundred and two riders who now spurred their horses over the last few hundred yards to the deeper darkness that was Delhi.

'I don't know what *you* think,' said Colonel Goatherd, a Martell in his hand, 'but *I* call it positively disgusting that this officer, a *Company* officer, I would add, and now a major, should kill three defenceless men—and princes, to boot—literally in cold blood. I call it murder.'

'Hear, hear,' said Garroway, ordering another whisky and soda. 'Disgraceful.'

'Neither of you gentlemen was there,' said Hodson, who had entered the mess tent. 'Otherwise you would have thought differently. It is true they were without personal arms. But they were surrounded by thousands of men.'

'But you had just disarmed them, too. Or so Mr Lang has informed us.'

'We had taken weapons from them, but by sheer force of numbers they could easily have overcome us all in seconds. And why extend such sentiments of mercy to men who have coldbloodedly and deliberately murdered and pillaged and organized a revolution for their own gain, when you order poor sepoys to be shot as though they were dogs, without any trial, without even considering that they are also human? Is it because these princes were more socially acceptable that you feel so deeply for them?'

He turned to Sir Theophilius Metcalfe.

'I hear, sir,' he said, 'that you are hanging mutineers—sepoys, of course—every day of the week, and even on Sundays. Why on Sundays?'

'Well,' replied Metcalfe, as though the question were ridiculous, 'I know Sunday is a Christian day of rest, but why should they eat rations for an extra day, until Monday?'

'Why indeed?' asked Hodson. 'I killed these three so-called princes because, if I had not, *we* would all have been killed. It was them or us.'

He turned and walked out of the mess. The night felt cool, and the stars glittered and winked in the sky. Lang fell into step with him.

'Did you hear that?' Hodson asked him.

'Yes.'

'Well? Why didn't *you* say something?'

'There wasn't much I could say. Frankly, I was not impressed with what you did out there. Shocked would be a better word. I didn't think it was them or us.'

'Then why did you not say so at the time?'

'I didn't know what you were going to do. *I* thought we would get the princes back easily. I know there were thousands of people shouting the odds, but we had only a few more hundred yards to go. One volley from us would have sent them scattering.'

'You don't understand,' said Hodson bitterly.

'What don't I understand?'

'So many things. The temper of the natives, the need for decisive action. And so many other things, too.'

He was thinking suddenly of Susan, and the few letters that she had sent and which had just reached him. They were not letters from a wife, but from a woman who happened to be married to him, as empty of love and passion as a child's account of what she had seen on her way to school.

He thought of the Guides, and the months of bitterness and frustration, when his enemies had pursued him with their lies about dishonesty and fraud. Bile rose in his throat, and he swallowed and it tasted as bitter as his thoughts. Why was it that *no one* seemed to understand him? They all seemed so eager to bait him, to criticize him. Only his mother had really understood him; and he would never see her again.

'That eunuch,' said Lang suddenly. 'Why did you shoot him?'

'I had to. I *had* to.'

Hodson heard the man's soft voice again in his tent on the previous night.

'*They say, sahib, that the sahib, in his infinite wisdom and mercy, has already taken money for the safe conduct of the Begum. They say that royal jewels have also been passed to the sahib.*'

'Well?' asked Hodson. 'What are you thinking about now?'

'Nothing, really,' said Lang. But this was not quite true. He was thinking of Nicholson leading his charge, knowing he must almost inevitably be killed—but desperate to transform certain rout into certain victory.

Of Hodson, making two forays to bring out the most wanted men in the Empire, who could call on thousands to save them—but who had not done so.

Why had Hodson shot the princes? Why had he not shot the King instead—or as well? And that fleeing eunuch—why had he killed him? He was a contemptible creature, agreed, but did that alone make him worthy of death?

He thought of Bisharat Ali, hands outstretched for mercy as Hodson had shot him. He had offered no threat of violence, but did he, and possibly the princes, offer a threat of a more serious kind?

Some pieces of the mosaic of reason and intention did not fit, and Lang wondered why. The only two men in all India to whom he had brought introductions had taught him what many never learned in a lifetime, about courage and resolution. And, perhaps unknowingly, they had also taught him something else, something important.

He could not put a name to this unknown thing he had learned, so he said to Hodson: 'Nothing.'

But this was simply not so; for what Lang had learned was that, almost unknowingly, he had crossed a frontier. From being a boy, he had become a man.

All that remained to do now in Delhi was anticlimax to what had gone before. The streets stank of a mixture of burned wood and unburied bodies and jasmin attar. Looting parties were organized more systematically, for they had learned where treasure was most frequently concealed. The first thing they did on entering an abandoned house was to discover the religion of the owners by examining any books left behind.

In a Moslem house, they would dig under the floor for hidden valuables; in a house formerly owned by a Hindu, behind the walls. If any house had an earth courtyard, they would urinate on it or swamp it in water from buckets. Where the water drained away most quickly, they would dig, for here the soil had been recently disturbed.

In this way, some private soldiers dug up fortunes in jewels or cash; some officers discovered deed certificates

which were worth great sums. Lieutenant Garroway was
one of these; as a result he laid claim to whole streets of
houses and shops. These he let off at usurious rents to Indians anxious to establish themselves in Delhi.

In the rush for personal riches, other more important
tasks were relegated to second place. Even by day, jackals
fed on the unburied dead. Abandoned guns, cannons with
burned-out barrels, carts without wheels, littered the city,
inside and outside the walls. Some soldiers had been hastily buried in shallow graves, but rain and night-prowling
carnivores soon uncovered decomposing limbs, which
were worried by packs of wild, yellow-eyed dogs.

Vultures, too gorged to seek further prey, grew too
gross to fly, and could barely waddle away from their everlasting feast on the dead. The heat of the sun tightened
the stomach muscles of some corpses so that they sat upright, teeth bared in grisly grins, empty eye sockets surveying the city they had died to save.

The audience hall in the Red Fort, where the old King
had received his petitioners, where he had flung the carpet
into the faces of his sepoys, was now the Headquarters
mess. Here, officers sat after dinner, feet up on tables,
cigar in one hand, brandy in the other, exchanging stories
of the attack.

In ancient days it had been the harem. Its pale marble
walls were delicately inlaid with flowers of cornelian, and
under these blue blossoms ran the motto: 'If there is a
paradise on earth, it is this, it is this.'

24

General Sir Henry Havelock looked around the assembled officers in his tent outside Lucknow.

'Gentlemen,' he said. 'We attack Lucknow tomorrow. You know your orders and the dispositions of our troops. May God be with us and grant us victory. With Lucknow in our hands, now that Cawnpore and Delhi have fallen, the end of our troubles is at last in sight.'

Some months had passed since Delhi had been recaptured. The mutiny was now all but over. Already, in Calcutta, British residents who had still been fearful of events only weeks before, were now buying stocks of fireworks to explode on the day Lord Canning would announce that India from shore to shore, from Cape Comorin to the Himalayas, was once more at relative peace. But first, Lucknow, besieged since May, strongly fortified and defended by desperate men, had to be taken.

From across India, columns had marched here for this last and definitive battle. Giant naval guns, capable of flinging a shell weighing more than half a hundredweight, had been dragged by elephants and men from coastal bases, and now stood aimed at the walls of the embattled city. Other guns were dug in behind complicated emplacements. In what shelter they could find from the ceaseless rain, the infantry sharpened bayonets, oiled their muskets, and made sure that if all else were soaking, at least their cartridges were dry.

This could be the fiercest, bloodiest battle of all, for the

Indian defenders would fight, doped with bhang, until death overwhelmed them. No mercy could be expected from either side.

The monsoon had turned hard tracks to quagmires and the flat paddy-fields into lakes. Mules and horses and camels and elephants stood dejectedly in a downpour that they had already endured for months. The troops had survived malaria, fever, dysentery and cholera, and now their feet were rotting in their sodden boots; in many cases the stinking flesh actually lifted off their bones.

They had nowhere dry to shelter, except in the houses within Lucknow that still possessed roofs. And, with God's grace and their own audacity, plus the overwhelming support of their big guns, they would be inside the city walls and dry again within twenty-four hours.

Physically, General Havelock was a small man, five foot, five and five-sixteenth inches tall—very conscious of the exact five-sixteenths. But his small frame burned with energy and eagerness for action, when the most that other officers of his age and rank produced were new reasons for delay.

Hodson and Lang, listening to him now, knew that, like Nicholson, he also possessed individual greatness. He had reached his rank at the age of sixty-four by sheer ability—and nothing else. He had been born poor. No influential friends had moved the levers of preferment. Indeed, he had not been promoted captain until his forty-third birthday.

For years, in cantonment after cantonment, he had been regarded as something of a joke, because of his efficiency. He was also a Baptist, and this was unfashionable; not quite so bad as being a Jew or a Roman Catholic, of course, but still a long way beneath the socially acceptable Church of England. But what made other officers smile was his enthusiasm for soldiering as a profession, not as a social activity.

As a boy, he had once asked to be removed from school because he thought that the headmaster was too lax. As a man, his troops were nicknamed 'Havelock's Saints' because, unlike most other British regiments, they were never drunk, and always appeared ready for battle, anywhere, in short order.

Havelock was proud of his position because he had achieved it himself; so proud that even at dinner parties, he would wear his sword and his campaign medals.

Now, posted from Madras, he had marched on Cawnpore, and then on to Lucknow.

Hodson had changed since Delhi, physically and mentally. His face looked leaner; he had aged ten years in a few months. Also, he felt almost constantly tired, and two sword nicks he had received in his right arm during a skirmish on the road from Delhi had obstinately and inexplicably refused to heal.

Although Neville Chamberlain told him in Delhi that he had been gazetted brevet major, the authority confirming this had not, in fact, been sent back to the War Department in London. No one knew why, but, somehow no one had sent the necessary letter.

Sir Colin Campbell, the new commander-in-chief, who had travelled to Lucknow to see the situation himself, had assured Hodson that the authority was on its way. But why the delay, Hodson wondered? Had he *still* enemies in important positions who were envious of what he had achieved?

Also, despite General Havelock's brave words at his conference, Hodson deplored the strange personal conflict that existed between Havelock and yet another general, Sir James Outram, who was Havelock's senior in service, and who, in addition, had just been appointed Civil Commissioner for Oudh.

At Cawnpore, Havelock found himself superseded by Outram, but then Outram had published an unprecedented divisional order in which he renounced his own right to the command until Lucknow should be relieved.

He explained that he appreciated the efforts which Havelock had already made to relieve the city—a direct attack had failed—and he declared that he wished Havelock to have the credit and the glory when he finally succeeded.

Hodson took a more realistic view of this odd situation. He realized that Outram, in renouncing his right, as the senior officer, to command, was probably also renouncing his chance of a baronetcy, a generous share of prize money, which could amount to thousands, and a higher pension, which would undoubtedly be the reward of the general who actually commanded the force that successfully relieved Lucknow.

But, by not accepting command, Outram would also avoid the inevitable criticism and contumely that would result from a second failure to capture Lucknow. Also, Outram constantly gave what he called 'advice' to Havelock, which could be held to be helpful or harmful, but which, in either case, cleverly protected his own position.

If Havelock followed his advice and succeeded, then Outram could reasonably claim credit for the plan. If Havelock followed it and failed, then the failure was Havelock's, not Outram's. And if Havelock did not follow it and still failed, then, again, his was the error, and his would be the downfall.

Because the weather was cooler, Havelock wanted his men to march without tents for these were only an extra encumbrance. Outram overruled his order. They took their tents—and lost days on the march.

Outram wished to leave all the heavy artillery some way outside Lucknow. Havelock, who knew the fear that their tremendous shells would arouse among the besieged natives, refused to follow this request, but by then the tracks were so treacherous that many of his guns sank in the mud.

No one really knew who was in command; the army was as divided and confused as it had been outside Delhi. They had leadership now, agreed, but the leaders had two heads and spoke with two voices. Gone, with Nicholson, were the days when he, by sheer force of character and intensity of will, had decided what would be done and when and where.

And then there was Susan. Nothing had changed in Hodson's relationship with her; probably nothing ever would. He had spent a leave with her in the hills, and she had appeared pleased to see him, for he was a celebrity now; after all, not many living men had a regiment named after them. But their relationship was almost platonic; they might simply have been friends.

He had brought her some ear-rings from Delhi. She looked at them closely and then put them on one side.

'Haven't you heard the rumours?' she asked him.

'What about?'

'About all the jewels you took in Delhi from the Begum. They say you made a fortune there, accepting jewels and money—and all you bring back to me are these little ear-rings.'

'I made no fortune,' replied Hodson. 'But I grant you, I *could* have done. I have paid my debts. I have won back my majority. That is all. Such rumours are ridiculous. They are just lies.'

'Why do we only hear lies about *you,* Willie? How is it that rumours like these don't circulate about other officers—only about you?'

'Perhaps they do.'

'No. I would have heard them. They also say you killed the princes, not because your life was in danger, but for some other reason.'

'What possible reason could there be?'

'That the princes knew about these bribes. That you feared they had proof and would talk. Why do people—your brother officers, who were there with you—say these things, Willie, if they are not true?'

'I have no idea,' Hodson said dully. 'I just don't know.'

And he genuinely did not know; that was the tragedy of it. Because if he could only discover how and why his personality aggravated other people, why he should arouse such raw jealousy in others richer and more influential than he would ever be, then he could try to change his personality. But somehow whatever he did attracted detractors, and the knowledge gnawed at his confidence like worms.

Now he sat in his tent, while, outside, his men buckled on their belts and pouches, and swung themselves astride their steaming horses. Hodson was not leading his Horse today. The assistant surgeon had warned him that to do so would open his wounds further.

This was only the second time that Hodson had not led his Horse since they had been formed—it seemed ages ago—in Amballa. He had a strange feeling of non-involvement, as though command had permanently passed from his hands.

'Good luck,' he called out to Lang and Gough.

'Thank you,' they called back, and raised their swords

in salute. About twenty horsemen, left behind in camp, also waved to them; then they were swallowed by the rain.

Suddenly, through the streaming spears of rain, thick as a wall of water, they saw a great column of mutineers advancing towards them from the city. Most of them were infantry, still in the Company's red uniforms, but with them stalked two elephants pulling artillery.

If they could lay these guns, then they could rake the British camp at virtually point-blank range, and the battle for Lucknow would be lost before it had properly begun.

'Charge the guns!' Lang shouted. The sowars galloped forward, lances parallel with the ground, their horses throwing up a screen of red mud behind them. But they were too late. The mutineers had already unhitched and laid the first gun. They fired point-blank at the charging, shouting riders.

The grape disintegrated a dozen horsemen, scattering bone and hair and leather. One moment, the line was firm; the next, it showed a great gap, and those on either side were spattered red with blood and flesh. They broke order. Their horses, nostrils wide, eyes flashing, plunged desperately to escape the terrible cannon before it could fire again.

The sepoys now dropped down on their right knees, firing coolly at them as they scattered. Their charge had been deflected; it could now disintegrate, and if that happened, then the horsemen would break and run.

Hodson, watching the catastrophe in horror from the mouth of his tent, shouted to his groom, his wounds forgotten.

'Get me my horse!'

The animal was already saddled, and the groom ran with it from the lines. Hodson leapt into the saddle, holding the reins in his hand through the sling. He drew his sword with his other hand. More riders were saddling up behind him.

'Follow me!' he ordered, half looking back over his shoulder. As their canter broke into a gallop, his shout carried back through the streaming rain.

'Charge!'

He could see the sepoy gunners frantically ramming more powder and shot down the steaming barrel of their

gun. Their stripped bodies shone like polished ebony in
the rain. As they jumped away from the muzzle, and the
firer raised his flickering portfire, Hodson reached them.
His sword scythed through the air and separated the
man's arm from his body.

His severed hand, wick taper still gripped flaming in its
fingers, rolled uselessly in the mud. Down and up swept
the swords; in, turn, twist and withdraw, went the sharpened lances.

Other riders of Hodson's Horse, who had scattered,
now saw their old commander miraculously out in front
again, and rallied and charged the second cannon. The
mutineers fled. Those who fell headlong in the slime and
mud were ridden down by their thundering hooves.

The charge had succeeded. Hodson wheeled his horse
round, and headed back to camp. As he did so, half a
dozen rebel cavalrymen came riding towards him from another direction.

He had not seen them, for he was weary and ill, and
the rain fell thick as cloudy glass. His injured arm felt as
though it were being torn apart, as the wounds opened.
He was slow in turning; the leader of the rebels was almost on him, and he had no time to swerve.

Hodson saw the upraised tulwar, the horse's nostrils
flared like funnels, mouth white-rimmed with foam, the
rider's face hard as a blackstone carving. And then suddenly one of his own horsemen, Kadir Ali, was between
them, sword raised, horse barging the man aside.

The sepoy's tulwar flicked, quicksilver in the rain, and
caught Kadir Ali in the right leg—a terrible blow.

Sickened, Hodson saw the man's foot, still in its riding
boot, fly through the air.

But astonishingly, Kadir Ali was still in control. He
swung around, and catching the mutineer off balance,
drove his own sword through the man's neck like a
skewer. The rider threw up his hands and rolled sideways
and down, and was immediately hammered to death by
hooves.

Kadir Ali turned now, grinning. His right trouser leg
flapped uselessly, his right stirrup was empty—but he
seemed unhurt, unperturbed, even delighted.

As he passed Hodson, he raised his sword in salute and

called out triumphantly: 'Ah, sahib, I *told* Lang sahib that
a rider does not *need* two legs—so long as his horse has
four!'

They were riding back then, through the powder-smell-
ing rain, over the churned morass of mud, to their tents.
Hodson swung himself down wearily, his wounds throbbing. He felt desperately ill. Where his soaking uniform
touched his flesh, he shivered. He must have a high fever.
He walked slowly and stiffly into his tent, and his orderly
helped him off with his uniform and into some dry
clothes.

How many of his Horsemen had died quite needlessly
simply because he had not been there to lead them? Lang
was brave enough, but he lacked experience; that would
come in time, but they had no time. All men needed leadership by someone who they believed, however wrongly,
could bring them victory, no matter what the odds.

Victory. Of what? Over whom? The word had a hollow
ring about it, like a cracked bell. He was tired, that was
all. After tomorrow, he really could relax. With Lucknow
theirs, the other outposts of disaffection were unimportant.
But what if they did not capture Lucknow? Havelock had
failed to do so once; he could easily fail a second time.

The plan was for a frontal attack against a triple line of
earthworks held by seventy thousand sepoys, backed by
probably nearly as many armed retainers belonging to feu-
dal chiefs, who had thrown in the weight of their resourc-
es with the mutineers, largely on Nana's suggestion, hoping to squeeze more concessions from the British.

These defenders would fight with immense ferocity, for
their entire future depended on the outcome. If they lost
and lived they would be stripped of their titles and their
land. So they would fight to win; no half measures; no
mercy; no retreat.

General Campbell's intention was to charge this heavily
defended redoubt, while Outram attacked through the
King's Garden, a suburb of the city, and turned the heavy
guns on the earthworks spread to the south. Then Havelock, with his siege guns, so heavy that they required
twenty bullocks each to move them, would batter the Residency—and attack on a third front.

Few slept long in camp that night; none slept well. The

smiths spent the dark hours sharpening swords and bayonets. Cooks in smoky field kitchens boiled huge cauldrons of rice and eggs and brewed gallons of tea. All the while, rain streamed down over besieged and besiegers alike.

Just before dawn, the attack began. The huge guns leapt like living things against their trails, and the blaze of each explosion lit up the wet darkness with flashes of unexpected lightning. Through gaping holes in the walls of Lucknow, holes that the cannons steadily widened, the infantry ran like men demented: Highlanders in kilts, loyal natives and the other regiments who had marched up from Delhi, all yelling, bayonets fixed.

Hodson's Horse waited silently in the rain for the order to advance. Again they would ride without their leader; his wounds were too raw for him to take them in.

Lang went in to Hodson's tent to report that they were ready to ride.

'May God go with you,' said Hodson.

'I thought you didn't believe in God?'

'At a time like this, everyone believes,' said Hodson simply. 'And one thing before you go, Richard. If these wounds don't get any better, and the sawbones send me to hospital, as they keep on threatening, I may not be able to take all my kit. Could you look after a few things for me?'

'Of course,'

Hodson handed him a sepia photograph of his wife. 'I have carried this with me all through the campaign. Then, these boxes. There's not much else. Oh, yes, and my keys.'

He pulled a ring of keys on a chain from his fob pocket and handed them to Lang.

'These are for the boxes.'

'Won't you need them?' asked Lang. He was surprised that his commander should press these things on him at the very hour he went into action. But then Hodson was not well. The assistant surgeon had told Lang that his wounds were septic; this infection might be poisoning his body, and affecting his judgement.

'Give me back those keys,' said Hodson suddenly, his hand outstretched. He bent open the ring, removed one key, slipped this in his pocket, and then handed the rest back to Lang.

'What is the one you're keeping?' Lang asked him.

'For my tin trunk. My personal papers. Regimental files and so on. I may need them, even if I am in hospital.'

Lang handed the keys and the picture over to his orderly, and told him to carry the boxes to his own tent. Then he shook hands with Hodson, and went out and mounted his horse.

After he had gone, Hodson sat in the hot, humid discomfort of his tent, itching to be involved again, hating being on his own, with only his thoughts for companions.

His arm was throbbing badly now, and trying to take his mind off the action in which he could not be present, he began to write to his wife. The letter was more difficult to pen than he had imagined. His nib scratched on the paper, for his thoughts were elsewhere, out in the rain, close to the angry guns, up under the city walls.

It was no good; he could not keep away. He stood up and opened the flap and looked out towards Lucknow, through the rain and clouds of whitish smoke that shrouded the battle.

The guns were firing almost continually now, their voices complementary: chattering muskets, the heavy bull roar of the naval brigade's siege guns, the high clatter and shriek of mortars and rockets, screaming overhead.

Each weapon made its own distinctive sound, as each had its special part to play; to pound a thirty-foot wall until it crumbled to powder; to spatter the defenders with red-hot shot; to hammer their big guns before they could reply.

Hodson could not concentrate any more; the guns were talking to him, calling him.

He would write his letter later; there would be time then. He would go now and see what was happening in Lucknow. He could ride there easily enough, and if he rode gently, surely he would not worsen his wounds?

He picked up his sword and pistol, pulled on a cap against the solid wall of water, and called for his horse. As he set off, a sergeant staggered towards him, holding his left hand round his right forearm, blood running out between his fingers, mingling with the rain in long, red streaks.

'How goes the battle?' Hodson asked him.

'We are inside at three points, sir.'

'Where is the fighting heaviest?'

'The Begum's palace. There is only one gateway, and a mass of Pandies are inside, firing out. The engineers are waiting for powder to blow the place up.'

That was where he was most needed. That was where he would go. Hodson rode towards the Begum's palace.

Outside the entrance, it seemed that a whole battalion was waiting, bayonets fixed, uniforms soaked, faces red with exertion, steaming and streaming with sweat and rain. They weren't his men. They were Highlanders, red-haired, awaiting the order to charge. He dismounted and they parted for him respectfully, recognizing his gaunt figure. He drew his sword. A sergeant saluted.

'Where are the rebels?' Hodson asked him. He suddenly felt fit again. The rain must be cooling his fever. Even the pain in his arm had subsided. This was where he belonged, not skulking in his tent. Action was the best antidote he knew; the only antidote.

'Through that gate, sir.'

'Come on!' shouted Hodson, and waved his sword to the Highlanders. 'Follow me!'

The sergeant jumped at him and pulled him back.

'No, sir! *Wait!* It is certain death to go in there. They have their muskets aimed at the gateway. I have sent men for powder kegs. All we have to do is light them and roll them in, and kill the lot.'

'*I'm* not waiting,' retorted Hodson, and started to run. Instantly, three muskets cracked like whips, not behind him but in front.

For a second he felt nothing, then pain burned in his side; pain that grew like the roots of a giant tree spreading through his body, consuming him, until it was no longer inside him; he was inside it, drowning in a vast vat of agony.

He staggered on the slippery stones and went down. As though from a great distance, he heard the sergeant shout to the nearest section: 'Fire over his head!'

As the Highlanders' muskets cracked, the sergeant rushed into the gateway, grabbed Hodson by one leg, and pulled him out. At that moment, the runners arrived with the kegs of powder. A corporal lit a handful of lucifers, touched the fuse and then kicked the first barrel through the gate.

The men waited, heads turned away, bodies bent forward, hands over their ears against the monstrous bellow of the explosion. When it came, it blew the breath out of their lungs. Then the Highlanders were running, into the gateway, splashing through the rain, shouting Gaelic threats, the drum of their feet growing fainter.

'Is he dead?' the corporal asked the sergeant, nodding towards Hodson.

'No. But badly hit. Get a *dooli*.'

Some bearers, stripped to loincloths, bodies like black seals in the rain, ran out with a covered stretcher. Gently, they lifted Hodson into it and carried him away, stumbling in the liquid red mud, between the corpses of men and animals, back to his tent.

'Did he say anything?' asked the corporal.

'Yes,' said the sergeant. 'When he was hit he called out, "My mother." And then, "My wife." '

'The sawbones will patch him up,' said the corporal hopefully.

The sergeant said nothing. He had seen the blood seeping through the front of Hodson's uniform, and the huge stain it had already made on his back. It was impossible to say how seriously he was hurt internally, but he was bleeding heavily.

They carried him into his tent, laid him on his trestle bed, cut away his jacket and took off his boots. He was groaning slightly, and only semi-conscious.

'Fetch a surgeon,' said the sergeant.

Rajib Ali ran out into the rain and found Cartwright amputating a Highlander's right leg, while an orderly held a canvas screen above him to keep off the worst of the rain. The man was unconscious, his face the colour of paper. The surgeon finished sewing up the flap of skin he had left over the stump, and not looking round, asked: 'Well?'

'Major Hodson, sir. He's badly wounded.'

'I am just coming.'

He followed Rajib Ali at a run to Hodson's tent, and knelt down beside Hodson. He felt his pulse and examined the wound. Some blood had congealed: the wound itself looked small, but he was still bleeding heavily inside.

Hodson opened his eyes and saw the surgeon, and moved as though to sit up. At once, the blood spurted crimson through this deceptively small wound with every beat of his heart. An artery had been severed. There was nothing that could save him. Hodson looked at the surgeon, and read the verdict in his eyes, and sank back again.

Outside, the cannonade grew fainter. The British were inside Lucknow. Their assault had been sustained. The last battle was all but over.

Dusk was darkening the afternoon when Lang rode back with the remnants of Hodson's Horse. He dismounted and unbuckled his sword. Then he lifted the flap of Hodson's tent and peered inside. The hurricane *butti* was not on the table as it usually was, but by Hodson's bed. And then he saw Hodson, and Rajib Ali standing like a sentinel over him, and in the amber light of the oil flame, he saw tears in Rajib Ali's eyes.

As Hodson heard Lang arrive, he looked up, eyes barely able to focus, and asked faintly: 'How went the day?'

'Well. Lucknow is all but ours.'

'It is over, then?'

'Very nearly.'

It seemed to Lang that they were talking not of one thing, but of two: a victory in battle, and a life ebbing away with each beat of a brave and tiring heart.

Hodson lay in silence for a few moments, and then, sensing rather than seeing that Lang was still there, he said, in a voice so soft that both Lang and Rajib Ali had to bend close to hear him: 'I feel I am dying. I want you to send my love to my wife. I want you to tell her . . .'

He paused. His forehead shone damp with sweat in the lamplight; the tent felt insufferably hot and full of oil smoke. His face was grey, already like a death mask. Outside, rain drummed furiously on the stretched canvas, and a horse neighed; someone was shouting orders.

'Tell her that my last thoughts are of her,' Hodson went on. 'Make sure of that, whatever you do. I trust I have done my duty.'

His lips still moved, but he could not speak. Lang gripped Hodson's wrist. The flesh felt cold. The pulse was dead. He stood up.

'It is over, sahib?' asked Rajib Ali.

'Yes. It is over.'

Lang walked out of the tent, into the rain. He felt numb inside, beyond feeling or thought. Nicholson dead; Hodson dead. And if both had only held back for but a moment longer, both could have lived. But to hold back, to delay, to follow the tepid timid counsels of caution, formed no part of their philosophies. They could only live in action, for action. And, when their time came, it was in action that they had died.

He went into his own tent. His bearer had spread some dry clothes out on his bed, a bottle of whisky stood on the table. The hurricane *butti* was lit, and night moths fluttered in its gentle glow.

Lang poured out half a pannikan of whisky and drank it neat. Then he sat down, without changing. He was too tired to eat or even to undress. For a long time he sat thus, head forward on his chest; and, presently, he slept.

In a cave carved into the hills, some miles out of Lucknow, half a dozen men crouched sheltering from the rain. They had made a fire of what dry sticks they could find and this smouldered sullenly, the smoke stinging their eyes, making them cough.

Nana Sahib sat on the ground, his back against the wall. Azi Mullah, watched by a handful of others who had followed them from Cawnpore, stirred a sooty cauldron over the reluctant flames.

Another man sat a little way off from the rest. He was naked save for a loin cloth, and his hair was matted with grey ash, his body daubed with yellow ochre. He was the holy man who lived in the cave and who had given them shelter.

They had been on the road from Cawnpore for weeks now, at first in a fairly leisurely way, with camels carrying treasure. But villagers, who until recently would have kissed the dust beneath Nana's footprints, now came out with staves and spears and demanded bribes or they would tell the British, the conquering, returning British, that Nana and his men had passed by.

So gradually their treasure had dwindled. They had bought time with gold, and then with rubies, and finally with the camels themselves, until here they were, with their only possessions what they could carry on their backs, in a cave, like hunted animals, grateful for any refuge.

The holy man would not give them away, because he was above all thought and hope of material gain. He would gather his rewards in the next world, and not in this.

'What do you see in the future for us?' Nana asked him now.

'Nothing for your comfort,' he replied. 'A long journey, a road without an end.'

'Will I be caught?' asked Nana.

'I do not see that. I only see you moving for the rest of your days. Often without friends, without trust, without a home. I see this country in a turmoil, as that cauldron bubbles on the fire. Yet not now, but later. A long time later.'

'Will I see the British driven out of India?' asked Nana Sahib.

'No,' replied the fakir. 'Not you, nor your sons. But *their* sons will see them sail away.'

'What about me?' asked Mr Todd, the Eurasian clerk.

'I see nothing for you,' said the fakir shortly.

'Mr Todd,' said Nana gently. 'Go back to your own people. They will receive you.'

'I have no people,' replied Mr Todd with pathetic dignity. 'I belong half to one country and half to another.'

'Choose England, then. Say you have been my prisoner. Tell them what stories you like about me. They will believe anything, and you will assure yourself of a future— of a sort. But if you stay with me, you will have nothing.'

'I feel I am betraying you if I go. You have been kind to me, Nana.'

'You are an honest man,' said Nana, taking the Eurasian's thin bony wrists in both hands. 'I, too, have enjoyed your company. I will think of you often, and sometimes when I meet a problem, I will ask myself "What would Mr Todd have thought the English newspapers would say about that?" Go now, while you have the chance. If they catch you with me, you will have none.'

Mr Todd stood up in the mouth of the cave.

'Thank you,' he said in his peculiar Welsh sing-song voice. 'Goodbye.'

'Goodbye. My thoughts travel with you.'

Mr Todd went out of the cave into the rain, and began to climb down the mountain's slippery spine.

Azi Mullah ladled some of the goat stew into an enamel dish and handed it to Nana.

'This is what we are reduced to,' said Nana bitterly. 'And I could eat off gold and silver plate every day!'

'It is the food you eat, not the plate,' pointed out the holy man.

'I will also go,' said Azi Mullah between mouthfuls. 'The British will be looking for two of us. It will be easier if we split up.'

'It would have been much easier if we had split up long ago, before you ever persuaded me on this mad course.'

'For a time we did succeed, and then things went wrong. I never thought . . .'

'They are sad words—*I never thought . . .*' said the fakir. 'The epitaph of empires, and of fools.'

'Yes,' said Nana. 'It is so.'

No amount of thought could save them now, or bring back any of the dead on either side; or the trust that had died with them.

'Good-bye, then,' he said. 'Take your servants and go.'

'And what about you? How will you fare?'

'I will stay with Nana,' said Ram Gupta from the back of the cave.

'I have nothing to give you, subedar. No honours. Not a pension. Nothing.'

'All I ever asked you for, Nana Sahib, was advice, and you gave me that. For years, I took the Company's money, and I was the Company's man. Then I became my own man. Now I am too old to go back in my footsteps. I will follow you. Even the rich need a friend, Nana Sahib.'

'I am not rich, subedar. I have no more money now than you. Probably less.'

'Then our need for each other is the greater. As the Lord Buddha says: "Victory breeds hatred, for the conquered is unhappy. He who has given up both victory and defeat, he is contented and happy." Let us therefore go in search of that contentment, Nana Sahib. If we do not seek, we shall never find.'

'It is as you say,' agreed Nana. 'I have distant relations in Burma. We will reach that country and ask them for help. The British are also in Burma, but they will not know us if we take other names and grow our hair.'

He paused, head sunk down on his chest.

'What are you thinking about?' asked Azi Mullah, gathering his few possessions around him; an army pack, a cloak, a wooden staff.

The fire was almost out now; only a few embers and sticks glowed in the grey ash. The cave felt very cold; wind began to moan around its mouth, blowing the bitter smoke farther inside.

'Whoever my real parents were,' replied Nana Sahib slowly. 'However lowly their station might have been, I still could not have sunk to a more wretched condition than I have now reached—and from a maharajah's palace. An outcast, without even a shelter or refuge for the night, save what others may grant me. I wish the old maharajah had never adopted me. If he had let me stay wherever I was, whoever I was, how *could* I be worse off than I am now?'

Suddenly, Nana put up his hands to his face and wept, and the sound of his sobbing echoed down the long tunnel of the cave and ran with the rain. The others listened, embarrassed and uneasy. No one had ever known a maharajah weep.

The fakir was also thinking. Only a few months ago, when his home had been a cave some miles outside Delhi, the English magistrate had come to him alone, his horse lame, and had sought shelter humbly, and he had helped him.

Now the enemy of the English had also sought him out, weary and pursued, and he had taken him in to give him what comfort he could. In time of war and trouble a holy man was trusted, for he was above all conflict, neutral as the clouds that ride above the earth; and it was good that this was so.

He could have betrayed both men, but then he would have also betrayed himself. Instead, like a shattered gong, he had uttered nothing, and he was at peace within himself. These two hunted men had done their duty, right or wrong, well-advised or ill-advised. He had also discerned his own duty, and he had been faithful to it. He was content.

'Sleep now,' he told Nana Sahib gently. 'Rest, and then rise before dawn, when the English slumber, and be on your way.'

'*I* will go now,' said Azi Mullah. He stood up, and went out into the darkness and the rain. Nobody said good-bye.

Lang heard the bugler call reveille, and walked stiffly out of his tent, still in his soaking, sweaty uniform, that had only partly dried on him, still unshaven, with mud in his matted hair, his mouth thick from whisky, his brain weary. Something terrible had happened, and he had forgotten what it was.

Then he remembered, Hodson was dead.

Gough saw him and came across to talk to him.

'So you have heard?' asked Lang.

'Yes,' said Gough sombrely. 'I would rather have heard anything than that.'

Lang nodded. He felt unable to clothe his feelings with words, for words had only one dimension, and Hodson's character had possessed as many dimensions as a diamond. He turned back into his tent. His bearer had put out a canvas basin of rainwater on its stand. He pulled off his jacket, washed and shaved.

His face, reflected in the polished metal mirror, had changed in the months he had been in India. There were lines now where before the skin had been young and smooth. His eyes were harder, more wary; his jaw set firm. And there were other changes in his mind, in his outlook, in his thinking, which were even more basic. These lines on his face were only the visible contours on the map of his experience.

An orderly presented himself at the tent mouth and saluted.

'Mr Lang, sir, the colonel's compliments. Would you please report to him immediately?'

Lang walked out of the tent and across the soggy marsh that the camp had become. Unexpectedly, the rain had stopped and the ground was steaming; distant tents were already enveloped in vapour.

An orderly outside the colonel's tent saluted as he went in. The colonel was sitting at a table, a map spread out before him.

'Ah, Lang,' he said. 'I have had a report that Nana Sahib, this monster who organized the Cawnpore massacre, and probably the evil genius behind the whole mutiny, has been seen in this area.

'I want you to take a patrol of as many men as you see fit, and bring him in. He is said to be alone except for a few servants or hangers-on. But take no chances. If they are armed and make a fight of it, kill him. Don't let him get away. He is one man of whom we must make a most stern example.'

'Who has reported him, sir?'

'One of his former followers, apparently. He ran away, fearful of his own skin, of course. But no doubt he'll be back to collect his blood money if Nana is caught.

'Fellow called Hazara Lal, though that means nothing. Used to be a shoemaker in Delhi. Says he wants to claim the reward to open his own shop. Extraordinary! Christ was betrayed for thirty pieces of silver, and this feller will sell his leader's life to spend his own making *chaplis!* Had some cock-and-bull story that he'd saved two English-women in Delhi, but then they all say that now. I paid no attention to that.

'Anyhow, all that is unimportant. No loyalty among these natives, you know. Nana is said to have been seen in or near a ruined temple three miles west of this camp. It's on the map. Here.'

He pointed to the ordnance survey sheet on his table. 'Any questions?'

'No, sir.'

'Well, good luck.'

'Thank you, sir.'

Lang saluted, and went back to his tent. How many times had he set out with Hodson on some patrol or skirmish, tingling at the prospect of adventure, of a ride under the hard, bright sun, over the burnt grass, breathing that strange unforgettable smell of India: heat overlaid with spice and jasmin and honey; the scented ashes from a million graves where bodies had blown to dust down the centuries.

Now he was on his own, and his stomach was not in

the journey. However, he had to go. He had followed the
drum so far, and when it beat, he must march.

He called for Rajib Ali.

'Reports say that Nana's been seen,' he told him. 'I am
taking twenty men. Would you recognize him if you saw
him?'

'Yes, sahib. I have seen him many times. I do not think
he is still in the area. Probably this is some relation. These
informers know the highest reward is on Nana's head, so
they will try to pass off anyone as him.'

'Well, I still have to see. Come with me to identify him
and to interpret.'

They rode out of the camp in silence, two leading
where three had ridden before. And it seemed to both
men that Hodson still rode with them in spirit. He seemed
so close that more than once Lang turned sharply, thinking he had heard his familiar voice.

The camp lay shrouded in steaming morning mist. Orderlies were carrying back wounded on *doolies*. The dead
were piled high on bullock carts, in all the terrible positions of mortality. Guns were firing somewhere, but on
which side and where, Lang could not see; and somehow
their anger now seemed unimportant, as impersonal as
distant thunder on an English summer day.

A few overgrown tombs and wayside shrines with faded
flowers in green tin vases marked the edge of the track
which twisted and turned away from Lucknow into high
ground. Ahead, on their left, Lang soon saw the temple, a
small sandstone building with a crude mud tomb and a
wall built round it. What a place to shelter a man who
had commanded fifteen thousand pensioners, a great palace, and stables of hunting elephants, he thought ironically.

A handful of Indians squatted on their shanks in the
shade against the wall. They must know that someone of
importance was inside; or maybe they were his servants?
Lang turned in the saddle and addressed the troopers.

'Draw your swords. See your pistols are cocked. I do
not know how many men are in the mosque, and they
may make a fight for it. But no one is to fire until I give
the order. Understood?'

'Understood, sahib.'

They rode on to the gate. The Indians, poor, thin men

in shabby loincloths and turbans, hands flattened, fingers spatulate from years of labouring in the fields with wooden ploughs and harrows, stood up and salaamed respectfully.

'Who is inside?' Rajib Ali asked one of them.

'I do not know, sahib. It is a holy place. We are just resting from the sun.'

Rajib Ali pointed his sword at the man's throat.

'Speak the truth, you dog, or die.'

'It is as I have said, sahib,' gasped the man, falling down on his knees. 'We are only poor people. We seek the shade. I do not know who is inside, I swear.'

'Let them go,' said Lang. He was sick of slaughter and death and the carrion smell that was beginning to hang over Lucknow, as it had lingered for so long over Delhi. The smell of rotting bodies and powder-smoke too heavy to be blown by the wind; of burned buildings and fouled wells. The smell of battle, of victory and defeat, the underside of glory, the stench of the dead who had followed to the last drumbeat.

'Go!' ordered Rajib Ali. 'Go from hence!'

The men shambled away, looking back fearfully.

Lang dismounted and walked through the gate into the little courtyard. It had a well in one corner and a few chickens scratched hopefully in the dust.

'If there is anyone hiding inside, come out,' Lang called in Hindusthani. No one replied. The doorway of the temple was a black oblong in a sunbleached wall.

'I will count three and then fire,' Lang went on.

'Take aim,' he told the troopers. A rattle of muskets, a crash of hands on butts, and twenty barrels pointed unwavering into the darkness of the doorway.

'One!' he called. A little trickle of sweat began to run down his neck between his shoulder blades; his serge uniform was almost unbearably hot. He felt overlaid with immense depression, his spirits heavy as his helmet and the ridiculous uniform intended for a winter climate. How many more volleys would he have to order, how many more men would he have to kill—for what? Simply to stay alive himself? And to think that once he had felt concern because he had shot one man, only one, in Meerut!

'Two!'

In the darkness, he heard a faint rustle. He drew his sword, suddenly conscious that he presented a direct target to anyone inside. But it was too late to move now. He could not retreat.

Then his heart jumped and tightened inside him as he saw a movement within the shadow. A young man came out, a bared sword in his right hand. He wore white trousers, a long white jacket with buttons to the throat. He threw his sword on the dusty ground. It clattered as it fell, frightening the chickens. They ran away, squawking.

'My God!' said Lang. 'You!'

The man's eyes narrowed against the unexpected brightness of the sun after the tomb, and then they focused on Lang in equal astonishment.

'Mr Lang!' said Kalyan Singh. 'After so long, we meet again.'

He took a step towards him.

'Stay where you are,' said Lang. 'I did not come to seek you, but Nana Sahib. Where is he?'

'I do not know,' said Kalyan Singh. 'I last saw him days ago. He was in flight from Cawnpore.'

'Where is he now?' asked Lang.

'I have told you, I do not know.'

'I have twenty men with muskets who may be able to refresh your memory.'

'I have nothing to gain from lies. And I have nothing to lose but my life. If you wish to tell your men to shoot, then shoot.'

'Prepare to fire!' shouted Lang. His mind fumed with surprise and doubt and worry. That this man, who had appeared so friendly on the voyage from Bombay to Calcutta, could now turn out to have been some high officer on the other side, was incredible.

That he might have connived at the massacre of those helpless women and children in the boats at Cawnpore, drove every other thought from his mind. He was not worth taking back as a prisoner. He would shoot him and let the vultures pick his bones clean. An eye for an eye, a death for the dead.

As he turned to the troopers to give the last command to fire, a girl's voice suddenly shouted from inside the tomb. 'Stop! For God's sake, stop! *Don't shoot!*'

She called in English, and at her voice the troopers instinctively lowered their muskets. Lang drew his pistol. If this was a trap, he would shoot Kalyan Singh from where he stood, and in the guts. That way, he would take the longest time to die. Some of the women and children in the boats at Cawnpore had taken hours to die.

A girl ran barefoot from the door towards him. She wore a red sari and her head was shrouded by a red silk shawl, edged with gold. She ran right up to him and then pulled back the shawl.

He looked Arabella in the eyes.

'*Arabella!* I thought you were dead! All the other women in the Fort were killed.'

'You don't mean that?'

'I do. Yet you've survived, my darling! Was this man keeping you prisoner?'

'No.'

'Then what are you doing here with him?'

'He saved my life.'

'When?'

'In the Fort. He took me away with him. If it weren't for him, I'd be dead. Don't shoot him, Richard. For God's sake, *don't shoot!*'

'All right,' said Lang, putting his pistol back in the holster. He still stood a yard away from her; yet he was engaged to marry her. Somehow, there seemed to be a barrier between them. Something had happened since that night at Five Mile Place; she had become a different person, wilder, yet more mature, more aloof; someone he did not know at all, someone he would never know now. And perhaps he also was different. In Dorset he had been a boy; now he was a man.

'We'll take him prisoner then, instead of shooting him. He can stand trial.'

'For what? Saving my life? For helping the other women? For getting us a doctor and food, and milk for the children?'

'I know nothing about that. I mean for being involved with Nana Sahib, in the murder of hundreds of defenceless people at Cawnpore, who had accepted Nana Sahib's word of safe conduct.'

'Kalyan Singh wasn't even there.'

'How do you know?'

'Because he was in Delhi.'

'If it is as you say, then he should have little to fear.'
He paused. 'I did not have one letter from you, all this
time.'

'I did not write, Richard. I couldn't.'

'Of course not—not from the Red Fort, but before—did
you write then?'

'No.'

'But why not? I sent you so many letters. Every day on
the voyage, I wrote to you. And you never replied?'

'No. I—couldn't.'

'Why not?'

'I couldn't write what I did not feel, Richard.'

'Oh. I see.'

The answer was so obvious; if he had been honest with
himself, he had suspected it for months; probably all the
time.

Lang turned to the troopers; he was forgetting the purpose of his visit.

'Arrest that man,' he said. 'See he does not escape or
take his own life.'

Three jumped down from their horses. One untied a
rope to bind Kalyan Singh's wrists. They would make him
run like a dog behind them, tied to one of their saddles.

'Listen,' said Arabella urgently, in a tone Lang had
never heard before. She put out her hands and gripped his
shoulders. 'You *can't* do this to him. Because if you do,
you are doing it to me.'

'What on earth do you mean?'

'What I say. We are married. He is my husband. *Now*
do you see?'

'My God.'

Lang uttered the words in an agonized whisper.

'You must be out of your mind,' he said gently. 'All
you have been through has deranged you. I have heard
that your father and mother were both killed, that you've
lost your home and everything you possess. This man has
helped you, so you say. But you *cannot* be married to
him.'

'But *I am*. On the way here, we were in a village, and
the villagers would have killed me if we had not married.'

'But that was only a native ceremony,' said Lang soothingly. 'It doesn't mean anything. Some heathen mouthings of words. Mumbo-jumbo.'

'Perhaps that is what they say about *our* marriages? In a' church, with a man wearing a pointed-tail coat and the bride in white—something old, something new, something borrowed, something blue. That is mumbo-jumbo, too.'

'But that is different,' protested Lang.

'No,' said Arabella. '*I* am different. *He* is different. He did everything he could to help all of us in Delhi. It's not his fault if they didn't get away. *He* tried to save life. All *you've* done is to take it.'

'That's unfair,' cried Lang. 'For goodness' sake, woman! Who started this mutiny? Who starts a fire—the tinder or the flint? Or the man who wields them?'

'Leave us, Richard. You have my word, Kalyan Singh has harmed no one. We will make our own life together. Just give us this chance. That is all I ask. Is it too much?

'I am sorry to hurt you like this, Richard. I *did* want to marry you and be your wife. You must believe me. But then I met my—husband, and there was nothing else I could do but what I have done.

'I cannot put my feelings for him into words. I can only say from the depths of my heart how I hope that one day you will know how I feel—and that some other woman will feel the same way about you.'

'But your relatives? What will they say?'

'I only have an uncle now. I do not care what he says.'

'He will inherit Five Mile Place,' said Lang, suddenly remembering the plump man with the big shirt cuffs at his engagement party. *His* engagement party! How ironic it all seemed now.

'Let him. It means nothing to me. That is not my country, nor my home, any more. My country is here. My home is here, too.'

Lang suddenly remembered Colonel MacDonald's warning about the Indian princeling his daughter had become attracted to. Of course! How slow and stupid he had been—especially when Kalyan Singh had told him on the voyage from Bombay that he knew Arabella.

Arabella let go of Lang's shoulders, and walked to Kalyan Singh and took his arm.

'If you must shoot,' she said, watching Lang's face, 'shoot us both. Now.'

'You don't know what you are saying, or what you are doing. If you stay with this man, you will be an outcast for ever. You will be ostracised in every cantonment. Your name will be a byword. Can't you *see* that?'

'What is there in any cantonment for me, anyhow? Bridge parties. Flirting. And endless complaints about the native servants. I know. I've spent my life in that world. But not any more.'

'Your children will be half-caste.' Even as Lang said the word 'children' he felt an ache in his own guts. To think of this man mounting Arabella; to think of their bodies entwined; to think of everything. It was almost a physical pain, and yet it was also quite extraordinarily a relief, a release. He was not engaged to be married any more; he was free.

'You will be denied by your own people and not accepted by your husband's. How can you do this mad thing if you are not out of your mind?'

'Because I love him,' Arabella said simply. 'That's why. *Now* do you understand?'

They stood looking at each other. To Lang everything—sandstone temple, Kalyan Singh's silent figure, the well, the shimmering burnished blue background of sky—merged into a mist of unreality.

No one was left in all the world but Arabella, and then even she faded out of focus, and he was alone. But as she turned to Kalyan Singh he saw in her eyes a look that had never been there whenever she had looked at him. It was as though a lamp burned inside her that he had never been able to light.

Land felt almost unbearably lonely; yet the feeling was curiously tinctured with relief. One emotion would pass; but which one?

He remembered Nicholson, always out front, in command. And always on his own. He remembered Hodson, writing long letters each day to his wife, hopefully asking the *dak* wallah whether there were any letters for him. He knew now how lonely they had felt; a little of how they had felt, anyway. He had all his life to learn the rest of it.

He turned away slowly and put his sword back in his scabbard.

'Are you taking him prisoner, sahib?' asked Rajib Ali.

'No,' said Lang.

'The colonel sahib said that Nana was to be brought back, sahib, or shot.'

'I know what the colonel sahib said. But this is not Nana. This is someone else.'

'You are young, sahib,' went on Rajib Ali in an urgent whisper. 'Do not think I mean disrespect, but letting this man go free could affect your whole future. Are you *sure* you know what you are doing?'

'I know,' said Lang. 'For the first time in my life, I am sure.'

He walked to his horse, mounted, and then turned and looked at the couple in the courtyard. They were still standing very close together, holding hands. The sun winked and glittered off the sword on the ground in front of them.

'You do know what you are doing?' Lang asked Arabella.

She nodded.

'I know.'

'Follow me,' Lang told his troopers. In silence, they turned and rode silently down the hill.

Arabella watched them go, little plumes of dust thrown up by the horses' hooves. They did not look back. She turned to Kalyan Singh. His two hands enfolded hers. Then he bent down and picked up his sword.

Lang dismounted, unbuckled his belt, took off his helmet and walked into his tent. He felt as though he had suddenly grown old; as though whole years had been somehow compressed into the events of a single morning.

Rajib Ali followed him in.

'You have acted with mercy, sahib, and that is a blessed thing to do.'

'I wonder if the colonel would agree,' said Lang, but somehow it did not seem to matter much whether he agreed or not. He had made his own decision. If others wanted to take Kalyan Singh prisoner, then let them go out after him. He would have no part in it.

'Hodson sahib would have approved,' said Rajib Ali.

'I am glad you say so. There is a time for war and a time for peace. We have had the former time, Rajib Ali. Now let us share the latter.'

'It is right. Especially as Hodson sahib's funeral has

been arranged for tomorrow morning. They have decided what they will write on the stone above his grave.'

'I can imagine lots of things that people would like to write there,' said Lang bitterly. 'What is the final choice?'

' "Here lies all that could die of William Stephen Raikes Hodson." '

'That is better than I thought.'

'In your religion you believe in eternal life, sahib?'

'I was taught to,' said Lang. 'But now I don't know what I believe. I feel there is an immortality by which brave acts, kind deeds and warm generous spirits are remembered. That is the immortality I strive after.'

'The sahib speaks wisely. Would you like to say a last farewell to Hodson sahib, before the funeral?'

'I should,' said Lang. 'But I hate goodbyes. One of the comforts of believing in eternal life is that we feel we will all meet again.'

'I hope that is so, sahib.'

Lang followed Rajib Ali out of the tent, across the swamp, into Hodson's tent. It was apparently just as when Hodson was alive, and yet it was inexplicably different. The nervous energy, the enthusiasm, the vitality had gone; it was only a tent now, nothing more.

Hodson's few possessions were neatly laid on the camp table. A revolver in a holster, a small volume of Milton's works, some unfinished letters, under a smooth flat stone, and, on its own, a key. Idly, Lang picked it up. Of course. It was the key to Hodson's personal trunk.

Hodson's body lay on his camp bed, his face turned away from the light, eyes closed. He might almost have been asleep.

'Would you, sahib, like to say a prayer to the Christian God for Hodson sahib?' asked Rajib Ali hesitantly.

'I will try.'

Lang knelt down by the canvas bed. He reached out and took his friend's cold hand in his.

'Oh, God,' he said haltingly, 'Who looks down on all nations and on all people, have mercy on all who fight each other in your name. And especially grant mercy and peace everlasting to this brave man, who served you in his own way, as we all should seek to do.'

'Amen,' whispered Rajib Ali. He stood for a moment

awkwardly, then he said, 'That key, sahib. What about the papers in the trunk?'

Lang had forgotten those. He had better open the trunk and see if there was a will, and begin all the dreary business that had to be gone through when a friend died. He bent down, put the key in the lock and turned it.

The trunk was so full of papers that the lid sprang open. It was crammed with regimental lists, pay statements for the men, copies of daily orders. And there were other pieces of paper that caught Lang's eye, pages written in spidery Indian hands, and canvas bags that jingled as he lifted them. He ripped one open. It was filled with golden coins. He opened another: jewels.

He picked up the first sheet of paper and read aloud.

'By reason of the seven thousand rupees which I, the Begum, Zeenat Mahal, hereby present, I am guaranteed safe conduct through the British lines.'

There was no signature, but it was dated. He remembered that day, when the fakir had come to Hodson's tent.

So had the rumours about Hodson been true? *Had* he been taking bribes on an enormous scale?

Images flashed uneasily through his mind. Hodson burning the I.O.U.s in the money-lender's box at Khurkund, and then shooting Bisharat Ali as he begged for mercy.

The King's eunuch reminding Hodson that the princes had proof of his bribery.

Hodson shooting the eunuch as he galloped away through the scrubby grass outside Delhi.

Hodson shooting the three princes in the cart, only minutes later. No one had been left alive who could speak against him.

Was that the reason he had shot them all? Or was he simply storing these coins and jewels, keeping these documents in a safe place, to produce them at the trial of the King of Delhi, as evidence of Indian perfidy and corruption?

Some would say one thing, and some another. But, remembering the past, most would say that Hodson the brave, the wise, the audacious had also been Hodson the corrupt. He would stand up for his friend's memory, of course; but what would one voice be against so many, more powerful, more venomous?

Rajib Ali and Lang looked at each other, an infinity of understanding between them. Lang bent down, pushed all the papers back into the box, locked it and gave Rajib Ali the key.

'He was a great man, sahib,' said Rajib Ali gently.

Lang nodded.

'Yes, and that is how he will be remembered. Throw away the key. Then wait until dusk and dump the box in the river. There is no guard on this tent, so anyone could have stolen it. But watch that no one sees you. And never speak to any man of this thing.'

He held out his hand. Rajib Ali took it, and then turned away so that Lang would not see his tears; men did not weep.

Lang walked across to his own tent. The mist had lifted now. The sun had dried some of the dampness from the soil, but the rains would start again, possibly within hours. For the moment, though, the atmosphere was warm, like an English August day after a sudden storm.

He sat in his tent, thinking, until the sun climbed slowly down the sky. The shadows of cannon grew far longer than themselves; tents stretched large as pavilions.

The firing had stopped completely now; Lucknow must be entirely in British hands. He stood up, poured himself a whisky, threw back the flap and looked out on the scene, glass in his hand. He had not yet reported to the colonel about Kalyan Singh. He must do so before others spoke for him, and put the wrong complexion on his action.

He could see British troops riding by. Some carried bottles of whisky. Others held unusual and useless objects they had looted from houses; cracked mirrors, a wicker chair, a silk curtain, a broken clock. Looting was a crime when you were vanquished but overlooked when you were victorious. They were as bad as each other; the Indians and these ruffians. Only the colour of their skins was different.

A great cheering came suddenly and unexpectedly from the shattered city walls. On a makeshift mast above the Residency, Lang saw the Union Jack go up slowly. It was tattered and shot through, but the wind took the flag so that it stiffened bravely.

So they had won. The British were back, and this flag would fly there for as long as they stayed in India.

But what did this victory *really* mean at that moment?

It meant thousands without homes, and cows in the fields unmilked, for the farmers were dead. It meant crops destroyed or never planted, houses shattered, burned, stripped of a lifetime of humble possessions. Then it meant another march through other country to another town, where the same process would be repeated.

It meant speeches in a Parliament thousands of miles away by politicians who had never known discomfort or personal danger, and who had never travelled farther east than Barking Creek.

It meant knighthoods for the wrong people for the wrong reasons; honours for cowards and fools, and a share of prize money strictly according to rank, so that those who had faced the least danger drew the largest sums.

It meant widows and orphans and hunger and fear and loneliness for thousands on both sides. It meant everything and nothing; life and death, and beginning again.

Lang thought of Hodson running into the gateway, knowing almost certainly that death was waiting there to meet him. Perhaps he had guessed that eventually the contents of the tin trunk would be discovered, and any explanation he would give then would not be believed?

Or perhaps he had just wearied of his world, and did not greatly care whether he left it?

Perhaps Nicholson, shouting to the retreating British to follow him—again to his own death—had felt the same way. Both men had died defending a discredited military mystique they despised, and in which they could no longer believe.

The cautious despatch that carefully absolved the sender from any responsibility; the commander's terror of making decisions; the glittering outer shell of bought commissions and promotion, of influence at dinner parties; the inner rottenness of feebleness in the field, thousands dying, not really of wounds or cholera, malaria and fever and dysentery, but through a general's declension of will. These were the weaknesses they had abhorred. Would those left alive tolerate them much longer?

An officer was walking towards him, weaving drunkenly, almost tripping over guy-ropes, and then putting out one hand to steady himself, as though he was on a ship. He held a bottle of whisky in his other hand. Every now and then he stopped and drank. His uniform was unbuttoned and spattered with spirit. He wore neither sword nor pistol.

'Have you heard?' asked Garroway drunkenly.

'Heard what?'

'I have been recommended for promotion. To be captain! For all I have done to help rehouse the Indians in Delhi!'

Lang smiled at the irony. What had Garroway done, but to buy options on properties at a fraction of their worth and then rent them for a fortune to rich Indian merchants when they considered it safe to return? Yet at least he had not taken any lives; not even the enemy's.

'I am sure your future is assured,' he said sincerely.

'Absolutely,' replied Garroway smugly. 'I'll buy a majority next. Why, I'll be a bloody colonel before I've finished.

'And there's another bit of news. Mrs Bolivar has promised me her hand in marriage. Her husband, poor fellow, never returned from detachment near Meerut last May.'

'I congratulate you,' said Lang. 'I have seen you together on the Ridge. I am sure you are admirably suited.'

Garroway's fuddled mind dredged for something else to say in reply. This Lang was not altogether a bad chap. He had nothing against him personally. Not like Hodson. Then he remembered. Hodson was dead.

'Pity about your friend, Major Hodson,' he said clumsily.

'It's a pity about thousands of others, too,' replied Lang. 'On both sides. Thousands who died, all over the country, and quite needlessly, not only from shot and shell, but from hunger and disease. All because we didn't stop the mutiny before it had properly started. Because no one had the guts to act.'

'Oh, I say. You can't really mean that?'

'But I do.'

Garroway diplomatically changed the subject; no need to get into an argument.

'Have you heard what they're going to put on Hodson's gravestone? I thought it rather apt.'

'Yes. But I could think of something even more apt,' said Lang, remembering the ride back from Khurkund.

'What?'

'From one of Shakespeare's sonnets. "The fools of time, which die for goodness, who have lived for crime." '

'Are you trying to be funny?' asked Garroway, thinking Lang was alluding to his own business deals, to his arrangement with Mrs Bolivar, to a number of other squalid enterprises from which he drew a high percentage. 'I don't understand.'

Lang looked at him for a long moment, seeing in his mean, avaricious face, flushed and puffed with drink, his narrow eyes, the weak acquisitive mouth, everything he disliked and despised, the obverse of military glory.

'I do,' he said. 'Now.'

He raised his glass and Garroway raised the bottle.

'Let's drink to tomorrow.'

'To all our tomorrows,' said Garroway.

As they stood thus, the bugler sounded the last call of the day. Slowly, the Union Jack, so recently hoisted above the ruined Residency, began to come down.

Such was the size and extent of the British Empire, ringing the world in red, that, as the sun sank over one British possession, it rose above another. The sun was, therefore, never allowed to set on the British flag. It would rise again tomorrow, and the flag would rise with it.

And for Lang, what did tomorrow hold?

A memory of Arabella gradually fading, erased by years, by service in other campaigns; the road all soldiers marched with no signposts and no fixed destination.

This was his life, as it had been Nicholson's and Hodson's; as it was the life of Ram Gupta and Subedar Rao, of soldiers everywhere, in all armies, under all flags.

Like them, he would follow the drum.

But where, oh, where, would it lead him?

BEULAH LAND

by Lonnie Coleman

the tremendously engrossing saga of a great Georgia plantation in its golden age, and of the men and women, white and black, who were born and died there, knew every pain and pleasure, virtue and vice.

BEULAH LAND

where the old South as it really was is brought to intense life, in all its outward splendor and secret shame.

BEULAH LAND

the novel that everybody's reading, everybody's talking about — and you will never forget.

"A Gone With The Wind with sex!"—Chicago Tribune

A DELL BOOK $1.95